Hazel Gaynor is a bestselling, award-winning author whose work has been translated into several languages. Originally from Yorkshire, she now lives in Ireland with her husband and two children.

You can discover more about the author at www.hazelgaynor.com

THE LIGHTHOUSE KEEPER'S DAUGHTER

1938: When nineteen-year-old Matilda Emmerson steps from the pier at Cobh onto the TSS *California* headed across the Atlantic to New York, she faces an uncertain future. Sent away from Ireland in disgrace, she must stay with her reclusive relative, Harriet Flaherty, the lighthouse keeper in Newport, Rhode Island. Once there, Matilda discovers a discarded portrait that opens a window onto a secret that will change her life forever . . . 1838: When a terrible storm blows up off the Northumberland coast, Grace Darling, the lighthouse keeper's daughter, knows there is little chance of survival for the passengers on the ship battling the waves. But her actions set in motion an incredible feat of bravery that echoes down the century, and touches Matilda in ways she could never have imagined . . .

Books by Hazel Gaynor
Published by Ulverscroft:

THE COTTINGLEY SECRET

HAZEL GAYNOR

THE LIGHTHOUSE KEEPER'S DAUGHTER

Complete and Unabridged

CHARNWOOD
Leicester

First published in Great Britain in 2018 by
HarperCollins*Publishers*
London

First Charnwood Edition
published 2019
by arrangement with
HarperCollins*Publishers* Ltd
London

A catalogue record for this book is available
from the British Library.

ISBN 978–1–4448–4315–6

Published by
F. A. Thorpe (Publishing)
Anstey, Leicestershire

Set by Words & Graphics Ltd.
Anstey, Leicestershire
Printed and bound in Great Britain by
T. J. International Ltd., Padstow, Cornwall

This book is printed on acid-free paper

For courageous women everywhere.
You know who you are.

I am not afraid of storms, for I am learning how to sail my ship.
— Louisa May Alcott

There are two ways of spreading light; to be the candle, or the mirror that reflects it.
— Edith Wharton

Prologue

MATILDA

Cobh, Ireland. May 1938

They call it Heartbreak Pier, the place from where I will leave Ireland. It is a place that has seen too many goodbyes.

From the upper balcony of the ticket office I watch the third-class passengers below, sobbing as they cling to their loved ones, exchanging tokens of remembrance and promises to write. The outpouring of emotion is a sharp contrast to the silence as I stand between my mother and Mrs. O'Driscoll, my chaperone for the journey. I've done all my crying, all my pleading and protesting. All I feel now is a sullen resignation to whatever fate has in store for me on the other side of the Atlantic. I hardly care anymore.

Tired of waiting to board the tenders, I take my ticket from my purse and read the neatly typed details for the umpteenth time. *Matilda Sarah Emmerson. Age 19. Cabin Class. Cobh to New York. T.S.S. California.* Funny, how it says so much about me, and yet says nothing at all. I fidget with the paper ticket, tug at the buttons on my gloves, check my watch, spin the cameo locket at my neck.

'Do stop fiddling, Matilda,' Mother snips, her pinched lips a pale violet in the cool spring air.

1

'You're making me anxious.'

I spin the locket again. 'And *you're* making *me* go to America.' She glares at me, color rushing to her neck in a deep flush of anger, her jaw clenching and straining as she bites back a withering response. 'I can fiddle as much as I like when I get there,' I add, pushing and provoking. 'You won't know what I'm doing. Or who with.'

'*Whom* with,' she corrects, turning her face away with an exaggerated sniff, swallowing her exasperation and fixing her gaze on the unfortunates below. The cloying scent of violet water seeps from the exposed paper-thin skin at her wrists. It gives me a headache.

My fingers return defiantly to the locket, a family heirloom that once belonged to my great-great-granny Sarah. As a child I'd spent many hours opening and closing the delicate filigree clasp, making up stories about the miniature people captured in the portraits inside: an alluring young woman standing beside a lighthouse, and a handsome young man, believed to be a Victorian artist, George Emmerson, a very distant relative. To a bored little girl left to play alone in the drafty rooms of our grand country home, these tiny people offered a tantalizing glimpse of a time when I imagined everyone had a happy ever after. With the more cynical gaze of adulthood, I now presume the locket people's lives were as dull and restricted as mine. Or as dull and restricted as mine was until half a bottle of whiskey and a misjudged evening of reckless flirtation with a British soldier from the local garrison changed everything. If I'd intended to get my mother's attention, I had certainly succeeded.

The doctor tells me I am four months gone. The remaining five, I am to spend with a reclusive relative, Harriet Flaherty, who keeps a lighthouse in Newport, Rhode Island. The perfect hiding place for a girl in my condition; a convenient solution to the problem of the local politician's daughter who finds herself unmarried and pregnant.

At one o'clock precisely, the stewards direct us to board the tenders that will take us out to the *California*, moored on the other side of Spike Island to avoid the mud banks in Cork Harbor. As I step forward, Mother grasps my hand dramatically, pressing a lace handkerchief to her paper-dry cheeks.

'Write as soon as you arrive, darling. Promise you'll write.' It is a carefully stage-managed display of emotion, performed for the benefit of those nearby who must remain convinced of the charade of my American holiday. 'And do take care.'

I pull my hand away sharply and say goodbye, never having meant the words more. She has made her feelings perfectly clear. Whatever is waiting for me on the other side of the Atlantic, I will face it alone. I wrap my fingers around the locket and focus on the words engraved on the back: *Even the brave were once afraid.*

However well I might hide it, the truth is, I am terrified.

VOLUME ONE

founder: *(verb)*
to become submerged;
to come to grief

I had little thought of anything but to exert
myself to the utmost, my spirit was worked
up by the sight of such a dreadful affair that
I can imagine I still see the sea flying over
the vessel.

— Grace Darling

1

SARAH

S.S. Forfarshire. 6th September, 1838

Sarah Dawson draws her children close into the folds of her skirt as the paddle steamer passes a distant lighthouse. Her thoughts linger in the dark gaps between flashes. James remarks on how pretty it is. Matilda wants to know how it works.

'I'm not sure, Matilda love,' Sarah offers, studying her daughter's eager little face and wondering how she ever produced something so perfect. 'Lots of candles and oil, I expect.' Sarah has never had to think about the mechanics of lighthouses. John was always the one to answer Matilda's questions about such things. 'And glass, I suppose. To reflect the light.'

Matilda isn't satisfied with the answer, tugging impatiently at her mother's skirt. 'But how does it keep going around, Mummy? Does the keeper turn a handle? How do they get the oil all the way to the top? What if it goes out in the middle of the night?'

Suppressing a weary sigh, Sarah bobs down so that her face is level with her daughter's. 'How about we ask Uncle George when we get to Scotland. He's sure to know all about light-houses. You can ask him about Mr. Stephenson's *Rocket*, too.'

7

Matilda's face brightens at the prospect of talking about the famous steam locomotive.

'And the paintbrushes,' James adds, his reedy little voice filling Sarah's heart with so much love she could burst. 'You promised I could use Uncle George's easel and brushes.'

Sarah wipes a fine mist of sea spray from James's freckled cheeks, letting her hands settle there a moment to warm him. 'That's right, pet. There'll be plenty of time for painting when we get to Scotland.'

She turns her gaze to the horizon, imagining the many miles and ports still ahead, willing the hours to pass quickly as they continue on their journey from Hull to Dundee. As a merchant seaman's wife, Sarah has never trusted the sea, wary of its moody unpredictability even when John said it was where he felt most alive. The thought of him stirs a deep longing for the reassuring touch of his hand in hers. She pictures him standing at the back door, shrugging on his coat, ready for another trip. 'Courage, Sarah,' he says as he bends to kiss her cheek. 'I'll be back at sunrise.' He never said which sunrise. She never asked.

As the lighthouse slips from view, a gust of wind snatches Matilda's rag doll from her hand, sending it skittering across the deck and Sarah dashing after it over the rain-slicked boards. A month in Scotland, away from home, will be unsettling enough for the children. A month in Scotland without a favorite toy will be unbearable. The rag doll safely retrieved and returned to Matilda's grateful arms, and all

8

interrogations about lighthouses and painting temporarily stalled, Sarah guides the children back inside, heeding her mother's concerns about the damp sea air getting into their lungs.

Below deck, Sarah sings nursery rhymes until the children nap, lulled by the drone of the engines and the motion of the ship and the exhausting excitement of a month in Bonny Scotland with their favorite uncle. She tries to relax, habitually spinning the cameo locket at her neck as her thoughts tiptoe hesitantly toward the locks of downy baby hair inside — one as pale as summer barley, the other as dark as coal dust. She thinks about the third lock of hair that should keep the others company; feels the nagging absence of the child she should also hold in her arms with James and Matilda. The image of the silent blue infant she'd delivered that summer consumes her so that sometimes she is sure she will drown in her despair.

Matilda stirs briefly. James, too. But sleep takes them quickly away again. Sarah is glad of their innocence, glad they cannot see the fog-like melancholy that has lingered over her since losing the baby and losing her husband only weeks later. The doctor tells her she suffers from a nervous disposition, but she is certain she suffers only from grief. Since potions and pills haven't helped, a month in Scotland is her brother's prescription, and something of a last resort.

As the children doze, Sarah takes a letter from her coat pocket, reading over George's words, smiling as she pictures his chestnut curls, eyes as dark as ripe ale, a smile as broad as the Firth of Forth. Dear George. Even the prospect of seeing him is a tonic.

Dundee. July 1838

Dear Sarah,

A few lines to let you know how eager I am to see you, and dear little James and Matilda — although I expect they are not as little as I remember and will regret promising to carry them piggy back around the pleasure gardens! I know you are anxious about the journey and being away from home, but a Scottish holiday will do you all the world of good. I am sure of it. Try not to worry. Relax and enjoy a taste of life on the ocean waves (if your stomach will allow). I hear the Forfarshire is a fine vessel. I shall be keen to see her for myself when she docks.

No news, other than to tell you that I bumped into Henry Herbert and his sisters recently at Dunstanburgh. They are all well and asked after you and the children. Henry was as tedious as ever, poor fellow. Thankfully, I found diversion in a Miss Darling who was walking with them — the light keeper's daughter from Longstone Island on the Farnes. As you can see in the margins, I have developed something of a fondness for drawing lighthouses. Anyway, I will tell you more when you arrive. I must rush to catch the post.

Wishing you a smooth sailing and not too much of the heave ho, me hearties!

Your devoted brother,
George
x

p.s. Eliza is looking forward to seeing you. She and her mother will visit while you are here. They are keen to discuss the wedding.

Sarah admires the miniature lighthouses George has drawn in the margins before she folds the letter back into neat quarters and returns it to her pocket. She hopes Eliza Cavendish doesn't plan to spend the entire month with them. She isn't fond of their eager little cousin, nor her overbearing mother, but has resigned herself to tolerating them now that the engagement is confirmed. Eliza will make a perfectly reasonable wife for George and yet Sarah cannot help feeling that he deserves so much more than reasonable. If only he would look up from his canvas once in a while, she is sure he would find his gaze settling on someone far more suitable. But George will be George and even with a month at her disposal, Sarah doubts it will be long enough to change his mind. Still, she can try.

Night falls beyond the porthole as the ship presses on toward Dundee. One more night's sailing, Sarah tells herself, refusing to converse with the concerns swimming about in her mind.

One more night, and they'll be safely back on dry land. She holds the locket against her chest, reminding herself of the words John had engraved on the back. *Even the brave were once afraid.*

Courage, Sarah, she tells herself. *Courage.*

2

GRACE

Longstone Lighthouse. 6th September, 1838

Dawn blooms over the Farne Islands with soft layers of rose-tinted clouds. From my narrow bedroom window I admire the spectacle, while not trusting it entirely. We islanders know, better than most, how quickly the weather can turn, and there is a particular shape to the clouds that I don't especially care for.

After spending the small hours on watch, I'm glad to stretch my arms above my head, savoring the release of tension in my neck and shoulders before climbing the steps to the lantern room. Another night navigated without incident is always a cause for quiet gratitude and I say my usual prayer of thanks as I extinguish the Argand lamps, their job done until sunset. The routine is so familiar that I almost do it without thought: trim the wicks, polish the lenses of the parabolic reflectors to remove any soot, cover the lenses with linen cloths to protect them from the glare of the sun. Necessary routine tasks which I take pride in doing well, eager to prove myself as capable as my brothers and eager to please my father.

A sea shanty settles on my lips as I work, but despite my efforts to focus on my chores, my thoughts — as they have for the past week — stubbornly return to Mr. George Emmerson. Why I persist in thinking of him, I cannot understand. We'd only spoken briefly — twenty minutes at most — but something about the cadence of his Scots burr, the particular way he rolled his r's, the way he tilted his head when surveying the landscape, and most especially his interest in Mary Anning's fossils, has stuck to me like barnacles on a rock. '*Tell me, Miss Darling, what do you make of Miss. Anning's so-called sea drrragons?*' My mimicry brings a playful smile to my lips as I cover the last of the reflectors, idle thoughts of handsome Scotsmen temporarily concealed with them.

The lamps tended to, I walk once around the lantern to catch the beauty of the sunrise from all angles. From the first time I'd climbed the spiraling lighthouse steps at the age of seven, it was here, at the very top of the tower, where I loved to be most of all, the clouds almost within touching distance, the strong eighty-foot tower below keeping us safe. The uninterrupted view of the Farne Islands and the Northumbrian coast hangs like a vast painting in a private gallery, displayed just for me, and despite the growl in my stomach I'm in no hurry to head downstairs for breakfast. I lift Father's telescope from the shelf and follow a flock of sandwich terns passing to the south before lowering the lens to watch the gulls bobbing about on the sea, waiting for the herring fleet to return. The patterns of light on the surface of the water remind me of Mary Herbert's silk dress shimmering as she danced a reel at last year's harvest home ball.

Dear Mary. Despite our friendship, she and her sister, Ellen, have always thought me a curious creature, unable to understand how anyone could possibly prefer the wind-lashed isolation of an island lighthouse to the merry hubbub of a dance. *Will we see you at the ball this year, Grace? Henry is anxious to know.* Their dedication to the cause of finding me a suitable husband — preferably their brother — is nothing short of impressive, but the business of marriage doesn't occupy my thoughts as it does other women of my age, who seem to think about little else. Even my sisters, who now live over on the Main, perpetually tease me about being married to the lighthouse. 'You'll never find a husband if you hide away in your tower, Grace. You can't very well expect the tide to deliver one to you.' Time and again, I have patiently explained that even if I did marry I would merely be swapping the life of a dutiful daughter for that of a dutiful wife, and from what I've observed I'm not at all convinced the institution of marriage is worth the exchange. It is a point well-made, and one they find difficult to argue with.

As I make my way down to the service room which sits just below the lantern room, I pause at the sound of my father's voice floating up the steps.

'You coming down, Gracie?' Mam has a fresh loaf. She insists it needs eating before the mice get to it.'

His Trinity House cap appears above the top

15

step, followed by thick eyebrows, white as the lime-washed tower walls. I take his arm to help him up the last few steps.

'You're supposed to be resting,' I scold.

His breathing is labored. His cheeks — already rusted from decades of wind and sun — scarlet with the effort of climbing the ninety-three steps from the ground floor. 'I know, pet. But Mam mithers when I rest. Thought I'd be better off resting where she can't see me.' He winks as he sinks gladly into his favorite chair, taking the telescope from me and lifting it to his eye. 'Anything doing?'

'Mercifully quiet,' I remark, adding a few lines to the Keeper's Log about the weather and the sea conditions before recording the tides. 'A few paddle steamers and fishing vessels passed. The seals are back on Harker's Rock.'

Father scans the horizon, looking for anything unusual among the waves, interpreting the particular shape of the swells, crests, and troughs. It bothers him that his eyesight isn't what it used to be, glad to have me as a second pair of eyes. We make a good team; him the patient teacher, me the eager pupil.

'Seals on Harker's Rock, eh. Local fishermen will tell you that's a sign of a storm coming. Mam's already fretting about your brother getting back.' He focuses the telescope on the clouds then, looking for any indication of approaching squalls or incoming fogs or anything to suggest an imminent change in the conditions. My father reads the clouds and the behavior of the seabirds as anyone else might

16

read directions on a compass, understanding the information they offer about bad weather approaching, snow on the way, a north wind blowing. Partly by his instruction and partly by an inherent islander's instinct nurtured over my twenty-two years, I have absorbed some of this knowledge, too. But even the most experienced mariner can occasionally be fooled.

Father rubs his chin as he always does when he's thinking. 'I don't trust that sky, Gracie. You know what they say about red skies in the morning.'

'Sailors' warning,' I say. 'But the sky is pink, Father, not red. And anyway, it's far too pretty to be sinister.'

Chuckling at my optimism, he places the telescope in his lap and shuts his eyes, enjoying the warmth of the sunlight against his face.

It troubles me to see how he's aged in recent months; that he isn't quite as vigorous as he once was. But despite doctor's orders that he take it easy, he insists on continuing as Principal Keeper. As stubborn as he is humble, there's little point in arguing with him. Being the light keeper here isn't just my father's job — it is his life, his passion. I might as well tell him to stop breathing as to stop doing the familiar routines he has faithfully carried out here for decades.

'You look tired, Father. Didn't you sleep well?'

He waves my concern away, amused by the notion of his little girl taking the role of parent as I often do these days. 'Mam was at her snoring again. Thought it was the cannons firing from Bamburgh to signal a shipwreck.' He opens one eye. 'Don't tell her I said that.'

I laugh and promise not to.

Taking the telescope from him, I lift the cool rim to my eye, tracking a fisherman's boat as it follows a course from North Sunderland toward the Outer Farnes. Hopefully it is a postal delivery with word from Trinity House regarding our annual inspection. Waiting for the report always makes Father restless, even though previous reports have consistently noted the exceptional standards maintained at the Longstone light, declaring it to be among the best-kept stations in England. 'Pride goes before destruction,' Father says whenever I remind him of this. 'And a haughty spirit before stumbling. Proverbs 16:18.' He is not a man to dwell on success, only striving to work harder because of it. Among the many traits that I admire in him, his humility is the one I admire the most.

Hauling himself up from the chair, he joins me at the window. 'The hairs are prickling at the back of my neck, Grace. There's bad weather coming, I can feel it in the air. And then there's birds flying in through the window downstairs.'

'Not again?'

'Nearly gave your mam a heart attack. You know what she says about birds coming inside and people dropping down dead.'

'I'd rather the birds flew inside than knocked themselves out against the glass.' Too many birds crash against the lantern room windows, dazzled by the reflected sun. I've often found a stiffened guillemot or puffin when I step out onto the perimeter to clean the glass.

18

'Which one of us do you think it is then, Gracie, because I'm not in the mood for perishing today, and I certainly hope it isn't you? So that only leaves your poor old mam, God rest her.'

'Father! You're wicked.' I bat his arm affectionately, pleased to see the sparkle return to his eyes, even if it is at Mam's expense.

My parents' quarrelling is as familiar to me as the turn of the tides, but despite all the nagging and pointed sighs, I know they care for each other very much. Mam could never manage without my father's practicality and good sense, and he would be lost without her steadfast resourcefulness. Like salt and the sea they go well together and I admire them for making it work, despite Mam being twelve years my father's senior, and despite the often testing conditions of island life.

Father flicks through the Log book, adding a few remarks in his careful script. *September 6th: Sea conditions: calm. Wind: Light south-westerly. Paddle steamer passing on horizon at two o'clock. Clouds massing in the south.* He takes my hand in his then, squeezing it tight, just like he used to when I was a little girl walking beside him on the beaches at Brownsman, our first island home. The rough calluses on his palms rub against my skin, his fingers warm and paper dry as they wrap themselves around mine, like rope coiling neatly back into place.

'Thank you, Grace.'

'For what?'

'For being here with me and Mam. It can't be

easy for you, seeing your sisters and brothers marry and set themselves up on the Main.'

I squeeze his hand in reply. 'And why would I want to marry and live on the Main? Where else would I want to be other than here, with you and Mam and the lamps and the seals?' It's an honest question. Only very rarely do my thoughts stray across the sea toward an imaginary life as a dressmaker or a draper's wife in Alnwick, but such thoughts never last long. I've seen how often women marry and become less of themselves, like scraps of pastry cut away and reused in some other, less important way. Besides, I don't belong to bustling towns with their crowded streets and noisy industry. I belong here, with the birds and the sea, with the wild winter winds and unpredictable summers. While a harvest home dance might enchant Mary and Ellen Herbert for an evening, dear Longstone will enchant me far longer than that. 'The island gives me the greatest freedom, Father. I would feel trapped if I lived anywhere else.'

He nods his understanding. 'Still, you know you have my blessing, should you ever find a reason to feel differently.'

I take my hand from his and smooth my skirts. 'Of course, and you will be the first to know!'

I leave him then, descending the spiraling staircase, the footsteps of my absent sisters and brothers carried in the echo that follows behind. There's an emptiness to the lighthouse without the hustle and bustle of my seven siblings to trip over and squabble with, and although I enjoy the extra space afforded by their absence, I occasionally long for their rowdy return.

As always, there is a chill in the drafty stairwell and I pull my plaid shawl around my shoulders, hurrying to my small bedroom beneath the service room, where a cheery puddle of sunlight illuminates the floor and instantly warms me. The room is no more than half a dozen paces from one side to the other. I often think it is as well none of us Darling children grew to be very tall or large in frame or we should have had a very sorry time always bending and stooping. Against one wall is my wooden bedchamber, once shared with my sister, Betsy. A writing desk stands in the center of the room, an ewer, basin and candlestick placed upon it.

Crouching down beside a small tea chest beneath the window, I push up the lid and rummage inside, my fingers searching for my old work box, now a little cabinet of curiosities: fragile birds' eggs protected by soft goose down; all shape and size of seashells; smooth pebbles of green and blue sea glass. I hope the collection might, one day, be impressive enough to show to Father's friends at the Natural History Society, but for now I'm content to collect and admire my treasures from the sea, just as a lady might admire the precious gems in her jewelry box. Much as I don't want for a husband or a position as a dressmaker, nor do I want for fancy jewels.

Taking a piece of emerald sea glass from my pocket, I add it to the box, my thoughts straying to the piece of indigo sea glass I'd given to Mr.

Emmerson, and the generous smile he'd given me in return. *'There is an individuality in everything, Mr. Emmerson. If you look closely at the patterns on seashells, you'll see that they're not the same after all, but that each is, in fact, unique.'* He wasn't like Henry Herbert or other men in my acquaintance, eager to brag about their own interests and quick to dismiss a woman's point of view, should she dare to possess one. Mr. Emmerson was interested in my knowledge of the seabirds and the native wild flowers that grow along Dunstanburgh's shoreline. When we parted, he said he'd found our conversation absorbing, a far greater compliment than to be considered pretty, or witty.

'Grace Horsley Darling. What nonsense.'

I scold myself for my silliness. I am no better than a giggling debutante with an empty dance card to dwell on a conversation of so little significance. I close the lid of the work box with a snap before returning it to the tea chest.

Continuing down the steps, I pass the second-floor room where my sisters Mary-Ann and Thomasin had once slept in their bunk beds, whispering and giggling late into the night, sharing that particular intimacy only twins can know, and on, past my brother Brooks' bedroom on the first floor, his boots left where he kicked them off beneath his writing table, his nightshirt hanging over the back of a chair, waiting expectantly for his return.

At the bottom of the stairwell, I step into our large circular living quarters where Mam is busy kneading a bad mood into great mounds of bread dough at the table in front of the wood-burning stove, muttering about people sitting around the place like a great sack of coal and, Lor!, how her blessed old bones ache.

'At last! I thought you were never coming down,' she puffs, wiping the back of her hand against her forehead, her face scarlet from her efforts. 'I'm done in. There'll be enough stotties to build another lighthouse when I'm finished with all this dough. I canna leave it now though or it'll be as flat as a plaice. Have you seen Father?'

'He's in the service room. I said I would take him up a hot drink.'

'Check on the hens first, would you? I'm all dough.'

Taking my cloak and bonnet from the hook beside the door, I step outside and make my way to the henhouse where I collect four brown eggs and one white before taking a quick stroll along the exposed rocks, determined to catch some air before the weather turns and the tide comes in. I peer into the miniature aquariums in the rock pools, temporary homes for anemone, seaweed, pea crabs, mussels, and limpets. As the wind picks up and the first spots of rain speckle my skirt, I tighten the ribbons on my bonnet, pull my cloak about my shoulders, and hurry back to the lighthouse where Mam is standing at the door, frowning up at the darkening skies.

'Get inside, Grace. You'll catch your death in that wind.'

'Don't fuss, Mam. I was only out five minutes.'

Ignoring me, she wraps a second plaid around my shoulders as I remove my cloak. 'Best to be safe than sorry. I hope your brother doesn't try to make it back,' she sighs. 'There's trouble coming on that wind, but you know how stubborn he is when he sets his mind to something. Just like his father.'

And not unlike his mam, I think. I urge her not to worry. 'Brooks will be in the Olde Ship, telling tall tales with the rest of them. He won't set out if it isn't safe to do so. He's stubborn, but he isn't foolish.' I hope he is, indeed, back with the herring fleet at North Sunderland. It will be a restless night without him safe in his bed.

'Well, let's hope you're right, Grace, because there was that bird making a nuisance of itself inside earlier. It sets a mind to thinking the worst.'

'Only if you let it,' I say, my stomach growling to remind me that I haven't yet eaten.

Leaving Mam to beat the hearth rug, and her worries, against the thick tower walls with heavy slaps, I place the basket of eggs on the table, spread butter on a slice of still-warm bread, and sit beside the fire to eat, ignoring the wind that rattles the windows like an impatient child. The lighthouse, bracing itself for bad weather, wraps its arms around us. Within its proud walls, I feel as safe as the fragile birds' eggs nestling in their feather beds in my work box, but my thoughts linger on those at sea, and who may yet be in danger if the storm worsens.

3

SARAH

S.S. *Forfarshire*. 6th September, 1838

Sarah Dawson and her children sleep in each other's arms, unaware of the storm gathering strength beyond the porthole windows, or the drama unfolding below deck as Captain John Humble orders his chief engineer to start pumping the leaking starboard boiler. Discussions and heated arguments take place among the crew, but as they pass the port of Tynemouth, Humble decides not to turn in for repairs but to press on, tracking the Northumberland coast, his mind set on arriving into Dundee on schedule, just after sunrise the following morning.

Steadying himself against the wheelhouse door as the ship pitches and rolls in the growing swell, Humble sips a hot whiskey toddy and studies his nautical charts, focusing on the course he must follow to avoid the dangerous rocks around the Inner and Outer Farne Islands, and the distinctive characteristics of the lighthouses that will guide him safely through. He has sailed this route a dozen times or more, and despite the failing boiler, he reassures his chief engineer that there is no need for alarm. The S.S. *Forfarshire* limps on as the storm closes in.

Dundee, Scotland.

At a narrow table beside the fire of his lodgings in Balfour Street, George Emmerson sips a glass of porter, glances at his pocket watch, and picks up a small pebble-sized piece of indigo sea glass from the table. He thinks, too often, about the young woman who'd given it to him as a memento of his trip to Northumberland. Treasure from the sea, she'd called it, remarking on how fascinating she found it that something as ordinary as a discarded medicine bottle could become something so beautiful over time.

He leans back in his chair, holding the page of charcoal sketches in front of him. He is dissatisfied with his work, frustrated by his inability to capture the image he sees so clearly in his mind: her slender face, the slight compression of her lip, the coil of sunlit coffee-colored curls on her head, the puzzled frown across her brow as if she couldn't quite grasp the measure of him and needed to concentrate harder to do so.

Grace Darling.

Her name brings a smile to his lips.

He imagines Eliza at his shoulder, feigning interest in his 'pictures' while urging him to concentrate and tell her which fabric he prefers for the new curtains. The thought of his intended trips him up, sending a rosy stain of guilt rushing to his cheeks. He scrunches the sketches into a ball, tossing them into the fire before checking his pocket watch again. Sarah will be well on her way. Her visit is timely. Perhaps now, more than ever, he needs the wise counsel and pragmatic opinions of his sister. Where his thoughts often stray to those of romantic ideals, Sarah has no time for such notions and will put him firmly back on track. Still, she isn't here yet.

For now, he chooses to ignore the rather problematic matter of the ember that glows within him for a certain Miss Darling. As the strengthening wind rattles the leaded windows and sets the candle flame dancing, George runs his hands through his hair, loosens the pin at his collar, and pulls a clean sheet of paper toward him. He picks up the piece of indigo sea glass and curls his fingers around it. With the other hand, he takes up his charcoal and starts again, determined to have it right before the flame dies.

4

GRACE

Longstone Lighthouse. 6th September, 1838

Late afternoon and the sky turns granite. Secure inside the soot-blackened walls of the lighthouse, we each find a way to distract ourselves from the strengthening storm. Mam sits at her spinning wheel, muttering about birds flying indoors. Father leans over the table, tinkering with a damaged fishing net. I brush my unease away with the dust I sweep outside.

The living quarters is where we spend our time when we aren't tending to the lamps, or on watch, or occupied at the boathouse. Our lives cover every surface of the room in a way that might appear haphazard to visitors, but is perfectly organized to us. While we might not appear to have much in the way of possessions, we want for nothing.

Bonnets and cloaks roost on hooks by the door, ready to be thrown on at short notice. Pots and pans dangle from the wall above the fire like highwaymen on the gallows. The old black kettle, permanently suspended from the crane over the fire, is always ready to offer a warm drink to cold hands. Damp stockings, petticoats, and aprons dry on a line suspended above our heads. All shape and size of seashells nestle on the windowsills and in the gaps between the flagstones. Stuffed guillemots and black-headed gulls — gifted to Father from the taxidermist in Craster — keep a close watch over us with beady glass eyes. Even the sharp tang of brine has its particular space in the room, as does the wind, sighing at the windows, eager to come inside.

As the evening skies darken, I climb the steps to the lantern room where I carefully fill the reservoir with oil before lighting the trimmed wicks with my hand lamp. I wait thirty minutes until the flames reach their full height before unlocking the weights that drive the gears of the clock mechanism, cranking them for the first time that evening. Slowly, the lamps begin to rotate, and the lighthouse comes alive. Every thirty seconds, passing ships will see the flash of the refracted beam. When I am satisfied that everything is in order, I add a comment to the Keeper's Log: *S.S.* Jupiter *passed this station at 5pm. Strong to gale force north to northeast. Hard rain.*

As Father is on first watch, I leave the comforting light of the lamps, and enter the dark interior of the staircase. My sister Thomasin used to say she imagined the stairwell was a long vein running from the heart of the lighthouse. In one way or another, we have all attached human qualities to these old stone walls so that it has almost become another member of the family, not just a building to house us. I feel Thomasin's absence especially keenly as I pass her bedroom. A storm always stirs a desire for everyone to be safe inside the lighthouse walls, but my sisters and brothers are dispersed along the coast now, like flotsam caught on the tide and carried to some other place.

The hours pass slowly as the storm builds, the clock above the fireplace ticking away laborious minutes as Mam works at her wheel. I read a favorite volume, *Letters on the Improvement of the Mind, Addressed to a Lady*, but even that cannot hold my attention. I pick up a slim book of Robert Burns' poetry, but it doesn't captivate me as it usually would, his words only amplifying the weather outside: *At the starless, midnight hour / When Winter rules with boundless power, / As the storms the forests tear, / And thunders rend the howling air, / Listening to the doubling roar, / Surging on the rocky shore.* I put it down, sigh and fidget, fussing at the seam of my skirt and picking at a break in my fingernail until Mam tells me to stop huffing and puffing and settle at something.

'You're like a cat with new kittens, Grace. I don't know what's got into you tonight.'

The storm has got into me. The wild wind sends prickles running along my skin. And something else nags at me because even the storm cannot chase thoughts of Mr. Emmerson from my mind.

If I were more like Ellen and Mary Herbert I would seek distraction in the pages of the romance novels they talk about so enthusiastically, but Father scoffs at the notion of people reading novels, or playing cards after their day's work is done, considering it to be a throwing away of time (he doesn't know how much time my sister, Mary-Ann, throws away on such things), so there are no such books on our shelves. I am mostly glad of his censorship, grateful for the education he'd provided in the service room turned to schoolroom. I certainly can't complain about a lack of reading material, and yet my mind takes an interest in nothing tonight.

At my third yawn, Mam tells me to go to bed. 'Get some rest before your turn on watch, Grace. You look as weary as I feel.'

As she speaks the wind sucks in a deep breath before releasing another furious howl. Raindrops skitter like stones thrown against the windows. I pull my plaid shawl about my shoulders and take my hand lamp from the table.

'It's getting worse, isn't it?' The inflection in my voice carries that of a child seeking reassurance.

Mam works the pedal of her spinning wheel in harmony with the brisk movement of her hands, the steady *clack clack clack* so familiar to me. She doesn't look up from her task. Inclement weather is part of the fabric of life at Longstone. Mam believes storms should be respected, never feared. *'If you show it you're afraid, you're already halfway to dead.'* She may not be the most eloquent woman, but she is often right. 'Sleep well, Grace.'

I bid her goodnight, place a hurricane glass over my candle, and begin the familiar ascent inside the tower walls. Sixty steps to my bedroom. Sixty times to remember eyes, the color of porter. Sixty times to see a slim

31

mustache stretch into a smile as broad as the Tyne, a smile that had stained my cheeks pink and sent Ellen and Mary Herbert giggling into their gloves. Sixty times to scold myself for thinking so fondly of someone I'd spent only a few minutes with, and yet it is to those few minutes my mind stubbornly returns.

Reaching the service room I stand in silence for a moment, reluctant to break Father's concentration. He sits beside the window, his telescope poised like a cat about to pounce, his senses on high alert.

'You will wake me, Father,' I whisper. 'Won't you?' I've asked the same thing every night for as long as I can remember: will he wake me if he needs assistance with the light, or with any rescue he might have to undertake.

Candlelight flickers in the circular spectacles perched on the end of his nose as he turns and acknowledges me with a firm nod. 'Of course, pet. Get some sleep. She'll blow herself out by morning.'

On the few occasions he has required me to tend the light in his absence, I have proven myself very capable. I have my father's patience and a keen eye, essential for keeping watch over the sea. Sometimes I wonder if it saddens him, just a little, that the future of the lighthouse will lie with my brother, and not me. Brooks will succeed him as Principal Keeper because for all that I am eager and capable, I am — first and foremost — a woman.

A smile spreads across Father's face as I turn at the top of the steps. 'Look at you, Grace.

Twenty-two years of unfathomable growth and blossoming beauty and a temperament worthy of your name. Such a contrast to the rumpus outside.'

I shoo his compliment away. 'Have you been at the porter again?' I tease, my smile betraying my delight.

Taking up my lamp, I retire to my room, a shrill shriek of wind setting the flame dancing in a draft as a deafening boom reverberates around the lighthouse walls. I peer through the window, mesmerized by the angry waves that plunge against the rocks below and send salt-spray soaring up into the sky like shooting stars.

Picking up my Bible, I kneel beside my bed and pray for the safety of my brother before I blow out my candle and slip beneath the eiderdown. My feet flinch against the cold sheets, my toes searching for the hot stone I'd placed beneath the covers earlier. I lie perfectly still in the dark, picturing the lamps turning above me with the regularity of a steady pulse, their light stretching out through the darkness to warn those at sea and let them know they are not alone in the dark. On quieter nights, I can hear the *click click* of the clock mechanism turning above. Tonight, I hear only the storm, and the heightened beating of my heart.

5

SARAH

S.S. *Forfarshire*. 7th September, 1838

Sarah sleeps lightly in unfamiliar places and is easily awoken by a violent shudder. Her senses feel their way around in the dark, searching for an explanation as to why the engines are silent. Without their reassuring drone, Sarah hears the howling wind more clearly, feels the pitch and roll of the ocean more acutely. Her fingers reach for the locket at her neck, remembering how surprised she'd been when John had given it to her, wrapped in a small square of purple silk fabric, tied with a matching ribbon. It was the most beautiful thing she'd ever seen, made even more beautiful by the locks of their children's hair he had placed inside.

James and Matilda stir on her lap, rubbing sleepy eyes and asking why the ship has stopped and if they are in Scotland yet and when will it be morning. Sarah smooths their hair, whispering that it won't be long until they see their uncle George and that they should go back to sleep. 'I'll wake you at first light. We'll join the herring fleet as we sail into the harbor. The fisherwomen will be out with their pickling barrels. The fish scales will shine like diamonds on the cobbles . . . '

A chilling roar shatters the silence, followed by a terrifying cracking of timbers and the shriek of buckling metal. Sarah sits bolt upright, her heart racing as she wraps her arms tight around her children.

'What's happening, Mummy?' Matilda screams. 'What's happening?'

James starts to cry. Matilda buries her face in her mother's shoulder as the ship lists heavily to starboard. Dark, frigid water gushes inside at such shocking speed that Sarah doesn't have time to react before she is waist deep in it. Lifting her children, one onto each hip, she starts to move forward. Terror and panic rise in her chest, snatching away short breaths that are already strangled by the effort of carrying her terrified children. She shushes and soothes them, telling them it will be all right, that they're not to be afraid, that she will keep them safe. And somehow she is outside, the wind tearing at her coat, hard rain lashing at her cheeks as Matilda and James cling desperately to her. For a brief moment she feels a rush of relief. They are not trapped below decks. They are safe. But the water surges suddenly forward, covering her up to her chest and the deck is all but submerged. As she turns to look for assistance, a lifeboat, something — anything — an enormous wave knocks her off her feet and she is plunged underwater and all is darkness.

6

GRACE

Longstone Lighthouse. 7th September, 1838

I sleep in unsatisfying fragments, the storm so furious I am uneasy, even within the lighthouse's reliable embrace. As I lie awake, I remember when the lighthouse was built, how I was mesmerized by the tall tapering tower that was to become my home, three miles offshore from the coastal towns of Bamburgh and North Sunderland. '*Five feet thick. Strong enough to withstand anything nature might throw at it.*' My father was proud to know his new light station was constructed to a design similar to Robert Stevenson's Bell Rock light. It has been my fortress for fifteen happy years.

Father wakes me at midnight with a gentle shake of the shoulder.

Dressing quickly, I take up my lamp and together we make our way downstairs where we pull on our cloaks and step out into the maelstrom to secure the coble at the boathouse, aware that the dangerous high tide is due at 4:13 A.M. The sea heaves and boils. I can't remember when I have ever seen it so wild. Returning to the lighthouse, Father retires to bed, leaving me to take my turn on watch.

I take up my usual position at the narrow

bedroom window, telescope in hand. The sky is a furious commotion of angry black clouds that send torrents of rain lashing against the glass. The wind tugs at the frame until I am sure it will be pulled right out. My senses are on full alert. Neither tired nor afraid, I focus only on the sea, watching for any sign of a ship in distress.

The night passes slowly, the pendulum clock on the wall ticking away the hours as the light turns steadily above.

Around 4:45 A.M., as the first hint of dawn lends a meager light to the sky, my eye is drawn to an unusual shape at the base of Harker's Rock, home to the puffin and gannet colonies I love to observe on calm summer days. Visibility is terrible behind the thick veil of rain and sea spray, but I hold the telescope steady until I can just make out dark shapes dotted around the base of the rock. Seals, no doubt, sheltering their pups from the pounding waves. And yet an uncomfortable feeling stirs in the pit of my stomach.

By seven o'clock, the light has improved a little and the receding tide reveals more of Harker's Rock. Taking up the telescope again, my heart leaps as I see a ship's foremast jutting upward, clearly visible against the horizon. My instincts were right. They are not seals I'd seen at the base of the rock, but people. Survivors of a shipwreck.

Snatching up my hand lamp, I rush downstairs, the wind shrieking at the windows, urging me to hurry.

I rouse my father with a brusque shake of the

shoulders. 'A ship has foundered, Father! We must hurry.'

Tired, confused eyes meet mine. 'What time is it, Grace? Whatever is the matter?'

'Survivors, Father. A wreck. There are people on Harker's Rock. We must hurry.' I can hear the tremor in my voice, feel the tremble in my hands as my lamp shakes.

Mam stirs, asking if Brooks is back and what on earth all the commotion is about.

Father reaches for his spectacles, sleepy fingers fumbling like those of a blind man as he sits up. 'What of the storm, Grace? The tide?'

'The tide is going out. The storm still rages.' I linger by the window, as if by standing there I might let those poor souls know that help is coming.

Father sighs, his hands dropping back onto the eiderdown. 'Then it's of no use, Grace. I will be shipwrecked myself if I attempt to set out in those seas. Even if I could get to Harker's Rock I would never be able to row back against the turn of the tide. I wouldn't make it across Craford's Gut with the wind against me.'

Of course he is right. Even as I'd rushed to him, I'd heard him speak those very words.

I grasp his hands in mine and sink to my knees at the side of his bed. 'But if we both rowed, Father? If I came with you, we could manage it, couldn't we? We can take the longer route to avail of the shelter from the islands. Those we rescue can assist in rowing back, if they're able.' I press all my determination into my voice, into my eyes, into his hands. 'Come to the window to assure me I'm not imagining things.' I pull on his hands to help him up, passing him the telescope as another strong gust rattles the shutters, sending the rafters creaking above our heads.

My assumptions are quickly confirmed. A small group of human forms can now clearly be seen at the base of the rock, the battered remains of their vessel balanced precariously between them and the violent sea. 'Do you see?' I ask.

'Yes, Grace. I see.'

I place my hand on Father's arm as he folds the telescope and rests his palms against the windowsill. 'The North Sunderland lifeboat won't be able to put out in those seas,' I say, reading his thoughts. 'We are their last hope of being rescued. And the Lord will protect us,' I add, as much to reassure myself as my father.

He understands that I am responding to the instinct to help, an instinct that has been instilled in me since I was a child on his knee, listening to accounts of lost fishing vessels and the brave men who rescued the survivors. I feel the drop of his shoulders and know my exertions have prevailed.

'Very well,' he says. 'We will make an attempt. Just one, mind. If we can't reach them . . . '

'I understand. But we must hurry.'

The decision made, all is action and purpose. We dress quickly and rush to the boathouse. The wind snatches my breath away, almost blowing me sideways as I step outside, my hair whipping wildly about my face. I falter for a moment, wishing my brother were here to help, but he

39

isn't. We must do this alone, Father and I, or not at all.

Mam helps to launch the boat, each of us taking our role in the procedure as we have done many times before. Words are useless, tossed aside by the wind, so that nobody quite knows what question was asked, or what reply given. I struggle to stand upright against the incessant gusts.

Finally, the boat is in the water. Stepping in, I pick up an oar and sit down.

'Grace! What are you doing?' Mam turns to my father. 'William! She can't go. This is madness.'

'He can't go alone, Mam,' I shout. 'I'm going with him.'

Father steps into the boat beside me. 'She is like this storm, Thomasin. She won't be silenced 'til she's said her piece. I'll take care of her.'

I urge Mam not to worry. 'Prepare dry clothes and blankets. And have hot drinks ready.'

She nods her understanding and begins to untie the ropes that secure us to the landing wall, her fingers fumbling in the wet and the cold. She says something as we push away, but I can't hear her above the wind. The storm and the sea are the only ones left to converse with now.

Once beyond the immediate shelter afforded by the base of Longstone Island, it becomes immediately apparent that the sea conditions are far worse than we'd imagined. The swell carries us high one moment before plunging us down into a deep trough the next, a wall of water surrounding us on either side. We are entirely at the mercy of the elements.

Father calls out to me, shouting above the wind, to explain that we will take a route through Craford's Gut, the channel which separates Longstone Island from Blue Caps. I nod my understanding, locking eyes with him as we both pull hard against the oars. I draw courage from the light cast upon the water by Longstone's lamps as Father instructs me to pull to the left or the right, keeping us on course around the lee side of the little knot of islands that offer a brief respite from the worst of the wind. As we round the spur of the last island and head out again into the open seas, Father looks at me with real fear in his eyes. Our little coble, just twenty-one foot by six inches, is all we have to protect us. In such wild seas, we know it isn't nearly protection enough.

7

SARAH

Harker's Rock, Outer Farnes.
7th September, 1838

Light. Dark. Light. Dark.

In the thick black that surrounds her, the beam of light in the distance is especially bright to Sarah Dawson. Every thirty seconds it turns its pale eye on the figures huddled on the rock. Sarah fixes her gaze on its source: a lighthouse. A warning light to stay away. Her only hope of rescue.

Her body convulses violently, as if she is no longer part of it. Only her arms, which grasp James and Matilda tight against her chest, seem to belong to her. She doesn't know how long it is since the ship went down — moments? hours? — too exhausted and numb to notice anything apart from the shape of her children's stiff little bodies against hers and the relentless screech of the wind. Behind her, the wrecked bow of the *Forfarshire* cracks and groans as it smashes against the rocks, breaking up like tinder beneath the force of the waves, the masthead looming from the swell like a sea monster from an old mariner's tale. The other half of the steamer is gone, taking everyone and everything down with it. She thinks of George waiting for her in

Dundee. She thinks of his letter in her pocket, his sketches of lighthouses. She stares at the flashing light in the distance. Why does nobody come?

A man beside Sarah moans. It is a sound like nothing she has ever heard. His leg is badly injured and she knows she should help him, but she can't leave her children. The desperate groans of other survivors clinging to the slippery rock beside her mingle with the rip and roar of the wind and waves. She wishes they would all be quiet. If only they would be quiet.

The storm rages on.

The rain beats relentlessly against Sarah's head, like small painful stones. Rocking James and Matilda in her arms, she shelters them from the worst of it, singing to them of lavenders blue and lavenders green. 'They'll be here soon, my loves. Look, the sky is brightening and the herring fleet will be coming in. You remember how the scales look like diamonds among the cobbles. We'll look for jewels together, when the sun is up.'

Their silence is unbearable.

Unable to suppress her anguish any longer, Sarah tips her head back and screams for help, but all that emerges is a pathetic rasping whisper that melts away into gut-wrenching sobs as another angry wave slams hard against the rock, sweeping the injured man away with it.

Sarah turns her head and wraps her arms tighter around her children, gripping them with a strength she didn't know she possessed,

43

determined that the sea will not take them from her.

Light. Dark. Light. Dark.

Why does nobody come?

⋆   ⋆   ⋆

Minutes come and go until time and the sea become inseparable. The light turns tauntingly in the distance. Still nobody comes.

James's little hand is too stiff and cold in Sarah's. Matilda's sweet little face is too still and pale, her hands empty, her beloved rag doll snatched away by the water. Sarah strokes Matilda's cheek and tells her how sorry she is that she couldn't tell her how the lighthouse worked. She smooths James's hair and tells him how desperately sorry she is that she couldn't keep them safe.

As a hesitant dawn illuminates the true horror of what has unfolded, Sarah slips in and out of consciousness. Perhaps she sees a small boat making its way toward them, tossed around in the foaming sea like a child's toy, but it doesn't get any closer. Perhaps she is dreaming, or seeing the fata morgana John used to tell her of: a mirage of lost cities and ships suspended above the horizon. As the black waves wash relentlessly over the desperate huddle of survivors on the rock, Sarah closes her eyes, folding in on herself to shelter her sleeping children, the three of them nothing but a pile of sodden washday rags, waiting for collection.

8

GRACE

Longstone Lighthouse. 7th September, 1838

Our progress is frustratingly slow, the distance of three quarters of a mile stretched much farther by the wind and the dangerous rocks that will see us stranded or capsized if we don't steer around them. We must hurry, and yet we must take care; plot our course.

After what feels like hours straining on the oars, we finally reach the base of Harker's Rock where the sea thrashes wildly, threatening to capsize the coble with every wave. The danger is far from over.

Lifting his oars into the boat, Father turns to me. 'You'll have to keep her steady, Grace.'

I give a firm nod in reply, refusing to dwell on the look of fear in his eyes, or on the way he hesitates as he jumps onto the jagged rocks, reluctant to leave me.

'Go,' I call. 'And hurry.'

Alone in the coble, I begin my battle with the sea, pulling first on the left oar and then on the right, sculling forward and then backward in a desperate effort to stop the boat being smashed against the rocks while Father assesses the situation with the survivors. The minutes expand like hours, every moment bringing a bigger wave to dowse me with frigid water and render me almost blind with the sting of salt in my eyes. Mam's words tumble through my mind. *A storm should he respected, but never feared. Show it you're afraid, and you're already halfway to dead.* I rage back at the wind, telling it I am not afraid, ignoring the deep burn of the muscles in my forearms. I have never felt more alone or afraid but I am determined to persevere.

Eventually, three hunched figures emerge from the gloom. Men. Bloodied and bruised. Their clothes torn. Shoeless. Bedraggled. They barely resemble human beings. So shocked by their appearance, I take a moment to react, but gather my wits sufficiently to maneuver the coble alongside the rocks.

'Quickly. Climb in,' I shout, pulling all the time on the oars to hold the boat as steady as I can.

The men clamber and fall into the boat, one quietly, two wincing with the pain of each step, the flux in weight and balance tipping the boat wildly as they stumble forward. The two injured men are too stupefied to speak. The other thanks me through chattering teeth as he takes an oar from my frozen hands.

'I'll help keep her steady, miss.'

Reluctantly, I let go. Only then do I notice the ache in my arms and wrists and realize how hard I've been gripping the oars.

'How many more?' I ask, wiping salt water from my eyes.

'Six alive,' he replies.

'And the rest?'

He shakes his head. 'Some escaped on the quarter boat. The rest . . . lost.' Water streams from his shirtsleeves in heavy ribbons, puddling in the bottom of the boat where several inches of seawater have already settled.

My arms and legs tremble from my exertions as I clamber aft to tend to one of the injured men. He stares at me numbly, muttering in his delirium that I must be an angel from Heaven.

'I am no angel, sir. I'm from the Longstone light. You're safe now. Don't try to talk.'

The boat pitches and rolls violently as I tend to him, my thoughts straying back to the rock, wondering what is keeping my father.

To my great relief, he appears through the rain a moment later, staggering toward the boat with a woman in his arms, barely alive by the look of her. As he lifts her into the boat, she kicks and struggles to free herself from his grasp, falling onto the rocks. She crawls away from him on her hands and knees, screaming like an animal caught in a trap. Father scoops her up again, calling to me as he lifts her into the boat. 'Take her, Grace,' but she slips from my arms and slumps against the boards like a just-landed fish before clambering to her feet and trying to climb out again.

The uninjured man helps me to hold her back. 'You must stay in the boat, Mrs. Dawson,' he urges. 'You must.'

'You're safe now,' I assure her as she grabs at my skirts and my shawl. 'We're taking you back to the lighthouse.'

Whatever she says in response, I can't fully

47

make out. Only the words, 'my children' swirl around me before she lets out the most mournful sound and I am glad of a great gust of wind that drowns it out with its greater volume.

Back in the boat, Father takes up his oars, pushing us away from the rocks.

'What of the others?' I call, horrified that we are leaving some of the survivors behind.

'Can't risk taking any more in these seas,' he shouts. 'I'll have to come back for them.'

'But the woman's children! We can't leave them!'

A shake of his head is all the explanation I need and in a terrible instant I understand that it is too late for them. We are too late for them.

As we set out again into the writhing sea, the three remaining survivors huddle together on the rock, waiting for Father to return. But it is not to them my gaze is drawn. My eyes settle on two much smaller forms lying to the left of the others, still and lifeless, hungry waves lapping at little boots. I am reminded of my brother Job, laid out after being taken from us by a sudden fever. I remember how I fixed my gaze on his boots, still covered with sawdust from his apprenticeship as a joiner, unable to bring myself to look at the pale lifeless face that had once been so full of smiles. I turn my face away from the rock and pray for the sea to spare the children's bodies as I turn my attention to Mrs. Dawson who has slipped into a faint. I am glad; relieved that she is spared the agony of watching the rock fade into the distance as we row away from her children.

After an almighty struggle, the coble finally moves out of the heaviest seas and around to the lee side of the islands, which offers us some shelter. The relentless wind and lashing rain diminish a little and a curious calm descends over the disheveled party in the boat, each of us searching for answers among the menacing clouds above, while Father and his fellow oarsman focus on navigating us safely back to Longstone. I glance around the coble, distressed by the scene of torn clothes, ripped skin, shattered bones and broken hearts. I pray that I will never see anything like it again.

I tend to the two injured men first, fashioning a makeshift tourniquet from my shawl before giving them each a nip of brandy and a blanket and assuring them we don't have far to go. I return to Mrs. Dawson then, still slumped in the bottom of the boat, her head lolling against the side. I hold her upright and place a blanket over her. She wakes suddenly, her eyes wild as she wails for her children, her hands gripping mine so hard I want to cry out with the pain but absorb it quietly, knowing it is nothing compared to hers. 'My babies,' she cries, over and over. 'My beautiful babies.'

As she slips into another faint and the boat tosses our stricken party around like rag dolls, I hold her against my chest, my heart full of anguish because I can do nothing but wrap my arms around her shaking shoulders and try to soothe her, knowing it will never be enough. I wonder, just briefly, if it might have been kinder for her to have perished with her children, rather than live without them. Closing my eyes, I pray that she might somehow find the courage to endure this dreadful calamity.

That we all might.

9

SARAH

Longstone Lighthouse. 7th September, 1838

When Sarah Dawson opens her eyes, the sky is chalky gray above her. She looks at the young woman called Grace whose eyes are as gentle as a summer breeze and whose hands grip her shoulders. She watches numbly as the boat sets out again, back toward the wreck.

Her arms are empty. Where are her children? In a panic she struggles and falls to her knees. 'They are afraid of the dark, Miss,' she sobs, clinging to the young woman's sodden skirts, tearing at the fabric with her fingernails as if she might somehow crawl her way out of this hell she finds herself in. 'And they will be ever so cold. I have to go back. I have to.'

The young woman tells her she is safe now. 'My father will bring your children back, Mrs. Dawson. We have to get you warm and dry now.'

The words torment her. Why had she been spared when her children had not? How can she bear it to know they are out there in the storm, all alone?

Her body goes limp again as the noise and

panic of the sinking ship races through her mind. She can still feel the ache in her arms from carrying her terrified children, one on each hip, as she'd stumbled up the stairs that led to the upper deck, pushing past passengers she'd chatted with earlier that evening, and whose lives she had no care for in her desperate bid to escape the shattering vessel. Her mind wanders back to the warm summer day when the midwife told her the baby was gone. She sees the tiny bundle at the foot of the bed, blue and still. Now James and Matilda, too. All her children, gone. She tries to speak, but all that emerges is a low, guttural moan.

Giving up her struggle, she allows the young woman and her mother to half carry, half drag her along. With every step closer to the lighthouse she wants to scream at them: Why didn't you come sooner? But her words won't come and her body can't find the strength to stand upright. She crawls the final yards to the lighthouse door where she raises her eyes to pray and sees the light turning above.

Light. Dark. Light. Dark.

Matilda wants to know how it works.

James wants to paint it.

Too exhausted and distressed to fight it anymore, she closes her eyes and lets the darkness take her to some brighter place where she sings to her children of lavenders blue and lavenders green, and where her heart isn't shattered into a thousand pieces, so impossibly broken it can surely never be put back together.

Dundee, Scotland.

Late evening and George Emmerson waits, still, for his sister in a dockside alehouse, idly sketching in the margins of yesterday's newspaper to distract himself from dark thoughts about ships and storms. The howling gale beyond the leaded windows sends a cold draft creeping down his neck as the candles gutter in their sconces. He folds the newspaper and checks his pocket watch again. Where in God's name is she?

The hours drag on until the alehouse door creaks open, straining against its hinges as Billy Stroud, George's roommate, steps inside. Shaking out his overcoat, he approaches the fireplace, rainwater dripping from the brim of his hat. His face betrays his distress.

George stiffens. 'What is it?'

'Bad news I'm afraid, George.' Stroud places a firm hand on his friend's shoulder. 'There are reports that the *Forfarshire* went down in the early hours. Off the Farne Islands.'

George cannot understand, scrambling to make sense of Stroud's words. 'Went down? How? Are there any survivors?'

'Seven crew. They got away in one of the quarter boats. Picked up by a fishing sloop from Montrose. Lucky buggers. They were taken to North Sunderland. The news has come from there.'

Without a moment's hesitation, George pulls on his gloves and hat, sending his chair clattering to the floor as he rushes out into the storm, Stroud following behind.

'Where are you going, man? It's madness out there.'

'North Sunderland,' George replies, gripping the top of his hat with both hands. 'The lifeboat will have launched from there.' The impact of his words hits him like a blow to the chest as he begins to comprehend what this might mean. He places a hand on his friend's shoulder, leaning against him for support as the wind howls furiously and the rain lashes George's face, momentarily blinding him. 'Pray for them, Stroud. Dear God, pray for my sister and her children.'

★　★　★

Learning of his sister's stricken vessel, George throws a haphazard collection of clothes into a bag and leaves his lodgings, much to the consternation of his landlady, who insists he'll catch a chill and will never get a carriage in this weather anyway.

Not one to be easily deterred by frantic landladies or bad weather, within half an hour of learning of the *Forfarshire* disaster, George has secured a coachman to take him to North Sunderland on the coast of Northumberland. The fare is extortionate, but he is in no humor to haggle and allows the driver to take advantage of his urgency. It is a small price to pay to be on the way to his sister and her children. He images them sheltering in a tavern or some kind fisherwoman's cottage, little James telling tall tales about the size of the waves and how he

54

helped to row his mother and sister back to shore, brave as can be.

Partly to distract himself and partly from habit, George sketches as the coach rumbles along. His fingers work quickly, capturing the images that clutter his restless mind: storm-tossed ships, a lifeboat being launched, a lighthouse, barrels of herrings on the quayside, Miss Darling. Even now, the memory of her torments him. Does he remember her correctly? Is he imagining the shape of her lips, the suggestion of humor in her eyes? Why can he not forget her? She was not especially pretty, not half as pretty as Eliza in fact, but there was something about her, something more than her appearance. Miss Darling had struck George as entirely unique, as individual as the patterns on the seashells she had shown him. The truth is, he has never met anyone quite like her and it is that — her particular difference — which makes him realize how very ordinary Eliza is. It had long been expected that he would marry his cousin, so he has never paused to question it. Until now. Miss Darling has given him a reason to doubt. To question. To think. Cousin Eliza and her interfering mother have only ever given him a reason to comply.

The rain hammers relentlessly on the carriage roof as the last of the daylight fades and the wheels rattle over ruts, rocking George from side to side like a drunken sailor and sending the lanterns swinging wildly beyond the window. Exhausted, he falls into an uncomfortable bed at a dreary tavern where the driver and horses will rest for the night.

Disturbed by the storm and his fears for Sarah, George thinks about the cruel ways of the world, and how it is that some are saved and others are lost, and what he might do if he found himself on a sinking ship. He closes his eyes and prays for forgiveness for having uncharitable thoughts about Eliza. She is not a bad person, and he does not wish to think unkindly of her. But his most earnest prayer he saves for his sister and her children.

'Courage, Sarah,' he whispers into the dark. 'Be brave.'

As if to answer him, the wind screams at the window, rattling the shutters violently. A stark reminder that anyone at sea will need more than prayers to help them. They will need nothing short of a miracle.

10

GRACE

Longstone Lighthouse. 7th September, 1838

It is a different home we return to.

I have never been more grateful to see the familiar tower of Longstone emerge from the mist, but I also know that everything has changed, that *I* am changed by what has taken place. Part of my soul has shifted, too aware now of the awful fact that the world can rob a mother of her children as easily as a pickpocket might snatch a lady's purse. But it is the sight of Mam — steadfast, resourceful Mam — waiting loyally at the boathouse steps that stirs the strongest response as I become a child, desperate for her mother's embrace.

Her hands fly to her chest when she sees the coble. 'Oh, thank the Lord! Thank the Lord!' she calls out as we pull up alongside the landing steps. 'I thought you were both lost to me.'

'Help Mrs. Dawson, Mam,' I shout, trying to make myself heard above the still-shrieking wind. 'Father must go back.'

'Go back?'

'There are other survivors. We couldn't manage them all.' Mam stands rigid, immobilized by the relief of our return and the agony of learning that Father must go back. I have never raised my voice to her, but I need her help. 'Mam!' I shout. 'Take the woman!'

Gathering her wits, Mam offers Mrs. Dawson her arm. Too distraught to walk, Mrs. Dawson collapses onto her knees on the first step, before turning as if to jump back into the water.

I rush to her aid, speaking to her gently. 'Mrs. Dawson. You must climb the steps. Mam has dry clothes and hot broth for you. You are in shock. We must get you warm and dry.'

Again, she grasps desperately at the folds in my sodden skirt, her words a rasping whisper, her voice snatched away by grief. 'Help them, Miss. Please. I beg you to help them.'

I promise we will as I half carry, half drag her up the steps. 'My father is a good man. He will bring them back. But he must hurry. We must go inside so that he can go back.'

The two injured men limp behind, while the other, refusing any rest and insisting he is quite unharmed, sets out again with Father to fetch the remaining survivors. I catch Father's eyes as he takes up the oars. Without exchanging a word, I know he understands that I am begging him to be safe, but that I also understand he has to go back. I pray for him as I help Mrs. Dawson into the lighthouse.

Inside, all becomes urgent assistance and action. While Mam tends to the injured men, patching them up as best she can, I fetch more wood for the fire and fill several lamps with oil, it still being gloomy outside. I set a pot of broth on the crane over the fire and slice thick chunks of bread, glad now of the extra loaves Mam had made yesterday. I pass blankets and dry clothes around the wretched little group huddled beside the fire, grateful for the light and warmth it lends to their frozen limbs.

Having dealt with the most pressing needs, my attention returns to Mrs. Dawson. I fetch a screen to save her modesty before helping her out of her sodden clothes, peeling them from her like layers of onion skin before hefting them into a wicker basket. How broken and vulnerable she is, standing in our home without a stitch on her. She shivers and convulses, her skin almost gray in color, her fingertips and toes badly wrinkled from the salt water. I dry her as quickly and gently and respectfully as I can before helping her into the dry clothes. Our eyes meet only once during the long process of undressing and dressing. It is a look that will stay with me for a long time.

'How long is your father gone?' she asks, glancing anxiously at the window.

'He is a strong rower,' I assure her. 'He'll be back soon.'

She stands then, as if in a trance, staring at the collection of seashells and sea glass on the windowsill. 'Matilda will like the glass pebbles,' she murmurs, rubbing her fingertips over them. 'And James will admire the patterns on the shells. He loves patterns. He likes the repetition in things.'

I curl her shaking hands around several small shells. 'Keep them,' I say.

Her eyes are glassy and swollen from her tears. 'They were too cold,' she says in desperate hitching sobs. 'I couldn't keep them warm.'

Kneeling at her feet to lace a pair of old boots, I blink back tears that prick my eyes. I have to stay strong, have to suppress whatever fears I have about my father, still out there at the mercy of the sea.

I startle as Mrs. Dawson places a hand gently on my shoulder. 'I don't know your name, Miss. I'm Sarah.'

'Grace,' I tell her, looking up. 'Grace Darling.'

Sarah Dawson smiles a little through her pain. 'Thank you, Grace Darling. I will never forget your courage and your kindness.'

'You don't need to thank me, Mrs. Dawson,' I say, standing up. 'We only did our duty as light keepers. I thank God for enabling us to save at least some of you.' I drop my gaze to my boots. 'I only wish we could have done more.'

I fetch bread and broth, watching closely as Sarah Dawson eats, just as a mother might watch its child, swallowing every mouthful with her, knowing that with each spoonful her strength will return, and that somehow she will find a way to endure this. As I watch her, I notice a pretty cameo locket at her neck. It reminds me that someone must be waiting for her, perhaps already missing her.

'Do you have family, Sarah? A husband? Sisters?'

'I have a brother,' she says, as if she had forgotten. 'Poor George. He'll be ever so worried. He'll be waiting for me. We were traveling to Scotland to spend a month with . . . ' Her words trail away. 'I don't suppose it matters now.'

I press my hands against hers. 'We can talk later. Try to get some rest.'

Eventually, she sleeps, exhausted from shock and numbed a little from the good measure of brandy I'd added to her broth. While she rests, I take the sodden clothes to the outhouse, where I put them through the mangle, sea water spilling onto the floor until half the North Sea sloshes about at my feet. I am glad to be occupied, but it is tiring work for arms that are already sore from my efforts rowing the coble. With each turn of the handle I imagine myself still rowing, bringing Father safely home.

The clothes are put through the mangle three times, and still Father doesn't return. I think about the bird flying inside and how he'd joked about it. '*Which one of us do you think it is, Gracie, because I'm not in the mood for perishing today, and I certainly hope it isn't you . . .* ' Scolding myself for being maudlin, I carry the heavy basket of damp clothes back to the lighthouse, where I hang them on the line above the fire. Glad to see Sarah Dawson still sleeping, I place the letter I'd found in her coat pocket on the hearth to dry. I will remind her of it when she wakes.

★　★　★

It is eleven o'clock — almost two hours after Father set out again — before he returns with the remaining survivors. My heart soars with relief when the lighthouse door opens and the bedraggled group stagger inside. Not for the first

61

time this morning I have to blink back tears, rushing to assist, keeping myself busy to stop my emotions overwhelming me. This is not a time for sentiment. It is a time for common sense and practicality.

'The children?' I whisper as I help Father out of his sodden coat.

'Not enough room,' he replies, shaking his head. 'They are secured on the rock with the other lost soul.'

'Secured?' The puzzled expression on my face demands further explanation.

'Placed high above the waterline,' he explains. 'Where the sea will not reach them. I will go back when the storm abates.'

We both glance over to Sarah Dawson. I can hardly bear to tell her.

Once again, our living quarters become canteen, laundry, and hospital, and Mam and I become cook, nursemaid, and counsel.

I place a reassuring hand on her shoulder. 'We'll manage, Mam. At least Father is back safe.'

'Aye, pet. I suppose we must be thankful for that. I only wish your brother was here with us.'

Brooks has been on my mind, too. I tell her I'm sure he is safe on dry land, and silently hope I am right.

Nine survivors in total are rescued and brought back to Longstone. Eight men and one woman. Five crew and four passengers. Of all those aboard the steamer when she'd set sail from Hull, it hardly seems anywhere near enough. Mam is pleased to discover that in addition to the *Forfarshire's* carpenter, trimmer, and two firemen, we have also rescued Thomas Buchanan, a baker from London, and Jonathan Tickett, a cook from Hull. Mr. Buchanan and Mr. Tickett soon have fresh loaves baking and a stew bubbling over the fire. The lighthouse is so full of people I can hardly remember the quiet harmony the room usually holds. As always, dear Longstone plays its own part, somehow expanding to accommodate everyone. I take a moment in the stairwell to offer my gratitude to this place I am so proud to call home. I can imagine nowhere safer, or more welcoming, for the poor souls below.

A little later, while they are seated around the fire, the five rescued crewmen talk in hushed voices, each recalling his own version of events, remembering moments of good fortune that had seen them at the front of the ship when it struck the rocks, or moments of great despair when they had been unable to help others. I am troubled to hear them debating their captain's decision not to seek repairs in Tynemouth, shocked by their willingness to apportion blame and point the finger so soon after the tragedy. It doesn't sit well with me, especially not with the captain believed lost to the sea and poor Sarah Dawson close beside them, foundering in her grief.

I offer the men a tray of bread and cheese, putting it down on the table a little too roughly so that the plates clatter against each other. 'I will leave you, gentlemen. You must have many things to discuss.' There is no smile on my lips.

No softness to my voice.

Realizing they have been overheard, the men lower their voices, shuffling their chairs closer together. Guilt clouds their faces as I step from the room. I am happy to leave them to their ill-judged discussions.

By late morning the light is still that of evening and the many candles and lamps scattered about the place burn their wicks hungrily. After the initial melee of organization and the rush to tend to our guests' needs, a strange calm falls over the lighthouse as the hours wear on. One of the crewmen takes up a lament, a haunting tune which we all join in to the best of our ability. Playing its part in the performance, the cacophony of the storm rages on outside. It is impossible to even contemplate making the journey to the mainland to seek help or much-needed supplies. As the waves crash relentlessly against the rocks and the wind howls at the windows, my thoughts turn repeatedly to Mrs. Dawson's children, alone on Harker's Rock. At a point when I think the storm has abated a little, I ask Father if he might consider returning for them.

He shakes his head, placing a firm hand on my shoulder. 'I'm sorry, pet. It is still too dangerous. We must pray for their souls. That is all we can do for them now.'

'But I can't get them from my mind, Father. How can I ever forget their still little bodies, or poor Mrs. Dawson's suffering?'

'I'm not sure you can, Grace. Nor that you should. We all must face our maker when the time comes and those of us left behind must somehow find the strength to carry on. Our duty as keeper of the light is to warn, but it is also to rescue and to offer a place of shelter for those in need. We did our best, Grace, and you showed tremendous courage. I will write a report for Trinity House and make a note in the Log, and we will trim the wicks and inspect the lenses and the light will turn as usual tonight, and the world will turn with it. That, my dear child, is what we must do — carry on. Today, we have seen the very worst of life, and the very best of it.'

'Best?'

He sees the surprise in my eyes. 'Yes. The best. Look at these people — strangers — in our home, in our clothes, eating our food. Look at how they comfort and help each other. Look how much you care for Mrs. Dawson and her children, all of whom you'd never even heard of until a few hours ago. There will always be someone willing to save us, Grace. Even a stranger whose name we don't know. That is the very best of humanity. That is what puts my mind at ease on a day like today.'

His words, as always, fly to my heart, giving me the strength to keep going. Pushing all thoughts of tiredness from my mind, I tend to the fire, fill the kettle with water to heat for tinctures and tonics. As I work, the door blows open, the wind rushing inside, snuffing out lamps and sending yesterday's newspaper skittering along the floor.

The storm has brought unexpected visitors.

From her chair beside the fire, Sarah Dawson observes the new arrivals with a strange detachment. Where were all these people when she was struggling to stay afloat? Where were they when her children were still alive? Too late, she wants to call out to them. You are all too late. But she says nothing, only wraps her arms around herself, rocking backward and forward, singing to herself of lavenders green and lavenders blue and muttering how sorry she is that she couldn't tell Matilda about the lighthouse, and that James never got to use his uncle's paintbrushes.

Reaching up to scratch an itch at her throat, her fingers knock against her locket. With trembling hands, she unhooks the chain around her neck. The filigree clasp is already undone, the two sides of the locket as open as butterfly wings. Inside, there is nothing. No lock of pale barley. None of darkest coal dust. The sea has robbed her of the last piece of her children. Her past has been erased, her future stolen, her whole world shattered into fragments of what was and what might have been and what can never be again. Like Matilda's rag doll, she folds in on herself, head to knees, her grief so all-consuming she cannot imagine how she will ever move on from this moment.

Eventually she sleeps, her fingers unfurling like a summer rose until the locket falls into her lap and the piece of emerald sea glass Miss Darling had given to her drops from her hand and rolls a little way along the floor, where it waits patiently for some other hand to find it.

11

MATILDA

Cobh, Ireland. May 1938

As I step forward to board the tender, I curl my fingers around the piece of lucky emerald sea glass I keep in my pocket. The pier creaks ominously beneath my feet, the noise tugging at my nerves like fingers worrying at a loose thread. A portly gentleman in front of me bends awkwardly to retrieve his dropped ticket. As I wait for him to move ahead I glance at my fellow passengers, wondering how many of them conceal shameful secrets beneath their boiled-wool coats and the stiffened brims of trilby hats. Behind me, Mrs. O'Driscoll chirps incessantly on about how wonderful America is, and how she hopes the rain will hold off for the departure, and Blessed Heart of God, would yer man ever hurry up. Already weary of her endless commentary, I'm thankful the crossing will only take five days.

Our tender, reserved for those with tickets in Cabin or Tourist class, is half-empty as it slips its moorings and heads out into the harbor. I can feel Mother's eyes burn into the back of my neck, demanding me to turn and wave to her one last time. I fix my eyes dead ahead and focus on the horizon, trying to ignore the rising sense of

68

nausea in my stomach.

'Departures always make me tearful,' Mrs. O'Driscoll clucks, dabbing at her cheeks with a handkerchief as we move along the deck to find a seat. 'The Lord bless us all,' she adds, crossing herself and saying a Hail Mary. Rumor has it that a relative of hers perished on the *Titanic*, so her prayers are entirely understandable. Still, I wish she would stop. Prayers and tears make me uneasy.

Settling in a deck chair, I pull a blanket over my legs and take a book from my traveling bag. Mrs. O'Driscoll sits in the chair directly beside me, despite the fact that there are a dozen others she could take.

'I'm not going to fall in,' I snap, a little more harshly than I'd intended. 'You can leave me as soon as we're out of Mother's sight.'

A shrewd smile crosses her lips as she raises an eyebrow in a knowing arch. 'Well now, Matilda. You see, I promised Constance — your mother — that I would see you safely to America, and I intend to do just that. The sooner you accept that I'm here for the duration, the better the journey will be for the both of us.' She rummages in her handbag and lifts out a small paper bag. 'Humbug?'

I shake my head, and then wish I hadn't. With a tired sigh I tell her I will take a humbug, thank you.

She makes a satisfied harrumphing sound and passes me the entire bag. 'Keep them. They're a great help with the sea-sickness.'

A recently widowed bridge-playing friend of

my mother's, traveling to visit a relative on Long Island, Mrs. O'Driscoll had been appointed as my traveling companion despite my insistence that I didn't need anyone to accompany me, especially not a turkey-necked woman with a taste for tweed coats and velvet hats. Of course, my mother wouldn't hear of my traveling alone, accusing me of being deliberately obstinate just to upset her. 'If you'd been this uncooperative when it came to 'other matters' we wouldn't be in this dreadful mess in the first place.' Her words had stung far worse than the accompanying slap to my cheek. In the end my protests, like everything else I had to say about this trip, were completely ignored.

As the tender slips its moorings I open my book, hoping Mrs. O'Driscoll will take the hint and leave me in peace.

'What's that you're reading?' she asks, leaning forward and peering at the cover. '*Instructions to Light Keepers*. Never heard of it.'

'You wouldn't have. It's a family heirloom. Of sorts.' It is, in fact, an ancient volume which explains the operation of lighthouses in great and very boring detail. Passed down to me with the locket, it has idled in a drawer for years, the tell-tale freckles of age quietly multiplying on the unturned pages.

Mrs. O'Driscoll makes an unpleasant sucking noise with her humbug. 'Well, I suppose life would be fierce dull if we all liked the same things.' She takes a copy of *Gone with the Wind* from her own bag. 'Scarlett O'Hara. Now there's a woman to take your mind off a long sea crossing.' She chuckles to herself and opens the book at her marked page, instantly engrossed.

I turn my book over in my hands. The spine is cracked. The embossed title faded. *Instructions to Light Keepers. By authority of Trinity House and the lighthouse board.* While the subject of the book has never interested me, the inscriptions inside hold a particular fascination: *For dear Sarah. So that you might know. Grace* and beneath that, written in a different hand, *For my darling Matilda. From Mummy. x* Below these inscriptions, several other names record the various recipients of the book over the generations.

To discover there'd been another Matilda in the family had enchanted me. As a child I'd often imagined her, talking to her in my games of make-believe until she became real. When a great aunt had secretively explained that this other Matilda was my great-great-granny Sarah's daughter, tragically lost in a shipwreck with her brother, I grieved for her as if she were my sister. In a way, she'd become the sister I never had, the playmate I'd never laughed with or whispered secrets to. With so much of my childhood spent alone, and so much of my life having always felt strangely untethered, I found something comforting in the permanence of the book and locket. I'd brought the book with me not because I wanted to read it, but because its freckled old pages somehow anchored me to my past in a way other parts of my life never had. Something once owned by my great-great-grandmother and part of my family's past, helps me face the uncertain future I am sailing toward.

The transfer across the harbor is mercifully short. As the tender turns around the end of Spike Island I look away from the buildings of the British soldiers' garrison, refusing to dwell on the murky memories it provokes. I focus instead on the great transatlantic liner that looms dead ahead. My stomach lurches at the sight of it.

Mrs. O'Driscoll stands up, smoothing her coat with a brisk flick of her wrists. 'Fierce big, isn't she. Twice the height of Carrauntoohil if she stood on end. Plenty of space to lose me in, that's for sure.' There is an almost playful look in her eyes as she unexpectedly takes my hand and squeezes it tight. 'You may feel as though you're making this trip on your own, Matilda, but that doesn't mean you have to be alone.'

Her words strike an unexpected blow to my determination to dislike her. Growing up without sisters or brothers, and with a mother who couldn't care less what I was doing as long as I wasn't bothering her, being alone is what I'm used to, and yet I've always felt it shouldn't be. A sense of having lost something follows me like a second shadow, but like my granny when she walks into a room and can't remember why, I can never quite grasp what it is I'm looking for. Standing here with Mrs. O'Driscoll's warm hand in mine, I'm suddenly tired of being alone. I stare up at the enormous vessel, blinking away the tears that blur my vision.

'Come along so,' Mrs. O'Driscoll chirps, passing me a handkerchief without so much as a 'dry your eyes now.' 'We've a ship to board, young lady.'

With everyone aboard, the anchor raised, and the engines churning the water far below, three sharp blasts of the whistle signal our departure and we slip peacefully away with a gentle sigh carried in the ship's wake. We soon pass the Old Head of Kinsale, the proud lighthouse sending us on our way, the endless Atlantic Ocean stretching out before us. I stand at the railing and watch Ireland, my home, disappear behind a light sea mist.

'I'm a little tired, Mrs. O'Driscoll,' I say. 'I think I'll take a nap before dinner.'

She studies me carefully. 'Hmm. You do look a little peaky all the same. It might take a few days to find your sea legs. Best have a rest. We've an awful long way to go before we see Lady Liberty.'

Lady Liberty. New York. I can hardly believe I will soon see the famous soaring skyscrapers. I'm not as excited to see them as I'd always imagined I would be. The sight of them will signal the start of nothing short of a prison sentence.

I lie down on the bed in our cabin, trying to ignore the increasing sway of the ship as I map out the journey ahead in my mind. From New York I will travel to Providence, Rhode Island, and then on to Newport, to stay with Harriet Flaherty, a distant relative who was triumphantly rediscovered like a forgotten family heirloom as it dawned on my parents that Harriet offered the perfect solution to their problem. *Their* problem. Not mine. I wasn't part of their discussions and

73

plans, but I heard enough — Mother's voice, shrill as a tin whistle; Father's, turf-thick with quiet disappointment — to understand that Harriet Flaherty was something of a black sheep, so I suppose I will have that in common with her, at least.

The decision made, Mother had related the arrangements to me as if I were a maid being instructed to prepare the guest room. 'You'll stay with Harriet until the child arrives. She'll help with doctors and appointments and those things. The child will remain in America — your Father will make arrangements — you'll come home, and we need never speak of it again.' Like a tumor, the unfortunate little creature will be lanced from me, and we'll all breathe a sigh of relief and carry on as if nothing ever happened.

She made it all sound so simple. Too simple. I wonder at what point her neat little plan will start to unravel.

★ ★ ★

Despite Mrs. O'Driscoll's certainty that I'll find my sea legs, I don't. Three days into our journey I still spend hours every day hanging over the railings, reproducing my breakfast like a cheap circus act, the locket swinging like a clock pendulum at my neck, ticking away the interminable hours as the ship plunges on and my stomach heaves in endless protest. In this way, the days pass until Ireland becomes a full stop at the end of a long paragraph, impossibly small and far away, and still we don't reach America.

The farther the distance from home and the greater my sickness, the more I come to depend on Mrs. O'Driscoll. Far from being irritated by her, I am soon grateful for her patient concern, not to mention her endless supply of handkerchiefs and humbugs and reviving tonics. The truth is that in the brief time we've spent together, Mrs. O'Driscoll has already acted more like a mother to me than Constance Emmerson has in nineteen years.

I thank her as she helps me away from the railings once again. 'I'd be lost without you, Mrs. O'Driscoll. Or lost overboard, more like.'

She bats my gratitude away, but the blush to her cheeks belies her appreciation. 'You hush now with all that sentimental nonsense.'

But despite her words, she throws her arms around me and I press my face into the collar of her turf-scented coat, surprised to find that she isn't as stiff and starchy as I'd imagined. She holds on to me a good while, and I am happy to let her.

'Now, come and sit down,' she says, 'and get your breath back. You're as pale as milk.'

She takes the crook of my arm and leads me, like an invalid, to a deck chair where she tucks a blanket around my knees and tells a passing maid to fetch sweet tea and smelling salts, and to be quick about it because the girl is awful seasick, so she is. I pick at a loose thread on the royal blue blanket and smile to myself, admiring her no-nonsense efficiency.

75

The maid promptly returns with a silver teapot and the ship's best china. Mrs. O'Driscoll pours two amber-colored cups of tea, adding two lumps of sugar to mine. She sits with me until I drink it all and the color starts to return to my cheeks.

She places a floury old hand on mine and looks at me. 'A few more days, and you'll be back on dry land and the swaying will stop.' Her gaze drops knowingly to my stomach. 'The other sickness will pass, too. You should be over the worst of it soon enough.'

I clatter my spoon around my empty cup and bite my lip. 'You know?'

'Of course I know.'

'Did my mother . . . '

'She never said a word. Didn't have to. You've that look about you, and besides, those sudden American holidays with long-lost relatives? They're never that straightforward.' Although I'm embarrassed, I'm relieved that she knows; relieved to drop the charade. 'I don't need to be knowing the ins and outs of it all,' she adds. 'But I thought you might be glad of a bit of advice all the same.'

I think about my mother's refusal to talk, how she closed up like the Venus flytraps in her hothouse whenever I broached the subject of what to expect in the months ahead. I'm so used to not talking about it, I don't quite know what to say. 'Were you as sick as this?' I ask tentatively, sipping my tea as I feel myself slowly coming back to life.

'Suffered dreadfully on both my little ones.

But it passes, and then . . . ' She drifts off into some distant place of happy memories.

'And then?' For all that I don't want to accept my condition or know what happens next, a curious part of me does want to know. Very much.

Mrs. O'Driscoll looks me full in the face. Her pinched little eyes sprout an unexpected flurry of tears. 'And then your cheeks grow as round as peaches and your hair feels like gossamer silk. Your skin shines like porcelain and you feel as if all the goodness in the world belongs to you. It's a miracle.'

I stare into my teacup, ashamed to remember how exceptionally un-miraculous this child's conception was. Forbidden from courting Dan Harrington, the only boy I'd ever cared for but who wasn't considered good enough for me, I'd decided to show my mother how much worse my choice could have been. A British soldier, a Protestant, was the worst possible man for me to be with, so I went to the bars where I knew the soldiers garrisoned on Spike Island went when they came into town. Except a bit of harmless flirtation, intended to get back to my mother, developed into far more than I'd bargained for. I wonder what Dan Harrington would think if he knew the real reason for my trip to America. I doubt he'd care. It hadn't taken him long to fall out of love with me and in love with Niamh Hegarty, just like all the boys did, sooner or later.

'No matter how it happens,' Mrs. O'Driscoll continues, as if she can read my thoughts, 'it's still a miracle. When you feel that first flutter of life . . . there's nothing like it.'

I stir my spoon around my cup, watching the whirlpools in the liquid. 'Were you ever afraid?'

'Oh, yes. Of course! Fear is perfectly normal.' She pats my knee. 'Plenty of courage will see you through. It won't be easy, but it won't be the end of the world either.' She straightens the blanket across her knees. 'You never know, Matilda. Going to America. The child. It might even be the making of you.'

We talk for a long while that afternoon, Mrs. O'Driscoll glad of the opportunity to reminisce about her children as I hungrily devour her wisdom and experience, realizing how starved I am of any real knowledge about what lies ahead. By the time we sit down together for dinner that evening, I'm sorry to have wasted my first few days with her in sulky disregard. There are only two days left of our journey. Suddenly, it doesn't seem nearly long enough.

12

MATILDA

Newport, Rhode Island. May 1938

I smell Aquidneck island before I see it, the briny odor of the ocean leaching through the open windows of the bus from Providence. A suntanned woman in the seat across the aisle sees me place my hand to my nose. 'It's the kelp, honey,' she explains. 'You get used to it.' I smile politely, wishing Mrs. O'Driscoll was poised with her smelling salts.

I already miss her company and her funny little ways. After standing together on deck to watch Lady Liberty and the Empire State Building loom from the mist, she'd accompanied me to Providence, only willing to leave me when she was sure the bus wouldn't stop until it reached Newport and delivered me safely to Harriet Flaherty. She'd insisted on taking Harriet's address, giving me the address she would be staying at in return. 'If you need anything at all, just write,' she'd said, pressing the piece of paper into my hand as we said a surprisingly emotional goodbye.

As the bus rumbles on, I take the piece of paper from my pocket, and unfold it. Beneath the address of her relative on Long Island, she's written the word *Courage*. I lift the paper to my nose, inhaling the familiar scent of lily of the valley and wishing, more than ever, she was sitting beside me.

The bus takes us over a long stone bridge that spans the vast expanse of Narragansett Bay. I press my nose against the glass to get a better look at the view. Yachts and sailing boats speckle the water, stretching as far as I can see. My eye is drawn to two lighthouses on rocky islands in the bay, as I wonder which one Harriet Flaherty keeps. Everything looks pretty with the sunlight reflecting off the water. It is a warm welcome that momentarily shushes the nagging doubts and uncertainties that hang over me.

Over the bridge, the driver turns down a wide boulevard before taking a series of left and right turns down a labyrinth of narrower streets with pretty names like Narragansett Avenue and Old Beach Road, each lined with trees and colonial-style clapboard houses in shades of green and white and rusted pinks. Letterboxes stand on posts in front gardens. A yellow school bus rumbles past. It is all so . . . American. A quiet smile forms on my lips as I think about everyone back home in small provincial Bally-cotton. I wish they could see me. I feel a little proud, brave even, to have traveled so far.

With a crunch of brakes the bus stops at the end of a wide long street. The driver leans around his seat.

'This is your stop, Miss. Corner of Brewer and Cherry.' Hurrying to gather up my things, I make my way to the front of the bus and walk down the steps. He wishes me good luck in a way that implies I'm going to need it. The doors close and the bus rumbles off.

I am alone again. Like a guest suddenly aware they're at the wrong party, all my optimism and courage depart in a hurry.

Fidgeting with my gloves and tugging at the rayon crepe fabric of my dress that clings to my legs, I start to walk. The damp sea air sends my hair springing into childish ringlets beneath my hat. A quick glance in a shop window confirms that I resemble a crumpled sack of potatoes, but I'm too tired to care. I duck and dodge around people on the pavement, trying not to stare at the American women who wear their clothes in a way that makes me feel as dowdy as a nun beside them. As the first spots of rain speckle the tarmac, I run the final few yards to Harriet's house, stepping in beneath a white wooden porch.

I knock on the door. Wait. Knock again, a little more firmly. Nothing. As I open my purse to check the address, I see movement behind the screen door. It opens with a slow, grating screech, like fingernails running slowly down a blackboard. A tall woman leans against the doorframe, smoke spiraling lazily from a pipe that dangles from her bottom lip. She is dressed in a paint-spattered jersey sweater and navy corduroy trousers tucked roughly into welling- ton boots. A patterned headscarf frames her angular face. We quickly assess each other, forming judgments and opinions, measuring the actual against the imagined, wondering what this stranger might become to us in the weeks and months ahead.

'Matilda.' It is more announcement than question, a faint hint of surprise carried in the word.

'Yes.' I smile, remembering my manners even though I want to run back to the bus. 'Matilda Emmerson. All the way from Ireland.' She doesn't smile back. 'You must be Harriet?' The question in my voice betrays my meager hope that I'm at the wrong house, and will be sent next door to a sweet old lady who will welcome me with a soap-scented kiss and a warm apple pie. The woman in front of me looks like she's never baked a pie in her life.

She thrusts a nicotine-stained hand toward me. 'Harriet Flaherty. Welcome to America.' Her voice is low and gravelly, her accent an odd mix of Irish and American. She wraps her hand tight around my cotton glove, studying me closely as we shake hands like business partners sealing a deal. Her expression is serious, but there's something about the way she looks at me that makes me feel a little uncomfortable. 'Well? Are you coming inside then,' she says, striding back into the house. 'Or were you planning to stay in the porch for the rest of the summer?'

I pick up my bag and step inside, the screen door slamming shut behind me.

The cool interior of the house is a welcome relief after the stuffy bus ride. The room is sparsely furnished with a shabby-looking rug, two chairs, and a low coffee table. A sideboard to my left is covered with small boxes and picture frames, all decorated with seashells. A wireless in

82

the corner plays Ella Fitzgerald, accompanied by the *click click click* of a ceiling fan. A bunch of browned lilies sits in a vase on the table, withered petals scattered apologetically on the floor beneath. The smell of stale flower water mingles with the bitter tang of kelp, reaching into the back of my throat and sending my stomach bucking in familiar lurching waves. I glance upstairs, gauging the distance to the bathroom in case I need to make a run for it.

Harriet perches on a chair arm, rests her pipe on a rusting metal ashtray and stares at me, clearly as surprised to find me standing in her home as I am to be here.

'Nice locket,' she says.

I hadn't noticed I was fiddling with it. 'Oh. This. Thank you. It's been in the family for decades.'

'Yes. I know.' She motions toward the small traveling bag in my other hand. 'Is that all your luggage?'

'The rest is being sent on. From New York,' I explain. 'It should be here in a day or two.'

I can hardly remember what I'd packed, it feels like such a long time ago, but seeing how Harriet dresses I already know I've brought far too many pretty skirts and blouses. She looks almost masculine in her scruffy work clothes and her hair tucked inside her headscarf. In my neat primrose-colored cotton dress and matching hat and gloves I suspect I am precisely the sort of prim young thing that Harriet Flaherty loathes.

'Suppose you'll be wanting to freshen up,' she says, standing up. 'I'll show you your room.'

I follow her up a bare wooden staircase, telling her about the awful sea crossing and Mrs. O'Driscoll being so kind, but my attempts at small talk are ignored as she stomps ahead, leaving sandy imprints from the tread of her boots. Halfway along a short landing, she pushes open a scuffed white door. 'This is you. The bathroom's across the landing. The chain sticks so you'll need to give it a good hard yank.'

I step into the small bedroom and place my bag tentatively on the bed. A wardrobe, a nightstand, and a small chest of drawers are the only furnishings. There are no pictures on the walls. No photographs. Faded calico curtains hang limply at the window. A collection of painted shells on the windowsill lend the only sense of decoration to the room.

'Thank you,' I say. 'It's lovely.'

'Well I'd hardly go that far, but it's yours for the duration, so you might as well make yourself at home.' Harriet leans against the doorframe. She looks at me again with that same, slightly surprised expression. 'Will you be wanting something to eat? I made clam chowder.' I nod, even though the last thing on my mind is food, and I don't have the faintest idea what clam chowder is. 'I'll leave it on the table downstairs so. Help yourself to anything else you find.'

'Are you going out?' For all that I haven't especially warmed to Harriet, I don't want to be on my own in this strange cold house either.

She nods toward the window on the opposite side of the room. The ocean glistens beyond, the outline of a lighthouse just visible through the haze. 'Rose Island. Didn't they tell you I was a light keeper?'

'Yes. My mother mentioned . . . '

'That's where I spend most of my time. I told her to explain that you'd have to entertain yourself.'

'Well, she didn't.'

Harriet walks over to the window and picks up one of the decorated shells. She's younger than I'd imagined. I'd assumed I would be staying with an elderly relative, like Mrs. O'Driscoll, but Harriet can't be much older than forty. 'Probably just as well she didn't tell you. You'd most likely never have agreed to come.'

'I wasn't exactly given any choice.'

The acknowledgment of the real reason I'm here rushes into the room like a storm, hanging in the air between us. I perch on the bed like a bold child.

Harriet turns to face me, arms folded across her chest. 'Whose is it then?' she asks. I stiffen at the unexpected question, color running to my cheeks. 'What? Did you think we wouldn't talk about it? Spend our days drinking tea and saying our Hail Marys and pretend you're a good little Catholic girl?'

I stare at the whitewashed floorboards. 'Of course not. I just don't want to talk about it right now.' I glance up at her. 'We've only just met.' I try to sound matter-of-fact but the high pitch to my voice betrays my deep discomfort. I kick off my shoes, suddenly tired of everyone poking around in my life as if I were a pincushion. Exhausted from the journey, fed up with feeling nauseous, and missing Mrs. O'Driscoll more than ever, tears well up in my eyes. I bite my lip to stop them. I don't want Harriet Flaherty to see me cry. I don't want her to write to my mother to tell her I'm a homesick little fish out of water, just as she expects me to be. 'Besides,' I add, 'it's none of your business.'

Harriet blanches at this. 'Really? And there was me thinking you'd come to live in my house, which makes it very much my business.' Taking my silence as a refusal to be pressed any further on the matter, she walks out of the room, closing the door with a bang behind her. 'I'll be back at sunrise,' she calls, more as an afterthought than to offer me any reassurance.

After clattering about downstairs, she leaves with a squeak of the screen door, and I'm alone again. Alone with the awful feeling that I've just made an enemy of the one person I'd hoped would become my ally.

'That went well, Matilda,' I say, my sarcasm ripe as summer berries. 'That went *really* well.'

With nothing else to do, I sulkily hang up my few clothes, place my book on the nightstand, and freshen up in the small bathroom across the corridor. I notice one other room at the end of the landing, which I presume is where Harriet sleeps, if she ever does sleep here. I creep downstairs, pour a bowl of clam chowder down the sink, nibble a piece of bread at the table, and sip a glass of water. I feel like an intruder and retreat back upstairs to the miserable little bedroom where I sit on the end of the bed and look out the window, idly picking up the painted

86

shells from the windowsill. They are a mixture of scallop and cockle shells, all painted white and decorated in deep blue patterns of spirals and fleurs-de-lis. They remind me of the delft my granny once brought back from a trip to Amsterdam. The name Cora is painted on the inside of each shell. Whoever Cora is, she has a steady hand and an eye for beauty. Her delicate little shells feel out of place in this cheerless room, like they don't belong here. Much like myself.

Despite my exhaustion, sleep will not come. I flinch at every creak and crack, at every strange sound from the street below, at the sweep of light from the lighthouse as it passes by the window. Everything feels strange. The pillow. The bed. The bare room. The house. Even my body feels unfamiliar: my appetite, my emotions, my sense of smell all altered by the invisible child that I refuse to believe is real.

I toss and turn until the small hours, when I give up on sleep, flick on the lamp beside the bed, and pick up my book, wishing Mrs. O'Driscoll had been a faster reader and given me her copy of *Gone with the Wind*. I'm sure Scarlett O'Hara would be far better company than a stuffy old book about lighthouses. Opening the front page, I run my fingers over the neat inscriptions. The first, to Sarah from Grace. The next, to Matilda from her mother, and then all the recipients of the book since, each mother passing it on to her daughter, a list of distant relatives diligently recorded over the years as the book changed ownership. I've always felt sorry for poor Grace Rose, her name struck from the page so bluntly. I wonder who she was, and what happened to her. An infant, lost tragically young, no doubt.

At the back of the book is a folded piece of paper, speckled with age. I remember the first time it had tumbled from the pages into my lap, remember the thrill of reading the neat script, written so long ago by a woman who knew my great-great-granny.

Alnwick, Northumberland

September, 1842

My dearest Sarah,

My sister tells me you have written several times in the past while, and I must apologize for my lack of response. Since returning from a trip to visit my brother at Coquet Island in the summer, I have been rather weakened and am to stay with my cousin here in Alnwick for a while. They tell me I am a dreadful patient — far too eager to rush my recovery so that I can get back to Longstone. I do not sleep well without the soothing lullaby of the sea at the window.

I was so happy to hear that you have made a new life in Ireland. I believe it is a very beautiful country. I know you will never forget what happened, but sometimes a different view in the morning, a different shape to the day, can help to heal even the deepest wounds. I hope you will find peace there.

You might tell George that I was thinking of him, if you hear from him at all. I do think of him often.

Wishing you God's strength and courage, always.

Your friend,
Grace Darling

I have learned a little about Grace Darling through snatched fragments of conversation overheard at family gatherings, but I would like to know more. I return the letter to the back of the book, turn back to the start, and begin to read about lighthouse keeping. It turns out to be far more complex, and more interesting, than I'd imagined.

Eventually, I sleep, albeit intermittently. I doze and wake, doze and wake, the flash from the lighthouse playing at the window, my dreamlike thoughts drifting to Grace Darling and my great-great-granny Sarah, women whose lives are connected to mine and whom I know so little about. I also think about Harriet, an outcast, a loner. Like the little girl who made up stories about the people in the portraits inside her locket, my mind begins to circle and turn, wondering and imagining, eager to fill in the gaps.

Who are you, Harriet Flaherty? Whatever did you do?

13

HARRIET

Rose Island Lighthouse. May 1938

Sleep doesn't come easily anymore, and I don't particularly care for dreaming.

I pour a mug of tar-black coffee, listen to the shipping forecast, roll a cigarette. I imagine Cora beside me, her button nose tilted upward, exasperation in her eyes. 'Awful dirty things,' she called them, my smokes. She didn't care for the nicotine stains on my fingertips, said it wasn't nice to see mammy's fingers all yellow, or 'lello' as she used to say.

How many times had I promised to stop? Too many. Broken promises strewn about our lives like the fragments of seashells she collected and stuck together to make her little picture frames. Cora was clever that way, making use of the lost and broken things she found on the beach, carrying them triumphantly home in heavy clacking pockets. 'Look, Mammy! Look!' She loved to turn them back into something useful, painting her seashells until they became more beautiful than the original. If she found half a hinged shell she would look for a matching half and stick them together. Forever fixing and mending. Perhaps she always sensed something was missing.

My breath catches in my chest at the thought of her.

Cora. The sun to my cloud. The calm to my storm.

I walk over to the table, pick up the log book, and slump into the window seat, my back pressed against one side of the thick walls, the soles of my boots pressed against the other. A perfect fit if I bend my knees. Da used to say it was like the lighthouse was built around me it suited me so well. I understand things here, always have. The routine and order make sense to me: the ebb and flow of the tide, the rising and setting of the sun, the coming and going of ships and storms, all carefully recorded in the log book. *Walls whitewashed. Lamps cleaned. Delivery of supplies. Two persons saved from the wreck of a fishing vessel. Painted windows and stairs.*

I miss the old routines since automation has taken away the last of my duties. There are no oil reservoirs to be refilled. No clock mechanisms to be wound. No wicks to trim. Now, I turn the lamps on and off with a simple flick of a switch. They call it progress. I call it nonsense. Like a child all grown up, the lighthouse hardly needs me anymore.

Nobody does.

Apart from Matilda perhaps. Matilda Emmerson, with her pale little face and glistening hair, black as mussel shells. So full of doubt and questions. So unsure of herself. Just like I was at her age. I'm not sure what I expected when I agreed to her coming here — intrigue getting the better of my common sense — but there's something comforting about the lilt of her accent and the smell of turf fires captured in the fabric of her clothes. Matilda carries the echo of a life I thought I'd left behind; a life that perhaps isn't done with me after all.

⋆　⋆　⋆

I add today's entry to the log. *Lamps lit at 8:43 p.m. Seas calm with a slight swell. Light breeze from the east*, then I flick over the crinkling pages, all of them filled with my memories. *Cora caught a crab! Cora saw a shooting star. Cora said Mammy. Cora's fever broke.* I can barely remember the woman who'd written these words. Back then, I wrote as much about Cora as I did about the tides and the weather, family life captured in a few simple words that concealed so much more. If I'd written down everything I wanted to say, I'd have filled a dozen log books a year.

Just after four thirty, Joseph Kinsella, the Assistant Keeper, arrives. I fill him in on the night's events, as few as they are, pull on an old oilskin coat, and make my way outside, my boots crunching over the shale path. Freeing the rowing boat from her moorings, I take a last drag of my cigarette, crush the stub beneath the heel of my boot, jump into the boat, and push off with an oar against the landing wall. I scull around the island, toward the bay, the light sweeping across the ocean, regular as a heartbeat: a warning light to those in danger, a light of remembrance to those who couldn't be saved. By the time I reach the shore, the first rays of sun streak across the water, illuminating the boat and the notches etched into the wooden seat. Twelve in total. One for each life saved.

Only one — the most precious to me — lost.

14

MATILDA

Newport, Rhode Island. May 1938

Newport wakes me with shafts of mellow sunlight that stream through the window and settle against my cheek. I lie perfectly still beneath the cocoon of soft woolen blankets, tucked tight around me so that I can barely move my toes. Keeping my eyes closed, I enjoy the warmth and the light. The smooth scents of pipe tobacco and fresh coffee drift beneath the door, mingling with the briny tang of the ocean that sticks to the walls. Louis Armstrong plays on the radio downstairs, the lively jazz a pleasant change to Mother's warbling operatic arias. Outside, I hear people chatting. It makes me smile to hear the American accents I've only ever heard in the movies.

'America.'

I whisper the word to myself, enjoying the shape of it on my lips. Although I wish I'd come here in different circumstances, there's something exhilarating about waking up on a different continent, far away from my mother's sniping comments and obvious disappointment in everything I do. I can't explain it, but I sense that coming here was about more than it being a convenient place to hide away. It was important.

Necessary. Perhaps inevitable.

I prop myself up against the pillow, push back the blankets and stare at my stomach, unable to connect the biological fact that I am pregnant with the emotional void I feel when I allow myself to think about it. In darker moments I wish the little creature could somehow understand the difficulty it is causing and slip quietly away while I'm asleep. It has happened to plenty of women, so why not me? Mrs. O'Driscoll had said I would start to feel it move soon. 'It's like a distant flutter. Hardly perceptible at first, but you'll know it when you feel it.' The thought repulses and terrifies me. I pull the bedcovers back up and push the thought from my mind.

Downstairs, Harriet hums along to the radio while the kettle sings on the stove. I hear the clatter of crockery and cutlery, heavy footsteps pressing against the boards on the stairs, then a terse knock before Harriet enters, pushing the door open with her behind.

'You awake?'

'I am now.' I pull myself up fully, my head muzzy with lack of sleep and the all-too-familiar dizziness that accompanies my mornings now.

'Fixed you some breakfast, as the Yanks say.' Harriet holds out a cluttered breakfast tray. 'Coffee. Tea. Toast with butter, jam, and marmalade. Grits. Eggs — soft boiled, and hard. Wasn't sure what you'd prefer.' She says all this with the emotion of an iron girder. No 'Good morning. How did you sleep?' No reassuring smile as she plonks the tray onto the blankets, sending tea sloshing out of the spout. 'You can

95

eat it in bed, or I can leave it downstairs if you prefer to be more civilized.'

'Bed will be grand. Thank you.' Without her headscarf, I can properly see Harriet's face. It is sun-kissed and etched with fine lines. She has strong cheekbones and almond-shaped eyes. Not a complete ogre after all. 'And thank you for the blankets.'

She passes my gratitude off with a shrug, deep brown eyes studying me. 'Eat it all. You need your strength.' There's something of a well-meaning scolding carried in her voice, reminiscent of my granny. 'I'll fetch you some clean clothes since yours haven't arrived. Think I've some'll fit you. Sure, they'll have to do, either way.'

I dread to think what Harriet's idea of clean clothes consists of but I don't suppose I have much choice given the circumstances.

She closes the bedroom door with a clatter, thudding off along the landing until another door opens, closes, and all is silent.

My eyes settle on the unruly hotchpotch breakfast: generous slices of sourdough with crusts left on, black coffee in a chipped mug, a pot of strong amber tea. No elegance. No finesse. My mother would scoff and cast one of her most disparaging looks over it. This is food to devour, not to pick at like a nervous sparrow. Suddenly ravenous, I start on the toast, letting crumbs fall onto the bedcovers, not caring for table manners, or any sort of manners.

Harriet returns with a bundle of clothes, tossing them onto the foot of the bed. 'You look

96

like you're about the same size.' There's a moment, a beat, when something shifts in the atmosphere of the room, incomplete thoughts and unspoken words swimming around us. 'Not as fancy as your own outfits, no doubt,' she adds, 'but better than nothing.'

'I'm sure they'll be grand. Thank you.'

'You can fix them up if they're not. Presume you know how to use a needle and thread?'

'Of course,' I lie.

'I'll make an appointment for you to see the doctor later. I've already told him about you. Explained that your husband passed away recently and without close family in Ireland you've come here to have the child.' A cover story. I wonder if that was Harriet's idea, or my mother's. 'Right so. I'll leave you to eat and get dressed.'

She is about to leave the room when I have an overwhelming urge for her to stay. 'I'm sorry,' I blurt out, as much to stall her as to genuinely apologize.

She pauses in the doorway, a frown on her face. 'Sorry? What for?'

'For causing all this trouble and landing on your doorstep and being rude to you yesterday. I was tired after the journey. I really am grateful that you agreed to let me stay here, even if I don't seem like I am.'

Harriet hesitates in the doorway, as if she wants to say something, but changes her mind 'Well, aren't you here now, trouble and all, so we might as well get used to it. Now, eat your breakfast.'

She closes the door behind her.

After eating I dress quickly, ignoring the smell of mothballs and stale tobacco as I pull on a blue day dress that fits almost perfectly. I smooth my hair and pinch my cheeks to bring a bit of color to them. The cameo locket glimmers at the hollow of my throat as the sunlight reflects off the mirror. I touch my fingers to it and spin it around, watching the patterns of light that dance across the floorboards before undoing the fastening at the back and taking it off. I open the clasp and study the perfect little portraits inside: George Emmerson's noble brow and kind eyes; the demure face of the mysterious lighthouse girl. In my made-up stories they always had a happy ever after, but that innocent little girl grew up to know that real life rarely ends that way.

Fastening the locket back around my neck, I make my way downstairs.

'The dress fits perfectly,' I announce, giving a little twirl before perching on the edge of a faded flocked armchair and pushing back the lace curtains at the windows.

Harriet glances up from her newspaper and studies me a moment. 'I'm glad it fits,' she says, returning to her reading. I notice her gaze straying back to me several times.

The newspaper carries a headline about rising tensions in Czechoslovakia and the threat of invasion by the Germans. It reminds me of Mrs. O'Driscoll fretting about the political crisis in Europe and the possibility of another world war. Dear Mrs. O'Driscoll. I wonder if she thinks about me at all, and whether she kept the piece

98

of paper with my address.

'Do you think there'll really be another war?' I ask, admiring the clapboard houses across the street.

'If Hitler has anything to say about it, yes. Awful fecker of a man.'

'Europe's such a long way from America though. I think I'd feel safe here if war did break out.'

Harriet scoffs at this. 'You've no right to feel safe anywhere if there is a war. They said the last one would be over by Christmas, and look what happened.'

A gentle breeze shakes blossom from a tree in the garden next door. The trembling leaves remind me of my father's shaking hands. His experience of war still carried in his nerves.

Eager to change the subject, I stand up and ask what we'll do today. 'It looks lovely out.'

Harriet laughs. 'We won't be doing anything today. You'll rest, I presume. I have to go out.'

The discussions about me coming here had all hinged around getting away from Ireland as quickly as possible, and what would happen when the baby came. Nobody had thought about what I would do while I was waiting; how I might fill the weeks and months ahead. Now that I'm here, it seems ridiculous not to have thought about it. What *will* I do?

'I can't rest for the whole five months, Harriet. I'll go mad.' I fold my arms defiantly. 'I might go for a walk then. See the mansions.'

'Pfft. Seen one mansion, seen them all.' Harriet puts the newspaper down and walks into the kitchen through a door to the right. 'I have to go to the lighthouse. I suppose you could come with me.'

My ears prick up like a dog eager to be walked, but I hide my enthusiasm. I don't especially want to spend time with Harriet, but I don't particularly want to go sightseeing on my own either. 'Suppose I could,' I reply, picking at a loose thread on one of the buttons on the dress.

Harriet peers around the door. 'You're not to be asking endless questions though, or getting under my feet.'

'You'll hardly know I'm there. I promise.'

And so it is agreed. I will go with Harriet to the lighthouse and pretend I'm not there, and she'll tolerate this new relative she has temporarily adopted because, whether she'll admit it or not, I know she feels at least some responsibility for me. If she didn't, why tuck blankets carefully around me last night and place my book on the nightstand? Why whisper into the gray morning light that she was glad I'd come? Maybe my being here is as convenient for a lonely spinster as it is for an unmarried pregnant girl. Maybe Harriet Flaherty and I are not so different after all.

While I wait for Harriet to get ready to leave, I pick up *Instructions to Light Keepers* and turn to my marked page. *Lights must be exhibited punctually at sunset and kept lighted at full intensity until sunrise . . . When there is no assistant, the keeper must visit the light at least twice during the night between 8pm and sunrise;*

100

and on stormy nights the light must be constantly looked after. I read the letter from Grace to Sarah again, wondering who these two women really were. Like a curious child opening doors to rooms they are forbidden to enter, I tug on the distant threads that connect me to them, determined to unravel the tangled knots of the past so that I can find the place where their story ends, and mine begins.

15

GRACE

Longstone Lighthouse. 7th September, 1838

Relief floods my heart at the sight of my brother huddled in the doorway, buffeted by the wind as he urges others behind him to hurry inside. While I hadn't engaged in conversation with my fears for his safety, they had nagged and whispered to me over the past twenty-four hours. It is with much relief that I can finally silence them.

'Brooks! Thank goodness!' The kettle rattles against the hearth as I put it hastily down, rushing to him and throwing my arms around his neck, not minding the cold and damp that seeps instantly into the fabric of my dress. 'You're frozen.' Six other members of the North Sunderland lifeboat crew shake out their coats and hats behind him — William Robson the coxswain, and his brothers James and Michael; Thomas Cuthbertson; Robert Knox; William Swan — all of them soaked to the skin and shivering violently. 'How did you all get here?' I ask, urging them to move closer to the fire.

Through chattering teeth, Brooks explains how they have come from Harker's Rock. 'We learned of the shipwreck, but found no survivors.' He glances around the cluttered room. 'Though I see that you did.' Confusion clouds his face. 'How, Grace?'

'You need to get dry and warm,' I say, taking his dripping coat. 'There'll be time enough for explanations.'

Mam flaps at her face with the end of her apron, so thankful to see her youngest boy safe. Although now a young man of nineteen years, Brooks will always be the baby of the family. Mam wraps a shawl around him, rubbing warmth into his back as I imagine she did when he was an infant. With so many burly men added to the already crowded room, Mam's thoughts soon turn to the conundrum of where to put everybody. 'Yis'll have to be sittin' on the floor,' she announces, throwing her hands in the air in exasperation. 'I canna be conjuring chairs from thin air.'

Brooks calmly suggests that the lifeboat crew will take the empty outbuildings that were used by the workmen when Longstone was being constructed. 'We'll manage, Mam,' he assures her. 'Trust me, after being out in that storm, we'd happily sleep on a bed of barnacles.'

Satisfied with the solution, Mam sets to preparing another pot of broth, her eyes wandering often to Brooks who shivers beside the fire. She is utterly in thrall of him and I am ashamed to feel a prick of jealousy as I observe her, knowing she will never look at me that way. Daughters never hold their mother's affection the way their sons do. Daughters are dutiful, dependable and disposable. Sons are brave and admirable, essential to the continuation of the family line.

When the new arrivals are warm and fed to the best of our ability with the limited supplies that remain, questions and explanations are exchanged like cannon fire. My father and Brooks sit close together, sharing their stories of the previous hours. Brooks is especially astonished to learn of my part in the rescue.

'Grace handled the coble herself while I helped the survivors from the rock,' Father explains. 'She coped admirably.'

In the moment, it sounds almost matter-of-fact, but I know that neither my father, nor I, will ever forget the feeling of dread as he stepped from the boat and walked away from me.

Brooks considers me with renewed respect as I refill his bowl. 'Then I commend your bravery, sister. I know men twice your size who wouldn't have considered going out in such seas.'

'Bravery doesn't come into it,' I reply. 'Father couldn't go alone, and we couldn't leave the survivors to perish. Anyone would have done the same in the circumstances.'

Brooks spoons broth hungrily into his mouth. 'Maybe. Maybe not.'

'She insisted,' Father adds. 'And you know how stubborn your sister can be when she sets her mind to something. A child born in the year of the Battle of Waterloo is always ready to take up the fight. Isn't that right, Gracie?' He takes my hand, pressing a smile into it to assure me of his teasing.

The truth is we are all as stubborn as each

other. Life on a rock in the middle of the North Sea suits an obstinate personality. Being cut off from the mainland, entirely self-sufficient for weeks on end during bad weather, requires something different of a person. It is that difference which sees us through the long wind-lashed nights of winter storms when ships founder, and through the gray mornings which bring the bloated bodies of dead sailors lapping at the island's stone beaches. There is no shame in being called stubborn. It is a necessity to survive.

My brother looks at me a little differently after hearing Father's account of our rescue. I think, perhaps, he no longer sees me as the annoying big sister he'd teased for admiring her seashells, but sees — for the first time — the young woman I've become. A young woman in charge of her mind and her home. A young woman capable of matching the actions of any man, when the situation requires.

The hours pass quickly as I gather up heavy coats and sodden boots. I find dry blankets for the new arrivals, bank the fire, fetch water for the kettle, change makeshift dressings on wounds, and offer words of comfort and reassurance that we will get everyone back to the mainland as soon as possible. I ignore the dull headache that settles on my brow; ignore the ache in my limbs and the cold that seeps through my thin dress, all my shawls given to those who need them more. Only much later, when things are a little less frantic, do I take Brooks to one side and ask the question that has been on my mind since he arrived. Did they find any bodies on the rock?

'Three,' he confirms. 'A reverend and two children. They're secured on the highest part of the rock. We couldn't get close enough to land the boat. As soon as the storm calms, we will remove them and take them to the Castle.'

'To Bamburgh?'

He nods. 'There will be an inquiry. The coroner and jury will need to view the bodies.'

I motion to Sarah Dawson, who sits quietly beside the fire. 'Their mother,' I whisper.

Brooks offers to tell her, but I shake my head. 'I'll tell her.' I feel responsible for Mrs. Dawson. The poor woman is so fragile I can't bear for her to have to share her distress with anyone else. Taking a deep breath, my hands resting against my stomach, I walk across the room to her.

In many ways, the long hours I spent in the coble battling the heaving seas seem like a quiet scull around the island on a sunny day compared to the struggle I face as I crouch beside Sarah Dawson and look into her eyes. Being out in one of the worst storms we have ever known was certainly difficult. Telling a grieving mother that the bodies of her children, although safe, are still out in that storm, lashed by a relentless wind and hard rain, is by far the hardest thing I have ever done. I excuse myself after talking to her, retreating to my small bedroom where I finally let my tears fall and feel no better for having done so.

Over the course of the afternoon and evening, I catch snippets of conversation as my brother and the North Sunderland lifeboat crew coxswain, William Robson, give a full account to my father of events on the mainland. They explain how the lookout at Bamburgh Castle had seen the wreck and fired the cannons to let any survivors know they'd been seen. They describe how a fishing sloop had picked up nine survivors who'd escaped in one of the *Forfarshire's* lifeboats and how Robert Smeddle — chief agent of the Bamburgh Castle Estate — had ridden to North Sunderland to alert the lifeboat crew. Brooks explains that they had taken a small fishing coble rather than the lifeboat, thinking it would be easier to manage in the rough seas, and how they'd rowed for nearly three hours against the swell. Finding no survivors at Harker's Rock, he had proposed they shelter at Longstone until the storm passed. They had come ashore at an inlet south of the island and carried the coble across the rocks. 'It is believed that forty-three passengers and crew were lost. The captain and his wife among them,' he concludes.

It is a sobering account.

'I'll need to write up a report for Trinity House,' Father muses, thinking aloud as he rubs the whiskers on his chin. 'There'll be an inquest: questions to answer, people to hold accountable.'

Brooks nods his agreement. 'Smeddle will take charge of that, no doubt.'

Mam tuts at the mention of Robert Smeddle. As the chief agent of the Trustees who govern the Bamburgh Castle estate, Smeddle is generally considered to be the most powerful man in Bamburgh. He also holds a degree of governance over the lighthouses along the

107

Northumbrian coast and, as such, is well known to us. Well known, and not especially liked.

As the hours pass and the skies brighten a little, we learn that the survivors come from as far afield as London and Dundee, fate having brought them together to our sparse little island. A crewman, Mr. Donovan, is the most vocal of the group, turning the conversation repeatedly to one of accusation, talking about the captain being aware of a leaking boiler even before the ship left Hull. 'Humble should have called in at Tynemouth for repairs. He has death on his hands, make no mistake.'

Father quietly suggests that Mr. Donovan be careful what he says and that such accusations would be better held back until the official inquiry into the disaster. 'In any event,' he cautions, 'Captain Humble has paid with his life for whatever decisions he made. Rather than apportioning blame, I think we would do much better to offer our prayers to those lost.'

As always, my father's good sense prevails and he leads everyone in prayer, giving thanks for our food and shelter and for those whose lives were spared. 'We pray, especially, for all the lost souls, especially little James and Matilda Dawson, who are in God's arms now, and will remain forever in their mother's heart.'

But despite Father's admonishment, Mr. Donovan and the crewmen whisper among themselves in huddled groups and an uncomfortable air of tension settles between the lighthouse walls. Storms, it can shelter us from. Bad feelings, it cannot.

As the evening progresses, my body aches as it has never ached before, my mind too exhausted to think, and yet guilt and worry make for a restless bed that night, my mattress carrying the discomfort of all those below who sleep wherever they can find a place to lie. Nobody would hear of me giving up my bed, not even Sarah Dawson, who insisted she wouldn't sleep anyway and would rather sit by the fire and wait for the morning. I know she thinks of her children. How could anyone rest in the circumstances?

I lie awake, listening to footsteps above as Father paces the service room, setting the boards creaking and cracking. He insisted he take the first watch through the small hours, anticipating another restless night with the storm still raging. I wonder how many more ships will founder on the unforgiving rocks of the Farne Islands while we keep the light here. With the shipping industry booming, I expect the *Forfarshire* will, sadly, not be the last.

The rush of the wind and the crash of waves become a curious lullaby as I release the emotions I've kept locked away. In the pitch dark of my room I stop being the brave lighthouse keeper's daughter everyone believes me to be and allow myself to become who I really am; an exhausted young woman, greatly distressed by the events of the day. Like the sound of the sea trapped inside a conch shell, the events of the *Forfarshire* are forever part of me now.

★　★　★

Downstairs, in the living quarters of the lighthouse, Sarah Dawson cannot sleep. She stares numbly into the fire as the embers fade and die. Everything must leave her it seems, even the warmth of the flames.

The men all sleep easily, snoring wherever they have found a place to rest: chairs, benches, rugs. She envies them the escape of sleep while she must stay awake with only her anguish for company. The storm batters the island outside and she cannot rest, even though her body is bruised and exhausted.

Taking up the plaid shawl Miss Darling had kindly given her for warmth, she slips quietly outside. The strength of the wind almost knocks her over and she clings to the white lighthouse walls, feeling her way around it in the dark as her skirts and the shawl flap wildly against her. She isn't sure of her plan, of what she will do next, but there is something pure about the energy of the storm and she feels oddly calm amid its fury, her grief spoken for her by the violent wind. Her tears match the multitude of raindrops that soon soak her to the skin. *Let it tear me apart*, she thinks. *Let it finish what it has started.*

She wants to scream and shout. She wants to become the storm, but she cannot and as she opens her mouth all she can do is sink to her knees and weep inconsolably with the wind. Her legs cannot support her. Her heart cannot *cannot* endure this. She doesn't know how long she stays there.

Mr. Buchanan, having stirred from his slumber and noticed Mrs. Dawson missing, finds her outside, barely conscious. Like an infant, he carries her in his arms and sits her beside the fire, which he stokes until the flames lick hungrily again. He tells her the pain will go away. 'It'll blow itself out. Like the storm. It will come to an end eventually.'

But she cannot believe him and the storm howls wildly in response, as if to confirm that she is right not to.

North Sunderland, England

After a long and difficult journey, George Emmerson arrives in Bamburgh, from where he is directed to the small harbor town of North Sunderland, but he does not find his sister in any smoky tavern or in private lodgings or fisherwomen's cottages. All he finds are hushed voices and clouded faces and dark tales of a vessel tragically lost. The only fragment of hope he can find is in the survival of several crewmen who, he is told, escaped in one of the *Forfarshire*'s own lifeboats. Everyone else, they say, is believed lost. But until he has confirmation, until someone in a position of authority can tell him with absolute certainty, he refuses to give up hope. He feels Sarah, still. Senses she is alive. As for the children, he cannot tell.

He takes a room at the Olde Ship Inn on the quayside. On a clear day, the owner tells him, you can see the Farne Islands from the upstairs rooms. It is of no comfort. It is agony to be so

111

close to where Sarah might be, and yet he cannot get to her, nor she to him, the seas too violent for any ship or boat to set out in either direction.

He cannot sleep, cannot settle while the storm tugs at the window and sends his thoughts skittering about like blown autumn leaves. He reflects on how carefree he was only days ago, how happy he'd been at the prospect of Sarah's visit, and how captivated he had been by the young woman he'd discovered among the sand dunes and with whom he had conversed about sea dragons and sea glass. How quickly things change.

His fascination with Grace Darling seems suddenly childish; immature and foolish. Unimportant. Through the clutter and tumble of his concern for Sarah, he can hardly remember what Miss Darling looked like, certain he has remembered her wrong in his reckless sketching.

Through the long night, he tosses and turns and for the first time in many days he wishes Eliza were there to comfort him. She would know what to say. She would place a cool hand on his forehead and tell him not to worry so. She is a good woman and deserves better than for him to spend his days turning over images of another in his mind. Life has sent a harsh reminder of the cruel twists it can deliver at a moment's notice. As he lies fully clothed on the straw mattress, poised to run out should any word be sent, it occurs to George that rather than dwelling on a woman he knew for only a moment, he should get on with the business of marrying the woman he has known all his life.

He sits up, hastily scribbling a letter to Eliza to express his love for her, explaining how he has taken a coach to North Sunderland in hope of finding Sarah and the children. But the words sound hollow when he reads them back and with the fire dying in the grate he uses the page to set it going again, wondering about life going in many directions, and the wrong direction, all at the same time. The wind keeps him awake until dawn, when he eventually dozes.

He awakes, midmorning, to a curious calm. Without taking any breakfast, he sets out into the winding narrow streets, knocking on unfamiliar doors and stopping harried-looking women going about their business. He explains that he is desperate for any word of his sister and her children, believed lost in the wreck of the *Forfarshire*, but they cast their eyes to their feet and shake their heads. They can tell him nothing of a Sarah Dawson and her children. Nothing at all.

16

GRACE

Longstone Lighthouse. 12th September, 1838

The sun rises and sets over Longstone three times before the sea conditions are considered safe enough for the life-boat crew to return to Harker's Rock for the bodies, which they take to Bamburgh Castle before continuing to North Sunderland to exchange their borrowed fishing coble for the lifeboat. It is another two days before they return to take the survivors back to the Main. As Father had anticipated, Robert Smeddle arrives with them.

Mam grouses at the window beside me as we watch him step precariously from the boat, his black cloak flapping about in the breeze like wings. She still hasn't forgotten the bird that flew in through the window on the day of the shipwreck. A bad omen indeed. Folding her arms tight across her chest, she sniffs derisively. 'Might have known *he'd* come snooping about. Surprised it took him so long.'

Father patiently reminds her that it is Robert Smeddle's duty to remain informed in all matters relating to shipwrecks and wrecked persons. 'Not so much snooping, as doing his job, missus. Don't be forgetting that we are in Smeddle's employ, to one degree or another, whether we like it or not.'

Mam sniffs again. 'We do not.'

Suitably chastised, she nevertheless does her best to be polite to our guest, regardless of her personal feelings.

'Mrs. Darling! William! Young Grace!' Smeddle greets us all effusively, pressing three freshly baked stotties and a haunch of ham into Mam's hands. 'I bring supplies, Mrs. Darling. Barrels of fresh water, dried peas, tea, barley and wheat.' I can feel the tension in Mam's shoulders release with each item Mr. Smeddle mentions. 'And boats to convey the stricken survivors to the mainland and relieve you of their care. You must be exhausted, cooking and cleaning for so many. What a woman you are! You'll be wanting to put your feet up and get things back to normal, no doubt.'

A smile passes my lips as Mam fusses and fawns, putting on her 'elegant' voice as she explains how she is entirely wrung out with it all, and that she canna remember when she last rested her poor aching feet.

As Father leads Smeddle inside, I walk behind with Mam, who inspects the quality of the ham. Suitably impressed, she concedes that Mr. Smeddle isn't such a bad sort after all. 'At least he had a mind to bring provisions, which is more than can be said for some.' She has never forgiven the Herberts for arriving empty-handed one Whitsuntide, apparently having left a basket of food on the scullery table. She'd served them a measly supper that evening to make her point. They have never arrived empty-handed since.

Smeddle adopts his usual air of authority as he

strides into the lighthouse, addressing his comments to my father while handing his cloak and hat to me as if I were a maid-of-all-work. 'I'd already held an inquiry and written up my remarks for the Crewe Trustees, considering the matter to be closed, when your son, Brooks, returned with the North Sunderland lifeboat crew and recounted the remarkable events that had taken place here. Of course, I had to hear it for myself and came as soon as I could!'

After several days of quiet condolence and prayer, Smeddle's commanding voice feels too loud and harsh in the confined space at the bottom of the lighthouse. Unexpectedly, he then turns his attention to me.

'Young Grace. Your brother tells me you assisted with the rescue, by which I presumed he meant caring for the survivors when they were returned to Longstone, but he assures me your part in the event was far more than that of nursemaid. He tells me you set out in the boat with your father. Is it true?'

I squirm beneath Smeddle's scrutiny, wishing he wouldn't peer at me with his narrow eyes. Suspicious or excited, it is impossible to tell. Whichever it is, I don't wish to be the center of Robert Smeddle's attention, or anyone else's for that matter.

'Yes,' I confirm. 'I set out in the coble with my father to aid the stricken survivors.' I keep my voice light, matter-of-fact, as I place Smeddle's cloak on a hook beside the door where it dangles like a hanged man. I don't care for the ominous form of it. 'My father made the journey twice.'

116

Sensing my discomfort, Father intervenes to confirm the events of my brother's story. 'You have things correct, Robert. Grace was the first to see the wreck from her bedroom window. As usual, she was perfectly levelheaded and assisted ably in the rescue. As you know, she is an experienced oarswoman. I couldn't have made the journey without her. The seas were like nothing I've ever seen before.'

Smeddle's obvious incredulity settles in the creases and lines on his face, his unfortunate pallor reminding me of crinkles pressed into a puddle of warm wax. 'Of course, I know your daughter to be an active girl. I've often seen her rowing in the waters around the islands, or over to the Main or to Brownsman on clear calm days, but the seas on the night of the *Forfarshire* disaster place an entirely different perspective on matters. I suspected young Brooks of embellishing his sister's role in the rescue and will admit I'd dismissed his reports as balderdash, but perhaps I was a little hasty.' He turns to me again. 'And you steadied the coble yourself, Grace, while the storm raged and your father attended to the desperate survivors clinging to the rocks?'

His dramatic narrative wouldn't be out of place in one of Mary Herbert's romance novels. I do my best to remain polite, nodding my assent. 'Yes, Mr. Smeddle. That is how it happened, but I was only alone in the boat for a few moments. One of the surviving men took the oars while I tended to another who was badly injured, and to poor Mrs. Dawson, who was

117

distraught to have lost her dear children.'

Even with the assurance of us both, Smeddle appears incapable of fully comprehending what he hears. 'It's simply remarkable. I can hardly believe that a woman would even consider setting out in those seas, nor that your father would permit it. Pure folly, surely.'

I can tell my father is rapidly losing his patience with Smeddle's endless questioning. He stands up suddenly, the legs of his chair scraping against the floor, the noise voicing his frustration for him.

'Well, I *did* permit it, Robert. Indeed, it was Grace who insisted we attempt a rescue while I was initially hesitant. She set out in the boat with me and the rest you know.' He places his hands on his hips. 'Now, unless this is an official inquiry, I think we would all like to have something to eat, and put the whole episode behind us.'

Smeddle laughs, tipping his head back so far his hat tumbles to the ground. 'Put it behind us! Mark my words, William, there'll be no putting this behind you. The locals are already talking about Grace, and will talk about her for a long time yet, I'll wager. When the newspapers get wind of her role in the rescue she'll be the talk of the country. Everyone loves a romantic tale of a daring young heroine.' He stands up, grasping my hands in his, gripping them tightly. My skin recoils at the touch of his clammy flesh against mine. My heart races as he leans forward, lowering his voice as he stares at me with great intent. 'There'll be a silk gown for you for this,

118

Grace. A silk gown! You mark my words.'

I laugh, nervously, willing him to let go of my hands. 'Whatever do you mean?'

'You, Grace Darling, will be famous!' He bangs his hands on the table, making me jump. 'And what a name to accompany such courage. Grace Darling — Heroine of the Seas.' His hands sweep upward in a broad flourish as he speaks, as if he were a theater promoter announcing his latest play.

Smiling politely, I assure him he is quite mistaken. 'It is the duty of a lighthouse keeper to save those in peril.' I grab a book from the windowsill, flicking forward a few pages until I find the line I am looking for. '*It is the duty of light-keepers to aid wrecked persons as far as lies in their power,*' I read aloud. 'See, it is stated in the instruction manual to light keepers from Trinity House. What sort of a story could the newspapers possibly make of such a simple fact?'

Smeddle doesn't answer, only smiles a self-satisfied smile that sends shivers down my spine. 'In any event,' he continues, 'the official verdict on the incident was challenged, so a second inquiry must take place. Your official report will be important evidence, William.'

Father assures Smeddle that everything is in order on that front. 'A full report is already written and ready to be dispatched to Trinity House. There is nothing more to add, Robert. We assisted the stricken passengers, and now we will return them to the mainland and wish them a speedy recovery. Our part in the matter is closed.'

Smeddle cracks his knuckles and blows his nose in a vulgar manner, muttering to himself about matters never being quite that simple.

Unable to tolerate his company any longer, I excuse myself, but even seeking distraction in my chores can't stop the echo of Smeddle's words. *'The locals are already talking about Grace . . . When the newspapers get wind of her role in the rescue, she'll be the talk of the country.'* With the wind tugging at the ribbons of my bonnet, a brooding discomfort settles on my skin like a fine sea spray. I look toward the just-visible outline of the mainland and wonder if it is true: if people there are talking about me. Have the wild winds that battered our island really carried my name so far, so quickly? Even if it is true, names are easily forgotten. Like the storm, any interest in me or my family will soon move on.

I am quite certain of it.

17

GRACE

Longstone Lighthouse. 12th September, 1838

Almost as suddenly as they arrived, our unexpected guests depart.

One by one, the nine survivors of the *Forfarshire* prepare to leave Longstone. They are eager to return to their families while also anxious about returning to a life that is forever changed by what they have endured, and lost.

There are many exchanges of gratitude as the lifeboat readies to leave. I help where necessary and step back when my assistance isn't required. I've become accustomed to caring for this small group and it is difficult to say goodbye.

When it comes to Sarah Dawson, I cannot stop myself rushing to her aid, nor does she want me to. Terrified of being out on the water again and still terribly weak and frail, having hardly slept or eaten since her ordeal, she trembles as she steps nervously into the boat, reaching up to touch her hand to my cheek as she sits down.

'You and your family have been so kind, Miss Darling. I'll never forget it.' She presses something into my hand. 'A token of my eternal thanks.'

Seeing that she has given me her locket, I insist she take it back. 'It is too much, Sarah,' I urge. 'Please. I cannot take it.'

She refuses to listen to me, quietly closing my fingers over it and smiling gently. 'It used to hold a lock of each of my children's hair. It's too painful for me to see it empty. It's not worth a great deal, but it would mean a lot to me to know it is here with you, at the lighthouse.'

Such pain and torment cloud her face that I have no choice but to quietly accept it. 'I will treasure it. Thank you.'

'I'd have been very proud to introduce you to my little ones,' she continues. ' "This is Miss Grace Darling,' I'd have told them. 'One of God's angels on earth, and the bravest woman in all of England.' ' Tears form in her eyes as she speaks. 'Matilda wanted to know how the lamps keep burning all night, but I didn't know. You could have told her, couldn't you?' I nod, unable to find anything helpful to say. 'Five days and nights I've been without them now,' she continues. 'I've never been without them a day. Not since they first bloomed in my belly and kicked their little feet.'

My thoughts flicker to the stiff little bodies on the rock; little bodies that now rest at Bamburgh Castle, waiting for their Mam to say her last goodbyes. I grasp Sarah's hands in mine. 'And if I should ever marry and be blessed with children, I will tell them about you, Mrs. Dawson. What you have endured these past days . . . I only hope I can show such courage, should I ever need to.'

We share a final embrace and, with an ache in my heart, I stand beside my parents and watch, silently, as the sea that has robbed Mrs. Dawson and the others of so much conveys them back toward the distant shore, and the misshapen life awaiting them there.

★ ★ ★

With our guests departed, I feel as empty as Longstone's apartments. The rooms appear ten times bigger than before. Far too spacious for our simple needs. The lighthouse senses everyone's absence, too. A hesitance lingers in the air as we attempt to settle back into the normal routines that have been all but forgotten in the tumult of recent days. With the lighthouse empty, I complete my chores quickly and take advantage of the first reasonable day's weather in almost a week to take a stroll around the island. The storm has brought such devastation, leaving great mounds of driftwood and seaweed piled up here and there. Seashells and stranded starfish color the sand pink-orange in patches, like the flesh of ripe peaches, but it is the limp remains of dozens of seal pups that I find the most distressing evidence of the storm. The shape of Longstone Island, the feel of it, is changed by what has taken place here.

As I walk, my attention is drawn to an unusual piece of rock. Bending down to pick it up, I smile: the telltale spiral of one of Mary Anning's 'curies.' A fossilized sea creature. A piece of the past, washed up in the present. Running my fingers across the undulating pattern, I think of how Mr. Emmerson would like to see it and realize I haven't thought about him for days, my mind having been so occupied with other matters. Thinking of him now, I discover that I think no less of him. I still remember our conversation. How, when he'd asked if I'd seen Miss Anning's sea dragons, I'd remarked that sea dragons didn't usually swim in the waters this far north, it being too cold for them. His laughter was full of warmth that spread around me like the heat from a smithy's furnace. Even with the cooling distance of the weeks since, an ember of something glows within me still. I place the fossil in my pocket to add to my collection. Mr. Emmerson, I put away also, into a very private place in my heart.

I stand then for a long time, just me and my beloved island, the ribbons of my bonnet flapping in the breeze, my skirts billowing around me, swaying to and fro like a church bell. Steamers slip by on the horizon. Fishing boats come and go. Everything returning to normal.

Having dosed myself with a much needed tonic of sunlight and sea air, I pick my way carefully over the slippery algae-covered rocks, back toward the familiar landmark of the lighthouse tower. The lamps have been some-what neglected amid the chaos of the rescue. There is much work to be done.

It is only much later that I remember the letter from Mrs. Dawson's coat pocket. The envelope and letter are still laid out on the hearth, the pages as dry and crinkled as autumn leaves, the ink mostly smudged. I can't help noticing sketches of lighthouses in the margins as I fold

124

the page. I hesitate for a moment, imagining my sister Mary-Ann at my shoulder, urging me to read the letter. Mary-Ann isn't known for her discretion, but I respect Mrs. Dawson's privacy. Smoothing the page, I return it to the envelope and place it in my skirt pocket. I will return it to her as soon as I can take a trip to the mainland and make the necessary inquiries as to a forwarding address. As I place the envelope in my pocket, my fingers settle on the cameo locket I'd forgotten I'd put there earlier. Taking it out, I admire the delicate filigree clasp and the words etched onto the back: *Even the brave were once afraid*. I fasten the chain around my neck. I'd expected it to feel a little awkward, heavy with the weight of Mrs. Dawson's grief, but it sits pleasantly at the hollow of my neck.

That evening, as I sit by the fire to read a favorite volume on geography, my fingers absentmindedly twirl the locket around and around. My thoughts stray often to the little locks of hair that should be nestled safe inside, and then I think of Sarah Dawson, and eventually Mr. Emmerson, whose image settles so determinedly in my mind that I can almost sense him beside me, as invisible and definite as a gentle breath of wind against my skin.

North Sunderland, England

At the Olde Ship Inn, George Emmerson is restless, waiting for news of the safe return of the lifeboat that will bring his sister. He cannot settle, pacing the boards as he goes to the window and returns to his seat, still no sign of them. He rehearses his words over and over in his mind, but no combination will suffice. No words can aptly express what he wants to say. No expression feels right.

Eventually, word spreads that the lifeboat and the survivors are back. George rushes to the harbor where a mournful silence falls over the gathered crowd of onlookers as the desperate group emerges, one by one, up the steep steps. And there she is. His dear sister.

'Excuse me. Make way. My sister is there.'

The crowd parts to let George through. Sarah raises her head as she steps unsteadily onto the quayside, her eyes searching the faces of the gathered crowd until she sees him and it is the sight of him, her dear brother, which brings her to her knees. George throws his arms around her and they stand, huddled in a tight embrace, as the crowds move away, giving them some privacy in their grief.

Neither of them speaks. When it comes to it, there simply are no words.

Through the fabric of her cloak, damp with sea spray, George feels the convulsions of his sister's body. He understands that she is broken beyond repair, but he must be the one to try to fix her. He presses her body to his, praying that some of her pain will pass to him, praying that he might bear this for her.

After a long time, she lifts her face from his shoulder, her eyes red and swollen, her face hollow and pale so that she is almost unrecognizable from the vibrant woman he'd seen last Christmas. 'I must see them, George.' Her voice is a whisper.

He nods. 'It is all arranged.'

They walk slowly, quietly, to a waiting coach that will take them to Bamburgh, where Sarah will somehow find a way to say a final farewell to her children. As he walks, George wonders how the streets can be so quiet and how the fisherwomen can talk so easily about inconsequential matters such as the day's catch, and how it is that, for some, everything continues as normal when, for others, so much has changed so irrevocably.

Later that night, when it is done, Sarah sits by the fire in Eliza Cavendish's home, a cup of ale in her hand. She asks George for paper and ink.

'What for, sister?'

'So that I might write it all down. What I remember. Of the lighthouse, and those who saved me.'

He crouches beside her. 'It is over now, Sarah. You must try to forget.' He is patient; careful with his words.

Sarah disagrees. 'I must remember, George. We must never forget.'

Thinking her rambling in her distress, George placates her. 'Very well. I will get you some paper.'

'Thank you. We mustn't forget the brave people who came to our rescue. We must never forget her name.'

'Whose name?'

'The woman who saved me. Grace Darling.'

The fire crackles and spits, shooting an ember onto the hearthrug. George stoops to pick it up with the fire irons, tossing it back into the grate. The rug smolders, a scorch mark seared forever into the weave of the wool, and in a moment of clarity George realizes that is precisely what Miss Darling has done to him. Despite the brevity of their interaction, despite his betrothal to Eliza Cavendish, despite none of it making any sense whatsoever, Grace Darling has seared herself into the fiber of his soul. And no more than he can easily remove the scar from the hearthrug, neither can he easily remove the memory of her from his heart.

VOLUME TWO

heroine: *(noun)*

a woman admired and emulated for her
achievements and qualities

*Is there in the whole field of history, or of
fiction even, one instance of female heroism
to compare for one moment with this?*

— *The Times*, 19th September, 1838

18

MATILDA

Newport, Rhode Island. May 1938

Late morning and the strengthening sun illuminates the waters of Narragansett Bay, making everything shimmer like silk. I follow Harriet past great teetering piles of lobster pots and crab pots and thick coils of rope. I cover my nose as the pungent stench of harbor life settles in the back of my throat and turns my stomach to jelly.

Harriet unties a small boat from its moorings and rows us easily away from the harbor wall. Soon, we are gliding effortlessly across the bay, the gentle rocking motion of the boat no worse than that of a train carriage. Having prepared myself to feel seasick again, I am surprised to find myself quite enjoying being out on the water as Harriet sculls us toward a small island in the middle of the bay. I pinch my nose to block out the overpowering smell of the kelp. Harriet rolls her eyes at me and shakes her head. I ignore her and focus on the view.

Despite the smell, I enjoy the breeze in my hair, the sting of the wind against my cheeks, the glimmer of sunshine on the surface of the water, the soothing slap and bump of the waves against the hull of the boat. New sounds, new smells, new sensations. My skin prickles in response as I trail my hand in the water, remembering happy short-sleeved summer days when my father would roll up his trousers and take off his socks and paddle with me in the sea, jumping over the smallest waves as I squealed in delight. I'm still haunted by the look on his face when my mother told him I'd fallen into the worst sort of disgrace and hadn't I only gone and got myself pregnant. To watch him close the living room door so gently behind him was the perfect demonstration of dignity and control when I had demonstrated neither. I'd only ever wanted to make him proud. All I've succeeded in doing is to disappoint him in the greatest way imaginable.

While my thoughts wander back to Ireland, Harriet focuses on her rowing, until even she can't ignore the silence in the boat. 'You get used to it,' she says. 'The smell.'

Like a pet starved of attention I leap at the invitation to talk. 'I hope so. Is it always this bad? It gets right to the back of my throat.'

'That's Aquidneck for you.'

'Have you lived here long?' I ask. Harriet pulls on her oars. Four long hard strokes. She doesn't reply. 'Do you miss Ireland?'

She fixes me with a hard stare. 'I thought you weren't going to ask questions. Wasn't that the agreement?' There's an edge to her voice, a warning not to get too close.

I fold my arms defiantly, sit up straight, angle my chin. 'There's no need to be quite so rude. I'm only trying to make conversation because I'm sat with you in this stupid boat and because

I have to spend the next five months with you, and because it's common courtesy for people to get to know each other — especially if they're related.' My voice wobbles with emotion as the anger I've held inside me these past weeks spills out in a rush. I'm angry with my parents for sending me away when I needed them the most, angry with myself for getting into this ridiculous situation in the first place, angry with Harriet Flaherty for being such a disappointment. I am even a little angry with Mrs. O'Driscoll for abandoning me just when I was starting to feel more hopeful about everything. I think of the piece of paper in my coat pocket. The neat handwriting. The word courage.

Heat rises against the locket at my neck. Like Newport's kelp and the damp salty air against my skin, Harriet Flaherty has an almost physical effect on me. 'If you're determined to dislike me then fine, have it your way. I doubt you've ever had it any other, living on your own, shutting people out with your cutting remarks and your scowl and your ... your clothes from a menswear department of the 1920s.'

I'm trembling by the time I stop talking, but I'm pleased to have stood up for myself. I refuse to let Harriet Flaherty bully and intimidate me. I've had nineteen years of that from my mother and I didn't travel halfway across the world to have more of the same.

Harriet says nothing as she continues to row, never breaking her momentum. I could scream at her but I press my frustration into the wooden seat with the palms of my hands and stare at the

133

lighthouse ahead, blinking away the flood of tears that threaten to fall at any moment. The oars rattle in their brackets as Harriet pulls them out of the water and rests them on the edge of the boat. Silence surrounds us as we drift for a moment. After a long pause, she responds.

'So, you *do* have a bit of something about you after all. I thought you'd become a prissy little madam like your mam, but maybe I was wrong. There's nothing worse than a girl who doesn't have anything to say for herself apart from do you like this dress and that hat and when will I ever be married.' She leans forward. 'I'm glad to see you've a fire in your belly, Matilda. That's all.'

So, it was a test. She was provoking me.

'I don't know about a fire,' I say, sulkily, 'but there's something in my belly, all right.'

We glance at each other, and look away again, but not before I see the start of a smile on Harriet's lips. I hide my own smile behind a fake yawn and turn my face back toward the sun.

Infuriating woman.

★   ★   ★

After mooring the boat beside a jetty, Harriet strides up a flight of stone steps that lead to the lighthouse. The boat tips and wobbles as I move forward. If I weren't so stubborn I would call for Harriet's help, but I refuse to be seen as weak or helpless so I crawl out on my hands and knees until I make it onto dry land. The borrowed cotton dress clings to me like the limpets on the rocks as I follow Harriet up a winding shingle path toward the lighthouse.

Close up, it is much bigger than I'd expected. An octagonal white wooden tower stands proudly above a two-story clapboard keeper's dwelling. The lower story is white wood; the upper story a sloping tiled roof with three dormer windows on each side. A lantern room crowns the top of the light tower, surrounded by black iron grille work around the outside. I tip my head back, dizzy as I take in the height of the tower. The breeze is stronger on the island, exposed without the shelter of the buildings that hug the harbor wharfs. I hold my hand to my hat as I stare up at the lantern, so engrossed that I don't notice a dog bounding over to me until a wet nose nuzzles my hand.

I bend down to pet him. He's a sweet little black-and-white patchwork of a thing, his stiff tail beating frantically, swinging his whole body from side to side as I rub his ears. He gazes at me with adoring brown eyes until a shrill whistle sees him scurry away. Shielding my eyes from the sun, I watch him run toward a man who scoops the dog into his arms before he continues to make his way over to me.

'Sorry about that,' he says when he reaches me. 'Wants to be everyone's best friend this one does.'

I smile and assure him I don't mind. 'I love dogs, and this little fella is an absolute dote.'

The man tickles the dog's belly affectionately. 'You're a charmer, all right. Aren't you, Captain?'

135

'Cute name. It suits him.'

'Her.'

Laughing, I apologize for my mistake as Captain squirms in the man's arms. He puts her down and throws a sun-bleached piece of driftwood for her to chase. 'I'm Joseph, by the way,' he says, holding out a suntanned hand. 'Joseph Kinsella. Assistant Keeper.'

Joseph Kinsella is quite the American poster boy in his rolled-up faded blue jeans, deck shoes, and a college sweat-shirt. A shock of fair hair falls into eyes that match the color of his jeans. He reminds me of Mickey Rooney's Andy Hardy in A *Family Affair*, but a little wiser and older.

'Matilda,' I reply, shaking his hand. 'I'm staying with Harriet Flaherty. She's here somewhere.' I look around but can't see her anywhere.

A look of recognition flickers across Joseph's face. 'So *you're* the wild Irish girl!'

'Wild?' I blush furiously. Surely Harriet hasn't told him the real reason I'm here. What about the cover story she'd said we should stick to? Only then does it occur to me that if I'm supposed to have been married, I should probably wear a ring.

'Only teasing,' Joseph says. 'I'm a quarter Irish myself. Does that give me the right to tease?' His dimpled grin is hard to ignore.

'Just about,' I smile.

'You're staying with Harry for the summer, I hear.'

'Harry? Is that what you call her?'

'That's what she's always been known as. Got

136

the shock of my life when I discovered Harry Flaherty was a woman!'

'Well. Hardly.'

He laughs. 'First time in Newport?'

'First time in America. First time anywhere other than Ireland,' I say as Captain races back to us, proudly dropping the driftwood at my feet, her head tilted hopefully to one side.

'Looks like you're already made a friend,' Joseph says as he picks up the driftwood and throws it as far as he can, sending Captain skittering after it again. 'Which part of Ireland are you from? My relatives are in Sligo.'

I hesitate. Mother had me well drilled, insisting I wasn't to be telling people about myself or getting overly friendly with the locals. She is terrified that news of my condition will find its way back across the ocean to her narrow circle of judgmental friends. Being so far away from her, I suddenly couldn't care less.

'Ballycotton,' I reply. 'In County Cork.'

'Beautiful part of the country. Great beaches I hear, although we've plenty here to rival them.'

Captain returns with the stick, dropping it at my feet again. I rub her velvety ears and glance back to the lighthouse. There's still no sign of Harriet. I wouldn't be surprised if she'd rowed back to the house and left me here as another test. 'I don't suppose you'd know where Harriet might be?'

'Probably at the beach around the back. She likes to collect shells and such. I'm heading up to the lantern room. You're welcome to come with me if you'd like to look around.'

Joseph whistles for Captain to follow and heads up the path to the lighthouse. I follow behind, Captain at my heels, the sun at my back, and the breeze ruffling my hair. I've been in Newport less than a day, and I already feel as far away from my life in Ireland as it is possible to be. There's something delightfully uncomplicated about this little harbor island with its timber lighthouse, and for a few untroubled moments I'm not the politician's daughter who has disgraced herself and her family, but just a wild Irish girl on her American holiday, as free as the wind that ripples the water in the bay.

It is at that moment I feel a strange fluttering sensation deep within me, like a feather brushed lightly against my skin. I stop walking and stand perfectly still. I feel it again. And again. *When you feel that first flutter of life . . . there's nothing like it.* The significance of it takes my breath away as Captain pushes past my legs. Ahead, Joseph says something about a glass of iced tea. I start walking, my mind spinning as I reach the lighthouse where I lean against the door. Suddenly light-headed, I trip over the step and stumble inside, just like the cheap drunken whore of my mother's insults.

Joseph grabs my arm and helps me to a chair. He hands me a glass of water and says he'll fetch Harriet. I'm not sure I say anything in response.

Captain lies devotedly at my feet, and as I stare at my reflection in the glass I feel the flutter again. It is the gentlest of feelings and the harshest reminder of what I have done and why I

138

am here, and the only emotion I can summon is fear.

Sitting in this pretty little lighthouse, waiting for one stranger to fetch another, I realize that no matter how many distant relatives are unearthed, or how many well-meaning chaperones pass on their advice, I really am on my own. Harriet Flaherty doesn't know the first thing about me, she doesn't know what it's like to be sent away from everyone and everything you know. However convenient her American home might be, Harriet can't help me any more than I can help her.

In the end, the only person we can truly rely on is ourselves.

19

HARRIET

Rose Island Lighthouse. May 1938

Time doesn't heal, as they say. I still feel the gaps in my day where Cora should walk and breathe and laugh beside me. I come here every day to the little horseshoe-shaped beach, collecting shells and driftwood and other little oddities in Cora's memory, filling my pockets until they sag beneath the weight of my spoils.

For sixteen years we walked and talked and played together on this little island beach, the lighthouse standing tall behind us. This is where Cora fell in love with the ocean, where she figured out the complicated ways of the world, where she grew from an inquisitive child into a clever young woman. In three weeks, I will be without her for three years. It hardly seems possible.

It was always the two of us. Harriet and Cora. The lighthouse keeper and her daughter. 'Look, Mama,' she would shout, running over to me with a cockle shell, pushing hair from her eyes with sandy fingers. 'We're like two halves of a shell.' Without her, I'm not even half of what I was with her. I don't know how to *be* without her, so I've retreated from the world, like a hermit crab scuttling away to hide among the rocks.

But the world has found me.

As I always knew it would, my past has caught up with me. Why now, I don't yet know. All I can be sure of is that despite my hesitation and uncertainty, despite my awkwardness around her, Matilda being here makes sense. She gives me a purpose, a reason to carry on. For now.

When her baby comes in the fall, Matilda will go back to Ireland. So I must only allow myself to paddle at the edges of whatever relationship we might form while she is here. I will dip my toe. See how it feels. I don't trust it enough to immerse myself fully.

Not yet.

Maybe never.

20

MATILDA

Newport, Rhode Island. May 1938

The fluttering stops as suddenly as it began and I feel silly when Harriet rushes into the lighthouse, concern etched across her face.

'Matilda? Is everything all right? Joseph said you nearly fainted.'

They both stand in front of me, like worried parents.

'I'm grand,' I say, sipping my water. 'I felt a bit dizzy, but I'm fine now.'

'She's definitely got color back in her cheeks,' Joseph remarks. 'You went a bit white there for a while.'

I smile at them both, as convincingly as I can. 'Honestly, I'm grand. Apart from being embarrassed for causing such a fuss.' So much for not drawing attention to myself.

Harriet insists I drink sweetened iced tea, which she fetches from the kitchen while Joseph stands awkwardly beside me, as if he's afraid to leave me alone.

'You gave me a bit of a fright there,' he says, blowing out his cheeks.

'I'm sorry. And thank you for helping.'

He shrugs. 'As long as you're feeling better, that's all that matters.'

'I do. Thank you.'

'Maybe I'll show you the lantern room another time.'

I nod. 'Probably for the best.'

He hesitates for a moment before saying it was nice to meet me. 'I've a small art gallery in town. You should pop by if you're not too busy. Kinsella's. On Bellevue Avenue.'

I tell him I will, but I don't really mean it.

With Captain following behind, he heads back outside, his boots crunching over the shale path beyond the window.

While Harriet clatters about in the kitchen, I stand up to look around the room. A black stove, similar to the one at my granny's house, stands against the far wall, bellows and fire irons in a basket beside it. On the opposite wall, a mustard yellow dresser is filled with all sizes of plates and bowls, each hand-painted with pictures of seashells and lobsters and crabs. A small white table with two chairs sits beside the window, a pot of red geraniums adding a lovely splash of color as the sunlight catches them. Seashore treasures are laid out haphazardly on the windowsills: scallop shells, bleached driftwood, anemone, sea urchins, and sea glass. The whole place oozes with warmth and personality. No wonder Harriet likes to spend so much time here. It's just a pity some of the warmth and personality hasn't rubbed off on her.

I walk over to a picture hanging on the wall beside the stove. It is a framed page from *Harper's Weekly* dated July 1869, a striking portrait of a stern-looking woman in a

143

voluminous black silk dress. The ocean and a moody sky have been painted into the background. There's a wonderful intensity in her eyes; a look of pure determination. I reach up to straighten it as Harriet returns with the iced tea.

'Ah. You spotted Ida.' She pours us both a large glass, spooning three heaped teaspoons of sugar into each before gulping hers down in one go and rubbing her sleeve across her mouth. 'Some woman, that.'

'Who is she?' I ask, tentatively tasting the cold sweet tea which is surprisingly pleasant.

'Ida Lewis. Former keeper at Lime Rock Light, in the harbor. My father found the picture in a junk shop the day we arrived here. Ida's hung on that wall as long as I've been in Newport.'

'Did you meet her?'

'Ida! Lord, no. How old do you think I am? She was long gone before I ever got here. Boots met her, though.'

'Boots?'

'Used to be the Principal Keeper here. Tough as old . . . '

'Boots?'

Harriet nods, a half smile at her lips. 'Didn't mess with Boots if you knew what was good for you. He loved to tell stories about Ida. Said she was like three women rolled into one. Tough as cowhide. She took over as keeper at Lime Rock light after her father had a stroke. Saved some thirty souls in her time. Became a local legend.' Harriet sits on the edge of the table, her feet splayed on the floor, her hands resting on her knees. 'Not that Ida ever cared for all the fuss, or the medals they gave her. People flocked to Lime Rock in the thousands in the summer to see her. She hated the attention.' She stands up to refill her glass from the jug. 'They called her America's Grace Darling.'

I cough as I swallow tea the wrong way. 'Grace Darling? I know about her.'

'And so you should. Grace rescued your great-great-granny Sarah from a shipwreck near the lighthouse she lived in with her family. It must be a hundred years ago now.'

'I have a letter written from Grace to Sarah. It's in a book I brought with me. A sort of family heirloom. It passes down through the genera-tions from mothers to their daughters along with this locket.'

Harriet looks at me and then at the locket and nods as she lights a cigarette. 'I noticed the book on your nightstand. *Instructions to Light Keepers*. Were you planning on doing some homework? It seems like an odd choice of reading material.'

I walk over to the window and look out at the view. The sound of the ocean laps at the lighthouse walls. Sea salt seasons the breeze. 'I've always found old things fascinating, and I liked the fact that the book was inscribed to another Matilda before me.'

'That Matilda was Sarah's daughter. She and her brother were lost in the wreck. It seems that Sarah formed quite a bond with Grace Darling after the rescue. She had a bad time of it with her nerves after the trauma of the shipwreck and

145

the death of her children. I suppose it makes sense that she would want to keep in touch with the woman who'd saved her life.' She takes a long drag of her cigarette. 'And of course there are the rumors about Grace and Sarah's brother, George.'

'George Emmerson?' My fingers reach for the locket. I undo the clasp. 'This George Emmerson? The artist?' Harriet nods. 'So the other portrait is Grace?'

'Most probably. Again, only a rumor though. It could be a picture of his wife. Seems like they all took the truth with them to their graves. My granny collected all sorts of things about Grace Darling, and old Boots had quite a collection of things about light keepers, too. He left it all to me when he died, God rest him.' She crosses herself, and I do the same. 'There's an old tea chest in the front bedroom upstairs, full of newspaper clippings about Grace and Ida, and some other light keepers, women like Kate Walker and Abbie Burgess. We'd started to organize it all into scrapbooks but . . . ' She trails off, incomplete thoughts drifting up into the rafters with the winding trail of her cigarette smoke.

'I could sort it all out,' I offer. 'It would give me something to do. I like reading through old newspapers and stuff. My mother says I should work in a museum. She doesn't like talking about the past, or dwelling on family history. I hadn't even heard of you until a month ago. I'm not even sure *how* we're related.'

Harriet's hand hovers midway to her mouth,

146

the cigarette burning slowly away as a long tail of ash drops to the floor. The pause in our conversation expands, stretching out through the windows and across Narragansett Bay, all the way to the Atlantic and on, to the rose-scented garden of my home where Mother sips tea with her friends, telling them how happy she is for me to have had the opportunity to take an American holiday. And in that long pause I feel the nagging sensation of something misplaced and I wonder if Harriet might know what it is I'm missing.

She takes a last drag of her cigarette, blowing a long puff of smoke toward me. 'Well,' she says eventually, 'you've heard of me now. My Da was your father's cousin, one of a dozen. There's not much more to know.' I can tell she isn't in the mood to offer any more detail.

The smoke from Harriet's cigarette irritates my throat, making me cough.

'You never smoked, I suppose?' she remarks.

'Once,' I say. 'To try and impress someone.'

'And? Did you?'

I think about the British soldier's lips pressed roughly against mine, the scratch of mustache, fumbling hands grasping my thigh, the stale smell of whiskey. Andrews, they called him. I never found out his first name. 'No,' I say. 'I didn't impress anyone.'

'Sure, aren't all fellas a waste of time anyway. Better off without them if you ask me.' Harriet jumps to her feet and pushes the spent stub of her cigarette into an empty soda can. 'Well, I can't be sitting around talking all day. Things to do. We leave in two hours.'

Upstairs, I find two cozy sunlit bedrooms, both so much nicer than my miserable little room in the house on Cherry Street. The tea chest is in the bigger room where white painted beams crisscross a lofty ceiling and a warm breeze plays at the open window, rippling the blue gingham curtains. The bedroom is neat and tidy, functional and simple. Shell-decorated boxes are dotted about on the windowsills. Illustrations of sea-shells hang in a row of five on the wall opposite the bed. There is a pleasant calm about the room, the rush and roll of the ocean washing around me as I kneel beside the tea chest, undo the leather buckles and open the lid.

I cough at the dust that is disturbed as I lift up a pile of scrapbooks, each one stuffed with yellowing articles about Ida Lewis from ancient editions of local newspapers. As I rummage a little more, I find an old postcard with a dramatic picture of a young woman rowing a boat in stormy seas. The name Ida Lewis is printed at one end, Grace Darling at the other. The same portrait for two women. I remember Harriet saying that Ida Lewis was known as America's Grace Darling, so I suppose it makes sense. Next, I pull out another pile of old newspaper cuttings dated between September and December 1838, all relating to the events and subsequent inquiry into the tragic sinking of a paddle steamer, the *Forfarshire*. At the very bottom of the chest my fingers find the hard edges of a picture frame. Pushing everything else aside, I lift it out, rubbing away a thick layer of dust with my cardigan sleeve.

The frame is warped with age and the glass is cracked on one side, but the image of a young woman instantly intrigues me. She is caught almost in a moment of private thought, as if she wasn't aware she was being painted, but has just looked up from some other task. Her bonnet is tied in blue ribbons beneath a narrow chin. A green plaid shawl is wrapped around her shoulders. The intensity in her eyes makes me a little uncomfortable. It's almost as if she is looking directly at me. Sketches of seashells border the image, each of them different from the other. But the most unusual thing about the portrait is that it isn't finished. Only two-thirds of the woman's face is painted, the rest still in the faint outline of a pencil sketch. The background is also incomplete. The woman's clothing only half in color, half in the gray shading of pencil and charcoal. It's as if the artist gave up halfway through. But then, why have it framed? I notice the initials *G.E.* are signed in one corner, and I wonder. Could this be a portrait of Grace Darling? And if it is, did George Emmerson paint it?

★   ★   ★

Later that night, from the window of my bedroom at the house on Cherry Street, I watch the turn of the light from Rose Island. The old postcard of Ida and Grace rests on the windowsill beside the painted seashells. I think about these two women who kept the lights all those years ago. I think about the newspaper reports, and accounts of the courage they'd shown, not only in the rescues they carried out, but also in the face of unwanted fame. It strikes me that I need to find some of that courage myself.

The flutter I'd felt earlier has really unsettled me. Even with the doctor's confirmation that my suspicions of pregnancy were correct, none of it had seemed real until today. To actually feel another life within me is shocking, but it is something else, too. That flutter of life came from an act of pure defiance. Despite never being hoped for or wanted, despite all the arguments and upset it has caused, despite all the odds being stacked against it, the stubborn little thing has carried on. Completely alone and totally ignored, it has found its own way to be noticed.

Harriet clatters about downstairs as I slip beneath the bed covers, my mind turning over our conversation at the lighthouse. Finally, she had started to talk, and yet she closed up like a clam as soon as I pushed too far. My natural sense of curiosity wants to know more, about Harriet and the distant relatives from my past, all connected, it seems, through Grace Darling and my great-great-grandmother.

I sit up in bed as I read the accounts of Grace's daring rescue. I picture her following the procedures I've read in the instruction manual, lighting the lamps at the top of the Longstone lighthouse. I imagine the difficult conditions she must have lived and worked in.

The melancholic sound of the fog horn disturbs the silence, a stiff sea breeze picks up outside, and all the while the unfinished portrait, propped against the nightstand, keeps watch over me.

Whoever the young woman is, it is almost as if she is present with me in the room, asking me to remember her.

21

GRACE

Longstone Lighthouse. September 1838

September, 1838

Dearest Sarah,

I hope you will forgive my writing to you unexpectedly, but I was anxious to let you know I have been thinking of you these past weeks. Robert Smeddle made inquiries and kindly passed on the address of your cousin, Eliza Cavendish, in Bamburgh. I hope you can forgive the intrusion.

I enclose a letter that I found in your coat pocket while you were here, and a book I had intended to give to you before you left. It is a copy of an instruction manual, issued by Trinity House to light keepers. You mentioned that Matilda had wished to know about the workings of the lighthouses. I hope you will keep the book in her memory.

The seal pups you admired grow bigger every day. There must be hundreds of them now. I think of you whenever I see them.

You might write a few lines when you are

feeling up to it. I would be so pleased to hear from you.

Grace

Apart from the cameo locket at my neck and a few remarks in the Log, there is little to show that the storm or Mrs. Dawson or the others were ever at Longstone, the moody skies and angry seas returned to a blue melodic calm. Open windows send a brackish breeze washing through the lighthouse apartments, blowing away the lingering scent of grief. The bed sheets dance on the washing line like music hall chorus girls, while Father takes advantage of the good weather to hoist coal up the ladders and clean the external glass of the lantern room. But even as the familiar rhythms and routines settle among us again I feel myself changed, and as the weeks pass and the amber gaze of autumn turns fully upon the Farne Islands, the gaze of the world follows. Like buttermilk spilled across a table, the dramatic accounts of my part in the rescue continue to spread, and fingertips across the country are stained black from the ink of the newspapermen's words.

Robert Smeddle comes to the lighthouse most fair-weather days, bearing the latest news reports from the printing presses in great bundles rolled up under his arms.

'Didn't I tell you there would be a silk gown in this for you, Grace?' he crows, pompous as ever in his self-righteousness. 'They can't get enough of you!' A dull headache settles across my brow as I read a headline from *The Times* of London.

HEROINE OF THE FARNE ISLES: GRACE DAR-
LING'S DRAMATIC RESCUE. 'Reports of your
rescue are spreading like a spring tide,' Smeddle
continues with his usual theatricality. 'Rushing
down streets and spilling into kitchens and
sculleries and onto the lips of gossiping maids
and fishwives. Who is this Grace Darling, they
ask? Who is this brave young woman?'

My heart thumps beneath my apron, heat
rising to my cheeks despite the cool air of the
afternoon. My hands shake as I pick up one of
the pages. 'But this report is wrong, Mr.
Smeddle. That's not how it happened. The way
they write, you would hardly think Father was
there at all.'

'You would hardly think I was where?' Father
asks as he appears at the bottom of the steps.

'The newspapers, Father.' I push them toward
him. 'Look.'

Father places his spectacles onto his nose and
studies the reports, pulling at the silvered
whiskers on his chin before turning to stoke the
fire. 'They must always find something to fill
their pages, Grace. Best to ignore it. It will be
talk of the Chartists by next week. I heard they
were very raucous at a recent meeting in
Newcastle. Did you hear the reports, Smeddle?'

Father's attempt to change the subject works
for a while as Smeddle divulges his knowledge of
the latest Chartist activities in the northern cities
and towns. I, however, am not as easily
distracted by their talk of politics. My gaze strays
back to my name, printed in bold black typeface.
I imagine all the hands that will run over those

154

words and all the eyes that will settle on them until I can almost feel those same hands and eyes on me. A shiver runs over my skin as I pick up my Bible and turn to Deuteronomy 31:6. *Be strong and of good courage, do not fear nor be afraid of them.*

But the newspaper reports are merely the beginning.

Next come dozens of letters, sent by the public to express their admiration for my bravery, many enclosing a small token of respect — books, Bibles, silk handkerchiefs. Requests for a lock of my hair or a piece of fabric from the clothes I wore on the night of the rescue are not uncommon. The declarations of admiration, and the kind words offered in my support, both touch and overwhelm me.

Mam throws her hands in the air when I tell her what the letters say. She marches off to the pantry, returning with a knife.

'What's that for?' I ask, a little alarmed.

'If it's locks of your hair they want, it's locks of hair they'll be having. And then maybe somebody might tend to the lamp, or is it all to be letter-writing now?'

I suspect she is quietly proud of the public's interest in me. To have my mother's favor is a rare and wonderful thing.

Smeddle insists on sitting with me for long hours, familiarizing me with the conventions of formal letter-writing as he dictates appropriate replies to the more notable correspondents.

'There's really nothing to it,' he says, pulling his chair too close to mine as he flicks through

155

the latest batch of correspondence. The warts on his fingers remind me of the fat blisters on bladder wrack seaweed. 'A few formalities to open and close. A polite line or two of news. That's all. The personal letters don't require as much care, whereas this from the Royal Society, and this, see, from the Institute of Mariners, these need your undivided attention.'

When I ask Smeddle if I really must reply to them all, as well as sign my name on the dozens of blank cards he has provided (for which I can see no obvious purpose), he is astonished.

'My dear Grace. We wouldn't wish to offend, would we? While you are very much in the public's favor right now, they could turn against you just as quickly.' He presses his fat little fingers against mine. 'I'm sure you wouldn't wish the newspapers to claim you are ungrateful and aloof, would you? Too busy to respond to your admirers?'

'Of course not.'

'Very well then. We shall continue.'

I diligently follow Smeddle's instructions, writing in my best copperplate handwriting until the ink runs dry and my hand aches with a cramp. I enclose a small lock of hair or a piece of fabric from my collar or shawl where requested, expressing my gratitude for their kind words while insisting I only did my duty and emphasizing my father's bravery at every opportunity. When Smeddle is satisfied, he bundles the letters and signed cards into his coat pocket to have his clerk at the Castle send off immediately.

And so it goes on, day after day, until I begin to dread the endless scratch of my nib on the page and the prospect of more time spent under Smeddle's tutelage. I tire easily of his company. I don't care for the way his breath catches in his chest, nor for the cloying odor of porter and mustache wax he brings with him, and leaves behind.

The unwanted attention from the newspapermen and the public gives me a headache as the quiet days I've always known on my island home become smothered by a tide of unceasing demand to know more about me. As I extinguish the lamps each morning, I find myself wishing that the glare of public scrutiny could be quenched as easily. I no longer sleep easy in my bed, am no longer soothed by the velveteen lullaby of the sea, too anxious about what new drama might arrive with the dawn.

Mam seeks distraction in her spinning wheel, tutting about people who have nothing better to do with their time. Father is more reserved on the matter, observing it all with quiet perplexity, and among it all, the lighthouse stands, tall and unyielding. In rare moments alone, I rest my cheek against the thick stone walls, imagining the lighthouse to breathe with me, willing it to absorb some of my discomfort. And yet despite all the changes recent events have brought to our door, I am determined to carry on as before. I tend to the lamps and the Fresnel lens, fetch wood for the stove, polish Father's boots, check on the hens, scrub at the hems of brine-stiffened skirts, take a needle and thread to any garments

157

in need of repair, keeping my stitches neat and even as Mam had taught me. I take pleasure in mending things, in being purposeful and occupied. It is, after all, what I've been raised to do. The business of being a heroine I knew nothing about, despite what the newspapermen would have their readers believe.

★ ★ ★

'I've made arrangements for a sculptor and an artist to visit in the next few days,' Smeddle announces as he swoops into the lighthouse for the third time that week.

Now it is Father's turn to be confused. 'An artist. Whatever for?'

'To capture Grace's likeness.' Smeddle smiles at Father as if he were a child misunderstanding a simple arithmetic. 'Everyone wants to see her, William. To put a face to the name.' He watches me closely as he speaks, already assessing my physical appeal.

Mam mutters about how she might as well open the lighthouse up as an inn and offer board and lodgings.

'They won't stay for long, Mrs. Darling,' Smeddle assures her. 'If Grace sits well for them they could be done in a day. It really is a great honor. David Dunbar is one of the best sculptors in England. And Henry Perlee Parker is renowned for his seascapes.' He studies me with a quizzical eye, tilting his head first to one side, then the other. 'They'll make a good job of her. They can fix the imperfections.'

I feel like a stone sculpture already, an inanimate relic for people to stare at, not a person with thoughts and feelings. I cast a meaningful gaze at my father, who raises his eyebrows in reply. Without saying a word, I know what he is saying. *What are we to do about it, Gracie? Smeddle knows these matters best. If people want a likeness of you, we must give them one.* Excusing myself, I step outside, walking my frustration onto the pebbles along the beach, crunching seashells satisfyingly beneath my boots.

An unusual air of tension settles within the lighthouse walls that evening.

Father remarks that I seemed agitated. 'I think all these letters and whatnot are troubling you, Grace. Am I right?'

I am grateful for his concern, but have no desire to talk about it. 'I'm sure the letters and gifts will stop soon enough, Father. The marriage proposals, too.'

Mam jerks her head up from her darning. 'The what?'

'There've been a few marriage proposals in the letters, Mam. That's all.'

She is either horrified, or excited, I'm not entirely sure which. 'That's *all?*' she screeches. 'Proposals from who?'

'Whom,' Father interjects.

Mam scowls. 'This is no time for fussing over grammar, Father.'

'Nobody, Mam. Lonely men who believe what they read in the newspapers and think me to be far more than I am. Don't give it another thought. I certainly won't.'

'Maybe you shouldn't be so hasty, Grace,' she counters. 'There might be one or two who are serious.' She turns to my father. 'Did you see these proposals?' He shakes his head. 'Well then, I suppose we'll never know if it was dukes and earls offering their hand. We'll never know the life she could have had.' She returns to her darning, stabbing her needle crossly into her work as if it had done something to offend her.

Taking up my lamp, I stand and stretch out my back.

Father studies me carefully, his brow knotted with concern. 'Why don't you take off to the Main tomorrow, Grace? See your sisters. We can manage well enough here. A change of scenery will do you good.'

I concede to think about it as I bid my parents goodnight and climb the spiral steps to the lantern room. Father is right. I *am* exhausted. Not from any physical exertions but from the weight of expectation to live up to all the fuss and attention. I feel a great burden has settled on my shoulders, and I'm not sure I am strong enough to bear it.

Despite my exhaustion, sleep eludes me, my thoughts drifting and swirling like the delicate fronds of the anemones in the rock pools. I dwell on troubling thoughts of unwelcome artists staring at me, fixing my imperfections with their brushes and paints. I'm not like Ellen and Mary Herbert, or the ladies on the Main, who delight in having their portraits painted.

I recall something Mr. Emmerson had said

about artists. That even for those born with a natural talent there is much that can be taught: how to study shape and form, how to frame an object to bring about its truest likeness, how to draw the eye to the focal point. '*There's far more to being an artist than brush, palette, and canvas, Miss Darling. Those are merely the tools. The real artistry takes place in the heart and the mind . . . and the eye.*' I picture the smile that crossed his lips as he took the piece of indigo sea glass from me, but the memory soon dissipates as my worries about the present return.

I can think of nothing worse than sitting still for hours on end, apart from which I am sure the artists will consider me far too dull and ordinary, the reality of Grace Darling failing to match the image of the saintly heroine the newspapers have written about. I only hope Mr. Smeddle's friends will change their minds and find someone far more interesting and suitable to occupy their brushes.

I toss and turn for hours, sit up and lie back down again. Perhaps Father is right. A trip to the mainland will be good for me.

22

GRACE

North Sunderland. September 1838

With my letter and a package for Sarah Dawson tucked safely into my skirt pocket, I set out just after sunrise the following morning, taking advantage of the calm seas. It feels good to be out in the coble again, my oars moving easily over the water, the sun warm against my face. I stop rowing for a moment, the waves slapping gently against the boat as it bobs in the light swell. I draw in deep steady breaths. This is my fuel; my oil and wick. This is where I come alive, with the sun on my face and the wind at my back and the unfathomable depths of the sea below.

With a tinge of guilt, I admit that I'm relieved to be free of the routine of my chores; glad to hear the cry of the gulls and to feel the rush of the breeze against my skin; relieved to be away from the tedious business of letter writing and the incessant interference of Robert Smeddle. As I sit quietly in the boat, I reflect on what Father said the morning before the *Forfarshire* disaster — *'It can't be easy for you, seeing your sisters and brothers marry and set themselves up on the Main.'* — and my reply that I could think of nowhere I'd rather be than at Longstone. The more honest answer is that I've grown so accustomed to life at the lighthouse that I've never properly considered any alternative.

Sitting alone in the coble, the lighthouse behind me, the coastline of Northumberland ahead, I let myself wonder. Properly wonder. Perhaps there *is* another life waiting for me, running alongside the one I know, like the tracks they use for the steam locomotives. Perhaps I *could* marry, could devote myself to something or someone other than my parents and the dear old lighthouse. Brooks will take over from my father when the time comes, and when he marries — which he undoubtedly will before too many more years pass — what need will he have of me? What do I know other than tending the lamps and keeping the seven apartments clean?

And there it is. My greatest fear. Not of storms or rough seas, but of a life beyond the lighthouse. My reluctance to leave Longstone doesn't only come from a sense of duty, but also from a reluctance to go anywhere else; become someone else. The newspaper reporters might write effusively about my bravery and courage, but the truth is that I am as scared and as hesitant as anyone else. To be truly brave would be to leave behind the life I know, to row away and not return with the tide. The question is: do I have the courage to do it?

Picking up the oars, I row on, enjoying the familiar ache in my shoulders and forearms. I am out of practice after being confined to the lighthouse by the weather and letter-writing, but my muscles easily remember and I am soon lost in the rhythm of my stroke as the lighthouse slips from view and the battlements of Bamburgh Castle grow closer. I reach North Sunderland's small harbor in good time, running the coble up onto the shallows with the aid of the incoming tide.

The early morning light tints the sand golden as the fisher-women gather on the shore to see home the herring fleet. Hungry infants suckle at heavy breasts while young children pull at their mams' skirts or draw pictures in the wet sand with razor shells. Empty creels stand nearby, ready for the day's catch. The cockle collectors, already back from their morning's work, haul their cobles up onto the shore beside me. The smell of seaweed and brine paints the air as I loosen the ribbons of my bonnet and ease my shawl around my shoulders.

I love these mornings when the boats come in; love to see such industry and bustle. I notice one or two local artists on the harbor wall, keen to capture the play of light on the water and the way the rising sun falls against the women's faces. Too many times, I've seen those faces cloud with concern as news is relayed about a missing boat. Fishing communities along the east coast towns of North Sunderland, Whitby, and Craster thrive on the fleet, their lives prospering or foundering with the boats. This morning, the first sight of them prompts a great cheering and waving from the gathered families.

Anxious not to draw attention to myself, I stand to one side, watching the women as they expertly pack the fish before hoisting their laden baskets onto their backs, everything they need for their day's work inside: gutting boards, knives, paper for wrapping the fish for the customers. They are hardy women, out in all weather. Tough as iron and never a breath of complaint. The fishwives work on the quayside, splitting the fish in two before packing them tight in salt barrels, their eager daughters learning the trade alongside them. Just as I once stood at my father's knee and learned the life of a light keeper, so these young girls will, one day, take on their mams' creels. They'll never question the life they were born into, or ever consider any other. Fishing is stitched into their bones and the plaid fabric of their shawls.

Passing Swallow's Smokehouse, the scent of wood chip makes my stomach growl at the prospect of fresh kippers. Limestone burns in the kilns on the harbor as boats are loaded with quicklime to be shipped to Scotland for fertilizer. Crab pots teeter in lopsided piles outside the door of The Badger, the raucous noise inside carried out through the cracks in the windows as the crab fishermen linger by the open fire, warming their bones.

I make my way along the narrow streets toward the Herbert's house where I am surprised and delighted to find my sister Thomasin, making a morning call. I am especially grateful for the familiar feel of her embrace. I forget, sometimes, how much I miss her.

Ellen is beside herself to see me, and explains that Mary is out for the morning. 'She will be very sorry to have missed you, Grace. We were all so worried for you when we heard about the rescue. Come and sit by the fire and tell us all about it. Was it really as terrible as the newspapers say?'

I remove my bonnet and gloves and move closer to the fire to warm my hands. Dry as autumn leaves, they whisper as I rub them together. When I have warmed myself and recounted the events of the rescue several times to Ellen and my sister's mutual satisfaction, Thomasin shows me a page from *The Times* of London. I am horrified to see that some of the letters I've received are printed on the page, along with my replies. I am furious with Smeddle for putting my private correspondence on public display and plan to tell him so when I next see him.

'You write so well, Grace,' Ellen gushes, oblivious to my anger. 'Such humility after such bravery. Is it true your admirers ask you for a lock of hair?'

I confirm that they do, but I cannot share Ellen's enthusiasm for the requests which she claims to be a mark of how highly I am held in the public's regard.

'Grace? What is it?' Thomasin asks. She knows me too well for my sour mood to escape her notice.

'Everyone is making far too much of it, sister,' I sigh, worrying my hands restlessly in my lap. 'You know it was my duty to help. You'd have done the same. Anyone would. Even Ellen.'

Thomasin laughs. 'Ellen! Go out in a storm?

She can't even put her toes in the water on a summer's day.'

Ellen admits that she can barely tolerate the boat trip out to the Farnes. 'You do yourself a disservice, Grace. There are not many who would have acted as you did.'

Thomasin places a hand on mine. 'Ellen's right. What you did that night was exceptional, Grace. No wonder people are eager to read about you in the newspapers.'

'Well I wish they wouldn't. I'm tired of people writing about me and talking about me.' I slump back in the chair and rest my feet on a stool. 'And now they're even sending out boat trips, full of people wanting to get a glimpse of me. Of me!'

For a moment the room falls silent apart from the fire crackling in the grate. And then Thomasin snorts a laugh. Ellen follows. Soon, we are all doubled up laughing, tears spilling down our cheeks. It is a welcome release and I feel much better for it.

'You shouldn't take it so much to heart, Grace' Thomasin says. 'You're far too serious.'

Perhaps she is right.

'Robert Smeddle is arranging for some artist friends of his to come to the lighthouse to paint my portrait,' I continue when we are all recovered. 'Apparently the public want to know what I look like.'

Ellen sits beside me. 'Well, that isn't so bad. Just relax and sit still. It's quite enjoyable.' She takes a sip of tea. I envy her ability to be so blasé about something I'm so worried about. 'Talking of artists,' she continues, 'do you remember Mr. Emmerson who we met at Dunstanburgh last month? A friend of Henry's. You probably won't remember.'

My cheeks redden at the mention of his name. I lift my teacup, hoping to conceal my face behind it. 'I don't especially remember him. No.'

'Oh, Grace. You must. He hardly spoke to anyone else. Tall fellow. Scottish accent. Broad smile . . . '

'Oh, him. Yes, I remember now. What about him?'

'Did you know his sister was rescued from the *Forfarshire*? A Mrs. Dawson.'

'Sarah? She's George Emmerson's sister?' I can hardly believe it. My mind races back over our conversations. Had she ever mentioned him? Had I? Had she noticed my distraction?

'Such a strange coincidence isn't it? George has been staying at the Olde Ship since she returned to the mainland. Sarah is staying with a cousin of theirs, in Bamburgh. Eliza Cavendish. Pleasant little thing, if rather too meek for my liking.' I can barely concentrate on what Ellen is saying, my thoughts straying back to that afternoon at Dunstanburgh, and all the occasions I have remembered Mr. Emmerson since. 'At least the wedding gives them all something happy to look forward to,' she adds.

'Wedding?' I stifle a cough and take another sip of tea before putting my cup and saucer down to stop the telltale rattling.

Ellen looks me full in the face, her eyes shining. 'George and Eliza's. They are to be

168

married next month.'

I feel suddenly very hot. 'You really shouldn't bank the fire so high, Ellen. You'll have the chimney on fire again.'

Ignoring me, Ellen continues to share everything she knows about the Cavendish girl and how the family had all but given up on George ever asking her to marry him, but all I hear are the words '*They are to be married next month*' and for some inexplicable reason tears well in my eyes and I have to excuse myself to visit the outhouse.

When I return, I explain that I must be getting on with my errands. Thomasin says she has to leave soon, too.

At the door, Ellen presses kisses to my cheek, telling me, again, how immensely proud they all are of me. 'Will you give the harvest ball some thought, or if not that then at least Christmas?'

I promise I will.

Thomasin, as ever, is quick to notice the change in my mood, delaying me on the doorstep as Ellen walks back inside. 'Is there anything you wish to tell me, Grace? I noticed you became rather flustered when Ellen mentioned George Emmerson.'

Pulling on my gloves, I assure her there isn't anything I wish to tell her. 'I'm just a little tired of the attention, and dreading the artists' visits.'

'Are you sure there's nothing else?' She squeezes my hands as she'd once done when we were young girls sitting together on the rocks, watching the seal pups. Thomasin has always been able to get the truth from me.

My true feelings burn against my cheeks as I reassure Thomasin there is nothing else. 'I will write.'

She folds her arms across her chest, clearly unconvinced. 'Come and visit me in Bamburgh soon,' she calls after me as I turn to wave before ducking down a side street.

Before calling at the post office, I stop at the haberdashery to pick up some buttons and ribbon for Mam but I am only inside the shop a minute when the whispering starts. 'Is it her?' 'It is.' 'Go and ask her, then.'

Soon the shop is full of admirers as word spreads that Grace Darling is about.

'God bless you, Miss, for what you done. Could I trouble you for a lock of hair?'

'Would you touch my baby's blanket?'

'Could you spare a little square of material from your skirt, Miss?'

I try to be gracious and polite, but I become agitated and excuse myself, leaving the shop without buttons or ribbon, forgetting entirely about the package in my pocket and my intended trip to the post office. With my head down and my bonnet tied tightly, I rush back to the harbor, eager to return to Longstone where I can be myself, rather than the heroine everyone desires me to be.

I walk with quick steps, already regretting not telling Thomasin the truth. She knows me too well for me to keep things hidden from her for long, but on the matter of Mr. Emmerson I won't — can't — be pressed. How awful it would be for me to admit I have been thinking about a man I'd barely spoken to for more than a few minutes, not to mention a man who is engaged to be married.

It is better to keep this particular secret to myself.

★   ★   ★

In a smoke-fogged tavern near the harbor, George Emmerson stares blankly into an untouched glass of porter, wishing there was something he could do to help his grieving sister. The agony of her loss is unbearable and he cannot shake the shadow of guilt that hangs about his shoulders like a heavy cloak. After all, he had encouraged Sarah to take the trip to Scotland, nagging and pestering, insisting the change of scenery would do them all good. He was the one who had arranged the tickets, choosing the *Forfarshire* especially as he had heard it was such a fine vessel. He is to blame for James and Matilda's deaths. His mind taunts him with happy memories of the many times he carried them on his shoulders. He can still hear their squeals of joy as he mercilessly tickled their knees. If he cannot bear their loss, how on earth can their mother?

Of course Sarah will not hear of his talk of blame, but George wonders if the same thoughts cross her mind during the empty hours of the night when she wakes from a fitful sleep and remembers that her children are not safe in the bed beside her. How can he ever set things right? How can he ever take away her suffering?

171

He is, at least, grateful that Sarah is taken under the care of Eliza's family in Bamburgh. When he visits, Eliza tells him how Sarah stays up late at night, scribbling illegible pages about the *Forfarshire* disaster and Miss Darling's rescue, and how she sings in her sleep of lavenders blue and lavenders green. Her delirium is painful to watch, she says. With the tragedy having hit the family so hard, all talk of weddings has been temporarily stalled. Even Eliza's mother has been sensitive enough not to mention it.

George knows he must return to his studies in Dundee, but he hates the thought of leaving Sarah. Besides, he has no interest in canvas, brush, or charcoal. Every time he thinks of painting or drawing he sees only a page of dark water and storm-tossed ships and stiff little bodies held tight against their mother's. No color. No joy. He wonders if he will ever paint for pleasure again.

Amid his anguish, George overhears rumor and gossip about the sinking of the *Forfarshire*. Whispers pass between the lifeboat crew and the locals while self-important men conduct the official inquiry, discussing the whys and wherefores and looking for someone to blame. A man by the name of Robert Smeddle is in charge and from what George can gather, appears to be rather enjoying the drama and attention. What does it matter where the finger of blame lies? Nothing will bring back his dear niece and nephew. Nothing will heal his sister's broken heart. No accusation or attribution of blame can ever make this better.

Aside from the inquiry, conversations revolve around the extraordinary tale of heroism that has emerged from the Longstone lighthouse. Grace Darling is the name on everyone's lips. Who is she, they want to know? What does she look like? George listens to idle speculation as he takes lunch in one of the harborside taverns. *I know*, he wants to tell them. *I remember the earnest look in her eyes, the trace of a smile at her lips.* That Miss Darling had saved his sister's life is a coincidence he cannot ignore. He turns the piece of indigo sea glass over in his hands and sees her in its reflection.

Beside him, on the bar, the evening newspaper carries a small advertisement in the center column which catches his attention.

BOAT TRIPS TO LONGSTONE. SEE THE HERO-INE, GRACE DARLING. DEPARTS DAILY.

'Is this true?' he asks the publican. 'They're offering trips out to the lighthouse?'

The publican wipes the thick rim of a glass and nods steadily. 'People want to see her with their own eyes. Fishermen are always quick to spot an opportunity to make a bit of money.'

'But Miss Darling isn't a circus exhibit. It doesn't seem right for people to go to gawp at her.' He thinks about how fondly she'd spoken of her secluded island life, how intrusive she will find it for boatloads of onlookers to descend upon her.

The publican laughs and holds out his hand. 'Then give me the newspaper and don't go!'

Finishing his glass of ale, George takes the

173

newspaper and his hat and walks outside into the pale autumn sunshine. He must meet Eliza, as arranged. He wishes he could be more enthusiastic about her, but he isn't like the street entertainers he passes with their clever tricks and quick hands. He cannot summon absent feelings from a hat, or easily conceal feelings he shouldn't possess. He must become an actor then, play the part of devoted husband. What else can he do, other than cause distress to a young girl who deserves none? He would ask Sarah's counsel but she has enough to think about without his problems.

Scrunching the newspaper into a ball, he tosses it in an empty creel and turns to walk up the harbor steps. Boat trips he can do without. Brave heroines he must push from his mind. Eliza and Sarah are all that he must think about now.

Or they would be, if Miss Darling weren't standing directly in front of him.

23

GRACE

North Sunderland. September 1838

'Mr. Emmerson!'

'Miss Darling? What a surprise!'

The surprise is all mine. After imagining him so often and conjuring fragments of our conversation in the darkness of my bedroom, it is almost incomprehensible that Mr. Emmerson is standing in front of me.

'I was only thinking about you,' he adds, hesitantly.

'Me?'

'Reading the latest account in the newspapers.'

A quiet thrill blooms in my heart to hear the soft musicality in his words, just as I'd remembered, but apart from his voice, Mr. Emmerson isn't how I'd remembered him at all. Dark shadows lurk beneath his eyes. His lips are pinched and pale, his skin carries the sickly pallor of the sleep-deprived. 'Ah, yes. There are rather too many accounts in the newspapers, I'm afraid.'

'Not nearly enough, I'd say, after what you did.'

I fiddle with my gloves for want of something to do with my hands. My breathing is shallow, my thoughts leaping to Sarah Dawson as I feel the press of the locket against my skin with every quick breath.

'I am so very sorry, Mr. Emmerson,' I say. 'For your sister's loss. And yours.'

'How can I ever thank you for saving Sarah and taking such good care of her in her darkest hours?' He speaks slowly, without drama or hysteria, yet the strain of recent events is clear to see. 'She is so grateful for your kindness. She speaks very fondly of you.'

'And I of her,' I reply, offering a tentative smile. 'Your sister was so very brave. I will never forget her.'

The pause in our conversation is awkward. 'My apologies,' he says. 'I am delaying you.'

I assure him he isn't, explaining that I had been visiting the Herberts. 'I'm afraid my appearance in the haberdashers caused rather a fuss. It seems I can't buy so much as a button without drawing attention to myself. I am keen to get back to the island.'

A slight smile tugs at his lips. 'Perhaps I can escort you to the boat?' he offers.

I accept the invitation while worrying about the appropriateness of walking with a man betrothed to another.

'Sarah and the children were traveling to Dundee for a little holiday with me,' he explains as we walk. 'Her husband passed away in the summer and she had suffered other . . . difficulties. I pestered her until she agreed to come to Scotland. I believed the change of scenery would lift her spirits.'

'It is a very beautiful country,' I remark.

Mr. Emmerson pauses. 'The thing is, Miss Darling, that I feel responsible for the loss of Sarah's dear children. If it weren't for my interfering, they would never have been on the bloody *Forfarshire*.'

I flinch at his language, shocked by the anger and emotion he carries beneath his crumpled frock coat.

He looks at me, such loss and remorse in his eyes. 'Please forgive me, Miss Darling. I am not myself.'

'There is no apology needed. You have all been through a dreadful ordeal but you mustn't shoulder the burden of blame. It was a terrible accident caused by a violent storm. If you must blame someone, blame Mother Nature.'

We walk down the steps onto the beach, the fresh breeze nipping at my cheeks.

'Ellen mentioned that your sister is staying with relatives in Bamburgh,' I say.

'Yes. Sarah is with an aunt and cousin. I visit as often as I can, but it all feels rather lacking.'

The name Eliza Cavendish settles between us like a child waiting to be entertained. Why doesn't he mention her? Why call her his cousin, rather than his wife-to-be? It doesn't make any sense. None of this does, and I am thankful that we reach the coble which Mr. Emmerson insists on helping me drag to the water's edge.

'I believe they are sending boats out to Longstone so people can see you,' he says as we push and pull together. 'It must be quite an intrusion to your usually peaceful home.'

I tip my head to the sky and let out a long

sigh. There is so much I want to say but now is not the time to admit to my frustrations or to share unkind thoughts about the boatmen and their passengers. 'Apparently the public must see their heroine, Mr. Emmerson. I only hope they will not be too disappointed,' I laugh, trying to lighten the mood a little. 'I blame the newspapers. They have greatly exaggerated my part in the rescue. It is really my father who should be praised.'

'I am quite sure nobody would be disappointed to see you,' he says, his words sending heat rushing to my cheeks. 'As for the newspapers' exaggeration? Perhaps, but men like your father are expected to row boats in stormy seas. A young woman isn't.'

'But as the lighthouse keeper's daughter it is my duty to rescue wrecked souls.'

'And so it is the newspapers' duty to report interesting events. We must all have our heroes and heroines, Miss Darling. The world would be awfully dull without daring sea rescues and brave adventurers. I certainly don't find much to inspire in the listings for the price of corn and the schedule for the courts.'

I smile, despite myself. 'You make a very persuasive argument.'

'There is no argument from me, Miss Darling. Persuasion? Perhaps a little.'

And there it is again. That gentle smile. The unspoken something I'd felt so keenly as we'd walked at Dunstanburgh Castle. I briefly wonder if he senses it, too, if he has thought about me in the weeks since we met. But of course he hasn't.

He is engaged to be married and I am ridiculous to even entertain the idea. Am I starting to believe the newspapermen's version of me? Do I really believe I am worthy of thought and attention? I blush at my awful neediness.

As I step into the boat I remember the packet in my pocket. 'I wonder if you might pass this on to your sister. I'd meant to post it to her. Would you mind?'

'Of course. She will be pleased to hear from you.' He takes the packet from me. 'It was an unexpected pleasure to see you again, Miss Darling.'

'And you, Mr. Emmerson.'

'I'm especially glad to have had the opportunity to thank you in person. I had planned to write a few lines, but words were never my forte.'

'And I am grateful for it. I am drowning in letters. You have done me a great favor by reducing the amount by one.' I push against the rocks with my oars. 'Besides, what need have you for words when you have the talent to draw and paint?' My thoughts flicker to the imminent arrival of the first artists, my heart sinking into my boots at the prospect.

As the waves catch the boat and carry me away from the shore, Mr. Emmerson places his hand in his coat pocket and takes something out.

'I still have it,' he calls. 'My memento.'

The indigo sea glass catches the sun, glinting like a rare treasure. He *had* remembered.

'And I am still looking for sea dragons,' I call in reply, biting my lip to stall the rampant smile that urges to break free.

179

I row poorly, unable to coordinate my strokes, distracted by thoughts of Sarah Dawson and Eliza Cavendish and sea glass and sea dragons. Mr. Emmerson stands for a long while until he becomes a barely visible speck, and I, in turn, become part of the sea, a young woman and her boat, invisible from the shore, indistinguishable from the waves that carry her home.

Bamburgh, England

Sarah Dawson listens patiently as George tells her, with great enthusiasm, how he had bumped into Miss Darling in North Sunderland, and what a strange coincidence it was and how well she looked and how humble she was in regard to the newspaper reports written about her. Sarah quietly observes the high color in her brother's cheeks, the adoration in his eyes when he talks about Miss Darling. It is a look she has never seen when he talks about Eliza.

For the first time since the tragedy, she smiles. 'If you weren't engaged to be married, I would believe you had feelings for Miss Darling, George.' She teases, only a little.

He denies it furiously, but his demeanor belies the truth. And then Sarah remembers the sketches of lighthouses in the margins of the letter he'd written to her, his sentences full of admiration for this lighthouse keeper's daughter. She wonders where that letter ever went. Lost to the sea, no doubt.

'It isn't too late,' she ventures, no longer

caring for propriety or caution, nor for Eliza's feelings, or her aunt's reputation.

'Too late for what?'

'To change your mind.' She leans forward conspiratorially, placing her trembling hand on George's knee and lowering her voice. 'Eliza is a pleasant girl, but she is a breeze, George. A breeze. Your heart desires a storm. I can tell.'

He stands up, fussing with the buttons on his waistcoat as he throws on his coat and hat. 'I don't know what you mean, Sarah. But I'm afraid I must be getting back to the Olde Ship. The landlady fusses when I'm late. Can I get you anything before I leave?'

Sarah shakes her head. 'But you can promise me something.'

'Yes?'

'Think about them. The breezes and the storms. Think about your life, George, and what you really wish to do with it. It can, so suddenly, be snatched away. We must do our best with the time we have. Mustn't we?'

He kisses her cheek and says that yes, he supposes we must, before closing the door thoughtfully behind him.

Sarah is pleased to have said her piece.

Dear George. He has been so good to her. So considerate and caring. She knows he feels responsible for what happened, even though she insists he mustn't. And Eliza has been kind, too. Everyone has. They tiptoe around her as if she were a piece of finest porcelain, liable to crack and break at any time. Does she want anything to eat? Has she had sufficient rest? Is there anything she needs to make her stay more comfortable? She understands that they mean well, but she feels suffocated by everyone's good intentions and wishes they would all leave her alone.

Nevertheless, she tolerates their incessant goodwill and lingers in this halfway house, stuck between the past and the future. She knows she is an awkward and unexpected addition to the Cavendishes' lives. She tries to keep out of their way, making herself small and uncomplicated, but despite the whispers and hushed voices that follow her around, her grief is loud and ever-present, lending an air of tension to the rooms of the small house. Although she dreads the thought of returning to her home in Hull, and all the memories and reminders waiting for her there, she knows she must. Apart from anything else, she doesn't sleep well here. She hears voices in the night: lullabies and distant songs.

A little while after George's departure, Sarah remembers the package he had brought from Miss Darling. She is touched to discover a thick book inside: *Instructions to Light Keepers* along with a letter. *I enclose a letter that I found in your coat pocket while you were here, and a book I had intended to give to you before you left. It is a copy of an instruction manual, issued by Trinity House to light keepers. You mentioned that Matilda had wished to know about the workings of the lighthouses. I hope you will keep the book in her memory.* Sarah runs her fingers over Miss Darling's inscription

182

inside the front cover. *For dear Sarah. So that you might know. Grace* Beneath, she adds an inscription of her own. *For my darling Matilda. From Mummy. x*

Alone in her room, she starts to read, page after page, hour after hour, studying the tasks and routines until she can picture Miss Darling, busy in the lantern room as she cleans the lens with a feather brush to remove any soot and dust before wiping each part of the delicate apparatus with a linen cloth. Spirits of wine remove any spilled oil, and then she buffs everything until it gleams. When the job is complete, she places a linen cloth over the lens and draws the curtains around the lantern room to prevent any discoloration by sunlight.

As for how Miss Darling spends the rest of her day, Sarah must imagine, the instruction book lacking in information about how a lighthouse keeper might feel, or what they might think about during the long hours on watch. Perhaps Miss Darling places the locket beneath her pillow at night, remembering the events of that awful night. Perhaps she imagines a life beyond the island. Perhaps she longs to fall passionately in love with a student of art, or perhaps all she wants is to fade away from the public gaze and slip back into obscurity like a discarded fragment of sea glass washed from the beach. Whatever she desires, Miss Darling must learn to be the heroine everyone needs her to be. As a laborer's daughter, Sarah has always understood that choice in one's destiny is a luxury preserved for the upper classes. For a lighthouse keeper's daughter, as for a sea merchant's widow, there is only duty and expectation.

Sarah adds a few lines to her account of the *Forfarshire* disaster before climbing into bed. The darkness of the room envelops her as the distant singing grows gradually louder until she isn't entirely sure where it ends, and she begins.

North Sunderland, England

That evening, by the light of a guttering candle flame in his room at the Olde Ship Inn, George Emmerson's hands move quickly across the page. He doesn't work especially well with charcoal but it is all he has with him. His mind is a whirl, turning over his sister's words. '*Eliza is a pleasant girl, but she is a breeze, George. A breeze. Your heart desires a storm.*'

He blows the dust from the page in short puffs before holding his work at a distance to scrutinize his progress. He is a harsh critic, never happy with his work until it is just right. He is determined to capture her, to show that certain something that sets her apart. But how? How to re-create her on the page? Slightly below average in height, a slender figure, a gracefulness befitting her name. He sketches a wreath of gentle brown curls, a clear complexion, soft as buttermilk. And her eyes, so darkly expressive, revealing her emotions without disguise. How to capture that willful determination? The wistful smile at her lips?

He scrunches his page into a ball and tosses it

184

to the floor. Starts again. And again, until, finally, she begins to emerge on the page, but the light of the candle fades and he cannot finish it tonight. He writes her name on the back, packs his materials away, and stands the sketch against the window, where the light will catch it at dawn.

As he falls into bed and closes his eyes, he remembers a favorite line from Shakespeare's *A Midsummer Night's Dream: Love looks not with the eyes, but with the mind; and therefore is winged Cupid painted blind.*

He will continue by daylight, already accepting he will possibly never capture her on the page as truly as he sees her in his mind; already accepting that it will have to be enough.

24

GRACE

Longstone Lighthouse. September 1838

The skies to the north are bruised in shades of violet and ochre as I extinguish the lamps the following morning. My telescope drifts repeatedly in the direction of North Sunderland, as if of its own compulsion. I presume it expects to catch a glimpse of Mr. Emmerson still standing at the harbor, indigo sea glass in hand. But of course he is not. He has far more pressing matters to attend to. Matters that weigh on my mind when they have no business whatsoever to do so.

The shock of learning that Sarah Dawson is Mr. Emmerson's sister, not to mention the discovery that he is engaged to be married, kept me occupied through last night's stint on watch. But even more than these revelations, it is the very real presence of him that I can't forget. Like a spirit summoned to life, I had seen and heard him, touched him even as he helped me into the boat. It is this sensory experience that lingers most persistently, and somewhat maddeningly.

I had always dismissed as folly the dreamy distraction of my sisters as they'd fallen in love. I'd accused them of being overly dramatic, only imagining themselves to be light-headed and forgetful and not experiencing any physical symptoms at all. Now, I realize I was unkind to tease them. Now, I understand why we use the phrase *falling* in love; because the dizzying sensation I experience when I think about Mr. Emmerson is not unlike that of dropping into the steep trough of a swell, my stomach momentarily suspended above before swooping down in a sickening lurch to catch up.

'What absolute nonsense, Grace.' I scold myself as I stare at my reflection in the lens, pondering the miniature likenesses caught in its petal-like structure.

Fresh air will do it. Fresh air and a brisk walk will settle things.

Morning on the island has dawned bright and fresh. I am invigorated by the breeze as I walk among the rocks, taking advantage of the low tide to search for new shells to add to my collection. The mewling and barking of the seal pups is a familiar joy to my ears and I clamber higher to see them. There must be at least a hundred gathered on the beach around the bay. I watch them for a good while, observing the way the mothers care for their pups so diligently. I find myself wondering what it would be like to raise a child, to sustain another life. I've never felt the pull of the maternal urge like my sisters, or Mam, who brought nine children into the world in as many years (and has complained about it ever since). I think, perhaps, I am content to be an aunt, and leave the raising of children to those more suited to the task.

My mood restored to something more familiar

than that of a giddy schoolgirl, I return to the lighthouse to help Father with the flotsam salvaged from the *Forfarshire* over the past weeks, some of which still arrives with each new tide. I remember my intention to write a strongly worded letter to Mr. Smeddle, still furious with him for printing my private responses to private letters, but I am delayed from the task. Father is waiting for me at the lighthouse door, taking me to one side before I even have a chance to remove my cloak and bonnet.

'There's a gentleman come to see you, Grace.' Color flies to my cheeks. Could it be Mr. Emmerson? 'A Mr. Sylvester, sent as an agent of Mr. Batty, the circus owner.'

Disappointment drains the color from my face as quickly as hope had put it there. 'Does he say what he wants?'

'He said he would rather explain things to us together.'

Unexpected callers seem to be two-a-penny in recent days, so I'm not greatly surprised to learn of another. Longstone has seen a steady stream of spectators and newspaper reporters taking advantage of the good weather. The short sea crossing from North Sunderland can see them brought out to us and returned to the mainland within a morning or afternoon. I've grown mistrusting of the reporters' questions and the scratch of their pencils. The less said the better as far as commenting on my 'heroics.' The men in charge of the front pages will insert their own words regardless and make drama where there is none. But an agent of a circus owner is a new, and rather curious, development.

Mr. Sylvester is a stout man with an impressive handlebar mustache and mutton-chops that obscure most of his face. He half bows when I enter the room, offering a small, simpering hand, which I take, glad to have not yet removed my gloves.

'Miss Darling. What an honor it is to have your acquaintance.' He speaks with a heavy Scottish accent and I don't catch all his words. It isn't entirely Mr. Sylvester's failure to enunciate clearly, but my mind which dwells on Mr. Emmerson's lyrical Scots burr.

'You are very welcome to Longstone, Mr. Sylvester,' I remark as I remove my bonnet. 'I hope you had a pleasant crossing.'

'Very pleasant, thank you. The *Tweeside* brought me. The skipper tells me he takes three trips a week around the 'Romantic Groups of the Farnes,' as his posters state. He kindly permitted me to alight here before he proceeded to Berwick. It took all his authority to prevent a mob alighting with me.'

'We know the *Tweeside* well.' I smile, as graciously as I can as I reflect on the profiteering fishermen. 'I am aware of the posters.'

'I expect you find the boat trips a little intrusive,' he remarks, clearly attempting to win my favor. 'Although I suppose they will become fewer as the winter storms increase.'

'Yes. I expect so.' I have never wished more for winter storms.

'Mr. Sylvester has brought a sum of money, Grace,' my father explains. 'From a recent

189

performance of Mr. Batty's Royal Circus in Edinburgh. Twenty pounds, indeed.'

'Twenty pounds? From a circus? I don't understand.'

Father invites everyone to sit by the fire as Mr. Sylvester explains. 'My employer, William Batty, held a recent performance of the circus in your honor, Miss Darling. He wished for you to have the net profits from the evening, which drew an impressive crowd. Your cause is a most worthy one, and our patrons were very keen to support it.'

'But I don't have a cause, Mr. Sylvester.' I cast an urgent glance at my father who raises an eyebrow in reply, as confused as I am. 'How did the people know the proceeds of the evening were devoted to this cause?'

Mr. Sylvester shuffles slightly in his chair. 'Mr. Batty advertised the event as such. Perhaps you could think of the money as a gift from the good people of Edinburgh. They were very keen to donate.'

He places the twenty-pound note on the table where it sits as if it were one of Mary Anning's rare fossils while we all stare at it.

'It is very generous of Mr. Batty, and the people of Edinburgh,' Father says. 'You must send our sincere thanks.'

Mr. Sylvester takes an envelope from his coat pocket. 'Mr. Batty would be greatly honored if you would visit the circus, Miss Darling.' He passes the envelope to me. 'He wished to send on a few lines to ask if you would consider thanking the people of Edinburgh in person.'

I don't especially care for the way Mr. Sylvester's smile turns almost into a sneer, but I am too confused to think of any plausible excuse as to why I couldn't possibly do such a thing and hear myself say I would be delighted.

'Very well then. It is agreed.' Sylvester sounds rather too pleased with himself. 'Perhaps we can take a walk outside, Mr. Darling, while your daughter writes a reply to Mr. Batty?'

Left alone to write yet another letter, I struggle to find the right words. Why am I writing to a circus owner in Scotland? Why are people donating funds to a cause I know nothing about, at a performance being advertised in my name, without my knowledge? Everything feels horribly out of control. I hardly dare imagine what else is happening in the name of 'the heroine, Grace Darling.' She has almost become a separate person to me. Someone I vaguely knew once, but can't quite remember. Reluctantly, and not with good humor, I pen a few lines to assure Mr. Batty we will visit his arena in Edinburgh to oblige those who have shown concern for my welfare, and admiration for my part in the rescue. The force of my full stop almost punctures the page.

I am grateful when Father announces he will row Mr. Sylvester back to the Main. Mam is also pleased the visit is only brief, having taken an instant dislike to the man.

'I see we are to have circus folk traipsing sand onto my rugs now, are we?' she mutters, crossly. 'I suppose Father will be rushing off to Scotland with you to this circus?'

'I can hardly go on my own, Mam.'

She grumbles about the lighthouse going to ruin and the wind causing havoc with her joints and that she doesn't know what is to become of us all, honestly she doesn't.

* * *

That evening, with Father returned from the Main, all is quiet at the lighthouse. Mam is at her wheel. Father and Brooks mend an old sail. I sit beside the fire with my darning needle. I take a moment to absorb the perfect normality of it all, an autumn evening spent safely inside the thick walls of the lighthouse while nature throws another tantrum beyond. I am happy and secure, and yet I know it won't always be this way. I imagine the scene without my parents, Brooks with his wife and children sat around the fire while my chair is pushed out toward the cold edges of the room. An observer. No longer a participant. The thought unsettles me, as it often has of late.

As if reading my thoughts, Father suggests that I sleep through that night. 'I will share the watch with Brooks tonight. You look tired, Grace. You should rest.'

Reluctantly I agree, but before I settle for the night, I climb the steps to the lantern room to check on the oil reserves. All is in order. My brother must have been up to carry out the inspection already.

The wind sighs at the windows as the lamps turn above, as reliable and steadfast as ever. As I lay my head on my pillow, I ask myself if I am needed here as much as I once was. Has the time finally come when I need the lighthouse more than it needs me?

Bamburgh, England

From the upstairs window of her cousin's home, Sarah watches the distant flash of the Longstone light. This will be her final night in Bamburgh.

She keeps her silent vigil until dawn, when the lamps are extinguished. Another night navigated without mishap. Another night navigated without the haunting dreams that await her on the other side of sleep.

She dresses quietly and leaves by the back door where the coachman is waiting as arranged by the maid. As the hooves clatter over the streets, she says a private farewell to this peaceful little town and steels herself for the long journey home. In her hand she holds the piece of emerald sea glass for James and the light keeper's instruction manual for Matilda, gifts from Miss Darling. Her deepest agony is the knowledge that she leaves her children's graves behind, but their lives, their memories, she takes with her. Whatever lies ahead, she resolves that neither they, nor the name Grace Darling, will ever be forgotten. In her pocket, she keeps her account of the *Forfarshire* disaster, carefully wrapped in brown paper. She is glad to have written it down, glad to have emptied her distress onto the pages.

Eliza has looked after her well so that she

almost feels sorry for having planted such a fertile seed of doubt in George's mind about her. Had things been different, she doubts she would have meddled, but she feels so sure that George's future happiness exists not in his cousin's reedy embrace, but in the arms of another on a small island in the middle of the North Sea.

As the coach clatters on, she thinks of the letter she left with the maid, to send on to Miss Darling. She is pleased to have written with such honesty. What good does it do to keep thoughts and feelings hidden away? If she has learned anything from the past terrible weeks, it is that any chance of happiness must be grasped and held tight, not left to dangle and fall where it may. Whatever she can do to put things right, she will. What other reason can there be for having been spared when her children were taken so cruelly? She must matter, now. She must have a purpose.

The morning light strengthens as the coach leaves Bamburgh and heads south along the coast road, the glistening sea to her right, her future straight ahead. With each rotation of the wheels, Sarah feels a little brighter, a little more hopeful. She sings of lavenders blue and lavenders green and lets the rocking motion lull her to sleep where she dreams of a lighthouse at the edge of the Atlantic Ocean, and a new life waiting for her there.

25

MATILDA

Newport, Rhode Island. June 1938

Early June, and my days in Newport slowly unravel beneath a generous sun and the fragrance of beach roses and juniper bushes. The early sunrises and late-setting suns are a gift to the tourists and honeymooners, but for me they offer too many hours to feel the strengthening flip and tumble of the secret I hide beneath ever-slackening waistbands and loose-fitting cardigans. A quickening, the doctor calls it as he places his stethoscope against my skin.

'Looks like you've a lively little thing in there,' he says as I flinch in response to the cold press of metal. 'A real wriggler.'

He could be talking about a new puppy for all that his words affect me. I still can't emotionally connect the motion I feel with the fact that it is made by a human life. My child. Only once have I wondered what it will look like before I pushed the thought quickly away, afraid to let it linger too long.

As I dress behind the screen, the doctor tells me to make another appointment for around a month from now.

'You'll be into your third trimester then, Mrs.

Collins,' he says, enthusiastically. 'Not too much longer to go.'

I wince at my invented name. My fictitious husband would turn in his grave at all the lies I'm telling to stick to Harriet's cover story. She makes it all sound so plausible I almost feel sad for poor Mr. Collins and his tragic demise in a traffic accident.

I step out from behind the screen. 'Thank you again, Doctor.'

He peers at me sympathetically through the black-rimmed glasses perched on the end of his sun-reddened nose. 'I know it feels endless right now, Mrs. Collins, but you'll have your baby in your arms soon enough.' The words prick at my conscience, knowing that it will be some other woman's arms that hold this baby, not mine. Mistaking my silence for concern, he pats my arm reassuringly. 'You've nothing to worry about. The child is perfectly healthy and everything is progressing as normal.'

I leave the consulting room in a daze and make my next appointment, ignoring the receptionist who says a friendly goodbye as she lifts the needle that has stuck halfway through an Andrews Sisters record on the turntable beside the counter.

I walk the short distance home, my mind replaying Doctor Miller's words. '*Everything is progressing as normal.*' Nothing about this experience feels even remotely normal. I don't even know what normal is anymore. The physical changes to my body are terrifying, and the seesawing of my emotions is equally alarming. I burst into tears at the slightest thing — happy, or sad — swinging from carefree to desolate at a moment's notice. Even Harriet has started to bite her tongue.

Despite a testy start to life at the clapboard house on the corner of Cherry Street, Harriet and I have found a way to eat at the same table and share the same bathroom and breathe the same tobacco fumes and be civil to each other. We might look and act as different as a lobster to a clam, but beneath our hard shells I suspect we have more in common than we realize. There's an energy when we're together, a friction that makes the somber little house crackle with the force of us.

Harriet feels it, too. I know she does, because for all that she keeps her distance and pretends to be disinterested in me, I know she listens and watches. When I'd casually mentioned that I like the scent of lavender, a tablet of scented soap appeared in the bathroom. When I remarked on a particular flower I'd seen in a neighbor's garden, a posy of them was left in a vase on the table the next day. When I complained about my skin itching, a tin of powder was left on my bed. When I talked about how I'd loved cycling back home in Ireland, a rusty old bicycle leaned against the gate the following evening. There is never any fuss made, no explanation given or thanks needed. I understand that this is Harriet's way of letting me know that she *does* see me, and hear me, and takes notice of me.

And yet for all the weeks we've spent together, I know almost as little about Harriet Flaherty as

197

I did before I left Ireland. She occasionally talks about her Da and old Boots and the work of the light keepers, and she constantly complains about the automation of the lights and how things aren't the same anymore. But there's still a distance between us. Despite our family connection, despite the fact that we were raised among the same smoky rooms of our grannies' fires, there is a bridge over which she won't let me cross. Harriet, I've realized, is like an island, and I don't yet have the right map to reach her.

★　★　★

Since meeting Joseph at the lighthouse, I've found myself thinking about him more often than I probably should. Finding the incomplete portrait at the bottom of the tea chest gives me the perfect excuse to follow up on his invitation to visit his art gallery.

Kinsella's Fine Arts stands in the middle of Bellevue Avenue. It is a narrow redbrick building with bottle-green exterior paintwork. A large front window displays gilt-framed seascapes and scenes of the harbor wharfs. The shop sign swings on an ornate iron bracket outside, the wording painted in elaborate swirling lettering: *Kinsella's Fine Arts. Portraits, Commissions etc. Enquire within.* With the old portrait wrapped in brown paper tucked under my arm, I push open the door and step inside.

The interior of the gallery is cool and soothing. A record plays quietly on an old gramophone in one corner. Potted plants lend an air of a Victorian glass house. A ceiling fan whirs above as I call out a hesitant hello and wait for a reply.

Joseph appears from a little door at the back of the room, his face breaking into a wide smile when he sees me. 'Hey! Wild Irish! Good to see you. Thought you'd gone back to Ireland.'

Captain pushes past Joseph's legs, her claws clattering against the varnished floorboards as she races to me. I bend down to pet her, laughing as she shoves her wet nose into my hands.

'Sorry. I meant to call in sooner.'

Joseph holds up his hands. 'No explanation needed. I'm glad you came.' He smiles. I smile back. 'So? What do you think of the place?'

I stand up and turn around, admiring the displays. 'It's very nice. Very . . . elegant.' I walk over to a collection of watercolor paintings of lighthouses. 'I like these. Not that I know the first thing about art.'

Joseph walks over to stand beside me. 'That's the great thing about art. Everyone takes something different from it. You're as qualified to like them as any expert is to not like them. As it happens, you have a good eye. They're mine.'

'Really?' I turn to look at him, impressed by his talent.

A proud smile crinkles the corners of his eyes. 'Lighthouses were last year's obsession. I'm working on a collection of screen prints this year. A study of crustaceans and mollusks.'

'Mollusks?'

He bursts out laughing. 'I guess it sounds a

little obscure when you put it like that!'

I push my hair self-consciously behind my ear. 'Art isn't really my thing. I'm sure mollusks are very interesting.'

Joseph hops up onto a desk against the wall and lights a cigarette. 'You smoke?' he asks, offering me one. I shake my head and wish I was the type of carefree girl who smoked and drank beer from the bottle and knew how to have fun. 'So, what *is* your thing then if it isn't mollusks?' Joseph continues. 'What does a wild Irish girl do in her spare time?'

It's a good question and one I don't readily have an answer for. My mother's church luncheons and charity events were what I did in my spare time. Being the local politician's respectable daughter was what I did in my spare time. Drinking whiskey with a British soldier in the back of an army truck was what I did in my spare time.

My eye settles on a copy of Thackeray's *Vanity Fair* on the desk. 'Reading,' I announce, relieved to have remembered something I enjoy. 'I like to read. And walk. On beaches. I used to collect shells when I was a little girl.'

Joseph pulls something from his pocket. 'I still do.' He places a scallop shell on the desk. 'Picked this one up this morning.'

I take a clam shell from my skirt pocket and place it beside his. 'Same.'

He takes a thoughtful drag of his cigarette. 'Maybe we could collect shells together some-time. If you're not too busy reading.'

I say maybe, yes, that would be grand and call

Captain over to me, glad of the distraction.

Joseph hops down from the desk and flips the record over on the gramophone. He nods toward my arm. 'You brought me something, or do you always walk around with a package under your arm?'

I'd forgotten the picture. 'Oh, this. Yes! It's an old portrait I found in a tea chest over at the lighthouse.' I undo the string and fold back the paper. 'I think she's rather beautiful.'

Joseph takes the picture from me and lays it carefully on the desk, studying the image. He runs his fingers over the frame, pressing a glass to his eye as he peers at the artist's initials.

'She's pretty, all right. There's something about the look in her eyes.'

'I agree. I think she's lovely. What era do you think it is?'

'Definitely Victorian. You can tell by the clothing, and the style of the shells in the border. Classic Victorian botanical sketches. It would be a nice piece if it was finished.'

'I quite like the fact that it isn't,' I say, joining him at the counter. 'It's unusual. I feel sorry for her, half in a picture, and half out.'

'Or maybe she's faded away over time,' Joseph adds. 'Her story never told, her name never spoken. Discarded in the bottom of a musty old tea chest.' He puts down the eye glass. 'Now there's a romantic old fool for you! Either way, she's not going to earn you a fortune, I'm afraid. The artist's signature isn't one I recognize.'

'Oh, I don't want to sell it. I think the artist was a distant relative of mine. I was thinking of having it reframed. Spruce her up a little.'

'Well, I can certainly do that for you. Could be a week or two before I get to it?'

I say two weeks will be grand and can already feel the time dragging ahead as I wonder how many more forgotten paintings and old relics I can find to keep me occupied.

Joseph wraps the picture back up and checks his watch. 'I make it elevenses. There's a diner around the corner if you've time for a quick coffee?'

I have all the time in the world and although my head tells me it isn't a good idea to make too much of a friend of this impossibly charming young man, my heart tells my head to shush.

We head to Bernie's, where we drink strong coffee and Joseph tells me about a local candy called saltwater taffy and about the Gilded Age mansions on Ocean Drive. An hour passes easily in his company and although I shouldn't I flirt with him a little, laugh a little too enthusiastically, let my feet knock against his beneath the table. I forget I'm supposed to be grieving for a dead husband and happily ignore the squirming sensation beneath my dress. Twirling the locket at my neck and stirring sugar into my coffee, I enjoy the easy conversation and the chance to relax.

'What's the locket?' he asks, noticing my habitual fiddling.

'Family heirloom,' I say, opening the clasp. 'It belonged to my great-great-granny. Her brother was an artist in England during the Victorian era. I think he painted the portrait I brought for

202

you to reframe. That's him.' I point to the picture on the left of the locket as we both lean forward so Joseph can see the little portraits better.

'Huh. Handsome fellow. That's neat.'

'Sarah — my great-great-granny — was rescued from a shipwreck by a lighthouse keeper and his daughter, Grace Darling. We think the other picture is of Grace. But it might be George's wife.'

Joseph leans right across the table and rests the locket in his hand, studying the miniature portraits for a moment before looking up at me, his eyes so close to mine I can see my reflection in them. 'She's very beautiful,' he says. We stare at each other for a beat before he leans back. 'She looks like the girl in your unfinished portrait. Maybe it's the same person. Maybe he was in love with her.'

'Maybe,' I agree, my heart pounding as I stir the dregs of my coffee and wonder why it's suddenly very hot in here.

'What are your plans for the rest of the day?' Joseph asks after paying the check, running his hands through his hair and sending it sticking up every which way as we walk outside together.

I'm glad of the fresh air. I feel light-headed from the caffeine. 'I don't really have any plans,' I shrug. 'To be honest, I'd hoped Harriet would have more time to show me around, but she's always busy at the lighthouse.'

'Harriet Flaherty? Your friendly Newport tour guide? That doesn't sound like the Harriet I know!'

'It doesn't, does it?' I laugh, realizing now how

ridiculous it sounds.

'I could show you around,' Joseph offers. 'The gallery's quiet enough when the weather's so nice. I'd like to show Newport off to you. Take you to a clambake. Pretend I own half the homes on Ocean Drive.'

'You're kind to offer, but I'll be grand. Honestly. I have a bicycle now. I'm getting quite good at finding my way around.'

'Sightseeing on your own isn't much fun though.' He shoves his hands into his pockets. 'Look, Matilda. I'll level with you. I don't know the real reason you're here and I don't need to, but that grieving widow story?' He raises an eyebrow. 'Even if you have something to prove to your parents, or Harriet, you don't have to prove anything to me. So, the invitation still stands. No strings.'

The relief of shaking off the pretense is almost physical as I feel my shoulders relax. I want to tell him the truth, desperate to share the burden of my secret. But for all that he is friendly and impossibly charming, I don't know Joseph well enough to be sure how he'll react. Joseph Kinsella may be quickly becoming the closest thing I have to a friend here and I certainly don't want to frighten him away with my shocking secrets.

He holds out a hand. 'If you let me show you around, I promise I won't ask any questions. How about it, Wild Irish? Deal?'

I smile and nod. 'Deal.'

And on something as simple as a handshake between friends, so things change.

Over the following weeks Joseph and I spend most of his free time together. He takes me on walking tours of the harbor wharfs and the historic colonial buildings of the town. I learn about the Quakers and the taverns that were the favorite drinking haunts of the country's founding fathers. I see the homes of the first Irish settlers who established their own community in the Fifth Ward in the southern part of town. We watch confusing games of polo and croquet and eat clams and fresh lobster. We cycle along Bellevue Avenue and Ocean Drive, stopping to admire the Breakers, Miramar, Rosecliff, Marble House — the eye-wateringly opulent homes built by the Vanderbilts and the Astors on fortunes made in shipping and the railroads before the crash. We follow the winding trail along Narragansett Bay, Captain lolloping faithfully alongside, and out to Easton's Beach and Goat Island.

Slowly, steadily this salt-tinged city by the sea begins to wrap itself around my heart, and despite everything telling me it won't end well, so does a young artist by the name of Joseph Kinsella.

26

MATILDA

Newport, Rhode Island. June 1938

Dawn paints the sky lavender, and I rise with the strengthening sun. I stand at the open bedroom window, enjoying the soft breeze against my skin, absentmindedly picking up a handful of the painted seashells from the windowsill. I admire the intricate patterns, the careful brushstrokes, knowing I could never create anything as delicate and precise. The initials *CF* are marked inside several of the shells. The name *Cora* is painted with a flourish inside the larger ones.

Cora.

The name washes through the walls of this house like an echo I can't quite catch. On the rare nights she spends here, I've heard Harriet call out the name in her sleep. In moments of distraction, she allows the name to creep into our conversation, following it instantly with an abrupt pause. A sudden full stop. Whoever she is, or was, Cora is as present here as she is absent, and as with a loose button on a coat, I can't stop fiddling and pulling to find out why.

Putting the shells down, I pick up the old postcard from the nightstand, running my fingertips over the painting of Ida and Grace. One and the same. Perhaps it isn't so unusual for two such similar people to become indistinguishable over time; one blending into the other until history forgets that they were ever two separate individuals.

Dressing quickly, I leave my skirt half-unzipped to accommodate my expanding waist. My stomach is clearly rounded now. Although my bump is still neat enough not to be noticed by those who aren't looking for it, it is undeniably there, especially in the evenings when I swell up like an overinflated balloon.

I stand in front of the mirror and pull the fabric of my skirt taut, turning sideways to inspect my curious new shape. With a sigh, I let the fabric drop, yawning as I make my way downstairs. The regular performance of the child's nighttime acrobatics keeps me awake long into the night and my insomnia has seen me reading far more of the lighthouse manual than I'd ever intended. What I don't now know about the operation of Victorian-era lighthouses probably isn't worth knowing.

I eat a good breakfast, finishing up just as Harriet returns from the lighthouse. Her eyes narrow as she sees me dressed.

'Are you going out again?' she asks. 'Shouldn't you be resting?'

'I can't lie in bed like a porcelain doll. Anyway, I'm sure fresh air is far better for me than sitting around, 'resting.' I feel grand.' I feel vigorous at times. Far from the confined invalid I've watched other expectant women become.

'You've an appointment with Doctor Miller at four.'

'I'll be back in time.'

'Hmm. Make sure you are.' Harriet puffs on her pipe and coughs.

'You shouldn't smoke so much,' I remark as I take my coat from the hook beside the door. 'They say it isn't good for you.'

She scoffs at me. 'They say everything isn't good for you. Life would be fierce dull if we didn't have our vices.' She takes a long series of puffs on her pipe before blowing smoke toward me. Her point made, she stands up and flicks on the wireless. 'Anyway, stop fussing. You sound just like Cora.'

That name again. The same pause. The same friction in the air.

I have to ask.

'Who *is* Cora? You mention her quite a lot.'

A breath of wind blows through the open sitting room window, ruffling the sun-faded curtains. Harriet stands still, her expression one of almost physical pain. I bite my lip, and wait for the inevitable rebuke.

'Endless bloody questions,' she snaps, turning her back on me, and on whatever memories I have stirred. 'It's always the same with you.' She fiddles roughly with the radio, filling the room with the hiss of white noise between stations.

'I'm sorry,' I offer. 'I just wondered . . . '

'Well don't.'

Taking the last sip from my coffee cup, I push open the screen door.

'Where're you going, anyway?' she asks, softening a little as she sinks into her chair. 'Surely you've seen the whole island by now.'

'We're going to the lighthouse.'

'By 'we' I presume you mean Joseph?'

'Yes.'

Harriet looks at me, as if she wants to say something but changes her mind. 'Well. Go on then.'

I leave by the back door and head down to the jetty at the end of the boardwalk where Joseph is already preparing his little sailing boat.

He smiles as I approach. 'You came, then!'

'Of course. Why wouldn't I?'

'Woman's prerogative, isn't it? To change her mind?'

'Well, it isn't mine. Anyway, I've been looking forward to it.'

He beams from ear to ear. 'Me too.' He bends down to lift a basket into the boat. 'You look pretty,' he adds, without looking up. 'Blue suits you.'

I say thank you and turn to face the sea to hide my idiotic grin, glad to have changed out of the green I'd put on first this morning.

Hearing my voice, Captain bounds across the jetty, nearly knocking me over as she jumps up at me. I push her down, afraid she might hurt the baby, or that Joseph will notice the rounding of my stomach. I catch myself doing this now: worrying about the baby, thinking about the baby, imagining what the baby will look like. However much I might pretend not to care, the fact is that I'm constantly aware of the life I'm carrying, and feel increasingly responsible for it. When I make these emotional connections, the reality of it all terrifies me.

After unfurling the sail we step into the boat, Captain jumping in with us, and Joseph sets a direct course around the bay. The wind and the tide are generous and the boat glides easily over the water. I close my eyes, enjoying the sensation of freedom, smiling to myself as I remember clinging so pathetically to the railings on the *California* with Mrs. O'Driscoll at my side. I wonder how she's getting on on Long Island. I often think about her and the piece of paper with her address and the word written beneath. *Courage.*

'So, how are you enjoying America so far?' Joseph asks.

I pull my sunglasses on and lean back, stretching my arms along the edge of the boat. 'It's very nice. The people are friendly.'

'Your folks must be missing you?'

'Not so much. We had a disagreement before I left.'

'Sorry to hear that. But absence makes the heart grow fonder, as they say.'

'That's assuming you have a heart in the first place. My mother? I'm not so sure.'

'That bad, huh?' He adjusts the sail, making a complicated maneuver look easy.

I sigh. 'That bad.'

★ ★ ★

I waited for Valentine's Day to tell her, foolishly hoping that a day of love would soften the blow. I should have known better.

For the briefest moment after I said the words

210

I'd agonized over for weeks, I thought I saw a flash of concern in her eyes, but the only thing my mother was worried about was the family's reputation. Her face crumpled into a picture of disgust and disbelief. I'll never forget it.

'Don't be absurd, Matilda!' Smoke wound from the tip of her Mayfair cigarette, the ash curling and dying like the dregs of our already dysfunctional relationship. 'How in God's name can you be pregnant?'

'Do you really need me to tell you?' My contempt for her was palpable.

I sat on the end of my bed, stiff as a tailor's mannequin, as she walked toward me. Would she hug me? Would she tell me it would all be grand and we would muddle through together? Dropping her gloves onto the dressing table, she walked past me to the window, standing with her back to me, arms folded across her lemon twin set. Beyond the window, the distinctive outline of Cork harbor. In the windowsill, my cherished collection of seashells.

'Who is it?' she asked.

'Who is what?'

'The undesirable monster who got you into this mess.'

'Does it matter?'

Whipping around, she glared at me. 'Of course it matters. Your father will want to know who took advantage of his daughter.'

'But nobody took advantage of me, Mother. I quite enjoyed it actually.' I knew I had gone too far. I deserved the slap to my cheek.

'This might all be amusing to you now,

Matilda, but your life is ruined. *Our* life is ruined. What were you *thinking?* Clearly not about the family's reputation. Clearly not thinking about anyone but yourself. As usual.' Her hands trembled with rage. 'I'll talk to Sister Murphy in the morning. See what we can do to make arrangements.'

She rifled through my wardrobe, pulling out something for me to wear for that evening's party before picking up her gloves and tugging them on with brisk purposeful movements.

'Get dressed and do something nice with your hair. Make yourself presentable before your father gets home. He's very busy at the moment with elections coming up. He could well do without these . . . distractions.'

A distraction. That's what I was. In many ways, I'd always felt like an inconvenient intrusion in my mother's life. Her reaction to my pregnancy, the way she so easily condemned and disowned me when I needed her help, underlined everything I'd felt since I was a little girl making up stories about the people in my locket. Even then, when I didn't have the words to express my emotions, I felt like an unwelcome guest in my own home.

How apt then that it was arranged for me and my little problem to be sent away, discarded as easily as a piece of unwanted furniture.

★   ★   ★

'Penny for them?'
Joseph's voice stirs me from my daydreaming.

212

'Sorry. I was miles away.'

'Back in Ireland?'

I nod.

'Anything I can do to help? A problem shared and all that?'

I look into his eyes, the color of faded-denim and full of such kindness. 'I wish it were that simple.'

'Then make it that simple. Nothing's ever as complicated as it seems when we keep it to ourselves.'

I smile, despite the secret that weighs heavily on my mind and in my heart.

Dear Joseph. He makes every problem seem like nothing more difficult than a fly to be swatted away. I wish I could find the courage to tell him, but the words dissolve on my tongue and we travel the rest of the way to the lighthouse in silence.

★   ★   ★

At the base of Rose Island, Joseph moors the boat. The shells crunch satisfyingly beneath our shoes as we walk up the little path. It reminds me of walks on Ballycotton beach with my father and I think that perhaps all my childhood wasn't bad.

While Joseph attends to some tasks at the lighthouse, I set myself up with a chair and my box of paints and start to sketch the view, carefully observing the way the light plays on the water in the bay. The scent of the pink beach roses beside me is heavenly. Captain settles at my feet. Joseph sings Nat King Cole through an open window. For a few blissful hours, it is like I have always been here, safe beside the protective walls of the lighthouse, and nothing else matters.

The hours slip away as I paint. I doze for a while, warmed by the sun, my thoughts turning over everything that has happened since I arrived in America. I think about Harriet, so broad shouldered and tall, and how she shrank into herself like a hermit crab when I asked her about Cora, scurrying off to be alone somewhere where people don't pry or ask questions. It plays on my mind all morning, tugging at me like a persistent child pulling at its mother's skirt.

As Joseph shucks fresh oysters from the bay for lunch, my curiosity finally gets the better of me.

'Can I ask you something, Joseph?'

He looks up at me, pushing the hair from his eyes. 'Sure. Fire away.'

I hesitate for a moment, knowing that if I prize this secret from him, I might not like the truth. 'Who is Cora?'

His hands still for a moment before he puts down the oyster and knife. He wipes his hands slowly on a rag hanging from his belt and sits down cross-legged on the blanket.

He looks directly at me. 'Why do you ask?' His voice lacks its usual bright buoyancy.

'Harriet has mentioned the name a few times but she wouldn't answer me when I asked her who Cora is.' I wait for a moment. 'She calls out for her sometimes in the night, and there are some painted seashells in my bedroom with

214

Cora's name on them.' Joseph casts his eyes down at the blanket. It is clear that he is wrestling with his emotions, but I can't stop prodding and poking. 'She's clearly someone important. So, who is she?'

Eventually, he lets out a long sigh. 'Cora was Harriet's daughter.' He picks up another oyster from the plate before looking up at me. 'And I'd hoped she might become my wife.'

27

HARRIET

Rose Island Lighthouse. June 1938

The past is a funny place, so far away and yet always there, waiting to trip you up with its memories and regret.

I can still smell the fresh paint of the ship's railings when I made the long sea crossing from Ireland. I can still taste the salt of my tears on my lips as I walked up and down the deck, trying to soothe Cora and find the cause of her shrill little cries. I'd never needed my mammy more; never felt, more keenly, the gap left behind by her death during my infancy.

I can still hear the panic in my voice as I asked a woman with older children what she thought might be wrong with my child. She told me it was probably wind and showed me how to put the infant over my shoulder and rub her back, but Cora still bawled and mewled as if she knew something was terribly wrong, and wouldn't stop crying until I set it right.

I remember how some of the passengers cheered when New York first loomed through the fog, but for me the sight of Lady Liberty only left a hollow ache in my heart. When I'd boarded the boat in Cobh, I thought I'd known the worst day of my life, but stepping off it was far worse.

The distance I'd traveled from Ireland was emphasized by every unfamiliar accent and noise and smell. The truth of what I'd done struck me like a punch in the chest so that I could barely breathe as I walked off that ship. My guilt has walked beside me ever since.

But Cora and I found a way. I was far from the perfect mother, but I did my best for her. With Da willing to help out in any way he could, and even old Boots taking his turn at playing nanny, we somehow muddled through. When Da and Boots passed away, I didn't look for anyone to replace them. I didn't need anyone else, fiercely protecting the little unit of two Cora and I had become.

But the echo from Ireland has always haunted me.

As the long nights on watch were washed away by rosy clouds, the first thing I saw each morning was Cora's sweet little face, cheeks as pink as summer roses, hair falling across her pillow, like a mermaid underwater. I imagine her now, living in some underwater world, the reflection from the moon silvering her hair.

I might not be needed here like I once was, but I still come to the lighthouse, like a moth drawn to a flame, flitting about through the small hours of the night, moving things that don't need moving, wiping surfaces that don't need wiping, finding ways to remember her and to keep myself busy. The alternative — to sit idle and invite in difficult memories — is too frightening.

The skies darken early, the small room at the bottom of the lighthouse cast into shadow by the gathering clouds. I pause at the picture of Ida Lewis as I walk to the kitchen to make coffee. Her image has faded over the years, erased by the sun and the passage of time. She's been a sort of guardian to me, someone I've always looked up to. Ida was a true American heroine, her life was noble and proud. Mine is a fabrication, stitched poorly together between Ireland and America, and it is starting to unravel and fray.

I make coffee and sit by the window, watching the shifting tint and tone of the sky, letting my thoughts drift back across the years, the salt-tang of the ocean filling my nostrils as I breathe in deep. I see her in everything: in sunlight and shadow, in the white tips of the waves and the lingering strands of the sea fogs. For so long, Cora was my reason to wake up in the morning. Cora, and the light. The darkness of her absence is unbearable.

Matilda is my purpose now, for as long as she chooses to stay here. I am curious to know her, enjoy the little clues I pick up as we spend time together. I know that she likes to sing along to the wireless and that she likes the scent of lavender and beach roses. I know that she enjoys cycling and collecting shells from the beach which she keeps in a trinket box beside her bed.

I know these simple little things about her that make a person unique.

Simple little things I should have always known about her, if things had been different.

28

MATILDA

Newport, Rhode Island. July 1938

The two months I've been in Newport could as easily be two years, such is the difference I feel in my heart and see in the swollen lump my once petite body has become. I no longer balk at the smell of the kelp, or comment on how quickly the fogs roll in and out of the harbor. I barely notice the low moan of the fog horn that disturbed my sleep during my first weeks here and I cycle past the grand summer cottages on Ocean Drive as if they were a row of shops in Ballycotton. The extraordinary has become ordinary and Newport no longer feels like somewhere I'm visiting. It feels like home.

As the weeks pass, it becomes obvious that I can no longer conceal my bump. I spend more time at Rose Island, glad to be away from the scornful gaze of Harriet's nosy neighbors. I prefer to spend my days alone at the lighthouse, sorting through the hotchpotch history of light keepers in the old tea chest, reading and sketching, or walking on the quiet beaches. I can relax there in the comfort of loose-fitting cotton housedresses, and leave my swollen feet bare while Harriet tinkers with some old mechanism or other, unable to shake her nostalgia for the way things used to be.

The only problem is Joseph. Whenever he's around, I sit at the table, or curl up in a chair with a well-placed cushion. So far, I've managed not to draw attention to my expanding waistline, and whether he has noticed or not, he has been diplomatic enough not to say anything.

With time on my hands, I've thought a lot about Cora since discovering who she was. Her absence drifts through the rooms of the lighthouse and the house on Cherry Street, sitting like a shadow beside Harriet, walking beside me so that I sometimes expect to see another set of footprints in the sand. Harriet doesn't know Joseph has told me, but discovering that her daughter tragically drowned only a few years ago has softened Harriet to me. I think about the first day I arrived here, how she stood in the doorway all hard-edged and unwelcoming. Now, I see her differently. I can understand her short temper and her reluctance to open up. What I'd seen as Harriet being snappy and reclusive, I now see as her being vulnerable and heart-broken. A mother grieving for her daughter.

I look at the painted shells in my bedroom, the borrowed dress I'd worn on my first day here, the seashell frames and work boxes scattered about the place, knowing now that they belonged to a much-loved daughter.

'Cora was Harriet's world,' Joseph had explained after telling me who she was. 'I never saw a mother and daughter so close.'

The pain of his own loss was evident when he

talked about her, but when I apologized for stirring difficult memories he said it was a relief to talk about her again.

'Harriet can't bear to talk about her,' he explained, 'and I hate to feel as though we've forgotten her.' He told me how they'd been childhood friends, but as they grew up he'd started to see her differently. 'Cora said I was like the brother she never had. I foolishly hoped she would look at me differently one day.'

'Why foolishly?'

He looked a little bashful before replying. 'She was too good for someone like me. Too smart. Too pretty. Too eager to see the world. She'd have gone off traveling anyway if . . . Well. I guess we'll never know what she might have done.'

The more Joseph talked about her, the more real Cora had become until I imagined her sitting beside us, listening to our conversation, laughing at his memories of her, a little shy to hear how fondly he spoke about her.

'The worst thing for Harriet is that there wasn't a body to bury,' he explained.

'She was never found?'

Joseph shook his head. 'She was carried out to sea in a riptide. Harriet tortures herself, imagining Cora is still out there, crying for help. She still looks for her. I don't think she'll ever get over it.'

'And you?'

'I've made my peace. Said my goodbyes. What else can I do?'

Like a balm on a wound, Joseph has a

wonderful ability to soothe the most difficult situations. No wonder I enjoy his company after so many years of rampant hysteria from my mother. But there's something else. Joseph doesn't have an agenda. In a way that nobody else ever has, Joseph really listens to me.

Which is why, in the end, I tell him.

★   ★   ★

It's another warm day and my cheeks are damp with perspiration by the time I reach the horseshoe-shaped beach near the boat landing. I spread out my cardigan on the sand and sit for a while, thinking about my past and imagining my future, idly drawing circles in the sand with my bare toes. I've come to love this peaceful little beach. I imagine this is my private island where nobody will ever find me if I don't want them to.

With the gentle lapping of the waves and the warm breeze, I lie back and relax. Here, I can make sense of things. I can think.

Breathe.

Sleep.

The familiar wet nuzzling of Captain's nose wakes me with a start.

I open my eyes, scrambling to sit up, forgetting that I have to roll onto one side now, unable to maneuver myself as easily as I used to. I throw my headscarf over my stomach as I awkwardly right myself. 'Joseph! I didn't think you were coming over today. Harriet said . . . '

He stands awkwardly in front of me as I sit

222

self-consciously on my knees, both of us waiting for the other to acknowledge what is now very obvious.

I tell him he'd better sit down.

'It's okay. You don't have to . . . '

'Please, Joseph. I owe you an explanation.'

'You don't owe me anything,' he says, flopping down onto the sand and pushing his hair from his eyes. 'But if you need to talk, I'm all ears.' He wiggles his ears with his fingertips. 'Might not be my most attractive feature, but they sure make me a great listener.'

It's so typical of Joseph to make this easy for me, to peel away the awkwardness and the fumbling explanations. I'm so grateful that I burst into tears.

Through my tears and apologies, I open up like a clam and tell him everything: about my fraught relationship with my mother, about my lonely childhood, about my sense of never fitting in, about my misguided flirtations with a British soldier, about being sent to America in disgrace. He doesn't question or judge, just listens patiently as he rubs my back and tells me it's all going to be fine.

When I've blurted it all out he passes me a handkerchief.

I wipe my tears and blow my nose. 'How do you do that?' I ask.

'Do what?'

'Always know what to say, and when to produce handkerchiefs and adorable dogs.'

He smiles. 'I guess that's what friends do.'

I explain my mother's plan for me to give the

child up to the adoption agencies before I go back to Ireland.

'Seems like your mother has it all figured out,' he says, leaning back on the sand and propping himself up on his elbows.

'She likes to think so.' I wipe away fresh tears, knotting the handkerchief between my fingers.

'And what about you? What's *your* plan? What do *you* want, Matilda?'

'Honestly?'

'Honestly.'

I hesitate, summoning the courage to be honest with him, and with myself. 'When I first found out I was pregnant, I wanted nothing to do with the child. I couldn't even think about it as a child, let alone *mine*. The whole thing terrified me. Now though . . . ' I place my hands tentatively on my stomach.

'You feel differently?'

I nod, almost ashamed to admit to the emotional connection I've felt to the child recently. 'It doesn't make any sense though.'

'Why not?'

'I don't know the first thing about raising a child. I'm only nineteen. I should be thinking about the rest of my life, not settling down and playing mammy. Besides, the thought of being someone's mother? All that responsibility? It scares me.'

Joseph takes a long sip from his soda. 'My mom had me when she was only eighteen and she's the best mom in the world. You might surprise yourself, Matilda. Mom always says the things that frighten us the most are the things

224

that make us who we are.'

I think of Mrs. O'Driscoll. 'Someone else once said something like that to me.'

'Then maybe it's time you started to listen.'

He jumps to his feet and holds his hands out to me. I hesitate before grasping them and let him pull me awkwardly to my feet. We stand for a moment, holding hands, the glare of the sun silhouetting this kind understanding young man in front of me.

'Thank you for telling me,' he says. 'That took some guts.'

I let out a long sigh as six months of tension lifts from my shoulders. 'Thank you for listening.'

'We're all allowed to make mistakes. It's what we do next that's the true test of character. And for what it's worth, I think you'd be a terrific mom.'

He wraps his arms around me in a big bear hug and for a few perfect moments I stop worrying and wondering and let myself be a young woman, wrapped in a friend's arms, the sea lapping gently at my toes. For the first time since leaving Ireland, I don't feel afraid.

We head back to the lighthouse for lunch, after which I take a nap. When I wake, the sun is low in the sky. Before I head downstairs, I lift a conch shell from the windowsill, pressing it to my ear as I remember my grandfather telling me all the world's seas and oceans were kept inside. I'd laughed, imagining it to be another of his tricks like the coins he pulled from my ear, and yet there it was, held inside the creamy white shell: the unmistakable rush of the ocean. It was the most magical thing I'd ever known.

I listen to the sound now, breathing in time to the rush of the waves. Standing in this peaceful room, a path of sunlight stretching across the ocean beyond the window, a sense of calm washes over me as I consider my options. I can either accept my mother's plan to give the child up for adoption and go back to Ireland like a good girl, or defy her and raise the child alone, here in America.

What I have, who I am, and who I will become may be far from perfect, but as I rest my hand on my stomach I finally trust myself to find the courage to do the right thing, whatever that might be.

★ ★ ★

Dusk, and I sit at the window of my bedroom at Cherry Street, watching the sweep of the light across the water as a fog rolls in, understanding now how the lamp turns, the detailed mechanisms that keep it turning and flashing. And I understand more about the people who have lived here. I understand that a deep pain lingers in the walls, passing between me and Harriet like light through glass. I feel it as clearly as the sand between my toes. A source of friction, rooted in some other place, but carried here, disturbed now by others who walk these rooms.

Harriet remarks on my excursions with Joseph over dinner. 'Joseph Kinsella may be a fine thing and a pleasant distraction, but you can't ignore the child forever.'

I rest my fork on my plate and take a sip of iced tea. 'What do you mean?'

She rolls her eyes. 'You know very well what I mean. I see what you're doing. Carrying on as normal. Having fun with your new friend. Ignoring the fact that you're six months pregnant.'

I know she is testing me again. Provoking and prodding as she likes to do. 'He's a good friend,' I say. 'And I have to do something to pass the time.'

'Fair enough, and I can't say I blame you. But the fact remains that we have to start making plans. For the birth.'

I tell her I don't want to talk about it and take my plate into the kitchen, but I know she's right. I pour myself a glass of water and take long thoughtful sips.

Harriet leaves me for a moment before standing quietly in the kitchen doorway where she watches me and waits for me to acknowledge her.

'What?' I snap, turning to look at her.

And for the first time since I knocked on the screen door that May morning, Harriet Flaherty smiles. Properly smiles, and I see real compassion in her face. 'You're not the first woman to be afraid of giving birth, you know. But being afraid won't make it go away.'

I think of Mrs. O'Driscoll's lovely turf-scented hug on the ship and I so desperately want this to be the moment that Harriet wraps me in a warm embrace of her own and tells me it will all be okay, but I stand rigid beside the kitchen sink because I'm afraid that if I admit to my fears, I will drown in them.

'I'm not afraid,' I say, and wish I sounded more convincing. 'I'm tired and I don't want to talk about it right now.'

I march upstairs to the cold little bedroom and lie on the bed, staring numbly at my swollen belly, watching my skin ripple and bend as the child dances impatiently on. I turn onto my side, my gaze settling on the old postcard of Ida and Grace. I think about their acts of courage and selflessness, and how, were it not for Grace putting her own life at risk, I most probably wouldn't be here at all. I think about Sarah losing her two children, and yet here I am, a spoiled selfish girl, regretful of the perfectly healthy, vigorous child I carry.

I cradle my stomach protectively with my hands and close my eyes, and in the rose-tinted light of a perfect sunset I allow myself to admit to my greatest fear of all. Not of giving birth, but of having to give up my determined resilient child for someone else to raise. It is that which scares me most of all.

Finally I realize that to raise my child alone isn't something to fear, but to embrace with the same courage shown by those who came before me: my great-great-granny, Grace Darling, Harriet, even. I take the locket from my neck and read the words on the back: *Even the brave were once afraid*. And in a quiet moment in a small house in Newport, Rhode Island, I let the fears of a young Irish woman turn to courage, and I know what I will do.

29

GRACE

Longstone Lighthouse. October 1838

The artists come and go with the tides, endless waves of them sent by Smeddle to meet public demand for my portrait and the special commissions he has secured for friends in high places. The men get under Mam's feet with their easels and their paint boxes stuffed with tubes of paint and vials of pigment and oil, not to mention their many brushes and palette knives and the turpentine they use to clean the oils from their brushes which gives us all a headache.

As a fiercely practical man, my father doesn't have much time for these artistic men with their romantic ideals and fussy ways. Like the reading of novels, he considers the creation of art to be an indulgence of the upper classes. While not quite so scornful of them, and admiring of their talents, I am, nevertheless, uncomfortable to find myself the focus of their gaze.

Henry Perlee Parker is the first to visit. A whiskery, boisterous man with an intolerance for small spaces, he finds the light at Longstone poor and the cramped conditions difficult to work in. He concludes that while lighthouses are rather romantic from the outside, they are definitely not designed for making good art.

I find the entire process of portrait painting tedious. It is unnatural to be cooped up inside for hours on end, afraid to swallow or blink, hardly daring to breathe. My back and neck ache, my feet and hands itch to be occupied. I try to distract myself during my sittings by silently reciting passages from the Bible or watching the seabirds through the window, but that only makes me long to be outdoors among them. The weather will soon deteriorate, leaving little chance for walking. Even Mam remarks that my skin has paled from spending so much time indoors.

'They won't need to sculpt me if I sit much longer,' I grumble. 'I'll turn into a statue of my own accord.'

'You should be pleased so many people want to paint you,' she replies. 'You've a face to be admired, and there's not many of us can say that.'

'Well, I admire yours,' Father says, planting a rare kiss on Mam's cheek where a pink stain rushes to join it, as round and rosy as if Mr. Parker had placed it there with one of his brushes.

Mam walks a little taller for the rest of the day, incapable of hiding her delight.

As the days pass, still the men arrive. After Mr. Parker and a Mr. Carmichael come David Dunbar, a sculptor, and then an artist from London, commissioned to paint my portrait by Lord Panmure, who requests a portrait of Father, too. A very pleasant young man, Mr. Musgrave Joy, lodges with us for a week when he is stranded by bad weather. Mr. Reay from

231

Newcastle almost drowns on his way out to us when his boat founders off Holy Island. For the most part, they are all polite and patient, but I long for the day when the last of them will pack away their oils and we may never be bothered by artists again.

Following a change in the weather and a notice from Father in the local newspaper to state that anyone else desiring my likeness might obtain one from the printed copies of pictures and engravings already in circulation, the visitation of artists comes to an end. The shortening autumn days pass more freely as the temperature drops and the dear old lighthouse endures heavy seas lashing its walls as it shelters us inside. On such heaving seas the boats of opportunist fishermen cannot sail, and for a perfect fortnight Longstone belongs only to us once again. The storms that had brought such unwelcome attention to our humble home become the very thing that affords us the solitude I have craved in recent weeks. Yet as I tend to the lamps and take my turn on watch, my mind follows the beam of light toward the coastal towns and to Sarah Dawson, whose letter I received the day the first artist arrived. Shocked, thrilled and confused by its contents, I have read it a dozen times since. Sarah's words have painted a picture on my heart that I am afraid to look at too closely.

Dear Miss Darling,

I leave shortly for my home in Hull

(address below) but before I leave I wanted to thank you for returning the letter, and for your very thoughtful gift of the lighthouse manual. I am already learning much about the maintenance of the lamps. When Matilda and I meet again in Heaven I will have so many things to tell her.

There is also something else I must tell you before I return to Hull. You see, Miss Darling, in the letter you returned to me — which you had found, sodden, in my coat pocket — my brother, George, had written to me about you. He told me he'd met a lighthouse keeper's daughter while walking at Dunstanburgh. Since my return from Longstone, he has spoken often of you, and with great regard.

You might not know that George is engaged to be married to a cousin of ours, Eliza Cavendish of Hope Street, Bamburgh where I have stayed these past weeks. I don't wish to cause Eliza any distress, but I won't rest until I tell you that George struggles greatly with his conscience. While his hand is already promised to Eliza, his heart aches for you.

Please do not think badly of me for sharing this with you. I don't wish Eliza any ill will, but life looks very different when you've lost everyone you hold dear. We must grasp every opportunity for happiness, no matter how difficult it might seem. You may choose to ignore these words, or to act upon them. Only you can know if you hold

any affection for George in return. Either
way, I wish you well, Miss Darling.

I would be honored to hear a few lines
from you now and again, if you have time.

Your friend,
Sarah Dawson

A break in the weather the following week sees the wind change direction to a cold northeasterly that blows away the storms to the south and carries a small fishing sloop toward Longstone on a lively slate-gray sea.

I am enjoying a much-needed walk on the Whin Sill, the dark volcanic rock that forms our island. I step over the tributaries and fissures of the tidal channels, careful not to slip on the exposed moss and algae. The water at my feet is clear and pure; the air around me ripe with the smell of seaweed and the keening song of the gray seals. It is invigorating to be away from tedious matters of letter-writing and portrait painting and cutting curls from my hair.

Tracking the approaching boat with the telescope, my heart sinks as I suspect another boatload of gawping onlookers with eager hands reaching out to touch me if I will only stop to say hello. But as the boat gets closer, I see that it is almost empty, just the oarsman and a tall gentleman in a black frock coat, sitting rigid in the back of the boat, eyes fixed firmly on the horizon.

Even from some distance, I know it is Mr. Emmerson.

The boat slows as it reaches the base of the landing. Unseen from my vantage point, I watch as Mr. Emmerson stands up, lurching precariously from side to side as the boat bobs in the swell. He passes some instruction to the oarsman, tips his hat, shakes sea spray from his coat, and clambers out, as ungainly as a newborn kitten.

Smoothing my hair beneath my bonnet and wishing I'd chosen a better dress that morning, I rush toward the henhouse, busying myself with unnecessary tasks as I rehearse my surprise. *'Gosh. Mr. Emmerson. What a surprise!' 'Mr. Emmerson. How lovely to see you here.' 'Goodness! Mr. Emmerson. Whatever brings you to Longstone?'*

As he appears at the top of the landing steps I look up, shielding my eyes from the glare of the sun against the water. For a moment, words fail me entirely, but I recover sufficiently to say, 'Mr. Emmerson! What a surprise!'

His skin bears the unmistakable pallor of someone who doesn't travel well on the sea. He stands feet apart, hands on hips, drawing in deep breaths of air.

'Miss Darling. You must forgive me for arriving unannounced, and in such a state of disrepair.'

It isn't quite the romantic encounter I have — to my shame — imagined in the private hours of night, when such things seem so possible. Daylight casts a mocking eye over my ludicrous ideals.

'Do I look as green as I feel?' he gasps, taking

235

another deep breath.

I try to hide a smile, not wishing to mock. 'You are rather . . . discolored, I'm afraid. Was the sea a little lively?'

'According to the fisherman it is as still as a mill pond today, but yes, it was far too lively for a hopeless landlubber like myself.'

'It takes some longer than others to find their sea legs. Far better to be at the lighthouse looking out to sea than at sea looking at the lighthouse.'

He manages to stand fully upright, a smile playing at his lips. 'I could not agree more.'

Insisting he take his time to recover, I chatter on about the weather and the last of the migrating kittiwakes and the gray seal colony and how fortunate I am to have such a majestic view to wake up to every morning. I ask after his sister, who, he confirms, has returned to Hull. The content of Sarah's letter presses uncomfortably on my mind.

After ten minutes of invigorating sea breeze and the rigidity of land, Mr. Emmerson assures me he is feeling quite recovered.

'You must come inside then,' I say, my voice casual despite the pounding in my chest. 'I'll make nettle tea. It is the best cure for nausea. Mam swears by it, and she's put most cures to the test over the years.'

'You are most kind. And I am rather embarrassed.'

'Well, you shouldn't be. We have seen far worse reactions to the sea. Ellen Herbert takes at least two hours to recover after traveling out to us. She swears by the reviving properties of a glass or two of Madeira.'

Leading Mr. Emmerson toward the lighthouse, I feel the familiar tumbling sensation in my stomach that I've felt too often recently. I urge myself to retain my composure as we step inside the welcome warmth of the living quarters where I remove my bonnet and gloves and introduce our guest to my parents.

'This is Mr. Emmerson. He is the brother of Sarah Dawson.' I invite him to take a seat beside the stove.

Mr. Emmerson greets my parents with his usual charm and humility. 'I'm afraid I am a little discombobulated by the crossing. Your daughter is a patient nursemaid.'

While Mam fusses over our visitor, fetching an impressive plate of bread, cheese, and meat, I tend to the fire, taking twice as long as usual, all fingers and thumbs and dropping the fire irons with a great clatter against the hearth.

'I do hope you'll forgive my intrusion, Mrs. Darling. Mr. Darling. I believe your days are punctuated with intrusions of late.' His legs stretched out in front of him, Mr. Emmerson looks, for all the world, as though he has sat beside our stove all his life.

Father confirms that we are rather the sideshow fascination of late.

'But friends are always very welcome,' I interject, afraid that as soon as he's arrived Mr. Emmerson will feel obliged to leave again. 'Mr. Emmerson is a good friend of Henry Herbert's,' I explain. 'He is a student of art at the University of Dundee.'

Mam, always with her senses on high alert, detects something in the air. 'You two have met before, then, I take it?'

'I bumped into your daughter while she was walking with the Herberts at Dunstanburgh Castle some months ago. I was fascinated to learn of Miss Darling's life at Longstone. It isn't often one meets a lighthouse keeper.' He takes a sip of his nettle tea. 'And then, of course, the events of the *Forfarshire* brought my sister into your care.' We all mark the memory of that night with a respectful silence. 'I cannot thank you enough for your bravery, and compassion.'

A nod from my father is all the acknowledgment required. 'How is she bearing up?' he asks.

'Some days are better than others. She has returned to Hull and says she is happier to be at home, surrounded by memories of the children. She tells me she is becoming quite the expert in the workings of lighthouses with the help of the manual Miss Darling kindly sent. She is surprised there are so many procedures to follow.'

'It is a highly regulated profession,' my father adds. 'Much more to it than lighting a lamp once a day. It becomes an obsession as much as an occupation. Much like your painting, I imagine.'

Mr. Emmerson smiles warmly. 'You are absolutely correct.'

'We've been rather busy with artists recently,' I add.

'So I believe. I've seen some of their efforts.'

'Efforts?' I laugh. 'Are they really that bad?'

Mr. Emmerson squirms a little. 'I am being

disingenuous. They are a little lacking in energy.'

'Oh?' I can't help feeling a little disappointed. 'And they took so long over them.'

He raises his eyes to mine. 'Don't be alarmed. They're a perfectly acceptable likeness, but who wants to create something *acceptable*. Who wants to do *anything* that is merely acceptable?' He takes a long sip of tea, lost in his thoughts as he swirls the cup around. 'When I made similar remarks about the portraits to my sister, she insisted I stop complaining about others' failings and paint you myself. She was quite adamant. My coming here is all her doing,' he continues.

My thoughts turn, again, to Sarah's letter. I hope Mr. Emmerson doesn't notice the color that rises in my cheeks.

'Our Grace is sick to the back teeth of being painted,' Mam remarks brusquely as she clears plates from the table. 'There are plenty of likenesses in circulation. Mr. Darling said as much in a recent letter printed in the *Courant*. Perhaps you could make an appointment with Robert Smeddle.'

'Mam!' I stare pointedly at her. 'Mr. Emmerson isn't just another artist. He is Mrs. Dawson's brother. I needed a break from sitting still for a few days, that's all.' I turn my attention back to Mr. Emmerson. 'An appointment won't be necessary. You are very welcome to paint my likeness. Right now, if you wish. Did you bring your things?'

Glancing at my parents, Mr. Emmerson confirms that he has, indeed, been rather presumptuous and brought everything required.

239

Father smiles knowingly at me, amused by the sudden contradiction to the announcement I'd made only yesterday about hoping I never had to sit for another boring portrait as long as I lived.

'If you'll excuse me I have to check on the lamps,' he says. 'You might like to join me, Mr. Emmerson?' Like a proud parent with a new child, Father cannot resist the opportunity to show off his wonderful lantern room.

Mr. Emmerson says he would like that very much.

I explain that I must row over to Brownsman to collect provisions from our vegetable garden. 'I'll be back within the hour. Perhaps we can start then?'

Mr. Emmerson looks a little hesitant. 'You're sure it isn't an awful inconvenience?'

'Perfectly sure. One more sitting can't do any harm. I'm far less fidgety than I was a month ago.'

He smiles. 'Then ours will be a happy arrangement.'

The manner in which he says this renders my fumbling fingers incapable of tying the ribbons on my bonnet. I leave them loose as I step outside, pressing an enormous smile into my gloves as I walk like a drunken fool toward the boathouse.

30

GRACE

Longstone Lighthouse. October 1838

Mr. Emmerson does not require me to sit like a statue. With the glow of the fire gilding his cheeks, he explains that he wishes to draw me as he'd first seen me. 'With the wind in your cheeks and the sea reflected in your eyes. I find posed portraits so lacking in life,' he adds, pulling on his coat. 'I presume you don't often sit as still as a statue and gaze wistfully out of a window?'

'Not often,' I chuckle. 'No.'

'Precisely. Which is why I wish to observe you in your most natural state, when you're not being Grace Darling's portrait but are simply being yourself.' He peers out of the window, checking the sky for any threat of rain. Seeing none, he claps his hands together purposefully. 'Would you be able to take a walk outside?'

I glance toward the pantry where Mam is pretending to tidy jars of preserves.

She peers around the door. 'I'll keep watch from the window. I would come out with you only the wind got into my bones yesterday and I can't seem to shift it.'

I pull on my cloak as I wait for Mr. Emmerson to gather his materials from the small traveling bag he'd brought with him, but he walks to the

241

door without them.

'What about your things?' I prompt. 'Your brushes and paints.'

He laughs. 'A true artist paints first with his eyes and mind, Miss Darling.' He stands to one side. 'After you. If we're lucky we might spot one of those sea dragons.'

As we walk I tell him about the latest fossil I'd found just after the storm.

'You must have quite the collection,' he remarks, slipping on a clump of seaweed so that I almost put out my arm to steady him. 'Something new delivered with each tide, no doubt.'

'I have most of the shells common to these islands, but I would love to find some rare specimens to confound the gentlemen at the Royal Society.'

'And you are just the girl to do it! I can picture the look of consternation on their faces when you show them things they've never seen the like of before.' He talks excitedly, his accent difficult to follow at times over the rush and slap of the breakers and the strengthening wind. 'Not so different to Miss Anning and her sea dragons, after all!'

I point out the different seabirds and seaweeds and the foliage native to the area: pink sea campion and fiddleneck, the scurvy grass where the puffins make their burrows.

Gathering up a variety of shells, I set them out on one of the flatter rocks, explaining how some are bivalves and others gastropods. 'The bivalves are twin shells, hinged together. Like these mussel shells. I think of them as portly gentleman, dressed for dinner in top hat and tails. Then we have cockles and scallops — ladies at a dance with their grand skirts flowing.' Mr. Emmerson laughs at my descriptions. 'The oysters and Venus shells are the grand old dowagers,' I continue. 'I suppose they are a little like a locket when you open them.'

'Like the one my sister gave you.'

'Yes.' I open a clamshell in my hand. 'And sadly just as empty.'

'But it mustn't remain so. It must keep something you treasure. We will find you something.' I smile at his enthusiasm. 'And these must be the gastropods,' he adds, picking up a cowrie shell.

'Yes. They are more like snail shells.' I pass him a whelk and a periwinkle. 'But even in the broad groupings there are many varieties and colors of each. At first they all look the same, but when you look closer you notice each is a little different. See? Perhaps only slightly so, but they are all unique. One of a kind. It is the same with lighthouses.'

'How do you mean?'

'Each structure is unique. Each one as individual as a fingerprint. Each lamp has a distinguishing aspect to its light, a unique pattern of a flashing or fixed beam. Each tower also has an identifying day mark so that sailors can recognize each lighthouse and navigate by it accordingly. It's like a private conversation between the light and the mariner. Communication without words.'

Mr. Emmerson picks up several shells to inspect them. 'I hadn't appreciated the humble seashell before, but you are right. Each is a thing of perfect individual beauty.'

'There is so much beauty on these islands,' I say, standing up. 'I know there are some who consider us to live a very stark and basic life, deprived of everything people take for granted on the Main. But we have everything we need here. Each season brings its own joys and challenges. Each day is different.'

Mr. Emmerson doesn't say anything, only looks at me as I speak. Only when I stop talking do I notice the way he is studying me, head tilted slightly to one side, eyes slightly narrowed.

'Are you painting me, Mr. Emmerson?'

That smile. Those gentle eyes. 'I am, Miss Darling. Yes.'

I cannot imagine that any of Mary-Ann's romance novels could contain a scene more perfect or moving. Quite unable to think straight, I suggest we move on before the tide turns and sees us stranded.

As we walk, pausing occasionally to peer into the pools of water, I forget about the newspaper headlines; forget that I am Grace Darling: Heroine of the Farne Isles. For the rest of the afternoon, I am just an ordinary young woman, walking with a young man, looking into rock pools as if it is the most natural thing in the world.

'Do you think you could ever give it all up?' Mr. Emmerson asks suddenly as we stroll. 'Spend your days at crowded markets and hear

244

the neighbors squabbling? I'm not sure I could if I'd been raised somewhere so isolated and free.'

His question pricks at my conscience as I recall the words in Sarah Dawson's letter and can't help wondering if there is a greater question carried beneath.

'I've never seriously considered it,' I answer, honestly, hoping my face doesn't betray my emotions as it so often does. 'My sisters tease me for being so devoted to the light and my parents. I enjoy visiting the mainland, but I am always anxious to get back to the island.'

My skin prickles and a dull ache settles across my brow. Suspecting a change in atmospheric pressure and noticing how the gulls settle on the rocks around us, I sense bad weather approaching.

'I feel the weather turning, Mr. Emmerson. We should get back.'

Without waiting for a response, and quite afraid of what might happen if we spend any longer alone in each other's company, I turn and walk purposefully in the direction of the lighthouse.

Within the hour, it is clear a storm will soon be upon us and there will be no chance of Mr. Emmerson's fishing boat returning for him. For once, I welcome the dark clouds and the high winds, inviting in the storm that gathers above the lantern room along with that which gathers in my heart.

Before retiring that evening, I mend holes in a fishing net, grateful for a difficult task to distract me from the presence of Mr. Emmerson across the room.

'Might I have a word, Gracie?' Father asks, quietly.

I put down my needle. 'Of course, Father. What is it? Another request for hair? I shall be bald by Christmas!'

Smiling, he takes my hands in his. 'I received word this morning from my superiors at Trinity House. They have revised their regulations. Every light station must now have an officially appointed Assistant as well as a Principal Keeper.'

We have anticipated changes to the regulations for some time. Knowing what Father is about to say, I save him the anguish. 'And you will, of course, appoint Brooks as Assistant.'

He nods and lowers his gaze. 'I am afraid so.'

'Afraid? But this is wonderful news. Father and son, manning the light. What could be better?'

His eyes crease into a gentle smile, relief lifting from him like smoke from the fire. 'I was afraid you might be disappointed. That you were hopeful of the position yourself?'

I squeeze his hands, affectionately. 'And I would have been the proudest daughter in the country if I were permitted to take the position. But that is not the way of things, is it.' I pick up my needle. 'I'll congratulate Brooks as soon as he's back from the lamps.' As Father stands up, I ask one thing. 'I can still assist the two of you? In an informal capacity.'

'My dear Gracie. This lighthouse wouldn't function without you. This family wouldn't function without you. You, my dear child, are the

246

light around which we *all* turn.'

As his boots echo off the steps, I pick up the fishing net, searching for the next fault in the lines, but it is quite impossible to mend delicate holes in fishing nets when your eyes are blurred with tears. I excuse myself under the pretense of fetching my fossils for Mr. Emmerson, pressing my disappointment into each of the sixty steps as I walk to my room because despite my father's words, I know that the lighthouse *will* function without me.

Whether I can function without the lighthouse, is another matter entirely.

31

GRACE

Longstone Lighthouse. October 1838

A full hunter's moon hangs low on the horizon, the agitated sea glistening beneath its bewitching light. Unable to sleep through the storm that has pounded the island for four days and nights, I stand at my bedroom window, mindful of old mariners' tales of rings around the moon being a foretelling of rain. We are grateful no other ships have foundered in the dreadful weather, and I am also grateful for the storm extending Mr. Emmerson's stay at Longstone. For that alone, I cannot entirely wish for clear skies and calm seas.

His presence lends an unexpected brightness to the lighthouse, filling a gap I hadn't known was there. We all feel it. Mam, especially, delights in having another young man about the place to fuss over. She misses her sons since they departed for the Main and it pleases her to have another hungry mouth to feed. Father, too, seems a little lighter with Mr. Emmerson around, or rather George, as he insists Father calls him, happily dispensing with formalities. Another pair of hands about the place is always welcome, especially at this time of year, and Mr. Emmerson is eager to assist and learn. I enjoy listening to the two of them debating politics and philosophy. They briefly discuss the outcome of the second inquiry into the *Forfarshire* disaster, ruminating on how Captain Humble was found entirely to blame for failing to turn in at Tynemouth for repairs. Knowing how easily the disaster could have been prevented, I feel the anguish of Mr. Emmerson's loss more keenly.

'Trinity House are pressing the government to make changes to shipping laws,' Father explains. 'We can only hope that no life is lost in vain and that we will learn something, no matter how small, from each vessel lost. I am confident there will be a time, perhaps not within our lifetime, when no ships are lost at sea for want of warning.'

I draw a quiet sense of completeness from having Mr. Emmerson around; the hours we spend together while he works on his portraits are as pleasant as the hours we spend apart. I breeze through my chores, spurred on by the knowledge that we will all gather for supper that evening. I find myself listening for the sound of his footsteps descending the stairs each morning, anticipating the cheery greeting which sets me in good humor for the entire day. Our evenings are spent in quiet companionship, safe and warm within the lighthouse while the storm batters the rocks beyond. I am surprised to find myself thinking, on more than one occasion, that if married life is like this, then I might not have been so hasty as to dismiss the idea. The simple fact is that George Emmerson slots into life at Longstone as easily as a lace through a boot, which only makes it harder to accept that the temporary bonds we have formed must soon be untied and threaded back among the lives of others.

Mr. Emmerson's engagement hasn't been mentioned by him, and nor have I asked, yet Eliza Cavendish blows through the lighthouse like an unwelcome draft, leaving a chill lingering about my neck. No matter how many rags I stuff against the bottom of doors or against the window frames, still she persists in creeping through, tormenting my thoughts and my conscience, pricking at my morals and asking questions of my Christian principles. It isn't like me to think unkindly of another, but the energy of the storm and Mr. Emmerson's company have placed a sort of madness over me.

To fill the long hours of our confinement, Mr. Emmerson works on more sketches and portraits. I am far less fidgety than I was during the early sittings with poor Mr. Perlee Parker and the others, and quite enjoy the process now that I've learned how to sit still, to relax my jaw and not pick at the quick of my nails. I sit beside the window with my ankles resting one over the other, releasing the tension in my neck and shoulders, my face turned to the left slightly so that the meager light afforded by the dull skies falls fully onto my face.

Mr. Emmerson settles himself at his stool, palette in hand, assessing the light and the angles of my pose, humming and hawing to himself as he is apt to do when concentrating. 'Could you turn your . . . '

I turn my cheek slightly toward him.

'Thank you. You're a very good student, Miss Darling.'

'I've learned that it serves no purpose to shuffle and fidget. The job will be done much quicker without my interruptions.'

'Good art cannot be rushed, Miss Darling. Like the incoming tide, it will take all the time it needs.'

A slight smile at my lips, I settle myself, but despite the rigidity of my body, my senses skip about like a giddy child as I listen to the swish of his brush on canvas, the patient *dab dab dab* of detail and the long sweep of broader strokes. The room smells of the linseed oil he uses to mix the pigments, and the spirits he uses to clean his brushes. Mr. Emmerson has a habit of tapping his foot as he works, and he also licks his lips in concentration. I hear every swallow, every clearance of his throat, every quick sniff of satisfaction and tut of frustration. Without its ever touching me, I feel every stroke of Mr. Emmerson's brush like a feather against my skin. Without ever looking at him, I feel his gaze settle on my face. In this quiet, intimate way, hours slip by as the wind whips up a frenzy outside.

When he is happy with the session's work, he coughs three times and as if a spell is broken, I emerge from my frozen state.

'Goodness. I must tend to the lamps,' I remark, noticing how quickly the light fades outside. 'I'll ask Brooks to join you. You might teach him another ballad or two? Father will be delighted to play his fiddle again.'

'I would like that very much.'

I am pleased to see how my brother enjoys Mr. Emmerson's easy manner and good humor. Brooks is easily impressed with our guest's repertoire of ballads and far-fetched tales of Scottish folklore. 'I'll apologize in advance for my brother,' I add. 'He tends to prefer the bawdier tunes.'

Mr. Emmerson laughs. 'Your brother reminds me of myself when I was younger. Full of energy and ambition.'

'He has a good heart, and is a quick learner. He is to be appointed Assistant Keeper and will take over as Principal when Father is no longer able to manage things.' The hint of regret in my voice is audible.

Mr. Emmerson detects the truth in my expression. 'You would like to take the position yourself, no doubt,' he asks.

I put on my brightest smile. 'A woman does not decide her destiny, Mr. Emmerson. The men in her life do that for her.'

The pause in our conversation underlines the point rather more markedly than I'd intended.

'There's something about a storm, isn't there?' Mr. Emmerson remarks, thankfully changing the subject as he packs away his things.

'In what way?' I reach my hands behind my neck to ease the ache left there by the persistent fingers of an icy draft.

'So much energy. Such absolute insistence to be heard and felt. It is almost impossible not to be affected by it. I feel a little wild myself.'

I smooth my skirt, noticing that the hem is

frayed and making a note to mend it later.

'There is certainly a passion carried in the sea when the wind blows like this. The island never feels more alive than in a full-blown storm. Visitors in the summer remark on how pretty they find the islands with the turquoise seas and warm breezes, but I prefer the chaos of the later months with snow-storms and lightning crackling in the air.'

Mr. Emmerson wipes his brushes carefully. 'I couldn't agree more. Having spent the past few days here, I don't think this storm will ever quite leave me.' He stands tall, blocking the light from the window. 'I am beginning to understand what you said about the lighthouse enchanting anyone who comes here. There's something about this island, this place, you . . . '

His words waver like a guttering candle flame, the guilt of his thoughts draining all color from his face.

I pause at the bottom of the stairs, turning half a shoulder but keeping my eyes to the floor. 'Enchantment is a fickle mistress, Mr. Emmerson. We would all do well to be wary of her.' I lift the hem of my skirt so it won't trip me on the stairs. 'You will excuse me. I am needed in the lantern room.'

★ ★ ★

In the small room below Miss Darling's apartment, George Emmerson cannot sleep. He tumbles and turns among the bed-sheets until he is wrapped in them like an embalmed corpse, trapped by his emotions and indecisiveness. Only briefly do his thoughts stray to Eliza, no doubt despairing for his welfare, imagining him to be drowned and all her plans for their future dashed against the rocks. Perhaps it would be better if he *had* foundered in a wreck or become stranded on some island far from these shores where he could spend the rest of his days alone, rather than confront the confounding reality of the feelings he has for Miss. Darling.

He hears his sister's words carried on the wind, as if she stands now at the small window, reminding him. '*Eliza is a pleasant girl, but she is a breeze, George. A breeze. Your heart desires a storm. I can tell.*' Even in the pitch dark of the room, he sketches Miss Darling with his mind's eye. He sees so clearly the rounding of her cheek, the angle of her eyes, the shape of each perfect shell-like ear. He knows he must leave Longstone as soon as the weather improves, but is grateful all the same for these days he has been afforded. Still, Miss Darling has made it perfectly clear that she has no desire for a husband or a life on the Main. She is as duty-bound to her family and the lighthouse as he is to Eliza. Devotion and obligation — the things that must keep them apart while binding them irrevocably to others. There can be no undoing of any promises. He would not ask it of her.

Resigning himself to the impossibility of sleep, he gets up and walks to the window, watching the reflection of the light on the water. He knows Miss Darling is on watch in her room above, ascending intermittently to the lantern room to keep the oil topped up and to trim the wicks, ensuring the light burns brightly through these, the very darkest of hours. He feels a madness settle over him, knowing that the storm in his heart won't be silenced until he has spoken his true feelings.

32

GRACE

Longstone Lighthouse. October 1838

In the lantern room, the wind howls as I refill the oil reservoirs. The spray from the waves flies against the windows, rattling like stones. It reminds me of my father telling dramatic stories of waves so big they came crashing over the top of the lantern room one winter and how the whole lighthouse had swayed from the strength of the gusts. Those were the tales of my childhood, the tales I asked him to tell again and again as I sat, spellbound, beside the stove, eyes alight with fear and excitement, willing such a storm to visit us again. While my sisters didn't share in my delight for the storms we experienced during the worst winters, I was always drawn to the wildest weather, finding something terrifying and fascinating about the fury of the sea. My father once said if I were to cut myself it would be the North Sea spilling out of my veins, not blood. 'That is the way with true islanders,' he says. 'At one with the sea; willing participants in the coming and going of storms.'

I haven't been in the lantern room long when I hear footsteps. Presuming it is Brooks come to take over on watch, I am astonished to see it is not my brother but Mr. Emmerson who appears at the top of the stairs.

'Mr. Emmerson!' Flustered by his presence, I pull my shawl about my shoulders, fussing with the locket at my neck as it snags stubbornly on a loose thread. 'You gave me quite a fright.'

He smiles apologetically, his face lit by the hand lamp balanced precariously on the top step. 'Forgive me, Miss Darling. I'm sure it is entirely against regulations for me to be up here, but I couldn't sleep with the storm raging and I very much wanted to see the lamp in all its glory.' I am unsure whether I should insist he go back downstairs or be delighted by his interest. 'I'm afraid I have startled and interrupted you,' he continues, 'so I will bid you goodnight.' He picks up his hand lamp and turns to leave. 'Please, forgive my intrusion.'

'Since you are here you might as well stay,' I offer, regretting the words as soon as I utter them. 'It seems a shame to have made your way up all those steps only to start immediately back down again.'

'It does rather, doesn't it?' His effervescent smile is as distracting as ever, pulling one from my own lips despite the very improper situation I find myself in.

Hauling himself awkwardly up the last step, he apologizes again. 'Since your father showed me the apparatus I am like a child with a new toy. I only wanted to see it work.' He walks slowly around the lamps. 'It really is extraordinary. Look how perfectly the prisms fit together to send the beam of light farther. It reminds me of a physics lesson. The angle of incidence . . . '

'. . . equals the angle of reflection,' I add.

'Precisely. The universal law of science.'

That impish smile again. Surely it will be the undoing of me.

As calmly as I can and despite the almost audible thumping of my heart, I talk knowledgeably about the Argand lamp and the Fresnel lenses and explain how the soot from the candles dims the light if the lenses are not regularly cleaned. 'The Fresnel lenses have a stepped surface that bends the light,' I explain. 'I've always thought them rather beautiful.'

'They are beautiful indeed. Like rose petals unfurling around each other. Pretty enough in the singular, but something rather spectacular when multiplied and placed together so cleverly.'

'My father was a little doubtful of them initially,' I continue, standing to one side as Mr. Emmerson circles the lamps. 'A Scottish physicist first convinced Trinity House to adopt the new lenses. The light travels much farther because of them.'

'It's extraordinary.' He stands up, almost touching the roof of the lantern room as he turns to look out of the windows. 'What a privilege it is to be up here.' For a moment, we stand alone with our thoughts as the wind howls at the windows. 'It really is blowing, tonight,' he adds. 'It whips up a recklessness in a person, don't you think? It makes me want to run around in circles and chase the clouds.' He pauses and looks at me, a wild excitement flashing in his eyes. 'Could we?'

'Could we what?'

'Step outside.'

I laugh, shocked by the suggestion. 'In *this* weather? You would be blown back to Dundee, Mr. Emmerson!'

'Then at least I wouldn't have to suffer the agony of another boat trip. You would be doing me a great favor!'

There is something so infectious about his enthusiasm that I feel myself start to concede. The storm's wildness has found its way under my skin, too. I glance at the door which leads to the platform that runs around the perimeter of the lantern, from where we clean the windows on clear days.

'I suppose, since you're here, you might as well experience the full force of the storm. The wind will take your breath away, mind.'

Mr. Emmerson grins. 'Then let us hope I have plenty to spare.'

Opening the door, I tell Mr. Emmerson to follow me outside. We are instantly buffeted and blown so violently we have to grip the top of the iron grillwork to stop ourselves being blown away. I shriek and then laugh at the sheer absurdity of it all.

Mr. Emmerson tries to speak but his words are whipped away and all he can do is peer at me through narrowed eyes, laughing with the wind as we are pushed forward and pulled back, nothing but a pair of rag dolls. A sudden gust blows me sideways, causing Mr. Emmerson to reach out and steady me. My hair whips wildly around my face as I am buffeted again, glad of Mr. Emmerson's arm locked around mine like an anchor, securing me to him, and for a wild wonderful moment I want only to stay here at the top of my dear lighthouse, with Mr. Emmerson beside me and all of the North Sea's temper booming like cannons below.

The energy of it infuses me with a rare recklessness, and as Mr. Emmerson leans toward me I close my eyes, ready for the kiss I have imagined in my most secret, private thoughts. But his lips do not meet mine, only press close to my ear so that I can feel the warm touch of his breath against my skin as I catch the words ' . . . wonderful, Miss Darling! So very wonderful!' Beneath the noise, I cannot be sure if it is the lighthouse, the storm, or something else he is talking about.

'We must go back inside,' I shout, barely able to form my words through the wind.

We stagger forward like a pair of drunken sailors spilling out of a tavern, fighting against the strength of the wind to open the door before we stumble back into the lantern room, laughing and catching our breath.

Mr. Emmerson smooths his hair, sent every which way by the wind. 'I'm afraid I resemble an inmate of Bedlam, Miss Darling.'

'Then I must resemble one myself,' I laugh, straightening my shawl and tucking stray hair behind my ears as I catch my breath. 'What madness!'

'Beautiful madness though, Miss Darling.'

'Island fever infects us all, sooner or later.'

His quiet smile ignites the ember of intrigue I'd felt the very first day I met him at

Dunstanburgh. I feel it in the burning of my wind-whipped cheeks and deep in the pit of my stomach.

Desperate to return to more familiar ground, I tell Mr. Emmerson how my father gave me and my sisters lessons in astronomy up here in the lantern room. 'I once envied my brothers for being sent to school at the castle in Bamburgh, but not anymore.'

'I cannot think of a finer place to study the stars. Believe me, there is no worse place to learn anything than a frigid schoolroom with a teacher too eager to use his cane.'

'I can imagine. I feel very fortunate to have been raised here.'

Mr. Emmerson turns to look at me. 'No wonder the prospect of exchanging it all for a drab rectangular home on the mainland is so unappealing?'

The inflection in his voice carries the same question I'd heard when we'd walked among the rock pools earlier. It is a question to which I do not have a ready answer, and yet there it is, suspended between us like the spider webs that hang between the rafters in the boathouse.

I let out a weary sigh, wondering if he hears the regret carried in it. 'It would certainly not be an easy exchange, Mr. Emmerson. And certainly not one I care to dwell on when I am still needed here.'

I try to focus on the storm beyond the window but I see only how different things might be in less complicated circumstances. Might I then permit myself to give up everything I am in order

261

to know what I might yet become?

An uneasy gaze settles in Mr. Emmerson's eyes. 'Of course. We must always put duty first.'

And with that, as surely as an oar knocked clumsily against the boathouse rafters, the strands of what might have been are snapped, the fragments left behind to blow in the wind.

With my mind and my heart racing, I turn my attention back to my task. 'I must go to the service room to record the tides.'

He nods. 'I have distracted you long enough.' As he turns to leave, he notices a conch shell on a ledge beside the door. 'Your favorite, I presume? I've seen lots of them dotted about the place.'

'My father used to tell me the North Sea lived inside,' I say, picking the shell up and pressing it to my ear. 'He said even when I was far away, I would always be able to hear home, as long as I had a conch shell with me.' I smile at the rush of imaginary waves caught inside before handing it to Mr. Emmerson. 'You must take it with you, as a reminder of your time here.'

He hesitates. 'Would you speak into it, Miss Darling?'

I laugh. 'Speak into it? Whatever for?'

With his eyes fixed firmly on mine, he rests his hand on the shell. 'So that I might hear your voice, even when you are far away.'

A flush of heat rushes to my neck and cheeks. 'Mr. Emmerson, I . . . '

'Forgive me. I have said too much. I am not myself tonight.' Picking up his lamp, he starts to make his way down the steps. 'Your father said he expects the storm will blow through tonight.'

I nod, barely able to think or speak. 'All storms pass, Mr. Emmerson. Even the most passionate and persistent ones.'

The gentle acquiesce in his eyes is the only reply required.

I wait until I can no longer hear the echo of Mr. Emmerson's footsteps before I sink onto the stool, as dizzy as a new sailor at sea. With the wind shrieking at the windows, speaking my anguish for me, I accept that whatever my heart might fool me into feeling, and however convinced Sarah Dawson might be of her brother's true feelings, the irrefutable fact remains that George Emmerson is engaged to be married and even the wildest storm in the whole of Northumberland cannot, and should not, tear apart a commitment such as that.

At 4:00 A.M. Brooks relieves me from my watch and I sink into my bed, where I lie awake until dawn, no longer disturbed by the wind, but by the very absence of it. The storm has passed and with its departure Mr. Emmerson will also leave.

After all, I have given him no compelling reason to stay.

33

GRACE

Longstone Lighthouse. November 1838

The morning of Mr. Emmerson's departure arrives with calm seas and a breeze as soft as a child's whisper. I watch the sunrise from the lantern room, remembering the quiet September morning when Father and I had joked about birds flying into the living quarters downstairs, unaware that before we would see another sunrise we would encounter such drama and tragedy.

It strikes me, as I stand here only two months later, that life is a constant surprise. No matter how many charts and maps we study, or how cleverly we believe ourselves able to interpret the change in atmosphere or the shape of the clouds or the movement of the waves, we can never truly know what the day will bring; cannot plan for every eventuality. Only as each dreadful misfortune or delightful surprise unfolds can we choose how to respond; fleeting decisions made in an instant but which carry an echo across a lifetime.

After tending to the lamps, I take advantage of the clear day to take a walk along the tidal pools. A bitter chill laces the air and my cheeks soon flame from the bite of the wind and my exertions as I clamber over the exposed rocks. I pay no heed to the frigid temperature, only glad to be outside. I stand at the edge of the sea, throwing pebbles in looping arcs, watching the ever-spreading ripples. I am fascinated by the invisible force that propels them on long after the pebble has sunk from view. I wish I could do the same; sink back into the quiet days of invisibility when Grace Darling was an unremarkable young woman, known only to her family and those in her close acquaintance.

Lost in my thoughts, I don't hear Mr. Emmerson approach until he is beside me. He stands quietly for a moment as we watch the path of sunlight on the water.

'Such a contrast,' he remarks. 'It is hard to believe the storm of the past week was ever here.'

I turn to him. The early morning light paints his face golden, erasing some of the confusion and doubt I'd seen last night. 'That is the way of the island, Mr. Emmerson. Sometimes a lion. Sometimes a lamb. No two days ever quite the same.'

'I have fallen quite under Longstone's spell, Miss Darling. I envy your ability to say this all belongs to you.'

'Oh, it doesn't belong to us, Mr. Emmerson. We are only looking after it for a while. In time the lighthouse and the island will pass to another keeper and his family, and so on. People will stand here in years to come and never know the Darling family once lived here.'

He bends to pick up a handful of pebbles, throwing them absentmindedly into the water.

'But you are here now, and I have enjoyed your family's hospitality more than I can say. I shall be very sorry to leave.'

'And we shall be sorry to have an empty seat at the table tonight,' I reply, the lightness of my response concealing the depth of my sorrow.

'I am sure your mother won't be sorry to have one less mouth to feed. I'm afraid I have been rather an unexpected interruption to your lives.'

'A pleasant interruption all the same, Mr. Emmerson.' I throw a pebble of my own into the water before brushing sand from my fingertips. 'But we must now return you with the tide. I'm sure you'll have been missed while we have enjoyed your company. No doubt there are others who will be glad to have you back.' My invitation for him to mention his betrothal to Eliza is as brazen as bait dangled from a fisherman's hook, but he doesn't bite.

He throws another pebble in a high arc. We watch the splash of the water as I remark on the mesmerizing spread of the ripples.

'I like the sense of continuity,' I say. 'A small act of rebellion against the inevitable end.'

The waves lap at my feet, the pebbles on the shoreline rattling as the water slips over them before pulling them back in the undertow. The push and pull of the tide. The eternal ebb and flow. In the distance, I see my father preparing the coble to take Mr. Emmerson back to the Main. I notice how he coughs and struggles, making hard work of a task he once performed so easily.

The strengthening sun sets Mr. Emmerson's

face alight as I look at him. I smile despite the flicker of regret I see in his eyes. 'I see my father preparing the boat.'

He nods in understanding, and we turn away from the water in silence, our boots crunching over shells as we walk back to the boathouse, our shadows cast behind us, an impression of what might have been, lingering in our wake.

Before Mr. Emmerson steps into the boat, I take a small conch shell from my pocket. 'A memento,' I say, passing it to him. 'So that you might always hear the North Sea.' My voice catches in my throat. The tremble in my hand clearly visible.

He smiles, that same broad smile I've pictured so often in my mind. 'And I wish you to have something in return,' he says, pressing a mussel shell into my hands. 'To fill the empty chambers of your locket.'

Unable to say anything further, I hold the shell tight in my hand, wrapping my fingers around it as I watch my father guide the boat around the islands until I cannot see it anymore. The wind balloons out my skirts and sends the ribbons of my bonnet fluttering. The sky turns as pink as summer roses and I sense the coming of snow in the fat clouds.

The seasons move on, and so must I.

Later, in the privacy of my room, I open the mussel shell to find two tiny portraits inside, beautifully painted on thick paper. One of Mr. Emmerson. One of me, standing beside the lighthouse. My heart breaks and soars as I take the portraits from the shell and place them carefully inside the locket, a perfect fit. I close the filigree clasp and place the chain around my neck, holding the locket to my chest as I try to dam the rush of emotion that floods my heart, knowing what might have been, but could not be.

I remain in my room until dusk when I ascend the steps to the lantern room to light the lamps. Cocooned in the lighthouse's sure embrace I set to work, the sound of the sea at the windows soothing me like a mother calming an infant. *It is for the best*, it says. *It is all for the best.*

That evening, by candlelight, I write two letters. The first, to Robert Smeddle, informing him that, in agreement with my father, I will not be at liberty to sit for any more artists, nor will I require any further assistance with my correspondence as I am quite able to manage matters myself.

The second letter is to Sarah Dawson. I thank her for writing to me so frankly about her brother, and for explaining the matter of his forthcoming nuptials and I assure her that while I am very fond of George and enjoy his company immensely, I could not, in any way, permit myself to be associated with the breaking of a promise of engagement. I tell her that I wish Mr. Emmerson and Miss Cavendish a very happy future together.

I only wish that I believed my own words.

★ ★ ★

Late afternoon and the sun hangs low over the city of Dundee, illuminating the church spires and gilding George's small bedroom with a generous light. He takes up his pencils and starts to sketch, her face as clear as if she were standing in front of him, the shape of her features so familiar to him now. But it isn't just her face he can't forget. It's the particular sense of purpose and determination that dripped from her like honey from a spoon. So slender in form and yet so immense in personality and character.

He lifts the conch shell to his ear and listens, first to the steady rush of the sea and then to the bright echo of her laughter held inside. He closes his eyes, imagining himself as the lighthouse, tall and fearless. The beams of light become his arms, reaching out across the miles so that he might touch her once again.

His union with Eliza Cavendish was perhaps inevitable, their future alignment having been set upon by their parents from infancy, their lives having circled around the assumption that they would, one day, marry. He cares for Eliza very much, loves her even, but only in the way that he loves his sister — a love borne of familiarity. He doesn't love Eliza with the passion he now knows it is possible to love someone. He doesn't see Eliza when he closes his eyes; doesn't replay again and again the conversations he has had with her. His mind, his heart, his soul is full of only one: Miss Darling.

Which is why it torments him that he must forget her.

Like the light keeper at sunrise, he must extinguish the flame that burns so brightly within his heart and let the tides of duty carry him onwards.

But first, he must write down everything he was unable to say to Miss Darling in person. Picking up a pencil and a sheet of writing paper, he spills his emotions onto the page like a spring tide, rushing forth without end. Only when the inkwell is depleted and the torrent has eased does he seal the letter, writes *Grace* on the front and places it on the desk beside his portrait of her. It isn't finished, and yet it strikes him as he looks at it that its incompleteness perfectly captures how he feels. It is the beginning of what might have been, a moment in time captured and released, a representation in art of a friendship that must remain unknown; a question without answer, a journey without end.

As he stares out of the rain-speckled window, he suddenly understands that love, like art, may perhaps never match the ideal of one's imagination, that the endless search for perfection causes torment, and rarely any sense of satisfaction. In the spring, he will marry his cousin and childhood friend and he will find a way to be at peace, just as the artist must eventually be content with the image on his canvas, knowing it is the best he can do at that particular time.

Placing the envelope against the back of the portrait, he measures his backing paper before tapping in the fine nails to fix it in place. He wraps the picture in a blanket and places it carefully into a tea chest beneath the window. He blows out the candle then, plunging the room into darkness.

The light is extinguished.

It is done.

34

MATILDA

Newport, Rhode Island. August 1938

As the summer months pass, the newspapers and wireless reports are full of speculation about a Nazi invasion of Czechoslovakia and the British prime minister traveling to Munich for talks with Hitler.

I read the latest headlines as I bite into a ripe peach, letting the juice dribble down my chin. I can hear my mother criticizing me for being uncivilized. *'Use a knife, Matilda. It's inelegant to be sucking and slurping.'* I am glad her silly concerns are so far away, and suck a little louder. Harriet doesn't even notice.

'Do you think there'll really be another war?' I ask.

'Hmm?'

'The newspapers. They make war sound inevitable.'

Harriet shrugs. 'Sure, how would I know? I only read the headlines and listen to the wireless reports, the same as you.'

'I heard that Mussolini is ordering all Jews out of Italy, and that if Chamberlain can't reach an agreement with Hitler, war is probably inevitable. It doesn't sound great, does it?'

'No. It doesn't. But if it happens, I suppose

we'll all do our bit, same as before.'

I think about my father's night terrors. The uncontrollable tremble in his hand. 'Was it awful?'

Harriet looks at me although I think she is really looking into the past. 'You've no idea, Matilda. If there's to be another war like it, sure I'd rather walk into the sea and never come back.'

'Don't say that.'

'I'll say what I like. When you've lived through hell once, you sure as feck don't want to live through it again.' She refills her coffee cup, alternately slurping the coffee and taking long drags from the cigarette that dangles from her lip. I bite my tongue. I know better than to comment on her vices.

Harriet's quirks and habits are familiar to me now. The things that set my teeth on edge when I first arrived no longer bother me. Like a married couple, we've got used to the other being around, and I find myself growing fond of her peculiar ways. Like the old teapot I use each morning, Harriet is full of cracks and flaws. She doesn't cover things up with false smiles and put-on airs and graces. She is what she is, and there's something reassuring about that. I don't have to pretend when I'm with Harriet. I can be myself, and the longer I spend here, the more I feel the real me emerge.

'What are your plans for today?' she asks.

I fix my hair in the mirror, fiddling with pins and wispy curls and wishing it would stay neat like the elegant American ladies I see. 'I'm

273

meeting Joseph at the jetty. He's going over to the island to paint the woodwork. I said I'd help.'

'Joseph this. Joseph that,' she teases. 'He's a grand young fella. Can't say I blame you for setting your cap at him.'

'I'm not setting my cap at anyone,' I protest, aware that I hardly sound convincing.

She looks at me knowingly, but doesn't press the matter. 'There's a low tide due. Don't get stranded.'

I promise I won't, glad of her concern.

★ ★ ★

I walk slowly to the harbor, enjoying the sun on my face as I waddle awkwardly along. For all her talk of miracles, Mrs. O'Driscoll had failed to mention the difficulties of moving around, or that I could expect to spend my last couple of months feeling like a beach ball. I'm exhausted by the time I reach the jetty, glad to sit down for a rest.

Joseph has brought the painting with him. It is wrapped in brown paper, waiting for me in the boat.

'She scrubbed up real nice,' he says. 'I hope you're pleased.'

I can't wait to see it, but decide to wait until we're at the lighthouse to take a look, afraid to get seawater on it as we row over.

'And there's something else,' Joseph adds, pulling a small envelope from his back pocket. 'It seems that your Victorian lady was hiding a secret. When I removed the backing, I found this.'

I take the envelope from him. The paper is yellowed and musty, lightly freckled with age. The name *Grace* is written on the front in neat script. 'So the painting *is* of Grace,' I say, almost to myself. On the back of the envelope, a wax seal is still in place, firmly guarding its contents. 'It's never been opened.'

'No. And from what I can see, the painting was in its original frame. The name Grace and the date 1838 are written on the back.'

'So the letter must have been put there when the portrait was originally framed? By the artist?'

Joseph nods, a smile in his eyes. 'Kind of romantic, isn't it.'

As the boat gently rocks and a breeze ruffles the edges of my skirt, I run inquisitive fingertips over the old envelope, turning the fragile paper over in my hands. 'So if the portrait *was* painted by George Emmerson, then perhaps he was in love with Grace but couldn't tell her so he wrote it all in a letter instead.'

'Well?' Joseph prompts. 'Aren't you going to open it to find out?'

I laugh and place it in my pocket. 'Not yet. It's waited a hundred years. It can wait a little longer.'

At the lighthouse, I hang the newly framed painting on the wall beside Ida Lewis.

'Back where you belong, Grace,' I say. 'In a lighthouse. You deserve to be seen and talked about, not hidden away in a stuffy old tea chest.' I admire the carefully drawn lines and the intensity in her eyes. Whoever had drawn her had really seen her and understood her, most

275

probably loved her. I glance again at the envelope, my fingers itching to open it and yet I'm reluctant to pry into someone's private thoughts. I leave it on the table while I go for a walk outside.

The envelope sits on the table all day. A tantalizing pause between the past, and the present.

After lunch, Joseph can't stand it any longer. He pushes it toward me. 'Go on then. Let's see what it says. I can tell you're dying to know.'

I take a deep breath. 'More like *you're* dying to know! All right then. Here goes.'

Carefully, I break the wax seal, unfold the pages inside, and start to read. Grace watches over me as the words of a letter written to her a century ago are finally set free. I read in silence as the private revelations of a young man in love tumble from the page and settle on my heart.

'So it *was* George Emmerson.'

I feel strangely emotional as I reach the end, passing the pages to Joseph so he can read them, too. For a while, neither of us speaks, giving George's words the respect they deserve. I refold the letter, return it to the envelope and tuck it behind the portrait of Grace, wondering what she would have thought if she'd read the words herself.

'It's too sad that she never knew,' I say. 'I wonder what happened.'

During the afternoon, I sort through more of the newspaper cuttings in the old tea chest, reading fascinating accounts of brave women who kept the lights turning along America's coastline through times of war and raging storms. For women whose lives were expected to remain as rigid and tightly laced as the corsets that stole their breath from their lungs, I'm surprised to learn how readily they stepped beyond the conventions of society and took on the jobs their fathers and husbands had once done.

I read accounts of women like Hannah Thomas who kept the light at Gurnet Point through the long years of the American War for Independence, Kate Walker at Robbins Reef off Staten Island, and young Abbie Burgess in Maine, left to mind the light when her father was stranded in a storm. These women saved hundreds of lives among them, recovering the washed-up bodies of those they couldn't. They saw some of the worst storms ever recorded, living in the most unforgiving environments, their priority always to keep the lamps burning. On remote islands, alone in their towers of light, these resourceful women found purpose and independence and I have nothing but admiration for them.

I understand it a little, too. In the compact rooms of the lighthouse, there is space to think. In the grand rooms I grew up in back in Ireland, I only ever felt suffocated and small. Here, I feel like a giant, daring to have opinions, plans and hopes for the future. Just like the generations of female light keepers I've read about, the lighthouse gives me a sense of purpose.

While Joseph works, I walk to the horseshoe-shaped beach where I sit alone to watch the seabirds and the boats on the water. The child feels especially heavy today and I lie wearily back against the grass, spreading my arms to my sides like wings, the wind dancing between my fingers until I imagine myself lifted by the thermals, soaring among the clouds where I can go anywhere and be anyone I choose to be.

Too soon, Joseph says it is time to leave. As he rows steadily around the headland and the lighthouse fades into the distance, I promise myself that I will raise my daughters to be strong independent women, not decorative ornaments. My child will have hopes and dreams — a future — and I can't wait to share them with her.

I take in a sharp breath, blinking back tears as a wave of emotion washes over me.

'Is everything okay,' Joseph asks, noticing the tears that slip down my cheeks.

'Everything's grand,' I say, brushing the tears away. 'It's just. Y'know.'

He smiles. 'I know.'

I place my hands on my stomach and drum my fingers like raindrops; smiling at the kicks and tumbles she gives in reply, challenging me to acknowledge her, and love her, and let the world know she's on her way.

My daughter.

35

HARRIET

Newport, Rhode Island. August 1938

Matilda Emmerson.

My past, and my future, asleep in the room beside mine.

I'd forgotten how it feels to have someone else around; forgotten how irritating and rewarding it is to be part of a family. I hear the creak of the bedsprings as she tosses and turns in the night, unable to find a comfortable position to sleep in now that her belly grows. I hear her cough, the soft *pad pad* of her feet as she takes a midnight trip to the washroom. I listen as keenly as a new mother listens for the soft breath of her infant in the crib beside her.

I stand at the window, watching the muted flash of the Rose Island light through an incoming fog. Joseph has taken another shift on watch so that I can keep watch over the girl. Time presses on. Every sunrise and sunset brings Matilda closer to her time, and takes Cora further away from me. There'll be a day when the calendar ticks over another anniversary and I'll be without her longer than I was ever with her. Sixteen years. That was all I had. It will never be long enough.

At sunrise I take the boat out, back to the

place where I lost her. Alone with the waves, I finally let out the years of grief I've kept locked inside until my body aches with my loss. Why couldn't I save her when I'd saved so many others?

I have been many things in my forty years: A daughter. A lighthouse keeper. A mother. A coward. I think of the people I've rescued here, each one a temporary respite from my guilt because when you're saving someone's life, the mess you've made of your own doesn't matter, for a little while at least. But the shadow of my past has always been waiting for me, like a storm gathering on the horizon, not yet felt, but seen, and heard.

And now the storm is here.

Matilda Emmerson.

I have to tell her. Somehow, I have to find the courage to tell her who she really is, because even if I don't deserve her forgiveness or understanding, she deserves to know the truth.

36

MATILDA

Newport, Rhode Island. August 1938

I have always been curious, asking too many questions, always prying into other people's business. After spending so much time on my own, it's no surprise that I developed an obsession with other people's lives. As a shy child I would listen to conversations, sometimes hiding under tables, sometimes perched rigidly beside my mother, following the whispers and revelations that passed around the table with the sugar tongs and the milk jug until I forgot I wasn't supposed to be listening. 'Why did they do that?' I would blurt out. My mother would give me one of her most withering stares before laughingly explaining to her horrified friends that I was a peculiar little girl and she didn't know where she'd got me from, really she didn't.

But that peculiar little girl grew up, and my sense of curiosity grew with me, following me from nursery to schoolroom, trailing behind me as I walked into Mass, shadowing me everywhere I went as I observed the affection between other mothers and daughters and wondered what it was, precisely, that I'd ever done to make my mother so emotionally distant.

Perhaps it is that latent sense of curiosity

instilled in me since childhood, which sees me standing outside Harriet's bedroom. Perhaps it is a small sense of rebellion that sees me turn the handle. Perhaps it is that nagging sense of something missing that sees me step inside and close the door quietly behind me.

It is not the room I was expecting to find. It is neat and tidy, the bed covered with a pale yellow eiderdown, a pile of books and an overflowing ashtray on a nightstand beside the bed. Framed photographs on the walls show Harriet as a younger woman, a baby in her arms. In one image, she is standing outside the lighthouse, in others she is at the horseshoe-shaped beach, or beside the boat or at the harbor. In every picture she is smiling and happy, almost unrecognizable. An older man is with her in some of the photos — her da, I guess — and an even older man is pictured with her in others. Boots, perhaps? The baby, I presume, is Cora.

I walk quietly around the room. On the dressing table there are a dozen more photos of a pretty little girl beaming up into the camera, seashells in her hands. On the nightstand there is a single framed photograph of the same child, grown into a striking young woman of about my age, perhaps a little younger, standing at the lighthouse with a little white dog in her arms. I pick up the photograph to look closer and I can't stop staring because she looks so familiar. The shape of her face. The gentle curve of her lips. The way her hair curls in a calf's lick around her forehead. It is like looking in a mirror.

A creak on the stairs makes me freeze. Before I

have time to react, the door handle turns and Harriet walks into the bedroom. She is as shocked to see me as I am to see her.

'What in God's name are you doing in here?' she demands.

I'm so shocked I don't know what to say. 'I was just . . .'

She strides toward me, snatching the photograph from my hands. 'Just what? Snooping? What exactly are you looking for, Matilda? Corpses in the wardrobe?'

'No. I just . . . I'm curious.'

She puts the photograph into a drawer which she slams shut. The bang rattles a mirror that hangs from a chain on the wall beside the door. 'I invite you into my home and this is the thanks I get? You've no business being in here.' Her voice is low and threatening.

I have to tell her, if only to offer an explanation as to why I'm snooping about in her room. 'I know about Cora.'

She stares at me; through me. 'What did you say?'

'I know about Cora. Your daughter. Joseph told me — but only because I asked.' She turns her back to me and walks to the window, placing her palms flat against the windowsill. I watch the rise and fall of her shoulders as she takes deep breaths, partly afraid of her and partly pitying her. 'I'm so sorry, Harriet,' I offer. 'I didn't mean to upset you. But you call out for her in your sleep sometimes and whenever she's mentioned you clam up, so I asked Joseph.' I let out a sigh, relieved to have told her. 'Anyway, I know, so you don't have to pretend anymore.'

Harriet pulls a packet of cigarettes from the pocket of her trousers and lights one, tossing the box onto the bed behind her. 'You know nothing, Matilda. You don't know the first thing about any of this.'

'I know that she drowned,' I challenge, desperate for her to open up to me. The words hang in the air between us. 'You can tell me about it if you want. If not, I promise I'll never ask again.'

For a long time, Harriet stands perfectly still, her face turned to the window. I bite my bottom lip and fidget with my locket, wishing I'd never come into her room, knowing I've destroyed any trust between us by doing so. I'm about to leave when she starts to speak.

'She had a little dog. Pepper. He went everywhere with her. I laughed when he jumped into the water after a piece of driftwood, but he got caught in a riptide, and Cora ran in after him. I saw it all from the lantern room. By the time I got out to the boat, they'd both been swept out to sea. No matter how fast I rowed, I knew I would never catch up. There was nothing I could do to save her.'

'Harriet, I'm so sorry.'

She turns around, her face as pale as the clouds that dust the sky through the window behind her. 'So, now you know.' Her hand trembles as she lifts the cigarette to her mouth. 'I watched my daughter drown. Now, I suggest you get out of my room before I say something I'll regret.'

I close the door quietly behind me.

For a long time I sit in my bedroom, perched on the end of my bed. I spin the locket at my neck, the words engraved on the back pressing into my conscience as the child kicks wildly against my swollen belly. *Even the brave were once afraid.* A reminder that I have one month to go, and only Harriet here to help me. Just when we were starting to understand each other, I've messed it all up. Like I always do. Blundering in, asking too many questions, making a nuisance of myself.

Eventually, I hear Harriet open her bedroom door and walk along the landing. She pauses outside my room. *Please come in. Please make it all okay.* But she continues on downstairs. A moment later the screen door opens and then closes behind her and she is gone.

I stand up and walk over to the mirror, peering at my reflection, studying the shape of my face, the gentle curve of my lips, the way my hair curls in a calf's lick around my forehead. I sink back onto the bed, my heart racing, my mind turning over past conversations and memories, trying to make sense of the nagging voice that asks the questions I don't have the courage to answer: if Cora looked so remarkably like me, and if she was Harriet's daughter, then who on earth am I?

VOLUME THREE

beacon: *(noun)*
a source of light or inspiration

I thank God, who enabled me to do so much. I thought it a duty, as no assistance could be had, but still I feel sorry I could do no more.

— Grace Darling

37

GRACE

Longstone Lighthouse. November 1838

With the distractions of artists and storms and Mr. Emmerson, I had forgotten entirely about Mr. Sylvester, and Mr. Batty's circus, but the arrival of the supply boat with a postal delivery brings an unwelcome reminder of them both.

I don't quite know what to make of the letter when I first read it. It is a very earnest missive from a Mrs. Margaret Kirk, sent on behalf of a group of ladies in Edinburgh. With the letter, she has enclosed a cutting from the *Caledonian Mercury* in which Mr. Batty has printed a copy of the letter I'd written to him, and in which he makes grand claims about my planned personal appearance at the circus. Mrs. Kirk expresses her opinion about my interactions with Mr. Batty, saying he is not a man to be trusted and that she fears he will take my good name and turn it to his own advantage. *Please do not, for a moment, consider exhibiting yourself in this manner, Miss Darling . . . We are, ourselves, gathering funds to donate to your cause and have grave concerns that the goodwill toward you from the respectable people of our city will be damaged by your association with this dreadful showman.*

My hands tremble as I read Mrs. Kirk's words

for a second time, trying to absorb the full meaning of them. Tears of humiliation prick at my eyes as I rush to find Father at the boathouse. He studies the letter in quiet contemplation as I read it, again, over his shoulder. It only seems to worsen.

'Look, Father. Here Mrs. Kirk says the public will believe me to be courting popularity and that my name will be tarnished. I feel like such a fool.'

He folds the letter and places it in his pocket as he stands up. 'Well, you mustn't feel like a fool, Grace. Not for one moment. The only fool here is Batty and his unscrupulous actions. How dare he?'

I have rarely seen my father as furious. I rush after him as he strides hotly out of the boathouse, declaring Batty to be the very worst kind of shameless opportunist. 'I will write to him immediately — and to the newspaper — to state that your intentions were entirely honorable, unlike those of Batty and his disreputable agent.'

His letter written in haste, Father rows to the Main that afternoon to dispatch it, leaving me at Longstone to stew over Mrs. Kirk's words.

When Father returns and he has calmed down a little, he sits me down to explain that he has received other, similar, requests to Mr. Batty's. 'I didn't want to trouble you with them, Grace. Not while all the artists were here. But I think you deserve to know.'

He shows me a letter from a theatrical producer in London who sets out, in great detail,

290

his plan to produce a dramatic stage play of the *Forfarshire* tragedy, asking if I would consider starring in the production myself. *I wonder if she might wear the same dress as that worn on the night of the famous rescue.*

I can hardly believe it, unsure whether to be horrified or amused by such a ridiculous notion.

'I know their game, Grace,' Father says. 'They see that there is profit to be made from your bravery. They are nothing but a flock of screeching gulls following the herring fleet, waiting to devour whatever pickings they can get.' He assures me he has replied to tell them, in no uncertain terms, that I will certainly not be starring in stage plays or any such nonsense. 'Don't worry, Grace. They will turn their attention to something else soon enough.'

But a somber mood settles over Longstone that day. Even Mam resists the urge to say I told you so. Nothing can cheer me. Not the seal pups, nor the miniature portraits in the locket at my neck. I have never felt less like the courageous heroine everyone believes me to be. I am nothing but a naive fool who misunderstands the ways of the real world and is easily duped by the actions of unscrupulous men.

Like the rocks at low tide, I am exposed. A curiosity. Nothing better than a circus exhibit for all to come and peer at. A deep discomfort settles in my stomach as the sun dips behind the horizon and the lamps cast a path of light onto the dark seas beyond. With the tide on the turn, I feel washed away, as if the real Grace Darling doesn't exist at all.

★ ★ ★

Over the following days, my spirits are lifted by a series of rather more pleasant news. The first comes in the form of an envelope bearing the royal seal.

I watch Father open it with trembling fingers, rubbing his chin as he reads the contents, declaring, 'Well, I never did,' several times.

Mam is fit to burst, grabbing it off him to read it for herself as Father takes my hands in his and explains it is from Queen Victoria, who, after reading in *The Times* about the events of the *Forfarshire* and our rescue, wishes to donate fifty pounds as a token of her esteem.

Having absorbed the contents of the letter, Mam sinks into a chair beside the fire and fans herself with it. 'A letter from the queen! From the queen!' It is too much for her altogether and she has to take herself off for a lie down.

'Good riddance to the like of Mr. Batty,' Father says, a twinkle returned to his eye again. 'It's royalty you're dealing with now, Grace.'

I cannot suppress my delight. As an ardent admirer of our young queen, I could not be more honored to know that she has thought of me. I read the letter so many times I can recite it at will by the end of the day.

But that isn't all. Father also explains that a letter has arrived from the Duke of Northumberland. The duke — a nobleman of the Percy family — and his wife, Duchess Charlotte, are well known in the area, their family seat being the impressive Alnwick Castle, a little distance

292

along the Northumbrian coast. The duchess had acted as governess to young Victoria before she became queen, and is extremely well-liked and respected.

'The duke writes to say that he is aware of the circumstances of the *Forfarshire* and our rescue and has written to the Duke of Wellington at Trinity House,' Father explains. 'We are to receive ten pounds each and he also wishes to present us with gold medals, on behalf of the Royal Humane Society, of which he is president. We are to go to Alnwick Castle in person to receive the medals.' I sit beside the fire to warm my hands and feet as Father reads the letter out loud. When he reaches the end he leans forward, the fire dancing in his eyes. 'An invitation to the castle, Gracie!'

I have admired Alnwick Castle many times from the upstairs window of my uncle Marsden's grocery shop on Narrowgate in the town. Never did I think I would be the recipient of a personal invitation there. The thought fills me with excitement and dread.

'And Mam?' I ask. 'It doesn't mention her?'

Father shakes his head. 'Just the two of us. Anyway, you know your mam. She won't be bothered one bit about invitations to castles and meeting dukes and duchesses.' He winks. 'She won't mind at all.'

38

GRACE

Alnwick Castle. December 1838

The day of our appointment at Alnwick Castle, I wake to mercifully calm seas. I have worried about the trip all week, unable to settle on what to wear and worrying about conducting myself adequately in front of the duke and duchess. Mostly, I have worried about the weather, concerned that we might be forced to attempt a crossing in rough seas. Thankfully, no such decisions are necessary.

Father prepares the coble while Mam helps me into my best pink dress, taking extra time to wind my hair into a neatly braided crown on top of my head. I wince at her less-than-gentle touch, but try not to complain. Her nerves are frayed enough as it is without my tugging at them with my grousing.

After saying our goodbyes and promising Mam we will remember our manners, we push the coble away from the rocks and set out for the mainland. Mam stands loyally at the landing steps until she fades from view behind a light sea mist.

'We'll never hear the end of it you know,' Father remarks as he sets up a steady stroke on the oars.

'The end of what?'

'That time we were important guests at the castle and Mam wasn't invited.'

We both giggle. 'Poor Mam,' I say. 'She would have loved to come, wouldn't she?'

'Poor Mam, nothing. She would have loved to brag about it to anyone who'd care to listen. The poor duchess would have had her ear chewed off! It's better this way.'

He's right, of course. I relax in Father's company, where I only become more fretful in Mam's. We row in quiet harmony, happy to be out on the water together. Inquisitive seals follow the boat and the gulls cry out to send us on our way.

We make good progress to North Sunderland, from where we take a coach to travel the seventeen miles along the coast to Alnwick. It is almost a year since I visited my cousins and I've forgotten how impressive the castle is. As the coach rattles along the cobbled streets beside the castle walls, I peer out of the window, eager to get a better look as we rumble beneath the impressive gateway, guarded by baileys and tower turrets. The area outside the gate is crowded with stall holders, harried mothers with fretful children, serene ladies and gentlemen, and soldiers on horseback. It is a stark contrast to the solitude of the island and I can hardly stop myself gawping. Father sits quietly beside me, absorbing it all in his usual humble way.

'Do you think they'll have tea and cake for us, Grace?'

'I should hope so,' I smile. 'I'm famished.'

He takes up my hand, as giddy as a child at Christmas. 'Who'd ever have thought it? Summoned by the duke. Are you nervous?'

'A little,' I admit. 'I hope they don't make a terrible fuss.'

'They will of course. That's what dukes and duchesses do. But we will be patient and polite and grateful for their time. The duke is a very pleasant man. I know you'll make a great impression on him.'

Our names announced, we are escorted inside the castle and up an impressive staircase, the ceiling soaring above. I try not to stare but my eyes rove up and down and all around as we follow our guide, my shoes sinking into the soft rugs as we are led down a long corridor, past enormous gilded portraits of members of the Percy family, their expressions captured so perfectly I feel their gaze follow us as we pass. The air is rich with the perfume of hothouse flowers, displayed in ornate porcelain urns that stand on great plinths. Father squeezes my arm as we walk, his lips twitching as he tries to contain a delighted smile.

We enter a sumptuous saloon, decorated in rich gold brocades and crimson velvet, where we are presented to the duke and duchess with quiet dignity. The duke cuts a very impressive figure in formal military dress and the duchess is the most elegant woman I have ever seen, dressed in sumptuous midnight blue velvet with an intricate lace collar. I dare hardly look at her as she addresses me.

'Miss Darling. What an honor to meet you.'

She smiles so warmly and speaks so pleasantly that my shyness and worry instantly ease. I curtsey, remembering how Mam had shown me and glad to have practiced. There is only a slight, almost indiscernible, wobble as I dip my knee. Beside me, Father bows deferentially before the duke takes him to one side where they discuss the proposed changes to shipping laws following the *Forfarshire* disaster. The duchess reserves all her attention for me, expressing her admiration for my bravery.

'It was such a dreadful tragedy. We were all astonished to learn of your part in the rescue, Miss Darling. Even the queen was most impressed to hear of your bravery. As a determined young woman herself, it pleased her greatly to learn of your part in the rescue. I daresay she would have jumped into the boat to help you row if she had been there.'

I smile and say thank you and how very grateful I am for the queen's support. It hardly feels sufficient response to such an honor.

'I cannot think of many who would have shown such courage,' the duchess continues. 'My husband was adamant we acknowledge your bravery with the gold medals.'

'We are incredibly honored, ma'am. Any keeper at the many light stations around the English coastline would have done the same.'

'Perhaps so, but I can only think the nine survivors fortunate to have found themselves stranded by the Longstone light, and no other. I was especially sorry to learn of the poor mother who lost her children. Do you hear of her?'

'Yes, we have exchanged a few lines.' I blanch at the thought of our latest exchange regarding matters of romance and George and Eliza. 'Mrs. Dawson was exceptionally brave, ma'am. I often think it should be her the newspapers write about, and who receives medals and accolades.' I am still haunted by the image of those ragged little bodies, slumped on the rock, the sea lapping at their boots.

The duchess places her hand on mine. 'And that is precisely why you are so admired, Miss Darling. Not only were you extraordinarily courageous, you show humility in equal measure.'

We talk for a good while, the duke and duchess keen to hear our version of the events of that night. I let Father do most of the talking but when prompted by the duchess, who is especially keen to hear my thoughts on the matter, I speak as freely as I can, becoming more relaxed as the interview goes on. When they are satisfied to have heard the full account, and following the formal presentation of the medals, our hosts prepare to bid us farewell. The duchess presents me with a gift of a Paisley shawl.

'I should be very happy to think of you wearing it as you tend to your lamps, Miss Darling. I have often admired the work of the light keepers. I shall admire them all the more after meeting you and your father. It has been a great pleasure.'

I thank her profusely. 'I shall wear it with the greatest pride, ma'am.'

Father and I are escorted to one of the

housekeeper's rooms, where we are served tea and cakes and delicacies the like of which we've never seen before. We are made to feel very comfortable and most welcome and smile wryly at each other as we eat, barely able to believe that we have swapped our humble living quarters at the lighthouse for all this.

After the refreshments, we are given a tour of the castle apartments. I am especially impressed by the vast library, never having seen so many books. We also see the armory and the chapel, the staterooms and another impressive portrait gallery. As we walk, Father tells me that the duke has expressed his intention to act as my ward.

'He was troubled to learn of the interferences you have experienced recently, with Batty and the like. He proposes to establish and manage a trust fund to handle the sums of money being sent, and to offer protection from any further intrusions into your privacy.'

It is a surprising development, but not an unwelcome one. 'It is a very generous offer,' I say. 'It would certainly be a relief to have the duke manage things.'

'Indeed,' Father agrees. 'It is a pity, in some ways, that events have gone so far, but I told him I am in full agreement that such steps are now necessary.'

We are grateful for the tour and the exceptional courtesy we are shown, but as we are escorted into yet another ornate room I begin to feel my enthusiasm wane. I can tell Father feels the same. We are both a little relieved when the tour reaches its conclusion.

As we walk back to the castle gates, we talk, ten-to-the-dozen, recalling everything we have heard and seen and consumed, each of us remembering some other detail. But my excitement quickly diminishes as it becomes apparent that a crowd has gathered at the castle walls. They push and shove around me as we try to leave, fervent cries of 'Hurrah for Miss Darling' and spontaneous applause surrounding us as we are engulfed by a wave of people, clamoring to see me. Hands reach out to grasp at my skirts and shawl, my heart pounding as I cling to my father, who calmly expresses his thanks on my behalf and asks that they make way. The cacophony of noise and the fervor of the crowd frightens and bewilders me.

At last we reach the carriage, where I stumble inside, Father behind me, urging the coachman to close the door and to hurry about it. My heart thumps beneath my cloak, my hands tremble when I place them on my lap. As the wheels begin to turn and we move away, the hurrahs and cheers fade into the background, but I am shaken by the event.

Father places a reassuring arm around my shoulder. 'They mean well, Grace. They only wish to show their admiration.'

I sigh. 'I know, Father, and I don't mean to sound ungrateful but I wish they wouldn't. I wish they would stop. I wish this would all stop.'

He squeezes my shoulder. 'You're going to have to bear it just a little longer, pet.' He rubs the whiskers on his chin. 'Perhaps we should have brought Mam with us after all. She would have seen them all off with her rolling pin.'

The thought of Mam running through the castle gates brandishing her rolling pin makes me laugh until tears of frustration and relief fall against my cheeks.

Father brushes them away with his thumbs. 'That's more like it. Let it out, Grace. Set it all free. This will pass, I promise you. Like the storms and the seasons, nothing stays the same forever.'

As the coach takes us back to North Sunderland, Father outlines in greater detail the full extent of the duke's guardianship, explaining that he will manage all matters relating to formal correspondence and that any further donations of money will go through the duke's own lawyers. I am especially pleased to hear that the duke intends for three of the Crewe Trustees at Bamburgh Castle (excluding Robert Smeddle) to be appointed in charge of my affairs.

Despite the distressing end to the day, I try to put it behind me and close my eyes, lulled by the motion of the carriage and comforted by the familiar shape of my father's shoulder against my cheek. Soon, the only sounds are the clatter of horseshoes and the creaking of the carriage and I let myself slip away from it all beneath the welcome embrace of sleep.

★   ★   ★

That evening, after taking Mam through every minute of the visit in painstaking detail (she is far from content with the abridged version offered by my exhausted Father), I take first watch after sunset. After the whirlwind of the day, I take pleasure in watching the sky as it changes from blue to violet to navy. I scan the heavens, waiting for the first star to shine through the darkness, and then the next and the next until the sky is fully dark and I am covered by a perfect canopy of starlight.

The lamp turns, and my mind turns with it, back to the events of the day and beyond, to the recent storm and Mr. Emmerson's unexpected stay. Despite his departure, his deep affection for Longstone lingers in my heart and his words linger in my thoughts. *The angle of incidence equals the angle of reflection. The universal law of science.* The universal law of love, it seems, has no such scientific explanation. It is as unfathomable as the depths of the ocean and the height of the heavens and I must find my place between them, without him.

I open the locket, admiring the miniature portraits inside. I think about the absent locks of hair once held there and how Sarah Dawson must now find her place in the world without her children. I wonder how she is, and set my mind to write another letter to her in the morning.

★   ★   ★

Sarah Dawson spends quiet empty days among the rooms of her quayside home in Hull. She has too much time to think, so that sometimes she cannot be sure which parts of her day are real, and which are spent in the fabrication of her restless mind.

While she was pleased to receive the response to her letter from Miss Darling, she is a little disappointed to learn that there will be no romantic development with George. Sarah understands that Grace isn't like the ladies on the mainland, eager to catch a gentleman's attention, desperate to secure a proposal of marriage. Although only slight in build, she is possessed of a great strength of mind; a strength which needs no bolstering by the affections of a man.

It is settled then. George will marry Eliza Cavendish in the spring and he will make the best of things, and Miss Darling will remain on her island. It is a shame, Sarah thinks, certain that George and Grace would have been much happier together than they ever will be apart. But she has meddled enough. Destiny must play its hand now, and she must get back to the business of stitching together whatever scraps and fragments of her life she can find at the little house on Quay Street, where she still hears her children's laughter in their empty rooms and still feels the warmth of her husband's embrace as she stands alone in the scullery.

As sure as a drowning man will cling to a piece of passing flotsam, Sarah clings desperately to these memories. They, alone, are what buoy her; keep her afloat in the ocean of her grief. They are all she has now. If she lets go of the past she shared with her husband and children, she will surely never find a future without them.

She picks up a sheet of paper, dips her pen into the ink, and begins to write her memories down, capturing her family's too-short story in simple sentences until she is satisfied. Here they are, written in ink, a permanent record of John, Sarah, James and Matilda Dawson so that they might never be forgotten and their story often told in the years and decades ahead.

She sleeps then, dreaming of the sea and where it might take her.

39

MATILDA

Newport, Rhode Island. August 1938

Through the sticky summer nights when the heat steals sleep from the restless, I rest my chin on the windowsill, breathing in the salty air through the open window as I watch the turn of the light across the bay. It fascinates me to watch the way the beam of light changes the color of things. The black rocks become ink-blue. The blue sea becomes a five-day-old bruise, green and purple. In quiet uncomplicated moments like this, I imagine myself staying here with the baby and it feels so right, but telling Harriet my plan isn't quite so easy. When she is reading quietly or in one of her better moods, I feel the words on my tongue. 'Do you think ... ?' 'Would it be possible ... ?' 'Could I ... ?' but I can't summon the courage to speak the words out loud, imagining how her eyes will narrow and her lips curl. And then what?

After she'd found me in her bedroom, things were strained between us for a while, the atmosphere stretched and taut, like an overblown balloon about to burst at any moment. We haven't talked about it since, both of us too wary to scratch the itch. And yet I can't stop thinking about the photograph of Cora. Every time I look in the mirror my reflection demands to know the answer to the doubts and questions that cloud my thoughts. I also sense that Harriet wants to tell me something, often pausing as she leaves the room or as she heads into the kitchen, but whatever it is slips away and we carry on in our strange little world, leaving questions unasked and unanswered as we try to make the best of things.

As my time gets closer, I sleep in unsatisfying scraps, my misshapen body impossible to make comfortable, my mind a whirl of what-ifs and maybes. During the day, I clean and tidy in bursts of energy. Harriet says it is an instinct to nest in preparation for the child, but I am sure it is more an instinct to make up for her blatant disregard for homemaking. I make myself as useful as possible at the lighthouse, shadowing Harriet, learning the small little tasks that fill her days. When she grows tired of my endless questions, I retreat to the cozy little bedroom where I continue to sort through the jumble of newspapers and mementos in the tea chest. When I feel too weary or uncomfortable to make the boat trip back over the bay, we spend the night at the lighthouse. I sleep much better here, while Harriet paces the watch room above.

Over quiet suppers, and when she is in the mood to listen, I tell Harriet about my latest discoveries in the tea chest, showing her the scrapbooks I've carefully compiled from all the newspaper cuttings kept by her granny and old Boots. I read her a transcription of a letter, written by Grace Darling to a local nobleman,

306

the Duke of Northumberland, who appears to have become her guardian. '*I have not got married yet for they say man is master, and there is much talk about bad masters*, but some of the original wording has been struck out and replaced with, *for I have heard people say there is luck in leisure*.'

Harriet laughs. 'She sounds like a sensible girl. Marriage is overrated.' She peers at me over the top of her book. 'Husbands are hard work, Matilda. You're better off without one in my opinion.'

'You never married then?'

'Me? Married. Can you imagine it?'

'No. Not really.'

'Can't think of anything worse. I made my vows with this lump of rock. No time for a husband. If I were you, I wouldn't be in a hurry to find one, neither. Far more trouble than they're worth. Even Joseph Kinsella.'

I blush furiously at this, denying any such thoughts about Joseph, or anyone for that matter. 'Don't worry. I'm not looking for a husband. I've enough complications ahead of me without adding more.'

'Good.' Harriet puts her book down and leans forward. 'Don't ever let a man tell you what you can and can't be, or that you're not good enough or pretty enough or smart enough. You go out there and you make something of yourself, do you hear?' Her words carry an unexpected sincerity; emotion I haven't heard from her before.

'Yes. I hear you,' I say. And I do.

307

As the sun sets that evening, painting the sea in shades of a New England fall, I wrap a blanket around my knees and continue reading the newspaper articles from the tea chest, glad to spend another night with Harriet at the lighthouse. The more I read about the brave women who've kept the lights for decades, the more I admire and understand them until their sepia-tinted past doesn't feel so very far away, or their lives so very unusual. I think about my life back in Ballycotton: Mother's stuffy luncheons, the endless requirement for proper manners, every day a dull repetition of the one before: be a dutiful daughter, secure a good marriage, maintain the family's reputation. I'd always felt like a bystander peering in through a misted-up window, never quite able to understand what was happening, or why I was part of it. Surrounded by the calm waters of Narragansett Bay and the walls of the lighthouse, I feel as though I understand everything. Here, life makes sense, even at a time when it should make the least sense of all.

Taking a final rummage in the tea chest, I find a bundle of dusty old pages tied together with string. I flick through them, amazed to discover an account of the Dawson family of Hull, hand-written by Sarah Dawson. My great-great-granny. I pore over her words, surprised at how emotional I become as I read her memories of her children and husband and the happy times they had together before tragedy tore them apart. Among these pages are some others, the words *Forfarshire Disaster, September 1838* written on the front, but the names James and Matilda and Grace Darling are the only words I can make out. The rest is an illegible mess of ink blots and the incomprehensible rambling thoughts of a grieving mother. I place them back into the tea chest and almost wish I'd never found them.

That night, I dream of a young girl in a storm, rowing from a lighthouse to rescue survivors of a shipwreck, among them a mother and her two children. But the girl can't get to them in time and they are swept into the sea as the wind screams in great gusts around her. As she turns the boat around, desperate to get back to the safety of the lighthouse, I see the girl's face. It is me. The screams of the wind are my screams. But no matter how desperately I cry out, nobody is there to save me, and the waves grow higher around me until they crash over the boat, soaking my skirts and dragging me down into the watery depths.

I wake with a jolt and sit up in bed, my hands clammy. The bedsheets are sodden, my night-dress soaked through. It is then I feel the first wave of pain wash over me.

'Harriet!' I shout. 'Harriet!' She is there in a moment and I am so glad of her. 'My waters have broken. The baby is coming.'

40

MATILDA

Newport, Rhode Island. September 1938

The pains come in steady waves that build into peaks and take my breath away. I curl up on the bed, tucking my knees into my chest, pulling on the sheets to try to crawl away from them, but still the pains come.

Harriet insists I stand up. 'You need to walk. It'll make the baby come quicker, trust me.'

I have to trust her. I struggle to my feet, hunching over myself like an old woman. 'It isn't even time. Not for another month.' My fear turns to panic. I'm not ready. I can't do this.

'Babies have a mind of their own. They come when they're ready, and it seems like this one is in a rush. Whether you like it or not, I'll be delivering your baby, right here, right now. The sooner you make peace with that, the better.'

Another wave of pain engulfs me as I grasp the end of the bedstead, pushing against the cold metal, praying for it to stop. Between the contractions, Harriet presses a hot water bottle to my back. When that stops working she plays jazz, turning the volume up full on the record player. We sing along to Ella Fitzgerald, my voice reaching impromptu crescendos every ten minutes as I sing through the pain.

'No good holding it in,' Harriet says. 'Shout and groan. Curse if you must. Sure there's nobody to hear you.'

So I do. My embarrassment is silenced by the need to release the shock of the pain. I wail into the eiderdown and grasp at my nightdress, yanking it above my stomach, unable to bear the brush of fabric against my skin. I'm so desperate for this to be over, for the child to be out of me, that I don't even think about what will happen next. I just want the pain to stop.

Hours pass and still we go on until it feels like the night and the pain will never end. Through it all, Harriet never leaves my side. I wonder if my mother, faced with the same circumstances, would have done the same. In calmer moments between contractions, I ask Harriet how long her labor took. It's the first time we've spoken about Cora since Harriet found me snooping in her bedroom. We are both too exhausted to fight about it anymore.

'Two days,' she says, 'give or take a few hours.'

'Two days!' I shout my disbelief through another contraction as I walk up and down the bedroom, leaning against the wall until the pain briefly descends again.

'I started a lot slower than you,' she explains, counting me through the contraction, reminding me to breathe slowly, in and out, in and out. 'And I had two babies to deliver.'

Another contraction grips me hard before I can respond, my back and sides aflame with the shifting and stretching of muscles. Tears squeeze from my eyes as I try to embrace it rather than fight it, riding the peak of the pain like the surfers I've watched catching the waves around Newport's beaches. Already exhausted from my efforts, my body trembles and shakes.

'Nobody knew there was two on the way,' Harriet continues, flopping down into the chair beside the bed, as exhausted by my laboring as I am. 'I didn't even know there was one on the way for a good while.'

Sensing that she might open up to me, I encourage her to go on as she wipes a damp cloth across my face. 'What happened?' I ask.

'The war happened. I was nineteen. Same age as you. He was a local boy, one of the lucky ones who returned from France after the war. All it took was a few desperate minutes of fumbling to release all the years of suffering. He sobbed like a child afterwards. Told me it was his first time.' I breathe through another contraction, count to twenty, praying it will soon be over. 'Poor fecker died of the Spanish flu before I ever knew I was carrying his child.'

I haul myself up from the bed, forcing myself to walk despite the urge to lie down. 'What did you do when you found out?'

'I made arrangements to have the child . . . you know . . . seen to, but my da begged me to change my mind.'

'He wanted you to keep it?' I think about the look of disappointment in my father's eyes, the way he quietly closed the door behind him, shutting me out of his life in the process. How different everything could have been if he had supported me.

312

'After so much death during the war, Da said every new life was more important than ever. He sat me down one evening and told me about a cousin of his whose young wife couldn't have children of her own. Things were even worse for unmarried mothers then than they are now. Since I wasn't married it was agreed the cousin and his wife would raise the child as their own.'

I breathe through another contraction, releasing the pain in long breaths in and out as I pace up and down past the window, breathing in time to the flash of the light.

'I suppose it might have all worked out if I hadn't changed my mind,' she continues. 'What I hadn't considered when I agreed to Da's plan was how I would be affected by that little life squirming around inside me. The closer I got to my time, the more determined I was to raise the child on my own.'

'What did your da say about that?'

'I think he understood, in a way, but he said it was too late to change my mind. That it was all agreed. The cousin's wife had already told people she was expecting and taken herself into a false confinement. He told me she suffered from her nerves and it would be the undoing of her if she didn't get the child.' Harriet pauses to take a long drag of her cigarette. 'What nobody knew was that I was carrying twins. I delivered two perfect little girls. Almost identical. I begged Da to let me keep them both, but I knew it would be hard enough to raise one child on my own, let alone two.' As she looks at me I see a softening in her eyes, a flicker of affection. 'Letting one of

313

them go was the hardest thing I ever had to do.'

I think about the photograph of Cora as I push through another contraction, Harriet rubbing the small of my back in circles, trying to rub away the pain. Almost as unstoppable as the relentless waves of pain that will soon see my baby delivered, I know that the conclusion to Harriet's story will change everything.

For a while neither of us speaks. I climb onto the bed, my nightdress soaked with my sweat. I take sips of water and press a cool cloth to my face while Harriet disappears for a moment and returns with a wooden spoon.

'You're nearly ready to push,' she says. 'Bite down on this when the contractions come.'

I look at her, wild-eyed. 'Will it be okay?'

'The baby? Of course. Do as I say and you'll both be fine.'

The pains come thick and fast as I instinctively bear down with each fresh wave. Harriet soothes me through another big contraction and tells me it won't be long now.

'What happened to the other baby?' I ask, afraid to hear the answer, but afraid to hide from the truth any longer.

'I suffered a hemorrhage after the birth. When I woke up in the hospital there was only one baby in the cot. My da had taken the other to his cousin. As soon as I recovered we left Ireland to start a new life here in Newport. That journey was the longest of my life.' I push through another contraction. 'I've thought about that child every day since. Years passed with no contact between my father and his cousin. His

314

letters were never returned. I heard through another relative that the child was healthy. That was all I knew. That, and her name. I'd called her Grace Rose, but the cousin's wife changed it.'

The name Grace Rose spins in my mind. Why is it familiar?

'What did she call her?' I ask as Harriet tells me to push. I bite down on the spoon, pushing as hard as I can, my body on fire with pain and exhaustion. 'Harriet,' I gasp. 'What did she call her?'

As the final moments of my labor rob me of my words, it all makes sense. The way Harriet has looked at me and cared for me since I arrived. The way my mother has always acted like a distant stranger. The striking resemblance between Cora and me.

I push when Harriet tells me to push, and pant when she tells me to pant, until, with a final excruciating effort, my baby slips between my legs. After all these long months, and hours of labor, everything is reduced into a single moment of relief. As if I have been underwater I feel myself surface as my daughter is placed into my arms and I cannot fathom that this little person is mine. 'She's perfect,' I whisper. 'Absolutely perfect.'

Harriet holds her hand to my cheek and tips my face gently toward hers. 'She is. Absolutely perfect.' She takes a deep breath as the sea sighs at the window. 'They called my daughter Matilda. Matilda Sarah Emmerson.'

41

GRACE

Longstone Lighthouse. 1840

The arrival of a new year brings baby pink skies and the first snow of the winter. The north wind bites at my cheeks as I tend to the hens, more grateful than ever for the waterproof mackintosh cloak sent as a Christmas gift from the duke and duchess. They have been extremely generous since we visited the castle. Mam is beside herself with her gift of a silver teapot, using it at least four times a day. I am equally taken with my gift of a watch. It is quite beautiful although it makes me all too aware of the passing of time and the increasing distance between the simple life I'd once known, and the continued complications of public scrutiny.

Under the duke's wardship I am, at last, free of the incessant interference of Robert Smeddle. Once a week I sit to reply to any new correspondence. The letters are much fewer in number now and it is not the onerous task it once was. The duke writes often regarding the trust fund and legal matters concerning the sums of money held in my name. I have agreed to take no more than five pounds every six months. As I expressed in a recent letter to the duke: *My prosperity was neither expected, nor desired, sir.*

I wish only to carry on here in my duties, and to he a good daughter.

Although the initial fascination from the public has thankfully diminished a little, the summer months of the previous year had seen the profiteering fishermen resume their boat trips, the decks crowded with people eager to see Longstone's heroine. Reluctant to visit the Main, where my appearance always causes unwanted attention, I spend more and more time at the lighthouse, focusing on the job of maintaining the seven apartments and assisting my father and brother with the lamp when needed.

I write often to my sister Thomasin, to whom I have always felt the closest connection and who has offered the most understanding and common sense over the past year. She, alone, knows of my secret affection for George Emmerson, having eventually prized the truth from me. She knows how it both pains and delights me to hear news of him from Sarah Dawson. Time heals, they say, and yet I still feel an ache of regret when I open my locket and see the little portraits inside, remembering the calm morning when Mr. Emmerson had pressed the mussel shell into my hands.

Sarah sent word of George and Eliza's wedding the previous summer, it having been delayed by Eliza falling dangerously ill over the winter. Having nearly lost her appears to have only endeared George more to his new wife. *The wedding,* Sarah wrote, *was a very happy affair. There was much dancing and merry-making. As you know, Miss Darling, I doubted the union,* but they are very happy together and George is quite settled, much to the surprise of us all. I expect they will start a family soon. Eliza makes no secret of her desire for a large brood and George was always such a doting uncle to James and Matilda. It would be lovely to see him become a father.

I replied to tell her how pleased I was to hear all was well and that, having completed his studies in Dundee, George had taken a small gallery in Durham, where he and Eliza had set up home. I didn't write of how often I open the locket to study the little images inside, nor how often I remember the days Mr. Emmerson spent with us at Longstone.

The first weeks of this new year bring happy news that our sister Mary Ann is expecting a child in the summer. She has already lost four children, and the poor thing is understandably anxious. We do our best to reassure her, but we all worry, Mam especially. I pray for the safe delivery of the child, and for Mary Ann to safely navigate the perilous business of childbirth. Another reason, if one were needed, to avoid the institution of marriage.

As winter releases its grip on the Farne Islands and the puffins and kittiwakes return to their nesting sites, we are blessed with a clutch of adorable eider ducklings scampering about the place. I watch them whenever I have the opportunity, enjoying the peep and chirp as they call to one another. With the winter storms passed and the sun warming my bones as I go about my chores, I feel a lightness of spirit I had thought lost to me forever. But the joys of the springtime are short-lived and a deep melancholy falls upon the family as we learn of the sudden death of Mary Ann's husband. Mam insists she return to Longstone so that we can take care of her in the final months of her pregnancy.

The poor thing is inconsolable. We do as much as we can for her, but she weeps continually, her face pale as milk, her eyes devoid of their usual brightness. It is a pitiful sight to see her belly so swollen and to know that the child will never know its father. He was a good man. It seems that it must always be the good ones who are taken from us too soon.

Despite a difficult labor which we all assist with in one way or another, Mary Ann is delivered of a delightfully pink and chubby little girl in the summer. She names her Georgiann, for her departed husband, George. I am fascinated by the way the child squirms in my arms and mewls like the kittens we raised on Brownsman. I sit with her for hours, delighted by the way she curls her impossibly dainty fingers around mine so assuredly. I quite love her already. With Brooks then announcing he is to be married to an admirable young girl from Craster, Mam is at her spinning wheel all the hours of the day to make enough thread for the dresses and bonnets we shall all need.

By the autumn, Brooks and his new wife, Jane, are settled with us at Longstone. Our numbers swell with every spring tide, and I believe they will soon grow again with Jane walking about the place like a ghost, retching at the smell of bacon rind, her face as gray as the seals. Mam is delighted to have her family around her again, but I am not quite so enthralled.

I make light of it in my letters to Thomasin, remarking that market day in Bamburgh couldn't be as busy as the lighthouse with everyone's endless chatter and demands. With so many opinions to take into consideration and so many mouths to feed, I don't quite feel myself. It is an age since I searched for fossils or read poetry with any serious attention to the words. I am irritable and easily distracted, and unusually short-tempered. But I cannot entirely blame my family for my bad mood. Since Sarah sent news at the start of the year that Eliza is with child, I have been unsettled. In my reply to Sarah I expressed my delight for them, but my words betrayed the pangs of jealousy and regret in my heart.

During long hours on watch, I find myself wondering whether I might have felt differently about remaining here if my family had descended on the lighthouse a year earlier. Might I have felt less obliged to stay and assist my parents if there had always been so many able hands willing to help? Might I have given Mr. Emmerson some encouragement in his obvious affections for me?

But there is little point in wishing things were different. No more than King Canute could turn back the tide, can I stop the momentum of fate nor alter what is done.

★   ★   ★

320

A letter from Longstone lighthouse brightens Sarah Dawson's day, although she is a little troubled to read how Miss Darling feels the weight of her unexpected notoriety pressing on her shoulders. *I don't mind telling you that I wish to be free of it now, Sarah. It drags about me like a yoke around a milkmaid's shoulders and weakens me. I do not feel myself.* For a young woman who has spent her life living beneath the light, it is perhaps no surprise that she feels uncomfortable now that the beam has fallen upon her.

Without the demands of a family to keep her occupied, Sarah is grateful to have found a position in the past year as cook and cleaner for a local bookbinder, Eamonn Flaherty. There is something about the lilt of Mr. Flaherty's Irish accent that appeals to the singsong in Sarah's ear. He is a kind man, a widower himself, and treats her with the greatest respect, almost as ashamed to find himself in need of a woman to help him as Sarah Dawson is to wash another man's smalls. As something of a tentative friendship develops between them, Mr. Flaherty tells her of the green fields of Ireland and how he hopes to go back there one day to where his father keeps a lighthouse in Donegal on the Atlantic coast. It is the prettiest place in all the world, he tells her. Sarah says she would like to go there one day, and it sets his mind to thinking.

If only George could settle, she might almost consider herself content for the first time since the *Forfarshire* disaster, but he is distracted when he writes and even more so when he visits. Although he cares for Eliza very much, Sarah knows he doesn't love her the way he loved Miss Darling. He has admitted as much in his letters, saying how he hopes the child will improve matters when it arrives. Sarah cautions him, warning that an infant, no matter how precious, cannot fix what is broken and that he expects too much of a child not yet safely delivered into the world. It leaves Sarah ill at ease as she rolls pastry for the apple pie she is making for Mr. Flaherty's supper, wishing she could as easily make a happy future for her brother.

42

GEORGE

Durham, England. September 1840

George watches his wife bloom, aware that she grows ever more anxious about the birth. He soothes and reassures her, reminding her she is young and healthy. But as the day of the infant's expected arrival looms and then passes, even he becomes restless and fretful. Every cough, every hand placed to the small of her back, every time Eliza stands suddenly to relieve the pressure on her bladder he rushes to her, ready to fetch the midwife.

Unable to sleep, he sits at his easel and works by candlelight. It is far from his best work, but the night passes quickly beneath the formation of his seascapes. He works from rough sketches taken during the daylight, capturing the sense of life in the local harbor towns: the fisherwomen waiting with their creels on the beach, cockle gatherers in the shallows at sunrise, men gathered in their dozens to pull the lifeboat back up the beach, the sea at its foaming wildest behind them. He paints reflections into the puddles left by the outgoing tide, imagining Miss Darling peering into one of the rock pools, her smile caught forever in the water. He turns to his wife as she moans in her sleep, returning to his work as she settles. He adds another layer of color, painting Miss Darling away, erasing his memories of her beneath cerulean seas and ochre clouds.

On it goes, night after night, until a high-pitched gasp from the bed makes him start. Eliza sits up and leans forward, taking a moment to catch her breath.

Rushing to her side, he takes her hand. 'Is it time?'

She nods, fear in her eyes. 'Yes, George. Fetch Nancy. And hurry.'

He knocks over his palette as he pulls on his cloak, assuring Eliza he won't be long. He returns as quickly as possible with Nancy, the midwife, and leaves the women to it while he walks to the cathedral and sits quietly to pray.

At sunrise he starts to make his way home, unaware of the drama that has unfolded during the dark hours; unaware that the house he left as a fretful husband, he will return to as a father, and a widower.

Nancy is waiting for him at the door, ashen-faced as she grips his hands, weeping as she tells him she did her very best for Eliza but that she lost too much blood and slipped into a faint she couldn't wake her from. He rushes to his wife, unable to comprehend the cold stillness of her.

He forgets, for a moment, about the child. Only at the sound of her whimper does he remember.

He walks to the crib beside the fireplace where his daughter, weakened by the complications of her entry into the world, struggles to hang on to the thin thread of life she grasps in her tiny little rosebud hands. And he loves her more than he has ever loved anyone.

For two perfect days he loves her.

And then he loses her.

43

GRACE

Longstone Lighthouse. March 1842

Spring arrives like an apologetic guest late to a party, and Longstone gladly shrugs off the last of the season's storms with a grateful sigh. It is a day for sending washing flapping on the line. A day for tending to neglected chores. I inhale the warmth and the light as I enjoy an easy row across to Brownsman Island to turn over the soil in preparation for planting new seeds. All is purpose at the lighthouse and there are hungry mouths to feed at every mealtime.

My little niece and my new nephew grow as fat as dumplings. I am accustomed now to their familiar little shrieks and giggles and no longer surprised by their outrageous little tantrums when their faces turn as scarlet as summer strawberries. I have adjusted to my family being here, and enjoy their company very much, but occasionally — and increasingly so — I feel like a spectator sitting quietly at the edge of life, watching the rumpus go on around me, rather than being at the heart of things, as I once was. There are plenty of hands to assist now with the cleaning of the apartments and the polishing of the lenses. I often ascend the tower to find the wicks already trimmed and the oil reserves already filled and the dust sheets already hung, with care, over the lenses. Jane, especially, likes to make herself useful. As a new member of the family it is entirely understandable that she wants to help, and yet I find myself smothered by her. Without a husband or children to demand my attention and affection and give the same in return, it is difficult not to cling to the things I have always cherished as my own: the lighthouse and the lamps. I have, by my own admission, become something of a spare part. It is a truth that does not sit with me well.

With everyone packed into the lighthouse as tight as herrings in their pickling barrels, it is finally agreed that new accommodations will have to be built for Brooks and Jane and their expanding brood. Workmen are shipped over to the island, their hammering and hoisting and loud calls of instructions turning my quiet little home into a small industrial town. I find myself lacking in energy, stopping halfway up the stairs to catch my breath, too weary to continue the ascent. I say nothing to the family and yet my father notices the change in my demeanor.

'You are not yourself, Grace. I see how you withdraw from all the noise. I'd forgotten how many of us there are now.'

I am grateful for his concern, but ashamed of my inability to be more welcoming. 'I am glad they are here, but sometimes I don't have the energy for them,' I admit.

He smiles and takes my hand. 'Perhaps you should take a break from us all. You and Thomasin could take a trip to Coquet Island to see how your brother is getting on.'

I start to say that surely they cannot spare me being away, but I know very well that they can.

'Go, Grace. Put the wind back in your sails. It's a while since you and Thomasin spent time together. It will do you good to be with your sister, and William and Ann will be pleased to see you. Go. We can manage without you.'

It is those final words, more than any other, which see me agree to the trip. They can manage without me, and I, in turn, must learn to manage without them. I write to Thomasin to tell her I will arrive at North Sunderland the following Friday, from where we will take the steamer to Coquet Island. But it is with a heavy heart that I set out on the agreed date and as Longstone slips from view, I can't help feeling that I am not just leaving for a change of scenery, but that part of me will never return.

★　★　★

Coquet Island, situated a mile offshore from the fishing port of Amble, is a wonderful place and I know, at once, that it was the right decision to come here. It reminds me of Longstone in the quiet days before the events of the *Forfarshire*; reminds me of who I used to be. I hope that a brief spell among Coquet's white beaches and clear waters will see that happy carefree young woman return to me.

At low tide, when the low-lying rag stone is exposed, Thomasin and I walk around the island to the ruins of a Benedictine monastery. The

328

sandy beaches are incredibly bright in the generous sunlight, the water almost turquoise when the light catches it. Rabbits dart about among the dunes. Puffin and roseate tern nest in abundance, and I wish we could stay long enough to watch the little pufflings emerge from the burrows. My brother, William, tells me the seal colony that used to inhabit the northern end of the island has dwindled in recent years, frightened away by the pleasure-seekers brought out in the summer from the Tyne. I'm not the only one, it seems, to have been forced away from my home by unwelcome intrusions.

I write home to tell Father all about Mr. Walker's impressive lighthouse design and to reassure Mam that her dear Laddie — as William has always been affectionately known — is in fine health. I don't tell them how he walks about with his chest puffed out, so proud of his appointment as Principal Keeper here since the Duke of Northumberland ordered the recent construction of the new lighthouse.

Spending time on this peaceful little island with Thomasin is a tonic. I had forgotten what it feels like not to have a constant dread in my stomach when a boat approaches. It really is blissful, and although I miss the familiarity of Longstone, it is a shame when the time comes, too soon, for us to leave.

As the steamship slips away from the island, I stand on deck, watching the island shrink with each wave that washes us further away and closer to Alnwick. Thomasin urges me to step inside as a light rain shower becomes heavier, but I tell her

329

I don't mind the damp. As the rainwater seeps into my clothes, I feel cleansed, ready to return to the bustle and clamor of Longstone. I wrap my cloak around my shoulders until I eventually give in to the turn in the weather and reluctantly step inside to rejoin my sister. But despite the comparative warmth, I cannot shake the chill from my bones.

Thomasin chides me for staying outside so long. 'You'll catch an influenza, Grace, and Mam will blame me.'

'I promise you I won't catch an influenza, Thomasin. But you might make certain of it by fetching me a warm drink.'

She fakes annoyance and leaves me to fetch us a pot of tea.

I shiver all that afternoon and take to my bed as soon as I return to Longstone that evening.

Not even the dear old lighthouse can warm me.

44

GRACE

Longstone Lighthouse. July 1842

The summer limps on with gray skies and barely a change in temperature from the start of spring so that I never feel warm. When I'm not busy, I huddle around the fire like a woman twice my age, barely able to rouse myself even when father plays his fiddle and merriment echoes off the walls. The longer days and restless nights are peppered with a persistent cough and an ache to my chest that I cannot shake. It snatches my breath away when I exert myself and robs me of my energy so that halfway up the steps to the lantern room I have to sit down and wait for someone or other to find me, slumped like one of Georgiann's rag dolls. I have never suffered from any lingering ailment or illness so it is an unusual situation I find myself in, to be the recipient of everyone's concern.

I do my best to ignore it and continue in my work. Mam fills me with broths and hot drinks, prescribing an endless array of tinctures and poultices until the lighthouse resembles an apothecary's storeroom. I brush everyone's concern away, forcing a smile and ignoring the heat that rises, unprompted, to my cheeks.

A family friend, Mr. Shield, having heard of

my illness from my father, invites Thomasin and me to visit him in Wooler over the summer. He believes the pure air of the hills will help in my recovery. It is not yet decided whether I am strong enough to go.

Whenever I can summon the energy, I write to Thomasin who always has something encouraging or interesting to say in reply. I also begin to correspond with Mr. Emmerson again. I was desperately sad to learn of the passing of Eliza, and devastated to learn that his dear little daughter wilted like a flower without water and died only days after her mother. I was reluctant to write to him at first, but felt compelled to pass on my deepest sympathies. I am glad to have done so, as he replied quickly to say he was very pleased to hear from me and that it brightened his heart to know that old friends were well, and thinking of him during his darkest days. Our exchanges are polite and brief, without mention of what passed between us before, the years and events since having altered us both so that nothing can be as it once was.

Although my renewed correspondence with Mr. Emmerson revives my spirits, my condition does not improve. With the doctor's approval it is settled that I will travel to Wooler with Thomasin. We will stay with Mr. Shield and his wife for a few weeks, until I am feeling better.

'Return to us well, pet,' Father says. 'We would like to have the old Grace back again.'

'I would like to have her back too, Father,' I say, even though I am not even sure who the old Grace is anymore.

Perhaps Father thinks wistfully of the little girl at his knee, telling him earnestly about the eider ducklings that have hatched. Perhaps he means the contented young woman I was before the unwelcome interruption of fame, or the person he observed with a blush in her cheek when Mr. Emmerson arrived to paint my portrait. Whoever it is, I worry that she might be lost to us forever.

Wooler is a most agreeable place. It is generally agreed that the damp sea air isn't helping my condition, while the air in Wooler is crisp and clear. Thomasin assures me it will soon have me feeling well again. We take gentle pony rides in the Cheviots, where the scenery is breathtaking. I think how Mr. Emmerson would love to paint it, the bracken a burnished bronze, the sun a gold ingot dripping toward the horizon. I imagine his brow creased into a frown, the sigh and shuffle as he adjusts his posture, the little cough to indicate he is done. Whether it is the clarity of the air or the peace and space to think I cannot be sure, but I resolve to write to him again when we return to Longstone and invite him to visit. I am sure he would like to use the island as inspiration for the seascapes he has become renowned for. I confide in Thomasin as our ponies amble along the peaceful bridleway, admitting, when she presses me, that I also hope we might rekindle some of the passion we had doused through necessity.

I feel a little better that afternoon, invigorated by the fresh air and the pleasant pony ride, but still my cough won't cease and even a delicious supper of singin' hinnies and Craster kippers laid on by Mrs. Shield cannot tempt me. I excuse myself and retire early, intending to write a letter to George, but my hands ache too much to lift the pen. I fall into bed and slip away to a restless night of coughing and sweating, tossing and turning until I wake in the dawn to see Thomasin beside me, a map of concern etched across her face.

'I think we had better return home, Grace,' she whispers, pressing a cold compress to my forehead. 'You have a fever.'

There is no argument from me, apart from one. 'Will we go back to Longstone?'

She smiles and pushes my hair from my cheek. 'We will go to our cousins first, in Alnwick, since it is closer. But of course, dearest. As soon as you are recovered, Father will take you straight back to Longstone.'

It is some small reassurance. The best medicine of all is the knowledge that if I am to see my beloved Longstone, I must fight this fever with every ounce of strength I have left. If I am to go home, I must get better. But as Thomasin helps me dress, each touch of the fabric against my skin causes me to flinch and recoil, and I see the same question in her eyes that burns in my mind: What if I do not get better? What then?

★ ★ ★

From the sanctuary of the light keeper's cottage she now calls home, the new Mrs. Sarah Flaherty watches over her sleeping babies. She can hardly believe she was blessed with one, let

334

alone two, the twins having come as a great surprise to her and Eamonn. Her heart overflows with gratitude and love for little Grace Matilda and William James, named for those who once saved her, and for those whose lives were taken too soon.

It feels right that she has started a new life here on Ireland's rugged coastline. The light is different here, the air cleaner than that of the choking dockside factories in Hull. Finally, she is able to cast aside the dark melancholy she has carried with her these past years. The aching loss of her husband and children will never be forgotten, but these surprising new gifts — her gentle husband, her son and daughter, living at the edge of Ireland where America is the next landmass — have set things on a new course. She feels hopeful again.

She writes to Miss Darling to share her news, conscious that without the courage she showed on the night of the *Forfarshire* disaster, she would not be here at all, would not have had this second chance at life.

But Miss Darling does not reply, and as the weeks pass, Sarah has cause to wonder if all is quite well.

45

MATILDA

Newport, Rhode Island. September 1938

United States Weather Bureau

SEPTEMBER 9TH, 1938

Shipping data reporting tropical cyclone south of the Cape Verde Islands in the eastern Atlantic. Further monitoring to follow as necessary.

★　★　★

As the heat of the summer dissipates, the tourists close up their beach huts and holiday homes and return to their jobs and brownstone apartment buildings. Shorts and sneakers are swapped for collared shirts and heels as the carefree summer months become a series of fading memories captured in photographs on desks in the skyscraper office blocks and typing pools of the city. I watch them go with a sense of contentment, knowing that I am the lucky one who gets to stay. Even better, I get to share it all with my beautiful daughter, Grace, named for the woman who, in many ways, saved us all.

I still can't believe she is mine; that I get to keep her.

Harriet has agreed not to write to my mother since I am still a full month away from my time. 'There's no need for her to know yet,' she says. 'Have this time to yourself. Hide away if you like. There'll be time enough for other people to give opinions and advice.'

To have discovered the truth about Harriet being my birth mother should have thrown everything upside down, and yet it only seems to have set things to right. Like a house stripped of tasteless wallpaper and cleared of mismatched furniture, the space I inhabit finally makes sense. To learn that it was Harriet who had passed on the locket and the lighthouse manual completes the puzzle of the inscription to Grace Rose in the book. It is a wonder they were ever given to me at all.

'When I found them packed into the old tea chest we'd brought from Ireland, I sent them to Constance with a letter,' Harriet had told me one evening. 'I explained the family tradition of passing them on to the next generation, and what it would mean to me to know you had them. I can't say I really believed she would give them to you. I suppose she did that much right, at least.'

Harriet's revelations make sense of the distance I've always felt from Constance Emmerson. Perhaps I should feel angry about all the years of lies and fabrication, but in the flush of motherhood, I feel only pity for her. She'd never bonded with me because she'd never felt my kicks and tumbling turns, or worried about me as she lay in bed at night, or felt the agony of labor, or the exhausted ecstasy of holding her child in her arms. Constance took me into her home with the same emotional connection as a new sofa for the sitting room. A child was something she coveted, something she must have to keep up with everyone else, something she believed would fix the distance she felt toward her husband. But I was not the solution to her faltering marriage, nor to her fragile sense of self-worth, or to any of the other failings she tried to pin on my tiny shoulders. None of it was my fault after all.

Like a hermit crab casting off an old shell and finding a new one to inhabit, I adapt to the role of motherhood with surprising ease. For the first time in my life, I have found something I can do well. The maternal instincts I'd feared would be lacking rush forward in enormous waves of affection and worry. When I hold little Grace in my arms I feel the deep bonds of love I have craved all my life. Finding my mother and becoming a mother in the same intense moment has affected me profoundly.

We settle into our own rhythm, Harriet, Grace, and I. Harriet dotes on the child and I am grateful for her experience and advice and the long hours in the night when she takes over to let me rest. I sleep well, safe in the knowledge that my daughter is in my mother's arms, all of us cocooned in the embrace of the lighthouse on Rose Island. They are, without question, some of the happiest times of my life.

On warmer days, I push Grace's pram to the little beach at the north end of the island where I sit and watch the breakers and think about fate and destiny and the people we have in our lives and the people we don't. I think a lot about Cora, the sister I'd always sensed I was missing. I think of how easily our lives could have been swapped and who I might be now if I'd been the one to stay with Harriet. What might I have become if I'd grown up here? Questions without answers. All I know is that fate chose me to be the one to stay in Ireland, from where my daughter brought me back to my mother. Rebellion might have led me here, but courage, determination and love will see me stay.

Grace coos and gurgles on the blanket beside me. I lift her into my arms, rocking her in time to the rush and whisper of the sea. Harriet says I will have the child ruined, forever picking her up and carrying her around. I don't care. I scoop her up, savoring the feathery weight of her in my arms, delighting in her squirms and snuffles and the sweet nutty smell of her. I wonder who she will become, this surprise child of mine. Where she will go. It is in these quiet moments that I plan our adventures together, determined to be everything to Grace that my mother wasn't to me, determined to let her know how much I love her and that whatever storms might arrive, we will weather them together.

46

MATILDA

Newport, Rhode Island. September 1938

United States Weather Bureau

SEPTEMBER 16TH, 1938

Captain of Brazilian freighter reporting a gathering storm, north-east of Puerto Rico. Warning radioed at 3.42am. Tracking suggests it will make landfall across South Florida. Further updates to follow.

*   *   *

Early evening at the lighthouse and Harriet is knitting a bonnet for Grace. I smile at the unexpected domestic harmony of it all as I sit beside the window, watching Grace sleep, her rosebud hands curled into tiny fists at each side of her perfect little seashell ears. The radio crackles intermittently as the reporter drones on about the developing tensions in Czechoslovakia. It seems impossible that there can be talk of war when my daughter is so full of innocence.

'Hitler and Mussolini and all those other awful men should spend more time with babies,' I say. 'Maybe they wouldn't be so

340

intent on starting wars then.'

Harriet tuts. 'Men always think they have the answers,' she replies. 'They think they can invade whatever they like: countries, women's bodies . . . they thrive on the power it gives them, but they're not as smart or strong as they think they are. If we do go to war, the men will leave and it'll be the women who'll tend the lights and work in the factories and do all the jobs they don't think we're capable of doing during peacetime. It was the same last time around.'

Now that we can talk more openly, and Harriet is less guarded and more patient with my questions, I am eager to know about my family's past. 'Did you always want to be a light keeper?' I ask.

She shakes her head. 'I didn't want to be anything. I didn't have what you'd call ambition. I presumed I would become a wife and mother. Cook the dinner. Keep a tidy home.'

I raise an eyebrow at this. 'You? Really?'

She scowls good-naturedly in return. 'Falling pregnant was a blessing in a way. My da was a rare breed for his generation. He raised me on his own after mammy died in childbirth and supported me when most parents would have thrown their daughter into a mother and baby home.' I'd heard what happened to the mothers and the babies under the care of the nuns in the so-called homes. It was neither godly, nor good. 'I was lucky. Da brought me here with everything we owned in that old tea chest of his mam's. He was a good man, God rest him.'

341

I give her a moment as she crosses herself and says a little prayer. 'Where did he learn about lighthouses?' I ask when she picks up her knitting needles again. 'Has it always been in the family?'

'The Flahertys come from a long line of light keepers,' Harriet explains. 'Your great-great-granny, Sarah Flaherty — previously Dawson — dedicated her life to keeping the lights. She always said she owed her life to Grace Darling and her father. She remarried an Irishman, Eamonn Flaherty, several years after the *Forfarshire* disaster. They started a new life together in Donegal where he succeeded his father as light keeper. After her husband's death, Sarah carried on the role, and when she passed away her son became light keeper. He was reposted to Ballycotton light with his young wife just before my father, Eoin, was born. In time, he became the light keeper there until the war. Even the lights were turned off then to prevent the enemy identifying our ports and landmarks. And now, there's me. The last of the line.'

I'm fascinated to learn about the history of light keepers in the family, all stemming from my great-great-granny, Sarah.

Harriet glances over to me. 'Sure, you might consider a life in the lights yourself. I see that look in your eye when you turn on the lamp. It's in your bones. I can tell.'

She is right. Over the summer the lighthouse has become less of a landmark and more of a home, wrapping itself around my heart, holding me tight within its walls. In a funny way, it has always felt familiar to me, like a half-remembered dream. The curve of the winding stairs, the smell of salt in the walls, the smooth walnut sheen of the handrail, the steady click of the lamp as it turns. Like a living thing, I see different moods in its tapering walls: joyful in the late afternoon sun, more serious in the flat gray light of early morning, coming fully alive at night when the dark skies allow the lamp to take center stage and everyone's gaze is drawn toward it. The lighthouse has charmed me. There is no denying it.

'Would you teach me?' I ask. 'About keeping the light.'

Harriet looks at me, a wry smile on her lips. 'What do you think I've been doing these past months, bringing you over here, giving you the old light keeper's manual and newspaper reports to read and filling your head with stories of Ida Lewis and Grace Darling? You don't need me to show you, Matilda. You already know.'

* * *

The following week, after making a trip over the bay to check on things at the Cherry Street house, and to pick up some extra things for the baby, Harriet returns with a surprise.

When I hear the crunch of footsteps outside, I finish changing the baby, scoop her up into my arms, and make my way downstairs. The familiar smell of something floral tickles my nose. Lily of the valley?

'Mrs. O'Driscoll! But . . . how?' I am so shocked and pleased to see her that I burst into tears as I rush to her. She opens her arms, enfolding me and Grace in her turf-scented embrace. 'What are you doing here?' I laugh through my tears. 'I can't believe it!'

'I remembered your time was close so I wrote to Harriet at the address you gave me and didn't she kindly write back to tell me all the news and, well, here I am! But I see somebody beat me to it.' She peels back the swaddling so she can see Grace's face. 'Oh, my. She's a beauty. An absolute beauty.'

'Come and sit down,' I say, ushering her to one of the chairs and placing Grace into her arms. 'It's so good to see you. I've thought about you a lot since we said goodbye.'

She bats my hand away affectionately. 'You have not. Sure, why would you be thinking about me?'

If only she knew how many times I've picked up that scrap of paper and read the word she'd added beneath her address: courage. 'I meant to write to tell you about the baby but I haven't had a chance.'

'Well, no. I expect you've had your hands full.'

Harriet makes tea as we swap all our news and I confide in Mrs. O'Driscoll about my plan to stay here with baby Grace and not go back to Ireland. She isn't at all surprised.

'Well I'm glad,' she says as she coos and fusses over the baby. ''Tis only right that the child should be with its mother. I think you're a very brave young woman, Matilda Emmerson. Didn't

344

I say this could be the making of you?'

'You did. You didn't tell me how awful labor is though.'

She smiles. 'Of course not. I didn't want to put the fear of God into you now, did I? By the way,' she says, lowering her voice to a whisper as Grace falls asleep in her arms. 'I didn't come because your mother sent me, so don't be worrying. She doesn't even know I'm here, and I'm certainly not going to be telling her. That's your business. Not mine.'

I take her hand in mine. 'Actually, Mrs. O'Driscoll, there's something I have to tell you.'

★   ★   ★

Mrs. O'Driscoll agrees to stay for lunch and then for tea and then she agrees to stay the night. Harriet doesn't like the look of the waves and she knows the combination of the autumnal equinox and the full moon will bring a particularly high tide. I am delighted to have more time with Mrs. O'Driscoll and we talk long into the evening.

A flame-red harvest moon hangs low in the sky over Narragansett Bay. I sit at the window and watch the stars come out and I have never seen a sky more beautiful. I close my eyes as I rest my cheek against Grace's velvet-soft hair, rocking her in time to the song of the wind at the windows. I sing to her of lavenders blue and lavenders green and despite the gathering threat of war, here in my tower of light with the sea sighing below me and the wind circling the walls, the world has never felt safer, and life has never felt more perfect or peaceful.

47

GRACE

Alnwick, England. September 1842

We remain for a week with our cousins, the MacFarlanes, in Narrowgate, but the house stands in shadows and I feel myself wither like a plant devoid of sunlight. Learning of my continued illness, the Duchess of Northumberland arranges for me to be moved to a property in Prudhoe Street, much better positioned for sunlight and air. She also offers the expert medical advice of the duke's physician, Dr. Barnfather. He is a bespectacled gangling gentleman, who prods and pokes at me with various instruments while Thomasin and the duchess hover by my side, eager to learn of some improvement. But despite their prayers and hopes he confirms in a whisper that my symptoms leave him in no doubt that I suffer from the consumption.

The word hangs above us all like a thick fog, the darkened room silent apart from the ominous tick of the carriage clock on the mantelpiece, all of us suddenly aware of precious minutes disappearing. I ask them to leave me alone for a while, their evident distress only making mine worse.

In this way, long hours and days pass. I am

grateful that I am so well cared for, but I ache to return to Longstone.

'I am certain I would feel much better if I returned to the lighthouse, Doctor,' I explain.

But he insists the journey is too far for my body to cope with. 'I am sorry, Grace, but I cannot give my consent. It is too great a risk.'

How can I explain to a practical man of medicine and science that by being away from Longstone I feel like a stranded fish, starved of the things I need in order to flourish, to survive, to breathe? How can a man of the land understand my deep affection for rugged rocks and crashing waves? I think how easily I would once have made the journey, rowing the coble with ease between Longstone and North Sunderland. Perhaps I might have appreciated such simple pleasures more if I'd known how few of them remained. There are many things I might have done differently if I had known what these autumn months would bring.

I write a few lines to Sarah Dawson in Ireland, or Sarah Flaherty as I must now think of her. As I had once promised myself I would, now is the time for me to show the same courage that she once did, broken and huddled beside the fire at Longstone.

As I have seen too many times, life can change as quickly as the tide and despite the care of the best physician in the country, and despite the duchess kneeling by my bedside to offer her prayers for my recovery, I decline with each setting of the sun, and there is nothing to be done about it.

48

MATILDA

Newport, Rhode Island. 21st September, 1938

United States Weather Bureau

SEPTEMBER 21ST, 1938

Hurricane force gusts reported at Bellport, Long Island, with sustained winds reaching 120 mph. All instruments and information confirm a category three hurricane is on a direct collision course with Rhode Island. There is no time to send a warning.

★   ★   ★

I wake from a nap to see the blue afternoon sky has turned a curious shade of violet, like a deep bruise. Fishermen in the bay notice the same ominous sky and turn back to seek shelter in the harbor, their vessels rocked by a sudden and violent swell. On the beaches, visitors scramble to pack their picnic baskets away as sun hats are blown from heads, and parasols take flight while the seabirds shelter on the shore.

I place Grace gently in her cot where she sleeps peacefully and take up the binoculars from the table, scanning the water for any sign of

Harriet or Joseph, who should both be making their way back from town. The wind howls outside. The rain lashes the windows. The trees along the shoreline bend like bread dough. Mrs. O'Driscoll stands at the window beside me, both of us afraid to voice our fears.

Over the course of an hour, the skies turn from violet to black, and in the distance I hear the growl of thunder. Picking up the telescope again I scan the horizon and realize it isn't thunder. It is the ocean. A massive tidal surge races toward the shore, a wall of unstoppable water breaking over the beaches, rushing up to the lowest houses, wave after wave of angry gray water, reaching higher and higher until the clapboard houses on the wharf side are engulfed. I think about Joseph and Harriet, out there somewhere, and I know with a terrible certainty that the only safe place right now is here, in the lighthouse.

Downstairs, I hear a frantic barking, and a scratching and scraping at the door.

'Captain!'

I rush downstairs and open the door, the roar of the wind deafening as I scoop the little dog up into my arms, not caring that she is soaked. Pushing the door shut with my foot, I rush to the window, rubbing at the misted-up glass with my sleeve, looking for Joseph. I can't see him anywhere.

'Where is he, Captain?'

Dark thoughts clutter my mind as my instincts tell me to get as high as I can. I urge Mrs. O'Driscoll to follow me up to the lantern room, baby Grace clutched tight to my chest, Captain trotting faithfully along at my heels. As we reach the top of the lighthouse, I turn to the windows to see the storm surge, two stories high, is nearly upon us and in that moment, all the glittering lights from the houses along the shoreline flicker once before going out, plunging everything into darkness.

49

HARRIET

As I lock the door of the house on Cherry Street, the behavior of the birds first alerts me to something sinister. Great flocks head in from the sea, a dark mass flying overhead. People around me stop to look up, remarking on how strange it is, but I notice the color of the sky, the unmistakable hue of a storm. I hurry to the boat, my only thought to get back to Matilda and the baby at the lighthouse. I don't like the look of the water, but I have to try.

The rain falls in sideways sheets that land like needles against my skin. Heavy rollers crash against the harbor wall, sending the boats anchored there rearing and dipping like wild horses. The trees along the boulevard bend wildly as I run past them, the branches snapping easily, like tinder cracked over a bent knee. Fallen power lines sag like cooked spaghetti between swaying telegraph poles as street signs clatter wildly down the street. Leaf litter and garbage from overturned bins swirls around my sodden feet. The water is rising. I make a note of the time. Two o'clock.

Relieved to reach the boat and yet daunted by what confronts me, I push off from the harbor and brace myself for a battle. This is my storm, my chance to set things right. All the years of loss and anger are carried in the wind that screeches in great gusts and rocks the boat wildly. I tell myself not to fear it but to embrace it, pulling hard on the oars, relishing the deep burn in my arms because with each pull and each strain on my muscles, I move closer to Rose Island. One last battle, I tell myself. One last chance at redemption.

In my mind I see Cora and her little dog, drifting away in calm seas, caught in a rip too fast for me to react to. I set my course and my mind to the task ahead.

'You won't beat me,' I shout, the rain blinding me as a wave turns me head-on to the driving wind. 'Not this time.'

As the storm and I continue our duel, and as I slowly approach the lighthouse, the lamps burst into life and my heart surges with a fresh wave of energy because I know Matilda is there, guiding me home.

I struggle on, almost at the landing steps when she appears at the lighthouse door.

'Harriet!' she cries. 'Thank God. Hurry! It's getting worse.'

'Get back inside,' I yell as I struggle to control the boat. 'It isn't safe.'

Seeing that I'm in difficulty, she runs toward the landing steps. 'Harriet!' she cries, shouting above the violent screech of the wind. 'I'm scared. What can I do to help?'

Behind her a wall of water approaches, but she can't see it. 'Get back!' I scream. 'Get inside!' But my words are torn apart by the roar of the water and with a horrifying crash it is upon us.

My boat is thrown up into a great wave as Matilda is knocked from her feet and dragged into the water.

50

GRACE

Bamburgh, England. October 1842

October, and the late afternoon sun paints the waves gold around Longstone Island. The rays cast an amber glow against the lighthouse tower, illuminating the lantern room where Father is making preparations to light the lamp. Downstairs, Mam sits at her spinning wheel and rubs the dull ache at the small of her back. She would complain, but there is nobody about to complain to. Beyond the window, my brother oversees the construction of the cottages where he and his family will soon live, while my grieving sister Mary Ann takes the washing off the line. She misses her husband dearly, but keeps her grief hidden away, like a cockle inside its shell.

The feverish whirl of images keeps me company in my sister's home in Bamburgh, my father having insisted on moving me from the accommodations in Alnwick. I take some small comfort from being closer to home, back among the walls of the pretty sandstone village where I was born, but I wish, more than anything, to return to Longstone where the comings and goings of life are so familiar that even when I am not there, I can easily imagine that I am.

I miss the rhythmic breaths of the tide, the

355

soothing whisper of the sea, the happy cry of the terns and the kittiwakes. I miss the sense of this vast earth you only get when you stand at the very edge of it, as I have done since 1 was a child.

In my delirium, I lie in bed, drifting in and out of sleep. Occasionally, I hear a knock at the door, another well-wisher or reporter come to inquire about my health and to pass on their prayers for my recovery. They mean well, but it is tiresome for Thomasin to forever repeat the same sorry tale of my lack of improvement. I hear her weeping and wish I had the strength to comfort her.

The duchess visits often, sitting quietly by my bedside day and night. She brings posies of sweet violets to brighten the cheerless little room. She tries to be brave, but I know it distresses her greatly to watch me wither and wilt.

In the afternoon, I hear my sister converse with another caller downstairs. Gentle footsteps on the stairs beyond the bedroom door set the boards creaking like tired old bones before Thomasin pushes open the heavy door and peers into the gloom.

'Grace, pet? Are you awake?' Her voice is as soft as goose down. Everyone talks to me in whispers these past weeks, as if they might damage me with too much noise.

My eyes flicker weakly against the thin strip of light that plays at the edge of the shuttered window. It lends a becoming glow to Thomasin's face. I want to tell her she looks pretty in her new bonnet, ribbons the color of eider duck eggs, but I can't summon the energy.

She clutches a rectangular parcel to her chest. 'I've something for you,' she says secretively, walking toward the bed, where she leans down to whisper in my ear, holding back long enough to stir my pulse in anticipation. 'A gift from George.'

Joy rushes to my lips at his name, but I can't easily shape them into a smile.

'A book, by all accounts,' she adds, resting the parcel against the ewer on the washstand as she unbuttons her gloves. 'Although a very large book by the look of it.' She helps me to sit up briefly so she can plump my pillows.

'Is he here?' My voice is barely a whisper.

She nods and gently squeezes my hand. 'He is downstairs, but he bid me not to disturb you if you were sleeping.' A smile dances in her eyes. My sister knows the extent of my devotion to George Emmerson. She has sent word to him of my condition over the past long weeks. She knows that to see him will cause my heart to bloom like a summer rose. 'Will I tell him to come up?'

I nod.

There is a hushed exchange beyond the door before hesitant footsteps enter and he is here.

'Dear Miss Darling.' He sits at the little chair beside the bed, his hat in his hands, his eyes barely able to look at me, at the pale imitation of myself I have become. 'I will not stay long. I only wished to see you for a moment.'

I try to smile. 'I am glad.'

He looks at me with such sadness in his eyes.

357

'I should not have left it so long.'

'But you are here now,' I say and only wish I had the energy I'd felt on the night of the storm when we stood outside on the lantern gallery. What would I say if we could have those moments again?

His eyes settle on the locket at my neck. 'You still wear it,' he says.

I reach my fingers to the clasp, but I am too weak to open it. Seeing my struggle, his hands reach forward and he opens it for me, his fingers brushing fleetingly against my skin. He smiles to see his portraits keep safely inside.

'A perfect fit,' he whispers.

He sits for a long while as I drift in and out of sleep, my eyes flickering open to see him still sitting there, watching me, loving me.

'Are you painting me, Mr. Emmerson?' I ask as the light fades at the window.

'I am, Miss Darling. Yes.'

There is so much more to say and yet nothing to say at all.

When I open my eyes again the room is in darkness, lit only by the soft flame of a candle. Mr. Emmerson is gone.

Thomasin brushes her fingertips against my forehead, frowning at the intense heat she feels there. 'You're too hot, Grace. Can I get you anything? Water? A cold compress?'

I motion to the windowsill.

Understanding that I want the conch shell that sits there, she passes it to me with a tender smile. 'You and your shells,' she says with affection. 'You always loved to collect them, didn't you?'

The crack in her voice betrays her emotion. I smile weakly as she fusses at the counterpane, as if by tugging it free of its crumples and wrinkles she might smooth away my illness. 'Try to get some rest, pet. Doctor Barnfather is due a little later.'

I sigh at the prospect. He's a good man and it is very kind of the duke to arrange for his physician to attend me, but I am tired of the doctor's ministrations. I am tired of lying here in this bed, in this room, so far from home.

Thomasin sees the frown across my brow. 'Now, Grace. You're not to be grousing. Let him take care of you and he'll have you sitting up singing one of your sea shanties before the week is out. Then we can get you back to Longstone, where you belong.'

She smiles with the effort of a mother reassuring an anxious child, and closes the door quietly behind her, leaving me alone with my thoughts and the melodic hubbub of an ordinary market day beyond the window. Except nothing is ordinary anymore. Everything is laced with a strange poignancy. Will this be the last time I hear a market day beyond the window? Is this the last time I will see my sister's bonny face peering around the bedroom door?

Slowly, I turn my cheek to the right, my gaze settling on the rectangular parcel wrapped in brown paper, tied with string. 'A book, by all accounts . . . '

It isn't a book. Without opening it, I know it is his portrait of me.

I can still see his hands moving briskly over

359

the canvas, the gentle furrow in his brow, the way he licked his lips in quiet concentration, the shy glances we shared as he worked. I have never been looked at that way before, nor since. I hardly dared breathe, such was the intensity in his eyes. I remember how the breeze set the ribbons of my bonnet fluttering around my cheeks as we'd walked outside and how my skirts ballooned like a church bell swaying in the rafters, the motion setting my thoughts to his impending wedding and the bells that would ring out in celebration of the happy union. I remember so clearly the look on his face as he quietly observed me, remember his remark that I came alive outdoors. That I became something more.

Beyond the narrow window, milk churns clatter against each other as a cart rumbles over the cobbles. Peddlers shout their wares. The fishwives gossip on street corners, their creels full of fresh herring. Children laugh at a street entertainer. I close my eyes, too weary to do anything but press the creamy white edge of the conch shell to my ear and listen to the sound of the sea, and a lifetime of memories captured inside.

51

MATILDA

Newport, Rhode Island. September 1938

The last thing I see is Harriet's face as the great wave knocks me off my feet and I am thrown into the water. I gasp for air as I break the surface, my feet searching for the rocks around the bottom of the island. 'Harriet!' I shout. 'Harriet!' But I can't see her.

My pink housedress becomes heavy, tangling around my legs so that for all my efforts I don't make any progress as I try desperately to swim back to the steps. I turn onto my back, remembering my father's reassuring voice beside me when he taught me to swim. *'Keep kicking. I have you. I won't let go.'* But this is no gentle sunlit bay, and I am entirely at the mercy of the water.

A huge wave blindsides me, pushing me beneath the surface again before carrying me up, where I splutter and gasp for air, but the next wave comes immediately after and is bigger still. It lifts me up, rolls me over, and sucks me down on the undertow, pressing my face into the rocks before rolling me over and over so that I don't know which way is up. Beneath the water, I kick and flail, instinct insisting I fight for breath.

I surface again, and Harriet is in front of me.

We lock eyes for a moment as our hands reach out for each other, but the motion of the water pulls us apart and I go under again.

I open my eyes. The sweep of the light crosses the surface above me and I start to kick toward it, fixing my gaze on the flashes of alternating light and darkness, determined to get back to my baby, and from nowhere I remember a song my granny used to sing to me — ' *'Twas on the Longstone lighthouse, There dwelt an English maid, Pure as the air around her, Of danger ne'er afraid . . .* '

When I break the surface this time I am farther away from the lighthouse. My breaths are shallow, my arms and legs exhausted with my efforts. I tip my head back and open my mouth wide, gasping for air, but another wave takes me beneath the water and I am too weak to kick anymore.

Above me, the light turns and flashes once more before plunging the water into darkness and I feel the light within me flicker and begin to fade . . .

52

HARRIET

I jump out of the boat and reach for Matilda but my fingertips just miss the fabric of her dress as I am pushed under, and she rushes past me in a surge of water, and is gone.

Beneath the waves I open my eyes, frantically looking for her, above and below me, but the water is thick with silt and debris and I am blind. The muffled silence betrays the chaos taking place above. My lungs burn with the desire to breathe as I kick for the surface, and as I break through the water she is in front of me.

A wave pushes me toward her and for a moment we hold each other's gaze and all the lost years and all the heartache and despair distill down into that one final frantic moment. When faced with the ultimate choice of living or dying we perhaps know ourselves better than ever. I try desperately to grab her hands, but she goes under again.

With one last breath, I dive beneath the water and reach for her, my fingertips gripping her wrist as I drag her up until we both break free of the water. I flip onto my back and kick with every ounce of strength in my body, determined to save her, determined not to lose her again. A wave carries us forward, smashing us beside the horseshoe-shaped beach. I take my chance and scramble onto the rocks, not caring for the way the sharp edges scrape and tear at my skin as I drag Matilda behind me.

A dead weight in my arms I struggle to pull her out of the water. I grit my teeth and use all my strength, never more grateful for the swell that helps me haul her up and onto land. She slides from my grasp and slumps onto the rocks, her head hitting the stones with a sickening thud.

I fall to my knees and push her hair from her face and start pumping at her chest and breathing into her mouth. *One, two, three, four, breathe, breathe . . . One, two, three, four, breathe, breathe . . .* Her lips are the palest violet. Her skin gray as dust. Her hair is matted and speckled with sand that glistens when the beam of the light settles on us.

Leaning back on my heels, I grip my head, my fingers like a vice. 'Breathe, Matilda! You've got to breathe! Breathe!' I scream at her, lean forward, and start again.

One, two, three, four, breathe, breathe.
One, two, three, four, breathe, breathe.

I pump as hard as I dare while the wind howls above and I press my face to hers and will my child to breathe, to stay with me, gasping for air as I give her whatever I can spare, not caring if I give her my last breath, as long as she wakes up. And then a sudden jerk in my arms and she convulses violently as water shoots from her mouth. Quickly, I roll her onto her side, holding her head so she can eject the seawater from her lungs. Still it keeps coming as she gasps and splutters.

'That's it, Matilda. Breathe. You'll be all right now. Everything'll be all right.'

She coughs again as I shush and soothe her as she huddles against my chest, finding her breath, grasping on to the life that had so nearly left her. Gradually, her breathing regulates and the color returns to her lips and cheeks. Only then does she look at me, blue-black eyes fixing on mine, and without words or explanation, we cling to each other for all the years we have missed, and everything we ever needed is right there in our arms.

We stand up then, stumbling together toward the lighthouse as fast as we can, both of us convulsing with cold and shock, but I slip on the rocks as Matilda reaches the lighthouse door, and as I try to stand up another huge wave sweeps me back into the heaving ocean.

The water engulfs me, pulling me down. For a moment I struggle, but I know I don't have the energy to fight it and all I can think is that Matilda and Grace are safe in the lighthouse.

Quietly, I accept my fate.

Everything becomes strangely calm as I close my eyes and I know that for all my shortcomings and imperfections, I loved my children with the passion of a storm and that, in the end, it is perhaps all we can ever hope for. To have loved, and to have been loved in return.

When I open my eyes, Cora is there. She takes my hand and together we become the fragments of light captured on the surface of the water, carried eternally on by the tides.

53

MATILDA

Newport, Rhode Island. September 1938

For two hours the great storm tears apart the town that gave me a home and a place of sanctuary when I needed it most. For two relentless hours it releases its fury, and then it is over. The great storm leaves as suddenly as it arrived, the turbulent skies washed away by a warm and generous sun. Newport is ripped apart, and my heart with it.

Joseph is here, and Mrs. O'Driscoll. Baby Grace and Captain. I wake to them all, and to silence. The storm has said its piece.

'Hey, you.' Joseph sits by the side of the bed, a shy smile crossing his face when my eyes meet his.

'Is it over?' I ask.

He nods. 'It's over.'

He explains how he arrived at the lighthouse just before the storm surge hit. 'Captain jumped out of the boat. I'd seen Harriet set out behind me, so I went back to try and help her. The water was crazy. But I got caught in a rip and swept around to the far side of the island. The boat was damaged on the rocks so I sheltered in the old fog signal tower until the worst was over.'

I wince when I try to lift my head. 'Harriet?'

He lifts his eyes to meet mine and takes my hand. A slow shake of the head confirms what I already knew. 'I'm so sorry, Matilda.'

Tears fall down my cheeks. 'She saved me,' I whisper, my words choked by my sobs. 'She saved my life.'

Joseph wraps me in his arms. 'It's what a lighthouse keeper does, Matilda. It's what she dedicated her life to doing.'

In the stories I made up as a little girl, my characters always had a mother who loved them. Perhaps I imagined Harriet so hard that, in the end, she became real. Harriet offered me a home, knowing she was inviting far more than a pregnant young woman into her life. She cared for me without smothering me, and she brought my daughter safely into the world when everyone else only wanted to take her away from me. Harriet Flaherty saved me in more ways than I ever thought possible.

I give in to the deep well of emotion I've carried for so long and I cry until my bones ache with the agony of it all, until the storm of my grief subsides and I shelter in the harbor of sleep, safe in the arms of the lighthouse. When I wake up to see little Grace gazing back at me, I know it will somehow all be okay. In giving her life to save mine, Harriet has given this little girl a mother. It is the ultimate sacrifice, and I hope I would have the courage to do the same, if the same were asked of me.

I'm so glad Joseph is safe and glad, too, of Mrs. O'Driscoll, who takes charge of us all, soothing the baby while I sleep, feeding us all, tending to the nasty gash on the back of my head. We spend long days and nights together, cocooned at the lighthouse, until Joseph goes back across the bay when it is safe to do so, returning with shocking tales of death and devastation.

'The storm began as a tropical cyclone off the Cape Verde islands some weeks ago,' he explains. 'It hit the New England coast with the full force of a category three hurricane. The tidal surge was so powerful that nothing in its path was spared.'

All along the coast, from Providence to Connecticut, Martha's Vineyard and Long Island, entire communities have been swept away, a trail of devastation and grief left in the hurricane's wake.

Newport suffers its own pain. When I am eventually strong enough to row across the harbor, I can barely believe what I'm seeing. The houses on Cherry Street don't exist anymore, erased from their foundations like dirt scrubbed from a muddy trouser knee. Where warm homes stood only days earlier, there is nothing but a tangle of wood and debris. Like chicken bones left after a feast, the sea has gorged itself.

The death toll rises daily. Three hundred dead. Five hundred. Over six hundred is the final tally. Even so, there are too few of our loved ones to bury. We search for days, but we never find Harriet. I like to think she is with Cora again and I hope that in saving me, she was, in her final moments, finally able to find peace.

And so it is that among these flooded streets and flattened homes and boats turned upside down, I find my future. There is no greater turning point than a disaster on this scale. The choice of what I do next is mine. I have been given a second chance to put things right, to make amends, to live my best life. When I look into little Grace's eyes, I know that *she* is the reason I was spared — and I will not let it go to waste.

I write to Constance Emmerson to tell her everything and to explain that I will not be giving up my child or returning to Ireland. I tell her I don't expect to hear from her, but that — for what it's worth — I wish her well. To my father, I say only that I am sorry to have disappointed him, but that I can feel no remorse or regret when I have such a beautiful child in my arms. I hope that, one day, he might understand.

Mrs. O'Driscoll stays for a month, helping to set things right. Joseph salvages a few things from his home, moving temporarily into the lighthouse while the town is rebuilt. Together we create a sense of family, unconventional though it is. I like to think Harriet would be happy to hear these walls filled with love and laughter again. She was never one to follow convention. I think it would please her to see the four of us, muddling through together. In quiet moments, I reflect on how far I have come since leaving Heartbreak Pier, so uncertain and unsure of myself. I am happy to know that the loose threads of my past have finally been connected to my present. Like a found piece of a jigsaw puzzle or a stray button reattached, I am back where I belong.

The locket was spared by the water, but I am so sad to have lost the miniature portraits of George Emmerson and Grace Darling. I replace them with a lock of baby Grace's hair, the ripples of family history carrying on.

As things begin to settle into something like normality, I take George's letter from behind the portrait of Grace Darling and open the envelope again. I sit in a bright patch of sunlight, unfold the crinkled old pages, and read the words he wrote so long ago to the woman he loved but could never be with.

Dundee. October, 1838.

My dear Miss Darling,

I know you have quite had your fill of letters lately, but this one requires no reply, so please bear with me while I try to capture the landscape of my heart with my words, rather than my brush.

The thing is, Miss Darling, you have touched my soul these past months, especially during recent days as the storm raged beyond the lighthouse walls. I was not a bit sorry to be stranded. Delighted, in fact. While I captured your likeness on my canvas, you, in turn, captured my heart.

Just as your love of the island binds you to Longstone, so my engagement binds me to another. You tell me you will never marry because your duty lies with your parents and the light. Knowing that you are prepared to make this sacrifice for your parents only makes my affection for you even greater.

Although through circumstance we must be parted, please know that I did not leave Longstone easily. Indeed, my return to Dundee was, perhaps, one of the hardest journeys I have ever made. I doubted myself with every turn of the carriage wheels, wondering if I should have said more, wishing I had found the courage to tell you, Miss Darling, that I love you.

But like the storm that brought us together, the moment has passed, and now there can be only silence. As we may never know the true depths of the seas, so it must be that you will never know the true depth of my feelings for you.

I will remember you when I listen to the sigh of the sea held inside the conch shell and I hope you might remember me occasionally when you look at the portraits inside your locket. If I cannot be with you, I will take some small comfort from knowing that a little piece of me rests close to your heart.

Perhaps Mr. Dickens put it best when he wrote the words, 'I wish you to know that you have been the last dream of my soul.' I can say nothing more, Miss Darling. I only hope that having been parted from you, I *will find you, once again, in my dreams.*

> *Yours, always.*
> George Emmerson

George's words settle around my heart like a sign as I place the letter back behind the portrait of Grace. I hope she knew how much he loved her.

With my daughter settled in her pram, I take up a yard brush and begin to tidy the lower rooms of the lighthouse, Ida Lewis and Grace Darling watching over me as I work. As the sun begins to set that evening, I light an old hand lamp and ascend the steps to the lantern room.

There is much work to be done.

54

GRACE

Bamburgh, England. October 1842

There are many ways in which a person can be saved. Sometimes among raging seas and wild winds. Sometimes with nothing more than a paintbrush and a gentle smile sent through shafts of winter sunlight. I have known both.

Over a dozen artists came to Longstone in the months following the *Forfarshire* disaster, but George Emmerson was the only one to truly capture me in every way possible, before setting me free so that I might stay in the place I love more than any other. I rest my gaze on his portrait of me. When I look into my eyes, captured so perfectly on the canvas, I see a young woman full of vigor and passion and I am grateful to have lived my short life so fully. Just as the portrait is unfinished, so must be the long and happy life I had always hoped would be mine.

Thomasin tells me that George called in again on his way to Durham last week, but I was sleeping and he refused to disturb me. She tells me he sat at my bedside for over an hour in quiet contemplation.

I know I shall not see him again.

As I listen to the wind in the eaves and the

joyful sounds of life beyond the casement window, my thoughts drift back over my twenty-six years, seeking out memories of the people and places I have loved the most. Those unexpected days with George at the lighthouse were, perhaps, some of the loveliest I have known, full of moments so tender and precious they turn my heart to pure ruby to remember them.

They call me a heroine, but I am not deserving of such accolades. I am just a young woman who did her duty; a young woman who had more to lose from her fame than she had to gain. It is still incomprehensible to me that they write poems and ballads and plays about Grace Darling — Heroine of the Farne Isles.

In the weeks and months that followed the rescue, many words and opinions were printed about my bravery. That a woman could set out in such violent seas was the very essence of heroism. Now, in these quiet days at my sister's home, I understand that this is not about a single act of bravery. The name Grace Darling has come to represent courage, and it is that — not the trinkets and tableware bearing my name — which I can be proud of.

My sister tells me I am feverish and speak of strange things in my sleep. I hear her telling the duchess that I am become like snow, melting in the spring thaw. Nothing can save me from this disease that sets my skin aflame and steals the breath from my lungs as easily as a footpad might steal a lady's purse on the turnpike.

There is no more saving to be done.

The light fades against the window, and I, with it.

I have asked my family to come to my bedside. Those who can, come quickly, knowing there is not much time. Mam is here, and my dear father. My brother, Brooks. My sisters, Thomasin and Mary Ann. I have a small trinket for each of them, a little treasured something that they might remember me by in the years ahead: my gold medal for my father, my silver watch for my mother, a silk handkerchief for Thomasin, my plaid shawl for Mary Ann, my collection of sea treasures for Brooks. To Mr. Emmerson, I leave my collection of fossils and ask that he might give his portrait of me to his sister. The cameo locket that Sarah had so kindly given to me, I also ask to be returned, for her daughter to wear when she is old enough; the circle complete. As I pass it to Thomasin for safekeeping, I think of the inscription engraved on the back: *Even the brave were once afraid.*

I need more courage now than ever.

Late evening, and another golden day slips away with the setting sun. My father takes my hand in his and tells me to get some rest. I feel his fingers, warm and paper dry as they wrap themselves around mine, like rope coiling neatly back into place. I hold on as I close my eyes and wait for darkness to fall, when the lamps will be lit and Longstone will send out its

THE BERWICK ADVERTISER
29TH OCTOBER, 1842

The funeral took place on 24th October of Grace Horsley Darling who died at Bamburgh on October 20th at 8:15pm, surrounded by her family. At an early hour of the afternoon, gentlemen from a distance of many miles round, began to arrive, and at the hour appointed, 3 o'clock pm, the village was crowded with strangers, both rich and poor, many of whom had come a long way to pay their last respects to the memory of the deceased. An immense concourse of people of all grades in society followed the coffin to the grave, many of whom were observed to be bathed in tears. The scene, altogether, was deeply impressive and affecting. The coffin was carried by four young men of Bamburgh, and followed by four pall bearers, William Barnfather, her doctor in Alnwick, and a representative of the castle, Robert Smeddle, representing Bamburgh Castle and the Crewe Trustees, the Reverend M. Taylor of North Sunderland, and Dr. Fender, the Bamburgh doctor.

There was also a young man from Durham, who wore the mourning emblem of intimate friends of the family.

55

GEORGE

Bamburgh, England. October 1842

George Emmerson sits in the church for a long time, watching sunlight stream through the stained glass windows. He turns a piece of indigo sea glass over in his hands, wishing, with all his heart, that he could hold the hand that gave it to him. The treasure of the sea, she called it. *'I've always found it fascinating that an ordinary medicine bottle can become something so beautiful over time. Don't you agree, Mr. Emmerson?'* He recalls his reply. *'I suppose, in time, anything can become treasure to someone, Miss Darling.'* He pictures her slender face, the slight compression of her lip, the wreath of sunny brown curls on her head, the slight frown across her brow as if she couldn't quite grasp the measure of him and needed to concentrate harder to do so.

Grace Darling. Her name still conjures a smile, despite the ache in his heart.

As the generous autumn sun reflects a rainbow of color at his feet, he thinks about the short years in which he had the joy of Miss Darling's acquaintance. He wonders many things in those silent hours, but mostly he wonders if things might have been different if he had said everything he wanted to say, if he'd spoken aloud the words in his letter. If he'd had the courage to follow his heart, might she sit beside him now?

From the first time he met her among the sand dunes at Dunstanburgh, he sensed in Miss Darling a spirit that would not bend and bow to convention. She was a woman of her own mind, so that even after Eliza's death, he knew it would not be right to ask for her hand in marriage. It would have placed her in an impossible position, forced her to make an impossible decision. It must be enough then to have spent time with her, to have fallen quietly in love with her without the promise of anything more. Like sea-foam against the sand, promises can quickly dissipate. His feelings for Miss Darling transcend anything so impermanent.

What he feels for her is captured in the portrait he sketched of her that breezy day among the rocks where she so loved to be. It is imperfect, incomplete, but it is the truest likeness of her he ever saw. The questions in her eyes. The fluttering of her bonnet ribbons, as if she might fly away if she cared to. Like the seabirds chasing the wind, she would not be captured or pinned down. And he would not be the one to try.

Darkness falls across the church until the only light is that of a crescent moon and the distant flicker of the light from Longstone; a beacon of remembrance for a young woman who did so much for so many, and who never once considered herself to be anything other than a humble lighthouse keeper's daughter. It is that for which George admires her the most. Not for the courage she showed in saving his sister and the others, but for the courage she showed in the months and years that followed; the courage to remain true to herself and all that she valued in life. As he leaves the church, he pauses at her grave, knowing that life will always be that bit darker now without her in it.

He walks then. Somewhere. Anywhere. He takes a creamy white conch shell from his coat pocket and presses it to his ear. Within it, he hears the gentle sigh of the sea and the whispered words of a woman he loved with all his heart. In her memory he will live his best and most courageous life. He will live a life not of quiet breezes, but of the wildest storms.

That is his final promise to her.

56

MATILDA

Newport, Rhode Island. September 1939

The skies to the north bloom in shades of peach and rose, a glorious celebration of Grace's first birthday. She wriggles on my lap, eager to get into the water, my little mermaid child. I draw her close into the folds of my skirt as we watch the sunrise together.

The past year has been swept away in a blur of rocking and playing, worrying and loving. I can hardly believe how quickly she has grown, how she can already stand and take her first tentative steps. She is in a rush, it seems, to get on with life. Her enthusiasm is infectious.

I pick shells from the shore and pass them to her, watching her tiny fingers as they feel their way around the edge until she remembers how to grip them. She studies them for a moment, tries to eat them, and then passes them back to me, taking a far greater pleasure in her ability to give than to receive. She leans forward to grab the locket at my neck, mesmerized by the way the light catches it and how it spins when I lean forward. When she is old enough, I will give her the lighthouse keeper's book and the locket, and I'll tell her about her great-great-great-granny Sarah, and how she was rescued by Grace

Darling, and I'll also tell her about an artist called George, who loved Grace with all his heart and wrote it all down in a letter. And I will give her a photograph, taken on that quiet September morning before the storm. An image of a strong, courageous woman who would give her life so that I could live mine. I will tell her all about her brave granny, Harriet Flaherty, and all the brave women who came before her.

I am mammy and daddy to Grace, but I am not alone. Joseph is here whenever I need him and Mrs. O'Driscoll, too. Having settled on Long Island after the hurricane, she visits often, subtly advising and helping without ever trying to change or control me. Life will always be a little mis-shapen, but I sense the women from my past walking beside me, giving me the strength to go on, no matter how difficult things become. I am buoyed by the knowledge of them, and by the tiny footprints that pattern the sand beside mine.

I take Grace's hand and we walk to the edge of the shore and watch the gentle breaking of the waves. Grace grips my thumb, squealing with the thrill of the water splashing against her knees. My darling little girl. My bright beacon of light.

When she tires of her games I scoop her up into my arms and make my way back to the lighthouse, singing to her of lavenders blue and lavenders green. She gazes up at me with eyes the color of winter seas and I see in her some greater wisdom; as if she understands that she is not just my daughter, but the sum of generations of strong courageous women who came before her, an echo of them all lingering in her soul.

Epilogue

Longstone Lighthouse

Dawn tiptoes over the Farne Islands with soft layers of rose-tinted clouds, the morning light settling along the ripples in the sand. On the mainland the fisherwomen stand beside their creels, waiting for the herring fleet to return. At their feet, their daughters chase their shadows, blown along by a bright breeze.

I turn my gaze to the soaring tower of the lighthouse, its walls holding my family close within. I watch my father extinguish the lamps and stand at the window with his telescope, tracking a flock of sandwich terns as they soar past, their white bellies gilded by the rising sun. I rush forward, rising and falling on the thermals with them, swooping and turning, as free as the undulating waves below and the lively wind that surrounds me.

My father's face is etched with sadness. He feels an emptiness without me beside him.

But I am here, Father, I cry, wheeling and circling with the gulls. *I am here! Look!*

I am the soft breeze that ruffles the hem of Mam's skirts as she stands at the lighthouse door. I am the fragments of sea glass waiting for the eager little hands of my nieces and nephews to find me among the rocks and pebbles at low tide. I am the glint of sunlight that catches the surface of the sea, and the soft breath of wind felt against hands and cheeks. I am temperate summer days and wild winter storms. I am the light that shines to warn those at sea, and a light of remembrance for those who could not be saved.

I am a daughter, a sister, a name, a memory.

I am Longstone.

I am home.

Acknowledgments

No writer writes alone and I am indebted to the wisdom, guidance, and support of an army of publishing talent at HarperCollins: William Morrow in New York, and HarperFiction in London and Dublin. Special thanks to my publishers Liate Stehlik and Kate Elton, and to my editors Lucia Macro and Kate Bradley, who steered this particular ship with patience, enthusiasm, and care. Thank you also to the following teams: in New York — Jennifer Hart, Molly Waxman, Libby Collins, Diahann Sturge, and Carolyn Coons; in London — Kimberley Young, Emilie Chambeyron, Charlotte Brabbin, Eloisa Clegg, Louis Patel, and the inimitable Charlie Redmayne; and in Dublin — Eoin McHugh, Tony Purdue, Mary Byrne, and Ciara Swift. Thank you, also, to the HarperCollins family who publish my books around the world. As ever, I am so grateful to my fabulous agent, Michelle Brower, for her endless advice, cheerleading, and photos of Jonathan the puppy. Thank you also to Chelsey Heller and the foreign rights team at Aevitas Creative.

To my dear friend Heather Webb, thank you for your input at the early stages, and all the brainstorming during our epic American book tour, and for keeping me on course in our many Google Hangouts chats since. Thank you, also, to Catherine Ryan Howard, Carmel Harrington, and Sheena Lambert who know more about my daily thoughts and feelings than is probably wise, and who make me laugh, talk me down, and ply me with good gin at every possible opportunity. I am sure this book would never have been finished without your support. You are my people!

Thank you to Max, Sam, Catherine, and Helen for putting up with my excessive enthusiasm on our trip to Longstone and Bamburgh. And to Damien, thank you for giving me the time and space to do what I do. I promise it will all be worth it when we retire to our seaside mansion. To all my friends, neighbours, and family, thank you for keeping my feet on the ground while my head is in the clouds, and thank you to the writing community in Ireland and America who inspire and support me in equal measure.

A huge shout-out to the booksellers, librarians, bloggers, and Instagrammers around the world whose enthusiasm and passion for books is endless and infectious. Thank you for being our champions. Special thanks to Woodbine Books in Kilcullen for opening the best bookshop in Ireland very conveniently down the road.

And finally, thank you to you, my amazing readers, for your incredible support. You are the reason I do what I do, and I am more grateful than you can know. If you enjoyed the book, please tell me. It really does help while I'm writing the next one!

Author's Note

The idea to write a novel about Grace Darling first came to me a number of years ago, but as with every idea it needed time to percolate while I figured out how to tell her story and if, indeed, I should be the one to write it.

The answer to that particular question came in the summer of 2016 while visiting my sister in Northumberland. She took me to Barter Books, an enormous and very wonderful secondhand bookshop in Alnwick. Because Grace had lived in the area, I wondered if I might find something about her there, but where to even begin looking in the biggest secondhand bookshop in Europe? As I turned to a shelf to my right just inside the door, I saw a small green book, the title so faded I could barely read it. I picked it up. Why? Who knows? The book was called *Grace Darling — The Heroine of the Farne Isles*, published in 1875. I always say the story finds the writer, and this, surely, was a sign. That ancient little book was the start of *The Lighthouse Keeper's Daughter*.

I've always believed that historical novelists have a responsibility to not only portray the historical facts authentically, but to do justice to the people they choose to write about. To add emotion, words, and color to often emotionless black-and-white facts recorded in history books and biographies is both a challenge and a privilege, and I especially felt this responsibility in writing Grace's story. Although Grace was written about very widely at the time of her famous rescue, the more I read about her, the more I felt that we only saw a one dimensional version of her: that of the classic Victorian heroine. As a novelist, I wanted to dig deeper to know who Grace really was. I wanted to walk in her shoes and live her days in the confined spaces of her lighthouse home. I wanted to know what she thought about in the privacy of her bedroom because Grace wasn't just a heroine, she was a young woman with thoughts and feelings and desires. When I discovered a tantalizing suggestion that she had formed a romantic relationship with a young man from the area, possibly one of the artists who visited her at Longstone to paint her portrait, I was intrigued. Grace Darling in love? Now *there* was a story to tell.

As always, research was very important to me, not just to understand the events of 1838 to 1842, but to understand who Grace was before the *Forfarshire* disaster, and who she was behind the scrutiny of the public's gaze. My research and writing often take me away from my family in one way or another, but I also try to take them with me on my journey of discovery. This particular book saw the four of us become temporary lighthouse keepers during a weekend stay at Wicklow Head lighthouse in Ireland. We also traveled to the Farne Islands. To step inside Grace's lighthouse on Longstone Island, stand in her bedroom, climb the steps to the lantern, and walk along the rocks and beaches where she spent her life was very emotional. A trip to Bamburgh to see the wonderful Grace Darling Museum, her monument at St. Aidan's church, and Horsley Cottage, where Grace died, was also a wonderful source of fact, inspiration, and connection to this extraordinary woman.

But Grace was not alone. I was intrigued when I discovered another female light keeper, Ida Lewis, who became known as America's Grace Darling. It was this connection between the two women that led to part of *The Lighthouse Keeper's Daughter* taking place in Newport, Rhode Island, and to me reading more widely about the generations of women who kept the lights in America. Their stories are absolutely fascinating and inspired the character of Harriet Flaherty.

Some of the place names referred to in the book are now spelled differently, or known by a different name, particularly Harker's Rock (now known as Big Harcar) and North Sunderland (now known as Seahouses). Where possible, I have remained faithful to the known events of the time line of the *Forfarshire* disaster and the aftermath, and to the locations Grace visited. Any historical errors are entirely my own.

Sarah Dawson and her children were actual passengers on the *Forfarshire*, the children tragically lost as described in the book. However, Sarah's story following the rescue, and that of her fictional brother, George Emmerson, are a product of my imagination. It is believed that there was a George who had a romantic connection with Grace, and George Emmerson appears in a footnote of the book *Grace Darling* by Hugh Cunningham. It was too intriguing a connection to ignore! All the characters in the 1938 narrative are entirely fictitious (apart from Ida Lewis), and although Rose Island lighthouse does exist in Newport, Rhode Island, I have imagined the people and events there. The devastating hurricane of 1938 which hit the area without warning on September 21, did happen as written, with huge loss of life.

I hope that this book might inspire readers to learn more about Grace Darling, Ida Lewis, and the history of female light keepers. The following books were invaluable to me during my research, and may be of interest: *Grace Darling: Victorian Heroine* by Hugh Cunningham; *Women Who Kept the Lights: An Illustrated History of Female Lighthouse Keepers* by Mary Louise Clifford and J. Candace Clifford; *Grace Had an English Heart: The Story of Grace Darling, Heroine and Victorian Superstar* by Jessica Mitford; and *The Lighthouse Keeper's Daughter: The Remarkable True Story of American Heroine Ida Lewis* by Lenore Skomal. *Grace Darling, Her True Story* written by Thomasin Darling was another fascinating and invaluable source of research and insight into Grace's life. I also drew from *Britain's Working Coast in Victorian and Edwardian Times* by John Hannavy and the fascinating *How to Read Water: Clues and Patterns from Puddles to the Sea* by Tristan Gooley.

The Creation Of A Heroine

Given the point in history when the *Forfarshire* disaster occurred, news about the dramatic rescue undertaken by Grace and her father spread with surprising speed. But the journalists' eye for a good story was already at work. Even the earliest reports exaggerated Grace's part in the rescue, almost entirely eliminating her father from the episode, and adding sentiment where the facts had given none. Descriptions of Grace hearing the screams of the survivors from Harker's Rock, for example, are rather dramatic since it would have been virtually impossible for Grace to hear these given the distance and the raging storm. The myth and fiction of Grace's story was already at play. The sensationalizing of news events and the desire to create heroines and heroes from tragedies is clearly nothing new.

Grace was perfectly placed to fulfil the desire among Victorian society for romance and heroines. She was, by all accounts, a pleasant young woman in looks and demeanor. That she lived such an isolated life and wasn't easily accessible to the public or the journalists keen to tell her story only seems to have increased the desire for people to know more. Her name undoubtedly fed the more romantic narrative of her story. As I wrote *The Lighthouse Keeper's Daughter* I often thought that I would have been accused of overreaching if I'd given a fictitious heroine the name Grace Darling. Fact, once again, proves stranger than fiction.

As much as Grace is known for her courageous rescue, she is also known for her reluctance in accepting the fame that followed. It must certainly have been alarming for such a private woman to find herself under the public's gaze with the boat trips and the artists sent to paint her, not to mention the correspondence that was sent to her — similar to the paparazzi and their prying lenses who we see tormenting modern celebrities. From the portraits created by the artists who visited Longstone, Grace's image was easily transferred onto pottery and kitchenware, which, when mass-produced, found its way into homes across the country, ensuring that her name, her image, her story, and her fame continued to spread. The imagination of poets and writers filled the gaps in her story, romanticizing her time and again in plays, poems, and ballads. Even William Wordsworth penned his own tribute to her.

To many at the time, Grace really was an angel without wings. She offered the perfect vision of domesticity, a role model for the age. Outwardly, she was a devoted daughter, dedicated to spending her life with her parents at Longstone. But surely there was more to Grace. A woman who would set out in such a violent storm, and who saw death and tragedy, was clearly not the typical Victorian lady, prone to fainting. Grace had some gumption about her. And she was, after all, only human. So what of her feelings; her flaws? Surely there were people in her acquaintance who she didn't care for. Surely her parents and siblings sometimes frustrated her. Where was the Grace the reporters didn't write about, the capable young woman struggling to escape from the conventional role assigned to her, the passionate young woman in love? Those were the questions I wanted to answer in writing this fictionalized account of her life.

It certainly seems that fame did not sit well on Grace's shoulders and one can only wonder if the unwanted attention had some sort of psychological impact on her. Stress was not a word used by the Victorians, but could it have been that which led to her physical weakening and, eventually, to the consumption (or tuberculosis, as we would call it now) that killed her? What we can be certain of is that her death so soon after the events of the *Forfarshire* disaster, at age twenty-six, only fanned the flames of adulation as Grace Darling the heroine became something of a saint. Had she lived a longer life, married, and drifted back into domestic obscurity, perhaps we wouldn't know as much about her. Like Marilyn Monroe, Grace Kelly, or Princess Diana, the tragic death of a young woman in her prime only leaves us wanting more. Like the unfinished portrait in the story, Grace's story was, in many ways, incomplete.

Grace Darling was not only a heroine of her time, but someone who people of a certain generation will remember learning about at school. Whether through the Grace Darling song or the dramatic childhood tales of this classic

Victorian heroine, Grace's story has been told many times in the 180 years since she first came to our attention. I hope we will continue to share her story with younger generations and ensure that we remember women like Grace, forgotten heroines whose stories are confined to the shelves of secondhand bookshops and the records of the newspapermen who captured their stories.

After all, at a time when women still fight for equality, we all need our heroines. Perhaps now more than ever.

We do hope that you have enjoyed reading this large print book.

Did you know that all of our titles are available for purchase?

We publish a wide range of high quality large print books including:
Romances, Mysteries, Classics
General Fiction
Non Fiction and Westerns

Special interest titles available in large print are:
The Little Oxford Dictionary
Music Book
Song Book
Hymn Book
Service Book

Also available from us courtesy of Oxford University Press:
Young Readers' Dictionary
(large print edition)
Young Readers' Thesaurus
(large print edition)

For further information or a free brochure, please contact us at:
Ulverscroft Large Print Books Ltd.,
The Green, Bradgate Road, Anstey,
Leicester, LE7 7FU, England.
Tel: **(00 44) 0116 236 4325**
Fax: **(00 44) 0116 234 0205**

THE COTTINGLEY SECRET

Hazel Gaynor

Cottingley, Yorkshire, 1917: When two young cousins, Frances Griffiths and Elsie Wright, announce they have photographed fairies at the bottom of the garden, their parents are astonished. The girls become a sensation; their discovery offering something to believe in amid a world ravaged by war ... One hundred years later: When Olivia Kavanagh finds an old manuscript and a photograph in her late grandfather's bookshop, it sparks a fascination with the story of the two young girls who mystified the world. Delving deeper into the past, and the truth behind an innocent game that became a national obsession, Olivia begins to understand why a nation once believed in fairies. But can she find a way to believe in herself?

THE SILENCE OF THE GIRLS

Pat Barker

When her city falls to the Greeks, led by Achilles, Briseis's old life is shattered. Abducted and shipped to the Greek camp on the battleground at Troy, she goes from queen to captive, from free woman to slave, awarded to Achilles as a prize of honour. And she's not alone. On the same day, and on many others in the course of a long, bitter war, innumerable women have been wrested from their homes and flung to the fighters. As told in *The Iliad*, the Trojan War was a quarrel between men — over Helen, stolen from her home and spirited to Troy. But what of the other women in the story, silenced by their fates? Briseis and her fellow women are at last given voices to tell this mythic story anew.

THE CURSED WIFE

Pamela Hartshorne

Mary is happily married to a wealthy merchant, living a charmed life in Elizabethan London. But there's a part of her past she can't forget. As a small girl, she was cursed for causing the death of a vagrant child — a curse that predicts she will hang. Mary's carefully curated world begins to falter; her whole life is based on a lie. One rainy day, she ventures to London's Cheapside, where her past catches up with her. Suddenly, the lies and deception she has fought to bury begin to claw their way to the surface. As the wronged enact their vengeance, Mary must attempt to break the curse. Can she right the wrongs of her past before the curse wreaks its revenge?